MW00830344

Rhenn
THE TRAVELER
LEGACY OF SHADOWS

Rhenn
THE TRAVELER
LEGACY OF SHADOWS

TODD FAHNESTOCK

F4 PUBLISHING

Casebind Edition

ISBN 13: 978-1-952699-52-8

Cover design: Rashed AlAkroka

Cover Art by:
Rashed AlAkroka

Cover Design by:
Rashed AlAkroka, Sean Olsen, Melissa Gay & Quincy J. Allen

Map Design by:
Sean Stallings

DEDICATION

For Elo,
Who convinced me to look through the eyes of
each character in the party, not just Khyven's

For Dash,
Who is still my favorite superhero

For Jane,
Who kept me on track

MAPS

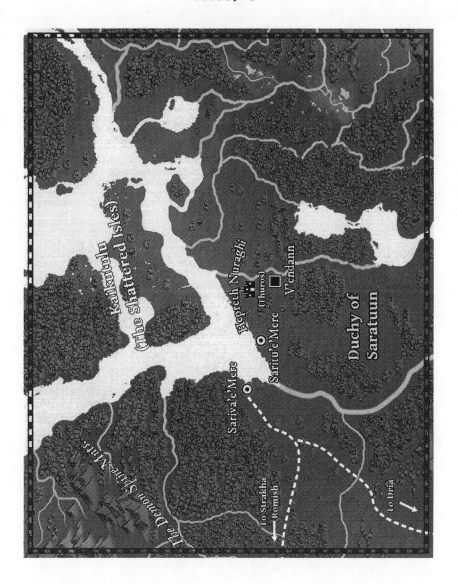

DEIHMANKOIOS

Thuroi Bakstadae'os

The Wyrm Lands

CH

Strakha
Strakha Ha
Strakha Heem
SOO KARI'MA
(Islands of the Dog Soldiers)
Strakha Khar
Strakha sun lo
Strakha Sangun
Strakha kamar
Cor
Strakha Vuul

RHO KARI'MA
(Hills of the Dog Soldiers)
Strakha Rekep
Calamath

Kemitayal
Var'Caspre

The Paekkomere Ocean
(The Devil's Sea)
Pakasai
THE RIKARI
NATIONS
Irinkarixal

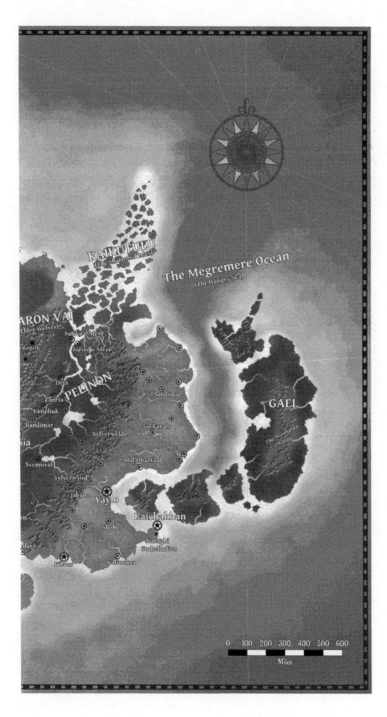

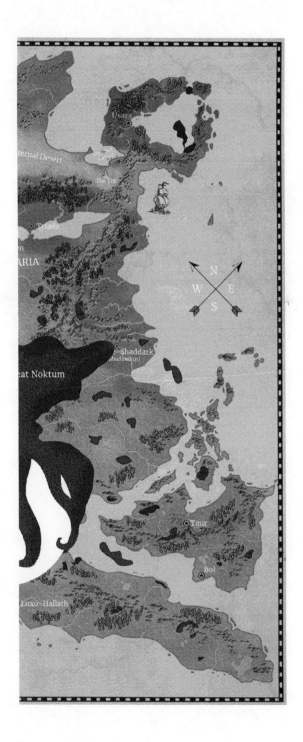

PROLOGUE

T he colors of the Thuros slid through Ventat Obrey's body. He took a swift breath and then his boots thumped on the stone dais on the other side. He glanced back at the Thuros room in Lord Tovos's castle, just past the archway, then into the dark room before him.

He had just stepped from one continent to another. He was literally walking in the footsteps of the Giants.

He took a deep breath, and humid air filled his lungs. Even though the room was dark—the slithering colors of the Thuros illuminated nothing—he knew he was in an entirely new land. He felt it.

Daemanon.

Most people thought the idea of multiple continents was a myth, if they had even heard those tales at all. But the continents were real, and they had once held great societies until the Humans had overthrown the Giants nearly two thousand years ago.

When Giants had ruled the world, Thuroi like this one had stood open all the time. There had been free-flowing travel between Noksonon and Daemanon. Daemanon and Lathranon. Lathranon and Pyranon and Drakanon and back to Noksonon. There had been commerce. Prosperity. A golden age of higher civilization.

Now the continents had been separated for so long they didn't even know about each other. Noksonon had fallen to the bickering tribalism of the Usaran, Imprevaran, Triadan, Demaijos, Luminent, Shadowvar, Brightling, and Taur-El kingdoms. Divided, leaderless, constantly warring.

The world needed correcting, and Ventat Obrey had been chosen by Lord Tovos to help correct it. Lord Tovos had taken Ventat from his humble hovel in Imprevar, lifted him up, and shown him the ways of magic.

Ventat opened his senses and felt the elemental power of this place. Daemanon was said to be the continent of life, of bursting vitality, of so many creatures it beggared the imagination. And beneath that was the richness of the elements themselves: stone, wind, fire, and so much water. Land Magic. Ventat's magic.

The lands of Imprevar were a desert compared to this place, and Ventat longed to play with this new land, to stretch out the fingers of his abilities.

He concentrated on the crumbled bits of stone on the floor at the base of the dais. Striking stone against stone could make a spark. Everyone knew that. But only a Land Mage could see that those sparks existed everywhere, in the very space between the air, waiting for the excuse to flare through the tiniest strike of rock on rock or the most powerful strike of lightning from the sky.

Ventat felt them now, hovering unseen in the air. He drew on his power, found a spark near his hand, and pulled it forth with a snap of his fingers.

A tongue of flame swirled in the air, and he cajoled the air around it to spin it, fuel it, shape it into a twirling fireball that illuminated the Thuros room. He kept the fire small as he recalled the words of his lord.

"Use only what magic you need," Lord Tovos had told him. "You have a mission. If you succumb to your personal desires, you will succumb also to a quick death. Daemanon has eyes everywhere."

"The Giants of Daemanon," Ventat had said.

"We have permission," Lord Tovos had continued, "to come to this place, to search for Rhennaria Laochodon of Usara. But it cannot be you who finds her, do you understand? You must use agents, work through them. If my counterparts hear that you are running around the countryside flinging fireballs with the magic *I* taught you, they will kill you."

"Yes, my lord."

"In addition, I shall be very disappointed."

"Yes, my lord," Ventat had responded. "I must leverage the locals."

"My war is with Humans, not with my brothers and sisters. That was where we went wrong during The Fall. I will not fight my own kind. All save one."

"Nhevalos the Betrayer."

"Queen Rhennaria of Usara is his new project, a new breed of Humans, what Nhevalos calls a 'Giantkiller.' She is a pestilence, and I want to eradicate her and all her kind. I have sent you and two dozen others to find her. So select your agent. Have them search for her. Have them destroy her."

"Yes, my lord."

"Nhevalos's machinations are deadly, but sparking a conflict with my own kind is even more deadly. Heed me, Ventat."

"An agent. Yes, my lord."

"Use them. Find her. Kill her."

Find her. Kill her.

Ventat returned from his reverie. He caressed the Plunnos in his hand. There was a heft to the coin, a solidness that begged him to hold it, to keep it. The oversized coin bore the symbol of Noksonon on one side—a pale sun being eaten by five tentacles of black—and the symbol of Daemanon on the other—a green demon skull with five horns pointed upward. The border of the coin was graven with symbols in ancient Giantish. Ventat could not read them, but the symbols on the Daemanon side indicated that it belonged to this particular nuraghi and one other. The symbols on the Noksonon side were the magical script for his lord's castle.

He tucked the Plunnos safely into a pocket within his robes and buttoned it shut.

That was when he felt movement in air. Its displacement had come from a distance, and none but a Land Mage would have felt it. Another gekurios might have dismissed it as the motion of some harmless creature, a rat or a raccoon that had found its way in.

But not Ventat. He had been warned.

His lord's voice returned to him.

"Beware the nuraghi," Lord Tovos had told him. "It was built by my forbears during an early war between the Daemanoi and the Noksonoi, a fortress controlled by us within Daemanon to protect the Thuros that gave us access to their lands. But the castle fell, and we lost control of that Thuros. To ensure we did not retake the castle, the Daemanoi left behind guardians. Some may still roam those stone halls. If you are from Noksonon, they will sense it. And they are highly attuned to magic, so if you use it, use it sparingly. They will be drawn to you, they will hunt you, and they will kill you."

"Yes, my lord."

The slight shifting of the air increased. Something was coming.

Ventat put his hand on the nearest wall, closed his eyes and focused on the stone of the castle, on the size of it. He searched for the closest wall that led to any great expanse of air beyond. The shortest distance between himself and the outside world.

It was down the hall to the left.

A low howl echoed through the castle.

Lords of the Dark! Either the thing was nearly upon him, or it was enormous.

Sending his spinning, tiny fireball before him, Ventat leapt from the dais, charged to the doorway, skidded into the hallway, and sprinted left.

Now even a normal Human could have felt the shifting of the wind. It ruffled Ventat's hair. The thing must be the size of the entire corridor, and it was coming fast. He could hear the pounding of giant paws.

Ventat didn't look back. He didn't want to know how big it was; he only wanted to escape. He couldn't afford to get into a battle with some ancient guardian. That was exactly the opposite of what his master had told him to do.

If the creature was a dark dweller—which likely everything in this nuraghi was—it had surely seen him, or at least his light.

Ventat plunged down the corridor, away from the approaching monster, and ran like he'd never run before. The end of the hallway split into a T-intersection, one passageway going to the right and the other to the left.

But the wall ahead was the outer wall. With the senses that came with Land Magic, Ventat felt where the stone ended and where the air began behind it. Freedom, except there was no doorway, no windows.

A chorus of howls filled the hallway now, so loud it made Ventat wince. An entire pack of supernatural wolves must be behind him.

The fireball cast jerky shadows all around as Ventat ran, and he frantically sent his attention ahead, dragging a finger along the stones of the hallway. In the outer wall there was a crack between the fitted, mortared stones. It was small, but he could work with that. He ran a finger along the stones of the hallway as he ran, urged the mortar to crumble and fall away, then he urged the stones to shrink and melt along that line.

His concentration on the stone caused his focus on the fireball to falter, and it spun away, flaring and then going out.

Ventat heard the excited panting of the wolves behind him. The thundering paws shook the ground. He cried out as he reached the end of the hallway and forced himself into the crack, turning his head sideways. The stone scraped his cheeks, his chest, and his back...

Then he was through into the starlight, falling to the ground.

He landed on a slope and managed to keep his feet just as the wall shuddered behind him. The creature—whatever it was—had slammed into it.

A huge, baleful eye looked through the barely human-sized crack. Ventat caught a glimpse of teeth as long as his forearm. Ropey saliva dripped down from the crack he'd created.

Part of him wanted to force-feed the beast a spear of fire. If he'd been in Noksonon, he would have, but those were not his lord's instructions.

Ventat smoothed his robes as that one huge eye glared at him from within its prison, then he turned away.

Select your agent.

Ventat had, of course, prepared himself before coming. He had studied the maps of the area. The largest city nearby was Saritu'e'Mere, where a religious sect attached to Nissra, a local goddess and one of Lord Tovos's counterparts, resided. To show respect to Nissra, Ventat would go there first. That was the place to start.

That was where he would find his minion.

Ventat withdrew a geode from another of his pouches. The rough, spherical rock had been cut in half, revealing a forest of crystals within. Ventat took a deep breath and closed his eyes.

The crystals of the geode came alive to him, the pure and structured nature of them, the way they caught and shaped light. He held on to that sense now, as Lord Tovos had shown him, and teased light out of the gemstones.

Ventat took a deep breath of the humid air and opened his eyes. An image hovered over the geode, the bust of Rhennaria Laochodon. She had a delicate but defined jaw, piercing blue eyes, and a crooked smile that seemed reckless and arrogant. Her gaze held the swagger of someone used to command.

Find her. Kill her.

"Yes, my lord." Ventat started down the slope and toward the city.

CHAPTER ONE

RHENN

Rhenn held up her hand, indicating that the others should stop. A'vendyr, the actual leader of the pentara, shadowed her gesture a half-second later. The scouting party came to a halt at his gesture, not hers, and A'vendyr shot Rhenn a dark look.

"Sorry." She mouthed the word and gave what she hoped was a charming smile. This wasn't *her* scouting party, wasn't her kingdom, wasn't even her continent. But old habits died hard.

He lifted his chin and dramatically portrayed a man sniffing the air. She wanted to roll her eyes, but she nodded with the others. That was why she'd called the halt, of course. The scent of decay. Not the normal decay of plant life sifting into the forest floor. Human decay. Someone had died nearby.

She watched the others in the pentara catch on. They were some of the best hunters Baron V'endann had, but their forest senses weren't honed like Rhenn's. Her nose had been trained to the woods of Usara, where catching elusive scents on the thin, dry air was an art form. Here, the humidity made everything reek. Scents lingered longer and drifted farther. In Usara, such scents were like words written in shifting sand. Here, they were like signs painted on a castle wall.

Slowly, silently, Rhenn peered out of the foliage. The fading golden light of the setting sun lent a softness to everything. It would be night within moments, but according to A'vendyr, the best time to catch water goblins was at dusk. He said the barely sentient beasts saw better in the dark, but they were also too stupid and too eager to wait for nightfall most of the time.

The local village, barely a mile from here, had lost half a dozen people in the last month. Four had simply vanished, never to be seen again. Two had been found chewed to the bone, laying in fields nearby the river.

Being a woodsman here was different than in the pines of Usara. This wasn't about honing endurance to move fast and far or learning how to step between dry leaves to stay silent. There were no dry leaves here. Like so many things here, it was all about water. Moving through the forest was a constant dance: bending, stretching, slithering through the trees so as not to disturb the poised beads of moisture. It was considered a warrior's dance.

And in the V'endann Barony, warriors were men.

Women didn't go running through the jungle. They didn't go hunting. They didn't wield weapons or serve in the military. They didn't set foot outside their doors unless as part of a protected caravan. Men went out into the world and did the physical things. Women stayed within the civilized areas and ran the domestics. City planning. Architecture. Growing or directing foodstuffs. Managing the household. Parenting the young children.

It was as though these people had split themselves down the middle based on gender, as if what someone had between their legs signified physical competence.

The quaintness of that had lasted for about five minutes for Rhenn, right up to the point where the matron assigned to her had draped her in one of the diaphanous dresses women were expected to wear. That hadn't been so bad, but when they'd brought out the shoes—the ridiculous shoes!—Rhenn had drawn the line. She'd taken one look at them and laughed, thinking it was a joke. They were torture devices, not footwear. The strappy things thrust the heel high into the air and perched it on a thin spike. No wonder women were perceived as less physically competent in this place—they were forced to tiptoe around on stilts!

All women in this place wore filmy dresses and ridiculous shoes while the men wore light, serviceable clothing: wide strips of cloth in a V shape tucked into their wide belts and kilts.

When the matron had tried to dress her that first time, Rhenn had endured the dress but politely refused the shoes. She'd then requested the far more practical kilt and tunic.

Eyes wide, the matron had said, "My lady, that would be… Wear a man's clothes? Please, put on your shoes."

Rhenn had refused, and the matron had left her alone to "think about her poor behavior."

So Rhenn had climbed out the window and run through the jungle in her bare feet. She'd come back soaked to the skin, dress ripped and plastered to her body. She'd left muddy footprints on the tiles and nothing to the imagination of all the open-mouthed V'endannians who'd witnessed her return.

Scandal? Clearly the matron had no idea what kind of scandal Rhenn could cause if she put her mind to it.

Two things had happened then. First, the matron had developed an undying hatred for her. Second, they'd given her "men's clothes": the jungle-running kilt and a specifically tailored top to keep certain "scandalous" body parts securely covered during the athletics of moving through the woods.

Rhenn was quite certain Nhevalos had had to pull a few strings to get them to acquiesce, but Rhenn didn't mind making life as difficult for him as possible. He'd kidnapped her. Caged her. And she had, of course, bent all of her will to escaping.

The problem was that this cage had no bars. The cage was the world itself. The only way back to Usara was a door she couldn't find and a key she didn't have. She was free to go anywhere she wanted, just not back through the Thuros.

But her plan, which in no small part included joining A'vendyr's pentara, was already in motion. Soon, Nhevalos's eyes would fly wide open when he realized she was gone. Then let him come find her. Let him try to take her when she was ready for him. He'd see a Giantkiller then.

Rhenn let her thoughts drift away, controlling her breathing as she waited for A'vendyr. She delicately ran her pinky finger along the curve of her jaw and removed the damp strands of hair stuck to her neck. In this humidity, her wavy hair had gone wild. Stray hairs popped loose and threatened to strangle her all the time. Of course, she had tried to force her hair into the intricate quadruple braid the locals used, but she had never been able to make her hair behave, even back in Usara.

"They're here," A'vendyr whispered. He motioned with two fingers.

She peered through the gap in the foliage. After so much talk, she was dying to see what a water goblin looked like.

Five of the foul creatures hissed and bickered with each other just beyond the natural duck blind. They were small—all between three and four feet tall—and vaguely humanoid, but no less intimidating for that. One had an old man's face with a bulbous nose, round ears, and puffy hands that he used to pry at the broken, exposed ribs of the dead woman at their feet. Another had octopus tentacles around his neck and a fish-like mouth. A third had a long nose and jaw that jutted like spears and tentacle fingers that grappled with a strip of meat he gnawed upon.

The fourth and fifth, one with four tentacles instead of legs and the other with a shark-like face and a dorsal fin, each had a fistful of the poor woman's blood-matted hair, still connected to her head. They snarled at each other, yanking the head back and forth as they fought over it.

A'vendyr roared and leapt from concealment. Rhenn's blood rushed as she stayed on his heels. Behind her, she heard the simultaneous *shing* of steel against scabbards as the other three warriors did the same.

The water goblins looked up. The stunned expressions on those bizarre faces might have been comical if not for the woman's blood all over their cheeks.

A'vendyr leapt into the heart of the beasts as though he would save the woman who had long since departed, but Rhenn went straight for the first water goblin to bolt, the one with the spear-like chin.

Spear-chin dropped his meat and ran for the river. A'vendyr had told her that water goblins never went far from a river, lake, or sea. Their advantage over humans grew three-fold in the water, and they knew it.

The stubby little goblin's legs were amazingly fast and Rhenn, who thought she'd be able to get a swing off before he was out of range, realized she had misjudged. She pelted after a squealing Spear-chin as he closed the gap to the water.

"No, you don't." She snatched her dagger from its sheath in mid-sprint, brought it overhead, and threw.

It wasn't the best throw.

She'd meant to sink it into the water goblin's lower back, but the dagger hit the back of its knee instead, pommel first. The thing staggered, stumbled, and the weapon got tangled up in its short legs. The goblin hit the ground hard, slid over the wet grass, up the rise of the riverbank, and dropped from view.

"No!" she cursed as she heard the splash on the far side. She crested the rise, gasping…

Just in time to see the pointy head floating downstream, barely exposed above the waterline.

She scanned the far and near bank for more water goblins. She couldn't see any. The water wasn't deep. Barely two feet. She could sprint along the bank, get ahead of the little miscreant, then jump into the water and intercept him. She would be in and out of the river in a second.

She let out a sigh. No. There was reckless and there was foolhardy. Rhenn prided herself on knowing which was which—though Lorelle had certainly disputed that often enough.

Sighing, Rhenn let the little water goblin go. She ran back, picked up her dagger, and went to join the fight thirty feet behind her.

But even in the twilight she could see it was already over. The growing darkness outlined the lumps of water goblin corpses and the four men of the pentara cleaning their blades.

B'ressyr, A'vendyr's *kahe*—the word for "second in command"—laughed as she approached.

"Ah, Fast Girl," he said. "Not so fast today, eh?"

"I didn't want to make you cry this time, B'ressyr," she said. "So I dragged my heels."

When Rhenn had become part of A'vendyr's pentara, B'ressyr had objected.

So Rhenn had challenged B'ressyr to a friendly duel. He'd laughed at that, but he'd agreed, patronizing her and lobbing glib jokes until they'd chosen their practice swords.

She'd made the duel quick and humiliating.

In the end, he'd sat there, nose broken, bruised arms wide with shock, looking very much like a full-grown baby with tears streaming down his face. That's when Rhenn had bowed and winked at him as she recalled one of the first things Lord Harpinjur had taught her about swordplay: "Do it right the first time—scare the piss out of your enemy—and you can win twenty battles with one. The others will fear to be next."

And he'd been right. Two things had happened after that battle: B'ressyr had developed a glowing hatred of Rhenn and no one else had challenged her.

B'ressyr smiled thinly. "I was just thinking that you might have caught him if you'd taken your sandals off and run barefoot."

Two of the other warriors chuckled under their breath.

"That's the way you prefer it, isn't it?" B'ressyr pressed his joke further, a sly smile on his face, as though she didn't know he'd just called her a whore.

"Sometimes," she said.

"Then it is as I thought," B'ressyr chuckled.

In the V'endann Barony, prostitutes never wore shoes, thus the barefoot reference. She sheathed her sword, picked up one foot and slid the leather strap off her heel. She did the same with her other foot and stood barefoot in the grass. The two warriors who'd laughed opened their mouths, eyes wide.

"Why such interest, B'ressyr? Is your bed empty? Are you hoping to drop coin to warm it?" She dangled the sandals from one finger and beckoned him with her free hand. "Come then, cold boy. Show me your coin, I'll help you out."

B'ressyr's face went beet red. He opened his mouth to say something, glanced at A'vendyr, then clacked his teeth shut.

"You're a disgusting woman," he finally said through his teeth.

"You want to fight me, B'ressyr? Draw your sword, then, and stop calling me names you think I won't understand. Name calling is for boys."

"You're calling me a boy?" He puffed up his chest.

"You shouldn't be ashamed that you lost to me," she said. "You should be ashamed that you aren't trying to improve. Ask me for tips. Ask me why I think you lost. Don't make some pathetic attempt to shame me." She shook her head.

B'ressyr looked like his purple face was going to explode. He took an involuntary step toward her. Her gaze went flat and she laid a hand on her sword hilt. That stopped him.

"Enough, B'ressyr," A'vendyr said in his deep voice. "Help the others throw the goblins into the river. We'll take this poor woman's body back home."

Rhenn kept her eyes on B'ressyr until he looked away, then slipped her sandals back on. It was refreshing, being part of a new culture. So many things to learn.

"Rhenn, if I may have a word with you," A'vendyr said.

"Of course."

He walked away from the men toward the jungle, and she followed him.

"Why antagonize him?" he asked.

"To train him."

"It's not your job to train him."

"Except that I'm in a unique position to do it."

"It's not helping him."

"He wants to believe he's a better fighter because—he thinks—women can't be as good as men. That's a weakness. It could literally kill him."

A'vendyr shook his head. "I let you join my pentara so you could help the group. What you're doing isn't helping."

"Oh, you don't believe that."

"Don't I?"

"When he called me a whore, you didn't interfere."

"I didn't think you wanted me to."

"I didn't. And you were right not to. But you didn't hold back because of what I wanted. You held back because warriors in a tight-knit group need to trust each other; they need to establish their pecking order. Can't do that if 'father' is constantly deciding disputes. So why are you jumping in to save B'ressyr?"

"That's different."

"Because I'm a woman?"

"His loss to you... his shame is greater, so he requires—"

"Maybe *you* need the lesson," she interrupted.

"That's enough," he said darkly. "Don't tell me how to command my pentara. I know how to—"

A ragged scream split the night. A'vendyr and Rhenn spun. Shadows dropped from the sky and fell upon the other three members of the pentara.

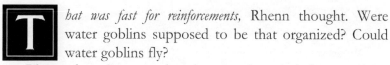

CHAPTER TWO

RHENN

T *hat was fast for reinforcements,* Rhenn thought. Were water goblins supposed to be that organized? Could water goblins fly?

Rhenn drew her sword and sprinted toward the monsters. Answers would have to come later.

The attackers looked like black sheets with claws; they weren't water goblins at all. They were something else. Something faster, stronger.

One of the pentara, El'rev, crumpled under his assailant. B'ressyr and C'eldon managed to stay on their feet, slashing wildly as the black sheets enveloped them. The creatures clung to their backs.

Rhenn shouted, a forceful blast of noise.

Two of the creatures flicked glances toward her, thank Senji. A moment's hesitation might save a life. B'ressyr took advantage of the tiny reprieve. He dropped, rolled, and dislodged his creature.

Senji's Braid, the thing looked Human! Rhenn had thought maybe they were giant bats, but the black-sheet effect was created by loose clothing, not wings.

One of the Human-like creatures turned toward her, hissing. It had a pale face and two long incisors. Its hands could have been bones for as thin and white as they were. Its claws were long, pointed, and blood red.

She feinted, lunging left as though its appearance had frightened her, but as she "cringed" she swung her sword to the right in a mighty arc.

The creature bought the feint. It leapt straight at her before realizing its peril, then it couldn't change direction. Its eyes went wide, and Rhenn's sword chopped deep into its side, slicing flesh and spine. Her sword almost came out the other side. The creature shrieked and fell to the ground, splashing blood everywhere.

She yanked her sword free. Hot blood flecked her face, and she stabbed the startled creature through the throat. It went down for good.

She immediately sought another creature. El'rev was on one knee, and one of the creatures undulated on top of him, head down next to El'rev's, as though it was taking great gulps of water.

She shouted again, trying to distract it, but it didn't even look up.

She stabbed it through the center of its back. It screamed, arching and spitting a waterfall of blood upon the unmoving El'rev.

Rhenn startled. That was a lot of blood! She clenched her teeth, whipped her sword around in a tight arc, and sliced the creature's head from its body.

The creature dropped; Rhenn spun away from El'rev. Until she knew the measure of her foes, she couldn't worry about the wounded. The threat had to be put down first.

B'ressyr had a new attacker. He was managing to keep it at bay, but he wasn't winning. He was on his back, dagger up defensively, scooting away from the thing.

Rhenn was about to aid him when she glimpsed A'vendyr out of the corner of her eye.

The pentara's leader was on his knees, mouth wide, sword lax in his hand. One of the creatures hunched behind him, thin fingers gripping his shoulders, mouth locked on his neck.

A'vendyr's glazed eyes stared at nothing. He didn't struggle, didn't even move, as though the creature had paralyzed him. His attacker made the same undulating motion as the first, as though it was sucking blood straight from A'vendyr's veins.

Rhenn unsheathed and threw her dagger in one under-handed motion. It was the least accurate way to throw, but the fastest. She had a sick feeling that A'vendyr wouldn't last more than a second with that mouth stuck to his neck.

This time she hit exactly what she wanted.

The dagger stuck into the thing's cheek, point first, and sank deep. The thing gasped, snatched the dagger out, and let A'vendyr go. Blood splashed everywhere.

Rhenn charged.

The creature's cowl fell away as it lurched to the side, revealing a gaunt face torn horribly by the dagger. It was a woman!

The rest of the creatures had looked like emaciated men, but beneath her black cloak, this woman had long blond hair and wore a light blue dress. Aside from her long incisors and pale skin, she was as Human-looking as Rhenn.

"You are outmatched," the woman gargled, blood dribbling through the ragged hole in her cheek.

"I hear that a lot." Rhenn thrust with her sword.

The woman leaned like a tree in the wind, narrowly avoiding the strike. She grabbed the blade and twisted.

Her fearsome strength dislodged Rhenn's grip. The woman yanked, surely cutting her hand to the bone, and the sword popped free.

The woman threw it aside and jumped six feet straight up, higher than Rhenn's head. That reminded Rhenn of Lorelle. Either the gaunt woman was exceedingly light or exceedingly strong.

Rhenn kept moving. In combat, you never stopped moving.

She dropped and rolled toward her sword with a grunt. The woman had obviously intended to surprise Rhenn with her speed and spectacular acrobatics, and land right on top of her.

But Rhenn had fought stranger than this, and she was just a blink faster. A claw scraped her back, but the woman didn't get a grip. Rhenn rolled over her sword, snatched the hilt, and brought it up, instinctively pointing it toward the sky.

She got lucky.

The woman was right there, descending so fast that if Rhenn hadn't made her assumption, there would have been no way to defend. But the woman came down on the point of the sword, impaling herself through the side of the chest. The blade punched through ribs and into vitals.

The woman screamed.

Rhenn kicked her in the jaw, then put her feet on either side of her blade and shoved.

The woman flew off and landed on her back, grabbing at her wound with both hands. Blood spewed everywhere, more than a human body should hold. It was like the woman was a punctured sheep's bladder.

Rhenn scrambled to her feet, trying to catch her, but the blond woman was too fast. She crab walked toward the trees a dozen feet away.

Damn she was fast!

Rhenn made her assessment in a flash. She couldn't catch the woman, even at a full sprint. And charging into that dark forest after this creature of the night would be suicide.

She watched until the woman vanished into the jungle then turned back to her pentara. Two of the creatures lay dead from Rhenn's own hand. One had fled into the woods, and the final was still trying to get its claws on B'ressyr's neck.

Rhenn shouted and ran at it.

With a hiss, the bloodsucker leapt away from B'ressyr. Its clawed fingers clenched and unclenched in frustration. Rhenn panted, lungs burning, but she ignored her fatigue. Hanging on just a moment longer could make the difference between victory and death.

"Lost your nerve?" she panted, trying to sound casual. Foes could often be unnerved by a show of unflappable confidence.

Her sword point weaved lazily in front of herself, as though she hadn't a care in the world.

"You…" the thing said from beneath its cowl, "will die dry and hollow."

"That's one I've never heard before." She put herself between B'ressyr and the bloodsucker as it clambered to its feet.

It pointed a finger at her and made a little swish, as though marking her, then it backed away.

Rhenn lunged forward and swung. The thing hissed and jumped back, but Rhenn sliced through the meat of its thigh.

It shrieked and leapt back a dozen feet on its one good leg, then hopped into the jungle.

She stopped her advance, waited a critical second, then put her hands on her knees and let herself pant in earnest, trying to regain her breath. She turned slowly, scanning the darkness for other shapes, other silhouettes trying to sneak up on them. She didn't see any, so she stood up and started back to B'ressyr.

"Nissra's Wrath!" B'ressyr exclaimed. "What were those?"

"You all right?" Rhenn held out her hand, and he took it. She pulled him to his feet.

B'ressyr stared wide-eyed at the jungle.

"B'ressyr!" Rhenn barked, and he snapped his gaze to her. "Are you all right? Are you hurt?"

He looked down at himself. He patted the two splatters of blood on his chest, but they didn't seem to be his blood.

He was fine. Rhenn turned and fell to her knees next to A'vendyr. The right side of his neck had two thin slices in it, and they leaked blood. But apparently the creature hadn't hit an artery. Rhenn had been fast enough.

She cut a strip from her kilt, folded it in half in one hand and pushed it on the wound. She hesitated, then laid her sword across A'vendyr's chest—within easy reach—so she could feel for a pulse on the other side of his neck. It was weak, but it was there.

"A'vendyr's alive," Rhenn said.

"They flew down from the sky," B'ressyr murmured. "The dropped on us like birds—"

"B'ressyr!" Rhenn barked again. He turned to her. Battle shock. Damn it. She needed him to snap out of it.

"Listen to me," she said calmly. "A'vendyr's alive, but I need you to come over here and hold this."

"Hold this…" he echoed.

"Right here." She nodded at the cloth on A'vendyr's neck, speaking smoothly and evenly like everything was fine, like this was the most normal moment in the world.

"Yes." He staggered toward her, walking like he was in a dream. He fell to his knees next to her.

"B'ressyr," she said, and his head wobbled as he blinked at her.

She narrowed her eyes, then reached up and put a kind hand on his cheek. He swallowed and smiled vaguely, like a child with his mother.

She slapped him hard with her other hand. His head jerked to the side, and anger flared in his eyes. She brought her hand to slap him again—

He caught her wrist before the blow hit, his brows furrowed. "What are you doing?" he growled.

She smiled. That sounded like B'ressyr. "I need you awake, B'ressyr. I need you able to fight. Are you up to it?"

He looked around, as though seeing the whole scene again. For a moment, she thought he would backslide into that daze again, but he swallowed and managed to hold himself together.

"Yes."

"They might come back," she said. "Be ready."

He nodded.

"Where's your sword?" she asked.

He groped at his empty sheath and realized he didn't have it. "It's…" He glanced back where he'd been crawling away from the bloodsuckers. "It's over there."

"Go get it, then come back here and hold this."

He did.

"Stay alert," she said. She cocked back her hand to slap him again, and he flinched away.

"I'm fine," he growled.

"All right."

Rhenn jumped to El'rev. The warrior's throat had been gashed wide open. His dead, half-lidded eyes stared at nothing. He was gone. She cast about, looking for C'eldon.

"They took C'eldon," B'ressyr said. "They hauled him up into the air! They can fly—"

"No, they can't," she replied.

He glanced at her. "They dropped from the sky."

"They're just really good jumpers."

He blinked at that.

"It's a surprise attack to make them seem more fearsome. And they're really good at it. But they don't fly."

"How do you know?"

"Because they didn't fly away when they were fleeing." She looked around. Damn, this place was dark. It was like someone had thrown a sheet over the world. "How far is the village?"

"Village?"

"Come on, B'ressyr. The village where that woman came from." She pointed at the corpse the water goblins had been feasting upon.

"Oh, that way." He pointed, and the light of hope came into his eyes. "Yes, that way. Only a mile or so."

"That's our plan," she said. "We're not going back into that jungle. We're headed for the village and we'll hole up until morning. Can you carry A'vendyr?"

"Carry him?"

"On your back. We can't both carry him, and you're the strongest. Can you carry him?"

"Uh, yes. I can." He glanced at El'rev's body. "What about El'rev?"

"We leave him," she said.

"We can't just leave him."

"It's him or A'vendyr. We need to get away from this place. And one of us needs to be free to wield a sword."

B'ressyr seemed to realize the sense of that, and he nodded.

"We come back for him and the woman in the morning."

"And C'eldon?" B'ressyr hefted A'vendyr onto his shoulders and stood up. Rhenn sent a prayer of thanks to Senji. Whatever else B'ressyr was, he was beastly strong.

"That," she said, "is going to be the next quest." She glanced to the horizon. "Which way?"

He pointed at the sky. "We head for the Star of A'vron."

The stars in Daemanon didn't match the ones she knew. Completely different constellations, completely different names.

"The bright one just above the horizon?" she asked.

"The Star of A'vron," he repeated, as though that helped.

She nodded and led the way, and it wasn't but a few minutes before they reached a road that angled almost directly toward the Star of A'vron. They made better time after that, and only a few minutes later, the lights of the village came into view.

"What's it called?" she asked.

"Padten," B'ressyr said. The man went silent for a moment, then said, "You saved my life."

She glanced over her shoulder, gave him a crooked smile. "Spotted that, did you?"

He didn't smile at the joke. "I… I wronged you."

"Yeah, well. Buy me a new pair of sandals."

This time, he did laugh, and Rhenn chucked him on the shoulder.

"You'd have done the same for me."

He shook his head. "No, I'd have been dead."

"Well, if you weren't dead, you'd have done the same for me."

"The way you fought," he said. "I've never seen anyone fight like that."

"No?"

"No."

"You'd get a kick out of meeting Khyven the Unkillable."

"Khyven the Unkillable?"

"Never mind."

"I would like…" he started, then hesitated. "I would be honored if you would teach me what you know. About swordplay."

"I'd be honored if you'd learn."

He gave a nervous laugh at that.

"Look," she said. "Don't strain so hard, B'ressyr. We're part of the same pentara. Let's just survive the night. We can talk about all this tomorrow."

"Yes."

They fell into silence and stayed that way until they reached the village.

CHAPTER THREE

N'SSAG

he door at the top of the landing opened suddenly and flooded the laboratory with light. N'ssag shouted and squinted upward.

"Shut that door, fool! Who do you think you…"

He trailed off. A priest of Nissra stood at the top of the landing, bright sunlight flooding around him. N'ssag peered at him like an unearthed mole.

The priest seemed like he wanted to retort to N'ssag's outburst, but he pressed a handkerchief to his nose, his horrified eyes wide as he gazed down at the gloomy, sunken laboratory.

A priest of Nissra. Here. Unannounced. This couldn't be good. The priesthood always sent a messenger first, a messenger who always knocked. So… the time had finally come. They were going to throw him out of the Order.

N'ssag watched the priest gaze at the laboratory with revulsion. Thankfully, the sudden sunlight hadn't ruined anything—N'ssag wasn't at a volatile stage of the process—but if the man had done this a day ago, he might have killed them both. The entire lab could have erupted into a pillar of fiery death.

But there were many paths to death. Apparently N'ssag had been indulged long enough by the Order. In all likelihood, this priest had come to strip him of his funds, confiscate his materials... Or...

Or was the priest here to kill him?

No one comprehended what he was trying to do. N'ssag was on the verge of greatness! It had just taken... longer than anticipated. He would bring vast power to Nissra's Order. He would make the goddess proud. He just... he had some refinements to make, that was all. They just had to give him more time...

"What is that horrific stench?" the black-haired priest gasped at last.

"It's the chemicals," N'ssag said.

The priest returned the cloth to his face and peered down at the shadowed figures on the slabs. "Are those *corpses?*"

So High Priest D'oreld—who had inducted N'ssag into the Order—hadn't told this priest about this project. N'ssag wondered if D'oreld had stopped mentioning N'ssag altogether, too embarrassed to reveal his recruiting mistake.

"Yes," N'ssag said.

"What are you doing with them?"

"You have a message for me from D'oreld?" N'ssag answered the question with a question. He might as well cut straight to the bad news. Then he could move on. Then he could get back to work.

The priest straightened. "It's *High Priest* D'oreld, acolyte. Where is your reverence?"

"Apologies," N'ssag said unapologetically. "What news from High Priest D'oreld?" N'ssag had already moved past the inevitable news he was about to receive. As always, his mind wandered back to his work, thinking of how he might continue funding his research without the support of the Order. There were ways...

The priest raised his chin. The skin around his eyes was deeply wrinkled, and N'ssag began to imagine what those watering, wrinkled eyes would look like dead. He could almost see the film covering them, their inert pupils vague and staring at nothing.

The priest would not be so uppity once N'ssag worked his magic into him, teasing the flicker of life back, bringing a bit of the priest's memories and sense of self to the surface, just enough to be useful, and then binding him to N'ssag's will. Dependent on him. Beholden to him.

But then, the priest's mind was undoubtedly inflexible, and so not ideal for the process. A resilient mind was much better. Rigid minds could snap. This priest would certainly have to be a plant rendering, and not a flesh rendering.

The flesh renderings—with their enhanced speed and strength—could become dangerous to N'ssag if they went insane.

"You are to serve your high priest this day," the priest said formally. "A messenger comes. A visitor to these lands. You are to host him. Give him your assistance." The priest paused, and the wrinkles around his eyes became even more pronounced. "Such that it is."

N'ssag snapped from his daydream. "Messenger?" He wasn't being thrown out of the Order?

"He has a task for you. High Priest D'oreld commands you to assist him. His name is Ventat Obrey."

What kind of a name was that? Some southern frill-wearer?

"Ventat Obrey," N'ssag repeated.

"I have delivered my message. Do not disappoint High Priest D'oreld." The priest of Nissra whirled on his heel and practically ran out the door. Of course he didn't close it, allowing the harsh, ugly sunlight to continue intruding on N'ssag's sacred place.

Ventat Obrey... N'ssag mused as he climbed the steps and slammed the thick door shut, plunging the laboratory back into darkness. Only the cowled candles flickered, barely illuminating the stone walls, his transition biers, and his sealed kegs of chemicals.

A foreigner. Perhaps from the very heart of King Stevan's ignorant, judgmental kingdom. Curious.

N'ssag went back to work, pushing down thoughts of the messenger and his impending arrival. He methodically sorted, prepared, and organized his work for his next transformation.

CHAPTER FOUR
N'SSAG

When the sun finally fell, N'ssag opened the caskets and released his flesh primes into the night. He sent them east to gather a new corpse for him. And, of course, to feed. It had been days for some of them. They looked gaunt.

He'd had to hold them back from feeding in the city lately because they'd taken too many drunks and wastrels from the back alleys of Saritu'e'Mere. Even a few of the living had spotted them. It wouldn't be long before the frightened whispers of the dregs made their way to the nearby merchant's section, then up the hill to the palace.

Once that happened, city guards would come looking for N'ssag's precious primes. He couldn't afford that.

Three days ago, he'd ordered his primes to stop feeding on the wretched of the city. Tonight, he was sending them into the country. They could cherry pick stragglers in the fields. If a few peasants went missing here or there, who of importance would care? And if the country folk described his primes to whatever authority might actually listen, who would believe them? Some new snaggle-toothed snark was always popping up in country folklore. N'ssag wagered his primes could feed for months without needing to move on. It was worth the extra time it took them to travel to the countryside.

In the beginning, N'ssag would have worried about his primes going so far away, that they might flee his protection, or that they might stay out too late and stupidly get caught by the sunrise, but that was before his masterpiece. The next level of his process. That was before L'elica.

L'elica was his most recent creation. Not only was she his most pure, his strongest and fastest prime, she was also smarter. Her resilient mind had retained her full living intelligence in the transition. She had understood N'ssag, saw the greatness of his purpose. She hadn't rebelled against her new body, her new abilities, or her new life. No. She had reveled in them, joining N'ssag not as a servant, but as a partner. She was glorious. It was she who led the others, protected them, and thought for them when N'ssag was not around to do the thinking.

No, N'ssag did not worry anymore.

But only a few hours after the primes had been turned loose, he heard a sound in the hidden part of the laboratory—which he called the catacomb—and he set down what he was working on. The catacomb was where the primes lived when they weren't hunting, and L'elica had not been ordered to return so early. She had made the decision to return early.

That meant something had gone wrong.

N'ssag jogged between the biers of corpses and human pieces and reached the iron door at the back of the laboratory. It was small, barely enough room for a person to wriggle through. It looked like the door of a furnace to throw off closer scrutiny. He unlatched it and flung it open.

"L'elica?" he called, and stopped short.

Her beautiful face hovered just beyond the doorway, half in shadow. In the pitch black, he caught the barest flash of her bare knees and her powder blue dress. She looked flush, like she'd recently fed, but a horrible gash had opened her right cheek. It was healing already, the flesh no longer raw, but her white teeth shone through the torn skin. It must have been a ghastly wound when she'd received it. Almost a killing stroke.

His heart skipped a beat at the thought of L'elica dying. He could barely conceive of it. Without her, his life would scarcely have meaning. She was his success; proof that he was on the verge of greatness.

He heard the sliding of a sarcophagus lid behind her in the dark. N'ssag had excellent night vision for a living man, but the back room where his primes slept was utterly black. From the location of the sound, he figured it was G'elreg climbing into his sarcophagus. He didn't hear any of the others.

"Where is everyone?" he asked.

L'elica moved toward the little doorway, and N'ssag stepped back. She slithered gracefully through the tiny doorway and stood up beside him. Her dress had spots of blood upon it as well as a few streaks of dirt. He reached up to touch the side of her face, but she caught his hand.

"Don't," she said. "Don't touch that. I don't... want you to see it." She turned her face so he could only see her pristine cheek."

"L'elica, you're scaring me. What happened?" he asked.

"It is my fault," she said. "We were glorying in the freedom of the countryside when we came upon three men leaning over the corpse of a woman. G'org attacked immediately, thinking only of the feast. And I... I didn't stop him. At a glance, I thought the same thing he did. Easy blood and three fine young corpses for you. But..."

"But what? What happened?"

"It was a fighting force. I didn't realize. One of the baron's pentaras."

"L'elica, I told you—"

"I know. I saw only three of them, so I didn't think of a pentara. But two had walked away, and I just didn't notice them until it was too late. But we would have killed them, master. We would have. All of them. If it wasn't for the woman."

"What woman?"

"A blade master of some kind."

"A female blade master? From Baron V'endann's holdings?"

"Yes."

N'ssag shook his head, confused. "Women aren't allowed to learn such things under the baron's rule."

"She killed G'org and B'uren."

"*Killed* them?"

"She was fast. Her sword was... everywhere. It was as though she could sense our vulnerabilities. She chopped B'uren's head off. She also wounded G'elreg, but he made it back with me."

"What about O'rsyyn?"

"I don't know." She shook her head. "He had the corpse we were to give to you. But he ran off. I thought it better to get G'elreg to safety than chase O'rsyyn."

"The sunlight will destroy him."

"Then he must have the sense to dig himself deep."

O'rsyyn didn't have much sense at all, actually. He was one of N'ssag's earliest primes. He barely had human level intelligence.

"This is..." N'ssag didn't have the words. "Catastrophic."

"I let you down," L'elica said.

"No," N'ssag said. "I sent you there. The fault is mine. But it is a heavy price for such a lesson."

"I will hunt this woman down and kill her," L'elica said. "She was fast, but she is only mortal. She surprised me. That won't happen again. She cannot see in the dark. She cannot look over her shoulder every moment."

"Not tonight," N'ssag said. "You need to regenerate, as does G'elreg. Did he—"

"He fed before I put him away. We stumbled across a drunk minstrel on his way out of the city."

"And you? Did you feed?"

"A little."

"Then go into the city tonight. Find someone who—"

A knock sounded at the door.

L'elica hissed. Her lips peeled back, revealing her fangs.

"Wait." N'ssag held up a hand. "I think I know who it is. It's a… It may be someone from the high priest."

"D'oreld sent someone to you?" Her incredulity mirrored his own, and it made him smile.

"I'll explain later."

"I won't leave you alone." L'elica slithered back through the furnace door and pulled it nearly shut, giving her a crack through which to watch.

It was ridiculous and endearing at the same time. L'elica was a far greater danger to him than the visitor was likely to be. If the visitor saw her and shouted or brought the city guard down upon this place, N'ssag would be hanged at the least. He considered pushing the door completely shut and latching it, but he didn't want to hurt her feelings.

He moved past his biers to the stone stairway, ascended, opened the door…

And looked up into the implacable gaze of a towering man, who had to be at least six feet tall, almost half a foot taller than N'ssag himself. N'ssag stepped back, nearly stumbling over his own feet and plummeting down the steps. He caught the handrail in time, thankfully, and steadied himself.

The man wore all black with a black cloak pushed back from his head and his shoulders. His black hair was pulled into a tight ponytail, accentuating the sharpness of his nose and his thick, black eyebrows. He seemed cut from the night itself. He stepped onto the landing without being invited, his cloak sweeping the floor behind him. His gaze flicked down, across the biers, the tables, the kegs of chemicals, then back to N'ssag's face.

N'ssag swallowed and was suddenly glad he hadn't shut the door on L'elica. His mind swirled as he tried to remember the name the priest had given him. Vander-something. Vangul. Venter.

"I am Ventat Obrey," the tall man said. "You are N'ssag?"

"Y-Yes," N'ssag said.

"Your high priest sent me to you. He told me I could expect your assistance."

"Yes, my lord," N'ssag said, not knowing whether this person was nobility or not, but choosing to err on the side of respect just in case. He certainly acted like a noble, entering without an invitation, carrying the air of command.

Ventat Obrey didn't correct him, so N'ssag figured he'd guessed right.

"D'oreld said you knew this area," Ventat said.

"I was born here, my lord."

"I'm searching for a woman."

"Of course, my lord."

He withdrew a halved geode from a pouch and held it forth in his gloved hand. The purple crystals inside the geode sparkled, then lit up. The bust of a woman formed out of purple light and hovered above the geode.

Land Magic! Powerful Land Magic to have rendered such exquisite detail! N'ssag marveled at it.

"Take it," Ventat commanded.

Surprised, N'ssag did so, holding it reverently in his hands. "This is the woman?"

"I have a strong reason to suspect she is in the area. In Saritu'e'Mere. Perhaps in the lands surrounding it. Do you know of the nuraghi to the northeast?"

"Of course, my lord."

"Do you know what a Thuros is?"

N'ssag hesitated. "A Giant's gateway, my lord?"

"That's right."

N'ssag's pulse quickened. By Nissra's beating heart, a Giant's Thuros? This man was steeped in magic. Why had D'oreld sent him *here*?

"I have been given permission by Nissra herself to utilize you to search this area."

"N-Nissra?"

Ventat narrowed his eyes, as though N'ssag was a simpleton. He hesitated, as though he was considering leaving this place and asking High Priest D'oreld for another assistant, but then he continued. "The woman's name is Rhennaria Laochodon, though she may be using a different name here. She was brought here by Nhevalos the Betrayer."

Nhevalos the Betrayer!

Ventat caught N'ssag's spark of recognition, and he raised an eyebrow. "You know who I speak of?"

"Of course, my lord. The blasphemer. The one who turned upon his own kind."

Ventat gave a nod. "Yes. If she is in this area, I want you to find her and kill her. There are many looking for her. But if Nhevalos brought her to this area, then you are my chosen agent. Find her, N'ssag. Kill her."

"Yes, my lord." N'ssag's mind spun. Nhevalos the Betrayer was a Giant! From legend. From a time before time. "Is he... is Nhevalos... here as well?"

Ventat ignored the question. "If you complete this task, clap your hand over the geode three times. That will alert me that the deed is done. If you do not find her because she was not here, then I will reward you for your time. If you do not find her and she *was* here, well... then I will reward you in a different way."

N'ssag swallowed. "I will find her, my lord."

Ventat turned and swept through the doorway into the soiled alley beyond and vanished into the night. In a daze, N'ssag stared after the man, then turned his focus on the geode. The woman had wild, wavy hair and an impudent smile. Shuffling up the steps as he memorized the woman's face—she was quite beautiful—N'ssag closed the door and latched it.

He turned to find L'elica standing beside him on the landing, and N'ssag started. He almost dropped the geode.

"L'elica!"

"That's her," she said. "The blade master. She is the one who killed the others."

N'ssag's eyes widened. "This one? You're sure?"

"It's her, N'ssag."

A chill ran up N'ssag's spine. What were the odds of that? It felt like the hand of Nissra had just moved through his laboratory, like N'ssag had suddenly been pushed into Fate's strong current. He shivered.

"I will kill her for you."

"Yes." N'ssag thought of how this would elevate him within the Order. How solving this so quickly for this powerful, foreign Land Mage would bring him up to full priest, maybe even priest of the second order, rather than a mere acolyte…

"No," he murmured.

"No?" L'elica asked, confused. "You do not want me to kill her?"

"No," he said slowly. The plan formed in his mind, succulent and delicious, and he grinned. "No, here is what we're going to do…"

CHAPTER FIVE

RHENN

Rhenn entered her room in Baron V'endann's keep, unbuckled her weapons belt, and tossed it on the bed. She wrinkled her nose. She should have cleaned that first. The blood upon the sheath and parts of the belt had dried, but...

Yuck.

With a sigh, she crossed to the bed, picked up the thick belt that held her sword and dagger, and took it over to her table. She gently laid it over the back of one of the chairs, unconsciously draping the sword such that she could draw it easily if needed. Better ready than dead.

After a month in this place, Rhenn wasn't expecting any of the baron's men to hurt her, but old habits died hard. She'd learned long ago that the moment you left your sword out of reach was the moment you needed it.

She turned, glanced at the little pallet in the corner that was her bed, and sighed. It looked so inviting. She'd been awake for almost two days. Her fatigue dragged her shoulders into a stoop. She shrugged and stood up straight.

The three survivors of the pentara had returned to Baron V'endann's keep this morning, and the baron's healers had taken A'vendyr to the infirmary right away, although the baron's youngest son had already seemed fine—a little fatigued but otherwise unhurt. The twin incisions on his neck were thin, almost unremarkable at this point. A'vendyr acted like a man who'd lost some blood. That was all.

But Rhenn's fatigue was twofold. The dull ache of physical exhaustion, but also the mental weight of loss. She'd lost men yesterday, and that was something Rhenn never took lightly. Two of her pentara would never open their eyes again.

But she'd saved some, too. That was something. If she hadn't been there, they'd all be dead. That was the one thing that buoyed her spirits. More would be dead if she hadn't been there. That would have to be enough for now.

That and a bath. Senji's Grimy Face, she longed for a hot bath, then to close herself in her room and fall into her bed for a day.

She drew a deep breath and refocused her mind. No. This was *not* her room. *Not* her bed. She must fight familiarity, fight the urge to get used this place, this routine, this rhythm. No doubt that was exactly what Nhevalos wanted.

This isn't your life, she reminded herself. *Don't make the mistake of thinking it is.*

She wasn't actually part of A'vendyr's pentara anymore than she was actually Baron V'endann's subject. She had a purpose, a plan. She was engaging with A'vendyr, the pentara, the other people of the baron's court, making friends, creating connections.

At the same time, she was encouraging that bastard Nhevalos she was settling in, accepting her fate. In the end, this wouldn't be his trap, it would be hers.

But she had to stay vigilant.

Rhenn had had plenty of practice playing parts. In fact, she'd played enough of them to know that if a person played a role long enough, it could become real. Especially at moments like this, when she was exhausted, when her guard was down. It would be so easy to convince herself that she should just treat this morning like what it was to A'vendyr, to B'ressyr. That she was just part of a pentara and needed to rest.

Now wasn't the time to rest. It was the time to wake up, to remember, to further her plan. Now more than ever. She couldn't afford to lose sight of what was most important.

Home. Getting home.

She let out a breath. "Come on." She shook her head and slapped her cheeks to give them color. "Time to be alluring."

The problem was she felt like a wet bag of offal squashed by a wagon wheel. Not the sexy wanton she needed to portray.

She cleared her throat, rolled her neck, and shook out her arms. When she had put on a smile and felt she meant it, she left her room.

Time to target her quarry.

The weapon smith E'maz took his bath late morning, which meant she was going to be late if she didn't hurry. A smith of exquisite craftsmanship, E'maz could form anything that was metal: plates and cups, swords and armor, jewelry and rings. The man was an artist, and his services were in high demand.

Rhenn had studied E'maz for two weeks now, had "accidentally" run into him in the halls, had casually flirted with him, and had visited his smithy once very much intentionally, that time allowing him to believe he was setting the pace of the flirting.

His near-royal status allowed him to work the hours he preferred, and he preferred late hours. Which meant he took his daily bath sometime around ten o'clock, barely half an hour from now.

She had to hurry.

Rhenn slipped quietly down the hallways of the keep. She didn't want to run into anyone, and luck was with her.

She stopped in front of the two archways: the women's baths and the men's. Neither were marked because some things in the V'endann Barony were just known, apparently. The right-hand archway led to the men's baths, indicating—she'd been told—that men were the strong right hand of the barony, doing all the strong things with their strong right hands. The archway for women was on the left-hand side because...

Senji's Braid, she didn't even remember. Because this ridiculous male-female oriented culture made her want to slap someone with her left hand, she supposed.

Still, today this frustrating aspect of their culture was going to work for her. There was no sign. No difference in the architecture. One was simply supposed to know, which made it entirely plausible that a stranger, like her, could get it wrong.

She moved quietly through the right-hand archway, listening intently. The first room was a storage and changing space, and no one was there. She stopped and stripped out of her blood-crusted kilt and top. Linen robes and towels were provided, so she snatched one of each and slunk into the baths. Steam enveloped her.

At this time of morning, based on her research, the baths were practically empty.

Good.

She slipped into the water, quickly and methodically washing clean. Only then did her racing heart slow down. Getting caught by someone other than E'maz—or getting caught by E'maz while she was blood spattered and bedraggled—had been her two greatest worries. But she'd passed that first hurdle. Now she just needed to wait and hope that E'maz didn't break his routine today.

She kept herself low to the water, her chin half-submerged just in case some other man came in first, but none did.

Mere minutes later, she saw a figure enter wearing a towel, a robe slung over one shoulder. She peered intently through the steam, waiting a moment to be sure, but it was E'maz. He was on time. Senji was with her.

As luck would have it, he turned left and headed directly toward her, though he hadn't seen her yet.

She turned in the water, facing away from him just as he drew alongside her. She walked up the steps, water streaming from her body, threw her hair back and wrung it out. She didn't look at him, pretending she had no idea he was there, but she imagined him stopping in his tracks, eyes widening. She gave him a good, long view, then turned.

She pretended to start as she saw him. "E'maz!" She didn't make any move to cover herself, as though she was too stunned to run for cover.

He spluttered, looking over his shoulder in panic like *he* was in the wrong place. He clearly spotted some landmark that reassured him that he hadn't walked into the women's baths by mistake, then spun back to her.

"Rhenn! What are you doing here?" he asked, his voice two octaves higher than usual.

She chuckled, still conspicuously not covering herself, as though they were just in his smithy, flirting. "Taking a bath."

He'd gone as red as a beet. His shock had turned to fixation as he stared at her.

There, she thought. *That's long enough.*

She bent down and picked up her robe, slipped it onto her wet shoulders, and wrapped it around herself. The effect on him was immediate. His mouth opened wider. Clinging clothes were, after all, more alluring than straight nudity.

Finally, his civility kicked in. Shock to fixation. Fixation to propriety. Bless him. He really was a nice man. She didn't like to use him like this, but she was in the middle of a war. She couldn't afford to pull punches.

"This is the *men's* bathhouse, Rhenn," he hissed quietly. Fumbling with the robe over his shoulder, he moved quickly forward and threw it over her shoulders. Through the steam, she got a good glimpse of his hard, muscled torso.

Well, she might feel guilty using him. But she wasn't going to hate it. The man had muscles on his muscles.

"This isn't the women's?" She looked around, seemingly bewildered.

"Rhenn… It's the men's. Right archway."

"I thought the men's was on the left."

He put his hands on her shoulders, and she felt a little jolt of lightning. No, this wasn't going to be difficult at all. She allowed herself to be guided to the changing room.

"You're going to cause a scandal. I swear you will," he said.

"I'm so sorry," she said, not sounding sorry at all.

"Are those your clothes?" He spotted her little pile of blood-crusted attire.

"Oh. Yes."

He wrinkled his nose. "Well, you're not going to put those on again." He grabbed yet another robe, and she allowed some of her smile to show when he draped it over her shoulders with the other two. She looked like a snowball.

"What were you doing? Butchering pigs?" He gave a sour glance at her clothes.

"Something like that."

He began to belt the robes, his arms encircling her waist, then he jolted and leaned back, looking up at her. She just watched him. He stopped himself, handed the ends of the sash to her. "Here… Well, you do it."

Calmly, she pulled the sash around her triple-robed waist and tied it. "Thank you. I think I'm well covered now."

"You've got to get out of here."

She moved toward the archway, but not in a hurry. At the archway, she turned. He was still staring at her.

"Oh, is it all right if I visit you in the smithy later today?" she asked.

"What?"

"I have something I'd like to commission. A decoration, really. A coin. Can you make a coin?"

"You want me to make something?" He looked nervously past her.

"Yes."

"Well, of course, Rhenn. Come by whenever. I'll make whatever you want. Just… you shouldn't stand there in just a—"

"I'm going." And she gave him a genuine grin. A grin of victory.

She left the bathhouse and, as luck would have it, nobody saw her except him.

That went spectacularly well, she thought.

She was still congratulating herself when she entered her room—

And found Nhevalos waiting for her.

CHAPTER SIX

RHENN

The Giant—disguised as a six-and-a-half-foot-tall Human—sat in one of her two chairs, the one without her weapons on it. A normal enemy would have put himself as close to her sword as possible, asserting his control, being a living obstacle to keep her from arming herself.

But Nhevalos wasn't normal, and his deceptive gesture was even more powerful. It said to her, "Take whatever weapon you want. It won't do you any good." She could fight and twist and rail against her situation, but she couldn't escape. Not until she possessed that oversized coin in his pouch—the key to opening the Thuros. The key to sending her home.

No, Nhevalos wasn't worried about her attacking him. He casually offered her the chance because he knew she'd lost.

And she knew it, too, because she'd tried. Six times.

Every time she'd failed, he could have killed her, but he didn't. No, she was no good to him dead. He wanted to use her. Nhevalos had revealed his plan to her, a crazy scheme that involved the entire world.

And her body. Her life. Her ability to choose her own course. All these were to be sacrifices to this "greater good."

She'd failed to kill him, yes. That had been her initial solution because she was good at that sort of thing. But Rhenn wasn't a one-trick pony. When she'd realized she couldn't best him physically, she'd pivoted and acted resigned. She'd seemed to slowly come around to his way of thinking, as though his rational arguments had taken root in her rational mind.

Clearly, Nhevalos was a master strategist, but Rhenn wasn't a novice. So she'd engaged him in a different contest. No swords or bloodshed here. It was her mind against his, a game of charm and deception, of setting traps or avoiding them, of twisting events until Rhenn had the high ground. At the end of *this* game, they would find out which one of them was more subtle...

And which was dead.

The Giant came and went as he pleased, so him being in her room wasn't a complete surprise. The people of the V'endann Barony treated him like some kind of holy prophet, and no one would question him entering whatever room he wished.

Nhevalos glanced at Rhenn's attire and raised a quizzical eyebrow. With three robes on, it was stifling in her room. Already, the prickle of sweat beaded at her neck, and a few trickles ran down her back. This eternally summer-like land was always hot. She'd planned to strip out of the robes the instant she got back.

Nhevalos had ruined even that little joy.

So she removed two of the linen robes and tossed them on the floor by her pallet. She thought about taking them all off to see what he would do, but she knew that answer. In all their interactions, she had never received any signal that seduction would work on him. He'd never stolen a glimpse at her body or shown even a flicker of desire for her. She had hoped for that weakness—for any kind of weakness—in him, but it simply wasn't there. Perhaps Giants considered congress with a Human to be bestiality.

She would have liked to find some chink in his armor, to have piqued his curiosity with her three-robed attire. If he had asked, "Why are you wearing three robes?" or "How did the sortie go?" that would have been something, at least, perhaps something she could use to get her hooks into him.

But he wouldn't. Nhevalos wasn't overmastered by curiosity. Or sentiment. Or friendship. Or pain. Or anything.

As far as she knew, there was a big fat hole through the center of him where a Human soul ought to be. He did not act as a normal man, not in anything she'd witnessed. He never seemed tired. He never seemed hungry. He was... inhuman, with a dozen minute mannerisms that set him apart.

Like the fact that it was impossible to hold his gaze. Just looking at his eyes gave her a headache. But she didn't stop trying.

She stared at him, ignoring the compulsion to turn away like she was staring at the sun.

"Would you like a drink?" He indicated a crystal decanter and two wine glasses. They loved wine in this hot land, but Rhenn had drunk wine before and didn't like it much. Her mother had enjoyed fine vintages imported from Triada, but Rhenn hadn't really had the chance to follow in her mother's footsteps much.

"I prefer whiskey," she said.

Nhevalos raised the decanter anyway, poured some into the wine glass. Whiskey sloshed in and settled. She narrowed her eyes at the decanter. The liquid was brown. A second ago, it had been red. She'd been sure of it.

That's what it was like, being in Nhevalos's presence. With every action, he illustrated how helpless she was, how far *beyond* her he was.

He played on the legends to heighten her fears. All part of the game. He wanted her to believe that he was all powerful here, that he could just point a finger at her and turn her into a bloodstain—or a goat.

Slayter could have changed wine to whiskey, she reminded herself. He could have done it. Probably after meticulous study and a complex symbol wrought upon one of his clay coins, but he could have done it.

She tried to tell herself that the subtle intimidation hadn't worked, but it had, damn him. It had set her off balance, set her to thinking about everything she was thinking now.

Nhevalos watched her with those dark, piercing eyes as he poured one for himself.

Wine to whiskey. Bastard.

She grinned, sat down in the chair, and picked up her glass.

"To you and your plan," she said. At first, she'd tried using the annoying nickname "Nhevie" with him, hoping to irritate him. But he'd ignored it, so she'd stopped after the first two weeks, pretty much about the same time she stopped trying to kill him. She quaffed the whiskey.

He sipped his. "Things are going well with A'vendyr," he stated. It should be a question, but it didn't sound like one, like he knew everything, like she was incidental.

"Tragic," she said.

"Tragic?"

The village had sent people to bring back the goblin-chewed woman and search for C'eldon, but she didn't expect them to find him. That bloodsucker had hauled him into the trees. He was certainly dead only moments after. "Three people are dead, two from A'vendyr's pentara. That's what we Humans call tragic."

"Ah," he said without an ounce of humor. Or remorse.

"And A'vendyr almost died," she said.

"But you saved him."

"So you know the story. You've talked to B'ressyr?"

"To the baron."

"So why ask me?"

"Because I'm not here for B'ressyr. Or the baron. I'm here for you. For as long as it takes for you to trust that I know what I'm doing."

"I *do* trust you, Nhevalos. I thought we already established that."

He didn't say anything.

"I took your advice, didn't I? I joined A'vendyr's pentara."

"And?"

"I think it's working. He's starting to warm to me. Aside from the fact that I, as a woman, don't possess any of the traits men in this culture admire—except for maybe the one—" She winked. "I think he and I are getting along famously."

"So you will do it," he said.

"Of course. I said I would. But these things take time, Nhevalos," she said.

And here it was, the crux of her captivity. Her sole purpose in being here. The only thing Nhevalos cared about.

A pregnancy. An important pregnancy, according to Nhevalos. Her pregnancy.

He'd brought her here to breed with A'vendyr. To mix her royal blood with royal blood of Daemanon. A'vendyr's blood.

And produce a baby.

Somehow, this would help Nhevalos's grand plan. He didn't seem to care how insidious and horrible and sick his request was. To a Human—to her—this was the worst kind of slavery. She'd even said as much when he'd first told her he wanted her to produce a child. He'd simply shaken his head like she hadn't understood the basic premise and told her his reasons why. Her son or daughter would be a Greatblood. Greatbloods were the key to defeating "bad" Giants—as though Nhevalos didn't fall into that category.

And his reasons for her pregnancy were compelling... if one bought into three key premises:

Number One, Giants were returning. Very well, fine. Clearly that was true. One was sitting across from her.

Number Two, Giants were going to overrun the world. Not so clear. How exactly was that going to happen? Rhenn had a hard time believing that even Giants were powerful enough to overrun all the kingdoms in Noksonon, let alone Daemanon and the other three continents he spoke of.

Finally, babies produced of certain bloodlines—apparently rich in Giant blood—could be transformed into Greatbloods. Giantkillers.

Well, that just seemed ludicrous.

She simply couldn't believe that Nhevalos's best-laid plan to stop a supposed Giant War was to impregnate women in the hopes that their babies came of age in time to be battle ready, with the right kind of inherent magic, to fight Giants.

There were so many holes in that logic she didn't even know where to begin. Or, well, that wasn't exactly true. When he'd first revealed this information to her, she'd known exactly where to begin.

She'd punched him in the face.

It was the only blow she'd ever landed on him. She'd completely surprised him, probably because she'd completely surprised herself.

After that, she'd tried to stab him, but he had handily stopped her. She'd tried to cut him down with her sword. No luck.

The problem was that Nhevalos was physically superior in every way. Rhenn was fast. He was faster. She was strong. He was a Giant. She was skilled with a blade, but Nhevalos had bested Khyven.

So she'd come up with her plan: act dejected, then slowly evince interest in his plan, then even more slowly "come around" to his way of thinking and "see" the danger he wanted her to see. Build a rapport with him, trust. Once she got to the point where his guard was down, she'd stick him for good, steal the coin, and go home.

She'd known from the outset that she'd have to spend time working up to it. That was no problem. All she had was time in this cage without bars.

"Have you chosen the time to breed?" he asked.

She chuckled. "You're thinking like a Giant again," she said as though she were fond of him, as though she enjoyed being this close to this inhuman creature who had stolen her, tormented her, and kept her like some damned pet. "Humans don't choose a time to breed. There's a natural flow to these things."

"Time is growing short."

"Not so short," she said. "I mean, if what you say is true, I've got nine months plus a few decades. I don't think a babe in diapers is going to wield your magic sword."

"It's not a magic sword," he said.

"Spear and magic helmet?" she offered.

He didn't say anything. The man was completely incapable of humor.

"Choose a time," he said.

"To get pregnant?"

"Yes."

She closed her eyes and put her fingers to her forehead like she was consulting an oracle. "Seven days."

"In seven days?"

"Sure."

He didn't get the joke. "Good," he said. "If you like, I will then take you back to Noksonon to raise the child."

"That's sweet of you," she said, and she actually managed to make it sound genuine. Below the table, she pushed her nails into her palm, practically drawing blood to keep herself from screaming.

Maybe, just maybe, this little farce would give her seven days before he came visiting again.

Seven days might be enough for her plan to come to fruition.

Nhevalos stood up and went to the door, where he paused, his face serious.

"It's going to start with you, Rhenn." It was the first time she'd ever heard any emotion in his voice. The urge to respond, to connect to him, was strong, like an insidious spell reaching out to her. Only her burning hatred for the Giant allowed her to resist. Everything about this creature was manipulating and false.

"So much rides on you," he continued. "You must trust me and you must learn. You must understand why Noksonon is the continent of night. If you are to lead your people in this war, you must know the darkness like no other Human before you. You must, or the path to victory will vanish altogether."

She turned in her chair, draping one arm over the back of it.

"Of course." She put as much earnestness into her voice as she could, leveraging that sudden desire to please him, to connect with him. She let it flow into her words. "I see the danger. I want to protect my people. And you're the only one who can guide us. You've shown me that, and I'm ready. A'vendyr is in hand. Don't worry," she lied.

He paused, watching her with that implacable dark gaze, then he nodded and closed the door behind him with a quiet *click* of the latch.

Conflicting emotions battled inside her. She turned to the crystal decanter. For the first time, she let her guard down and poured herself a drink not because it was part of the act, but because she needed it. She quaffed it in a single go, wanting to ease her fears and racing mind with that blessed euphoria that came with the burn of whiskey. It was a weakness, she knew, but she needed it, and she took another.

She felt she was doing all the right things, the only things she could possibly do. But then, Rhenn usually felt that way, even when she was wrong. That's where she'd always relied on Lorelle. Her sister could always point out the difference between Rhenn's oblivious confidence and her right-thinking decisions. She could set Rhenn back on solid ground when she'd wandered into the marsh.

My sister, she thought. *Am I doing this right? Oh, how I wish you were here.*

CHAPTER SEVEN

RHENN

The light smoke stung Rhenn's eyes as she stepped into E'maz's smithy, but she liked it. That scent and the constant ringing of his hammer made her feel comfortable in a land where nothing else did.

She spent her days walking a floor of needles, all of them trying to stab through her thin sandals. If she stepped just so, she could navigate it, but she could never relax. Every thing she said and every action she took had to be weighed, measured, and delivered with full conviction. She had to address every threat surrounding her: After all, A'vendyr might get frisky, trying to fulfill Nhevalos's "prophecy." A'vendyr's father, who hated her, could turn that hate into action. Nhevalos could uncover her deception.

It all had to remain perfectly balanced, or the needles would come punching through.

E'maz hadn't lit his lanterns yet, though the sun had already set. He always worked into the night, and she liked that. She liked standing in his workshop and watching his forge grow brighter as the light faded.

She wended her way through the front part of the smithy, imagining for a moment she was as stealthy as Lorelle. Rhenn crept around the benches and past the sturdy shelves on the wall, which held rows of gleaming helms, bracers, greaves, and carefully folded piles of scale mail.

She stopped at the doorway that led to the forge, where the smoke thickened. E'maz wore a sleeveless leather tunic covered by a leather apron. His thickly muscled arm rose and fell as he pounded on the beginnings of a sword blade. Sweat glistened on his skin in the orange glow of the forge, but he continued that rhythmic motion like he could do it all day long. Like the sweat and the exertion were simply normal.

She watched the beauty of his body and allowed herself to breathe deeply, tasting the bitter tang in the air, and she reveled in it. A week had passed since she'd disrobed for him in the bath house. The day after, they'd become secret lovers, and she'd visited him almost every night since.

At moments like this, she allowed herself a daydream about what it would be like if their courtship was real. What would her life be like if she spent the rest of it as his mate?

She allowed herself to imagine it in its entirety. Living out her days in this warm and humid land, the wife of a good-hearted blacksmith. No kingdom to rule. No Giant to outwit. No war. How easy that would be, how uncomplicated.

It was a pleasant fiction, but it faded quickly. The needles were pressing against her sandals, eager to get to her, eager for her to make a mistake.

This is a trap, she thought. *A trap of my own making, but no less deadly.*

Sweet, unknowing E'maz could be her downfall as easily as anything else. Perhaps him most of all. She'd duped him, cultivated him, and was exploiting him, but she also liked him. She looked forward to their time together more than she wanted to admit. Their passion and abandon with each other in the quiet… it was a stolen moment. She wouldn't have been able to do this back in Usara; it was a guilty pleasure.

Rhenn had taken lovers before. During her time in her rebel's forest as she'd built her war machine, she'd had a tumble here, a tumble there, all in good fun with no expectations beyond the heady rush of the moment. Lorelle had disapproved, of course. Lorelle had disapproved of anything out of her control, but she'd never said anything about Rhenn's lovers. The joys of being a rebel were few, and they'd each taken refuge where they could. Lorelle in her solitude and control. Rhenn in her flirtatious recklessness.

But once Rhenn had become queen, those days had stopped. Lorelle's wisdom wasn't a thing to be easily ignored. Rhenn had to play the role she'd fought so hard to claim, and the rules had changed. Bedding a queen was far different than bedding a rebel, and she'd had to treat it as such. Rhenn's lovers had ceased the moment the crown rested on her brow.

So this stolen moment with E'maz had been lovely, a welcome departure not only from her war against Nhevalos but her role as queen as well.

The blacksmith's hammer rang rhythmically.

Clang… Clang… Clang

Enough of this, she thought. *I can daydream when the work is done.*

She steeled herself, put on her alluring smile, and intentionally scuffed her sandal on the floor. The ringing stopped. E'maz looked up. A smile spread across his bearded face.

"Rhenn," he said in his deep voice, and she could hear the affection.

"I was standing in my room tonight, feeling like I'd forgotten something." She swayed her hips as she walked around the forge. "I kept turning around and around, trying to figure out what it was…"

"And?" The muscles in his forearm rippled as he lifted the glowing blade, pinched between tongs, and dropped it into the water trough. It hissed. A gout of steam billowed up.

"It was you. I was missing you," she said.

He smiled through that bushy beard. She loved that smile. It was part admiration, part amusement, a smile that made her feel wanted and clever at the same time. He came to her, and she leapt onto him, wrapping her legs around his waist and her arms around his neck. He held her like she weighed nothing. She pushed her fingers into his mane of hair and kissed him. It lasted a long time, then she lowered her legs and leaned back. His big arms encircled her and didn't let go.

"That was all," she said, slowly removing his hands, disentangling herself.

His eyebrows raised.

"That's all I came by to tell you." She started walking away.

He laughed. It was a deep, happy roar that filled the smithy. She sauntered to the doorway, turned, and winked.

"Wait," he said.

She raised her eyebrows.

"I have something for you."

Do you now? she thought. *What a surprise. What a surprise surprise surprise.*

Two nights ago, E'maz had mentioned that he'd almost finished her coin. Her carefully exhibited excitement at this news and the fact that she had "neglected" to visit him last night had no doubt fueled his passions to put the finishing touches on it.

He came forward with the four-inch coin laying in one wide, callused hand, and he presented it to her.

Senji's Spear, it was perfect! The symbol of Noksonon on the one side had been so lovingly rendered it almost looked alive. He'd enameled it exactly as she'd described, black tentacles reaching over the pale yellow sun.

He handed it to her and she didn't have to fake her enthusiasm. This was it. This was the key to her freedom. He'd done a masterful job. She flipped the coin over and looked at the demon head on the other side, what she'd come to learn was the symbol of Daemanon.

She couldn't be sure everything was exactly the same as Nhevalos's coin, but by Senji's Braid, it was close enough to make the switch. She wouldn't get better.

"E'maz..." she breathed. "It's exquisite."

"Well, I'm glad you like it."

"Now I have two pieces of you to carry with me everywhere." She laid a hand on the dagger he'd given to her three days ago. The magical dagger that she'd asked about, that she'd encouraged him to tell her about, down to the most minute details of how one worked magic into the creation of a weapon.

It was Line Magic, he'd said, commissioned by a visiting duke who'd had his own Line Mage with him. During the duke's stay at the V'endann Barony, the Line Mage and E'maz had worked together to imbue the steel with the requisite magic, then the duke and his mage had been called away before the project had been finished. They'd promised to come back and pay for the dagger. They never had, so E'maz had kept it.

Once she and E'maz had been together a few nights, she'd intentionally told him the details of her fight with the bloodsuckers, reworking the tale as needed. She'd nearly died in her version, and her last, life-saving strike had been with her dagger, which had snapped in half during that critical moment.

"All that stood between me and oblivion was that dagger," she had said.

The next day he'd presented her with the magic weapon "to replace what she'd lost."

"This one won't ever break," he had ensured her.

She had been appropriately stunned at his generosity.

What a surprise. What a surprise surprise surprise.

She kissed him again. "See you tonight?"

"It *is* tonight."

"Later tonight." She grinned.

"Yes."

She left him with a lingering caress of his cheek, then turned back to her work.

It was fun to play the giddy young lover. Rhenn had never been a giddy young lover before. As long as she could remember, her mind had burned with purpose. To dethrone Vamreth. To regain the kingdom he'd stolen from her parents.

Now, she was in Daemanon, and she burned with the same purpose. To get home. To reclaim that same kingdom.

She made straight for the baron's keep and went inside. Its dark granite walls moved past her as she glided up the steps toward her room. She even had a smile for Matron L'via as the unhappy woman looked disapprovingly at Rhenn's scandalous male kilt and revealing top.

Rhenn made it back to her room, lit a lantern, and gave herself a moment to celebrate her victory. She had them, the two pieces she needed to enact her plan. And tonight was the seventh day after her promise to Nhevalos. He would visit her tonight. He would ask her how things were going.

And she was going to kill him.

Rhenn had discovered long ago that rigid plans tended to break. The best plans had fluidity and contained little nodes of certainty floating in the uncertainty of the future. These nodes could pivot, could be moved, could be placed in the right spot.

It was just like battle. She hadn't looked at the cadre of bloodsuckers and determined in rigid detail how she was going to kill them. Likewise, she hadn't fallen prey to surprise or fear when the battle didn't play out as she'd envisioned.

She'd moved her nodes of certainty—her skill, her quickness and strength, and her experience with previous fights—to the right places until victory was achieved.

Now, her plan included a magic dagger, a facsimile of Nhevalos's coin, and a burning hatred that would fuel her to victory. She was taking the magical coin. She was going home to her family and her kingdom, and she was going to kill that bastard.

That's when Senji reminded her that there was no certainty about the future at all.

Rhenn turned and caught the silhouette hunching in her window. Four stories up. Someone was in her window.

A bloodsucker.

CHAPTER EIGHT

RHENN

The bloodsucker launched himself from the window, and time seemed to slow. Rhenn's mind spun in a frantic montage of thoughts.

First, she recognized the bloodsucker; it was the one who'd dragged C'eldon off into the forest. In the flickering lamplight, its fangs seemed longer than she remembered. Its tattered black cloak spread like wings; it really did seem to fly.

Second, she wasn't ready. Her mind had been far away, buried deep in a daydream about the future. The attack caught her completely flat-footed. She wasn't thinking fast enough, wasn't moving fast enough. Fear spread over her heart like sudden frost.

She was going to die.

The thing crashed into her, driving her to the floor, driving its needle teeth toward her neck. The impact slammed the breath from her, stunned her, and the bloodsucker's teeth broke her skin.

"Rrrrnnnoooo!" She shouted like an animal.

Then, somehow, the magic dagger was in her hand. Her battle instincts slammed back into place. She knew what to do.

Rhenn always knew what to do.

She stabbed, but her body was sluggish. The strike was weak, clumsy. It deflected off the bloodsucker's ribcage. An amateur strike. A dead man's strike.

A crackle of blue light sparked at the wound, and the bloodsucker jolted like she'd stabbed him through the neck.

He lurched back like he was on fire, opening his fanged jaws in a silent scream. His left arm and leg went limp. His right arm and leg thrashed a counterpoint as he fell to the floor and scrabbled wildly. His spasmodic flailing spun him around in a circle on his side. The limp arm and leg seemed like they had detached from his body, like they were hanging by a few strings beneath that amorphous black sheet.

Rhenn felt sluggish, like those teeth had almost paralyzed her. During her first encounter with these bloodsuckers, she'd watched A'vendyr kneel before his attacker, glassy eyed and helpless as it prepared to feast on him.

She shook her head, trying to clear the fog, and levered herself to her hands and knees. Her arms were heavy. Her balance was off, but she gripped the dagger tightly. Her hand on its hilt was the only thing behaving normally. The rest of her body seemed packed with mud.

I've been wounded, she thought. *I'm not in fighting shape. I should retreat.*

The bloodsucker thumped and thrashed in a circle, instinctually trying to flee the scratch in its side. The wound drooled blood, far more than it should have for just a scratch.

She tried to stand and toppled over, tried again, fell again. The floor refused to stay where it ought to.

Damn it!

She clenched her teeth and crawled like a worm toward the thing. When she grabbed its shoulder, it noticed her as though for the first time. Its eyes flew wide. It seemed about to flee, but then it came at her, snapping its teeth like a dog.

She meant to stab it before it could do anything, but her palsied hand was slow. It was only halfway to its mark when the creature sank its teeth into her forearm.

The pain made her jerk, but that actually helped. Her arm shot forward and she poked it in the neck. Weak as she was, it only went in half an inch.

The result was spectacular.

Blue light sparked again, and the thing's jaws released. Its head fell back, skull thunking on the floor as though she'd cut it from the body. Its thrashing stopped.

She grunted, withdrew the dagger and clumsily stabbed it in the neck again. She did it properly this time, but it was like she was stabbing a corpse. The bloodsucker didn't react. Didn't twitch. Didn't do anything.

Its eyes turned milky, as though this was suddenly a two-week-old corpse, rather than a freshly killed monster.

What *were* these things?

She tried to stand up again and failed. She could barely even climb to her hands and knees, so she lay there in a pool of blood, her head a mere foot from the thing.

This is disgusting, she thought. *I've got to get up, got to call for help.*

Her urgency froze on that thought.

No.

No, this was perfect! Nhevalos was coming tonight to check on her progress with A'vendyr. He was coming here.

She imagined him opening the door to this grisly scene. Blood splashed across the floor. The bloodsucker nearly on top of her. He'd try to help her. Perhaps lift her up. Amidst the mess, it would be the perfect time to make the switch. Open the pouch with the coin in it, make the trade. He'd never know, not until he went back to the Thuros and tried to go through it.

And she planned to be long gone by then, back to her kingdom where she would tear the Thuros down brick by brick, trapping him here as he'd trapped her. By Senji, she'd close off that entire subterranean room! She would—

Rhenn heard footsteps.

Moving numbly because of whatever poison was in those fangs, she rolled herself to the bloodsucker's corpse like it had leapt upon her. Its head lolled onto her shoulder.

Good. That was good. She smeared some of its blood over the wound on her neck to reinforce the deception, and laid her head back.

The doorknob rattled and began to turn.

The coin!

Senji's Spear, she'd almost forgotten to have the coin ready. She hastily fumbled with slick hands at her pouches, found E'maz's coin, yanked it out, and palmed it behind her back. It would be covered with blood when she switched it, of course, but she couldn't help that. She'd just have to make sure Nhevalos got a good swiping all over when he picked her up.

She laid back down, closed her eyes, and listened.

The door opened.

She waited for the hasty footsteps to rush to her, for him to throw the corpse off.

His boots scraped as he turned. The door thunked closed. Footsteps crossed the room and stopped at her table. There was no other reaction. No urgency. Nothing.

Did he think she was already dead?

She gave a little moan. Her forearm and neck hurt like blazes, so she didn't have to fake the pain. In fact, her neck wound had begun to feel feverish. It tingled.

She heard the creak of the chair as Nhevalos sat down.

"Innovative," he said in his deep voice. "But unwise."

She grunted painfully, like she was too weak to respond.

"You realize this creature's blood is magical," Nhevalos said. "It was a poor decision to let it mix with yours."

The tingle in her neck became a burn, and the swelling grew. She could feel it pressing on her windpipe. A chilling fear swept through her.

"Nhevalos..." she wheezed, refusing to give up on her gambit yet. "Help me..."

"Yes, I think I will have to." The chair creaked as he stood up.

She let her eyelids flicker open weakly, and she feared it was less of an act than she would have liked. Her limbs felt like lead bars.

His emotionless face hovered over hers. "You are driven. You use every tool at your command. This is why I need you." He peeled the body of the bloodsucker off and tossed it aside. It hit the wall like it was made of wet paper.

She waited for him to lean a little closer, just a little more.

"It was never going to work, your plan. Against a Human, yes. There's actually a touch of brilliance to it for one who sees only what his eyes reveal. But this is what you need to understand, Rhenn. I see the future. I knew what you were doing from the moment you thought of it. I have seen the future for thousands of years. My plans encompass continents. Accept this. Accept me, and we can move forward."

Finally, he was close enough. She tried to reach up—

But her arms wouldn't move. She was paralyzed. The thickening of her throat continued. She could barely breathe.

"You're going to die," he said.

She thought he'd stretched the word out to emphasize it, but she suddenly realized her ears had warped it. Nhevalos blurred, and she felt like she was falling down a long, slick tunnel into darkness.

The last thing she remembered was his hand reaching out, grasping her throat.

CHAPTER NINE

RHENN

Crackling lightning shot through Rhenn, like she'd been poked with a hundred needles. She gasped and jolted upright, almost falling out of the chair. Bewildered, she gripped the seat and looked wildly all around.

She was still in her room. Blood covered the floor and the base of the wall where Nhevalos had tossed the bloodsucker. It still lay there, crumpled like a bag of bloody bones. Another streak of red smeared across the floor from the middle of the floor to the chair where Rhenn sat.

Nhevalos sat across from her, the only thing in this room that wasn't covered in blood. He regarded her, as always, with a cold expression.

On the table between them lay two oversized coins, glimmering in the lamplight, both as clean as if they had been washed and polished.

Her heart fell.

She didn't have to pat her pouches to know that one of them was E'maz's coin. The other was Nhevalos's. The key to her escape. They looked similar enough, but it was easy—side by side—to tell which was the real one. It simply seemed… heavier. More substantial.

"It is an interesting spell infused into the blood," Nhevalos said. "Elegant in its simplicity. That is its power, I think. It's contagious on a basic level. His blood was attacking your blood, changing it. I think it might actually have overtaken you if I let it. You might have become one of them."

Rhenn didn't know if she was more afraid she'd almost become a bloodsucker, or that her plan lay in tatters.

"You knew," she said tightly.

"Of course I knew."

"About the coin."

"The coin. E'maz. Your plan to steal the Plunnos. To kill me if you could. I knew when you would have tried, what weapons you might have used, that you planned to return through the Thuros. What your life would have been if you had succeeded in killing me and giving yourself the chance to use the Plunnos and fail."

"Fail?" she said through her teeth.

"This Plunnos is keyed to me. If you actually managed to kill me, you'd have been stuck here. In that future, you would have become the enterprising wife of your blacksmith, creating a merchant empire throughout the kingdom of Pelinon. Selling trinkets."

She swallowed. It sounded like he was reading this from a history text, some future that had already passed.

"It's what Lore Magic does, Rhenn."

"So you knew. Seven days ago, you knew what I was planning."

He just watched her.

"Why let me go on with it, then? Why not stop me?"

"Because if I do that, you will not learn. You must come to this conclusion on your own."

"What conclusion?"

"That I know what I'm doing. That you can trust me."

"That I should just do what you say?"

"The V'endann Barony needs you—"

"They need me like they need a rock in their sandal. The baron hates me. Given his choice, they'd turn me into one of their porcelain dolls. I'm the queen of Usara, not the powdered bride of the V'endann Barony. You want me to understand your plan? Then understand this: I'm not going to work with you until you return me to my kingdom."

"I can't do that."

"Clearly you can."

"You must widen your gaze first, or all is lost."

"What exactly do you *want* me to see?"

"The truth. The world, for your kind, is doomed without me."

"I don't believe you!" she shouted. She shouldn't rage in front of him, shouldn't tell him what she really felt. He wanted her to believe that he knew everything she was going to do, and that had to be a lie. It was meant to trip her up, to make her feel helpless.

She didn't want to show weakness, but she couldn't see a path right now… All her planning. All her efforts…

For nothing.

He'd just been watching her like a parent watches a child throwing a tantrum. Had he seen her in the bathhouse when she'd snared E'maz? Had he seen her at the smithy when she'd first kissed him? In the bedroom when they'd first…

She felt sick and turned her face away. She couldn't bear to look at him, couldn't bear to see her pathetic self reflected in his eyes. A fumbling, bumbling idiot who had thought she was so clever.

Nhevalos reached out and carefully picked up the Plunnos— the real one—while leaving the fake on the table. She should grab his hand, scream at him, try to take it away.

But she knew she'd fail, and she couldn't bear another failure in front of this inhuman bastard.

"Your plans are incorrectly laid. Your goals are poor," he said as he put the coin back in its pouch.

"Are they?"

"I would warn you, but you won't listen."

"I have a hard time trusting people who kidnap me."

"Your dalliance with E'maz is a mistake."

"Because you'd rather I prostitute myself for A'vendyr?" She should stop. She shouldn't let her emotions control her like this. But she hated him. Oh, she hated him. And she couldn't fight him. She couldn't escape him. If she didn't lash out at him in some way, she would burst into tears, and that would be a horror.

"You will be at the center of coming events," he said. "An upheaval like you cannot imagine. These events will spin around you like blades. Those who are not integral to my plan will be cut down. Do you understand? You stand in the center of the storm, Rhenn Laochodon. You and a select other few."

"Like Khyven."

"Like Khyven," he said. "The world needs the two of you, so you will not fall because I will not allow it. But not for everyone else. So I tell you this once: take care who you beckon close. They will share your danger, but not my protection. E'maz is not a part of my plan."

"I don't care about your *plan*!" she shouted. Every instinct told her to leap at him, to tear at his face with her fingernails.

She sat there, impotent.

"You will." He stood up.

"By Senji, I would slit your throat if I could," she hissed. Her hands trembled where she pressed them flat on the table. Her lips twisted in a painful smile. "But I suppose you already know that, too."

He just watched her.

"I hate you more than I've hated anyone in my life."

"What you think of me is irrelevant. You'll see." He left the room, and the door thumped shut.

Rhenn's throat thickened with a sob, and she fought it. She pushed her knuckles against her forehead, harder and harder, until the pain took the tears away.

CHAPTER TEN

RHENN

She sat there for a long time. Long enough for the smell of the bloodsucker's gore to make her nauseous.

She stood up. She had to start moving. When one plan went foul, movement was the key. If she kept moving, another plan would form. It always did.

But this time standing up just made her heart heavy. She truly was trapped. If Nhevalos wasn't lying about the Plunnos, then even getting it from him was useless. Every flicker of a plan that flared in her mind only died a moment later.

For the first time in her life she could see no way out. Even after hers and Lorelle's parents were murdered, Rhenn had found a way forward. Her options had been few, and sometimes horrible, but she'd made the best use of them.

Now, everywhere she turned, she felt Nhevalos's cruel eyes following her. He might even actually have magics watching her everywhere she went. Her scheming had been laughably transparent to him. A joke.

For all her travels into the noktum, Rhenn didn't know much about magic. She'd tried to bolster her education the moment she'd won back her throne. She'd spent hours studying with Slayter, absorbing what he knew.

But this was beyond her. Probably beyond Slayter, too. This was Giant magic, beyond them all.

All except, perhaps, Khyven.

Nhevalos's own words defined Khyven as a Greatblood. A "Giantkiller." Apparently Khyven was a successful product of Nhevalos's scheme, birthed twenty years ago from Daemanon and Pyranon royalty.

This could explain Khyven's specialized magic, his "luck" in the Night Ring, his ability to find that single, nearly impossible path to victory every time.

Now more than ever before, she wished Khyven was here. And Lorelle. Slayter and Vohn. If her friends were here, they could smash a hole through this insidious trap. They could turn Khyven's Giant-killing ability upon Nhevalos, put that cold-eyed, arrogant creature in the ground.

But Khyven wasn't here. He was one more fanciful plan that lay just beyond her reach.

She tried to gather her thoughts. Wishing for the impossible didn't help her. She had to work with the tools at hand.

But she couldn't see them. She had nothing. Despair crouched behind her like a vulture, waiting, longing to get its hooks into her—

"You wish… escape," a quiet voice said from the window.

Rhenn lurched to her feet. The chair upended and clattered on the stone floor.

In the window crouched another bloodsucker, the blond-haired woman who'd bitten A'vendyr on the neck, the one Rhenn had stabbed in the face.

Rhenn glanced at the pool of blood on the floor where she'd lain. E'maz's magic blade lay there, a crimson lump in the shape of a dagger.

A strange kind of hope rose within her. This was battle. This, she understood. It pulled her mind away from the despair. The dagger was far, considering how fast the bloodsucker could move. Long odds. But Rhenn had faced longer, and her whole body itched to fight. To do something rather than spin in useless, impotent despair.

The moment the bloodsucker so much as twitched, she was diving for that blade. In the meantime, she needed a distraction, something to engage the creature and give her a chance to get closer.

"Your face looks good." Rhenn touched her cheek, taking a half step toward the bloody mess. She made it look casual.

The woman's face was smooth and pale, the wound gone. That wound should have taken weeks to heal. It should have left a jagged scar, but there was nothing.

"You are Rhenn the traveler," the woman said. "From another land."

"And you're Smiley the bloodsucker, who tried to eat my friend." One more step.

"I am L'elica, and I am not here to hurt you," the bloodsucker said, but rage simmered beneath her voice.

Rhenn chuckled. "Just like he wasn't here to hurt me." She tipped her chin at the crumpled, bloody bag of bones against the wall.

"O'rsyyn went rogue. He was… he didn't understand much. All he knew was that you killed his brothers."

"I'm like that when people try to suck the blood out of my body."

L'elica's lips retreated a little, flashing her long fangs. "We were hunting."

"You were hunting me and mine."

"We did not know who you were."

"So now we're friends?" Rhenn was nearly close enough to crouch and snatch the dagger.

"Please do not pick that up," L'elica said. "I have not attacked you. I will not attack you. I have been ordered to help you."

Ordered? So these creatures had a leader.

"So old O'rsyyn here was acting against orders?"

"He didn't know."

"Because he wasn't my friend yet, like you."

L'elica narrowed her eyes, perhaps realizing Rhenn was mocking her.

Rhenn stood over the dagger now. She slowly descended and picked it up, never taking her gaze off L'elica.

All right. That was better. Much better. Rhenn loosened her shoulders and relaxed. She calculated that the odds were in her favor now. She'd fought L'elica before. The creature was fast, but so was Rhenn. And now she had a weapon that had dismantled O'rsyyn with a scratch. Rhenn would bet that L'elica didn't know about the magic.

The bloodsucker seemed to sense the threat, though. She shifted her weight on the windowsill, poised to leap away, and for the first time Rhenn thought maybe she actually *wasn't* here to attack her.

"What do you want?" Rhenn asked.

"To help you."

"You realize how ridiculous that sounds, don't you?"

"Nevertheless, it is true. My master needs you. Likewise, you need us."

"Do I?"

"I overheard your conversation," L'elica said. "You wish to escape. I can take you away from here."

"I bet you can."

"To my master."

Rhenn chuckled. "Well, that sounds appealing, doesn't it? Is that where your master transforms me into a bloodsucker like you?"

"No, he wants you alive."

And that was an interesting thing to say, Rhenn realized.

"So you and O'rsyyn… You're dead?"

"Come with me," L'elica urged.

"Well, I would, but I'm just not dressed for company." She waved her hand at her blood-smeared body.

"You will want to meet my master. He is powerful. Powerful

enough to hide you from your mage captor."

"Is he?"

L'elica nodded.

"Well tell him I'll think on it. I'll go wash the remains of your friend off me and then I'll send him a pigeon."

"A pigeon?"

They didn't have carrier pigeons in Daemanon. Rhenn had learned that, to her surprise, in the first week, but she hadn't really meant for the bloodsucker to get the joke.

The bloodsucker narrowed her eyes, then said, "You have no plans to come with me, now or after your bath."

"Spotted that, did you?"

"You would be wise to take my master's offer."

"And see, I think the opposite."

"Consider it."

"You're a blood sucking monster who killed two of my friends. My answer, I think, is a solid 'no.'"

"You will never escape this mage by yourself. You will stay here, under his thumb, until you realize that my master is the only one who can save you."

Rhenn started toward the window, dagger in hand. L'elica faded back into the darkness.

When Rhenn reached the window, the creature was gone.

CHAPTER ELEVEN

RHENN

Rhenn stood at the window for a long moment, whether to see if she could spot L'elica—it was four stories down to the ground—or to see if the bloodsucker would return.

The whole encounter had been... odd. If Rhenn didn't know better, she'd have thought L'elica was telling the truth.

It was ludicrous, of course, to think she was. Her enticement was clearly a ploy to lure Rhenn away from the protection of the baron's keep into the dark where L'elica, and no doubt a dozen of her other bloodsuckers, could finish the job they'd started.

But if that was the case, why—

A knock sounded on the door. Rhenn pivoted to the side of the window, making sure her back wasn't facing the night, and reflexively brought her dagger up.

But no bloodsucker came bursting through the door. Instead, the hasty knocking came again.

"Rhenn?" A'vendyr's voice came through the door, muffled.

She let out a breath. Not a bloodsucker.

Of course, as she glanced down at her gore-splattered self and remembered the not-so-long-ago conversation between herself and Nhevalos, she realized one of the last people she wanted to see right at this moment was A'vendyr.

"What?" Rhenn asked.

"Are you all right?"

"I'm fine."

"Rhenn, open the door."

"You have hands," she said, though she was certain he wouldn't take the invitation.

The people of V'endann had an interesting cultural nuance. They didn't open other people's doors. Not to personal abodes, anyway. You couldn't just say, "come in" and expect the visitor to enter your room. You had to actually open the door for them or they'd just stand outside your door all day.

It gave her time to stride across the room. There was a teakwood rack next to the bed where she kept her clothes, and she was hoping she'd left a towel there so she could at least wipe away some of the blood.

"Rhenn," A'vendyr said. "Nhevalos told us you were in trouble."

"Trouble? What trouble?"

There was no towel, but she'd kept a robe from the bath house. Oh, the poor washing servants weren't going to like that very much, but she didn't have anything else. She picked it up, readying to wipe her body, but she realized she'd never get clean before A'vendyr started banging insistently, so she threw the robe over her shoulders and belted it.

"Please open the door."

"I'm stark naked in here," she said.

She heard a chuckle, not A'vendyr's voice. It was cut off abruptly as though A'vendyr had glared at whomever had dared to make light of Rhenn's comment. So there was more than just A'vendyr in the hall. Had Nhevalos sent a fighting force?

"Rhenn, I must insist."

"Oh very well. If you're insisting and all." She went to the door and opened it.

A'vendyr stood on the other side with three other V'endannian warriors. They all had daggers drawn. A'vendyr's eyes went wide.

"Rhenn!"

Apparently, the robe had done nothing except perhaps accentuate the bloody mess.

"It looks worse than it is."

"It looks like you've been ripped apart."

"Not me. Him." She jerked a thumb over her shoulder, now wishing she hadn't put the robe on at all. The sticky blood clung to her arms and legs, and it was hot in the room. She was now sweating and moistening the blood again. Senji's Teeth, she was going to vomit.

Three young warriors entered the room and fanned out, each of them checking corners. She knew them all, of course. Rhenn made it her job to know as many of the fighting men in V'endann as she could. She'd tipped a few glasses of wine with these three. They were all young, each gifted in fighting. Good choices to fill out the pentara.

In fact, if Rhenn had had to choose two warriors to replace the two A'vendyr's pentara had lost, she'd have chosen two of these. J'alas was young, fair-haired, and tall. She'd watched him in the practice yard. He was fast, and he had a good sense for objects in space around him. It was hard to sneak up on him.

G'rau was short with close-set eyes and dark, curly hair. He had shoulders like an ox, but moved a lot faster than you'd expect someone of his build—and stature—to move. He had a quiet way, and was almost bashfully respectful of everyone. Rhenn had liked him instantly.

T'ailfen was almost undoubtedly the chuckler. His dark brown eyes always twinkled with mirth, as though he knew the punchline to the joke of life and was just waiting for someone to ask him.

There were three new warriors here, except only two had died.

"Where's B'ressyr?" she asked.

A'vendyr stared at the crumpled bloodsucker against the wall, then glanced over at Rhenn. "What?"

"B'ressyr. He's not here. Where is he?"

"B'ressyr is on temporary leave. Rhenn, we have to get you to the infirmary."

"The bath house."

"Bath—? I think not."

"I'm not injured. Do you want me to disrobe and let you inspect me?"

"Rhenn, I… no. I'm just trying to… Look at your neck!"

"Oh, that." She rubbed where O'rsyyn had bit her and felt the cuts, two little slices. Beads of tacky blood clung to them, her blood this time, trying to form a scab. Strange that Nhevalos healed whatever stupor had overtaken her, but not the cut itself. Was there a purpose to that? It was Nhevalos, so probably yes, but she couldn't think of what the purpose might be.

"You are the most stubborn woman," A'vendyr said through his teeth. "I'm trying to *help* you."

"Oh please. If I was one of your male warriors and I said I was all right, you'd chuck me on the shoulder and grin at me for being tough. But I'm a woman, so you're clucking around me like I'm made of glass. Let's just imagine I'm part of your pentara."

"You *are* part of my pentara."

"My point. And I'm telling you I'm fine. Let's move on."

A'vendyr glanced helplessly at the men behind him. T'ailfen chuckled, then put a hand over his mouth.

"I…" A'vendyr's face darkened. He looked back and forth between the men of his pentara and Rhenn. "Leave us," he commanded. J'alas, G'rau, and T'ailfen hesitated only for a second, then exited the room and closed the door. A'vendyr turned to Rhenn.

"Is this where I get a lecture?" Rhenn asked.

He blushed even darker. "Rhenn, I have tried to accommodate your behavior because you are from another land. And I think I've been very open to your strange ways. Kalistar knows, no woman has ever served on a pentara before, yet I requested you be put on mine."

"Because Nhevalos told you to."

"Because..." He stumbled in his delivery. "Because I serve my father, the Baron of V'endann, and I do what a good son does. I follow the orders of my liege lord."

"And your father does what Nhevalos tells him to do."

"Nhevalos is the Prophet of V'endann. He is a sacred being."

"Nhevalos is a manipulating, lying bastard who—"

"Enough!" A'vendyr swiped a hand through the air, cutting her off. "You cannot spit in the teeth of all of our ways any longer, Rhenn. You cannot ignore the rules you don't like. You are an honored guest here, but our tolerance can only be pushed so far. My father is already..." He sighed, shook his head. "Do you know what it's like here with you wandering around? The ladies whisper about you every single day. They question their own place in the barony, revering you or hating you by turns. The warriors discuss you at length, at first due to your uncanny talent with a blade, and now because... Well, the stories are far more colorful since..."

"So you know about E'maz."

"I am my father's son. I know about *everything* in this barony," A'vendyr said.

Oh, I doubt that, Rhenn thought.

"You are here because you are the chosen of Nhevalos. The chosen! Do you know what an honor that is? You walk with the gods."

"Nhevalos is not a god." Rhenn's lip curled in derision.

"Rhenn, you are here to holy purpose. You are here because you are to... Because we are to be..."

Rhenn raised her eyebrow, wondering if he would say it.

"Don't you understand what you are doing?" he asked, dropping his voice. "You are meant to serve the highest purpose, yet you resist. You cut through the fabric of our society. If you were not Nhevalos's chosen, do you know what would have happened to you by now?"

"A public shaming?"

"A public flogging! Imprisonment at best!"

"For being slathered in blood in my room?"

"For disrobing in the men's bath house, Rhenn. For throwing yourself at E'maz."

"Throwing myself?"

"You'd be dragged to the stocks as a wanton. Commoners would throw rotten fruit at you. And rocks."

"E'maz didn't mind."

"Of course he didn't, he is..." A'vendyr trailed off, catching himself almost in time, but Rhenn heard the last word anyway.

"He's a man?" She floated the question lightly, like she *wasn't* about slap him.

"Rhenn, you are the consort of... You're meant to be for me." His face was beet red now.

"Because Nhevalos says so."

"Yes, because Nhevalos says so! How do you think it looks for me among the people? To have my intended whoring around with a common blacksmith?"

"He's hardly common..." Rhenn reflected in an appreciative voice.

"Rhenn!"

"Let's get our facts straight," she said. "First of all, no money exchanged hands. So you're going to have to come up with another slander for me than whore—"

"It amounts to the same thing! You are promised to—"

"Second..." She interrupted him. "I'm not yours to lose. I'm not your consort. I will never be your consort."

"Nhevalos has decreed—"

"If you were the last man in the barony, in the kingdom, on this entire continent!" she said through her teeth. "I would not be your consort precisely *because* of what Nhevalos has 'decreed.' Do you understand that?"

He straightened, his chin elevating.

"I have been kidnapped, A'vendyr! Have you even thought about that? Even for a second? You whine about your image.

You, the baron's son... Poor you, people will think poorly of you." She paused, lowering her voice. "I am *queen* of a kingdom that makes V'endann look like a backwater village. I was ripped away from my home and my friends, stolen in the middle of the night away from an entire people who need me. But *you* want me to assuage your pride by falling into your bed?"

"You are twisting the situation," A'vendyr said.

She laughed, a dark, ugly laugh. "One of us is, for certain. Tell me, A'vendyr, what would you do if this keep and these people were suddenly plunged into war and I yanked you away from here? Imagine you were thrust into a castle with me, unable to leave, unable to get back to them without any knowledge of what had befallen them, whether they were alive or dead. Your father, your mother, your brother and two sisters might be fine, or they might be corpses on pikes. And I told you, 'Just go along with it, A'vendyr. It's Senji's will. Just follow my laws, serve my needs, please me in my bed. Oh, and don't disturb the waters too much or my subjects might think less of me.' What would you do? Would you go along? I think not. And if you would, then you're a spineless coward. Where I come from, we fight when we've been wronged. We fight until there's nothing left."

Unlike her conversation with Nhevalos, Rhenn remained in control of this one. She let just enough emotion into her voice to hammer A'vendyr with her point.

His brow creased.

"I know it may be beyond you," she said. "But imagine for a moment that Nhevalos isn't a holy prophet."

"He is," A'vendyr protested.

"I know you believe that. But if you want to understand my side, then use your imagination. Use your own intellect. And then ask yourself what you would do in my place. Would you go meekly where you were led?"

She could see the war on his face as though, somehow, this had not occurred to him. That dawning realization clashed with his obvious anger at what he expected of her and how she had frustrated him. He opened his mouth to speak, closed it.

She raised an eyebrow.

"I…" he began, cleared his throat. He stood there, awkwardly silent, for a long moment. "I will have servants come to clean up this mess."

She glanced briefly over her shoulder at the remains of O'rsyyn.

He turned and went to the door, but stopped with his hand on the handle. "And I will fill a special tub for you, so…"

"So I don't make the communal baths a bloody mess?"

"Yes."

"Thank you."

"I will have it brought to the baths."

She nodded.

"The *women's* baths," he clarified, and this time he met her gaze. Was that a joke? He gave a tentative smile, and she realized it was. Maybe there was hope for him yet.

She grinned. "If you insist."

"I…" he began.

Just leave it, she thought. *A good ruler knows when to leave it alone.*

He hesitated, nodded, and left.

CHAPTER TWELVE

N'SSAG

N'ssag blinked against his fatigue. The chemicals stank of rotting guts and vinegar. The stench floated about his laboratory, filling his nostrils and saturating his very skin, but the batch was strong. That's what he wanted. It had to be strong. He'd discovered something important, and his flesh renderings were progressing. He couldn't stop now.

His creations, these dead people he'd brought back to life, had been improving with each new batch, each new adjustment, as L'elica's existence very clearly demonstrated. His original flesh renderings staggered around with little bits falling off of them. They hadn't been much more than moving corpses with a basic survival instinct.

Their successors—the "primes"—were a vast improvement. They could move faster than the originals and react like a human body would, but their intelligence level was somewhere just above a dog's. They sensed N'ssag was their master, which was good, but they only acted on three instincts: hunt, flee, or revenge. They couldn't make intelligent decisions in a crisis, and he'd had to do their thinking for them.

Until he'd created L'elica.

She'd become his field captain. With his adjustments to the chemicals and the light in the room, as well as the critical step of his own life-siphoning magic, he'd brought her to life with most of her memories intact, a true revival of body and mind without the sluggish responsiveness of the original flesh renderings nor the idiocy of the first primes. But N'ssag knew there was more to be had. He could sense it.

He could make a prime twice as fast, twice as strong as L'elica, and keep her human level of intelligence.

L'elica already evinced a speed and strength that outstripped most Humans, if only by a little. In life, she'd been the wife of a local baker, vital, young, and a mother of two. He'd taken her body only two days after her death. Hers was the freshest corpse he'd ever taken.

Her family had buried her the day after she'd died. He had exhumed her and had backfilled her grave that same night. L'elica had been dead less than forty-eight hours when he began the process, and her body had been in excellent condition. The swamp fever had hit her so fast she hadn't had time to atrophy. In short, she was perfect. That had been one key to his success.

The second key was the strength of the chemicals. He'd built the batch potent for her, spent three times as much money on the preparation of her body as he had the others. The vinegar was cheap, thank Nissra, as that comprised about ninety percent of the solution. A natural preservative, it helped the flesh remain strong while the binding agents of the *c'alynne* root and the *forsa* powder worked their way into the flesh. And the precious emerald drops, of course, were vital. That little green bottle had changed the entire process, but by holy Nissra it was expensive. Only with this specific combination of elements had he kept his primes from falling apart like the original flesh renderings.

But he didn't just want to bring his children back from the dead, to give them new life; he wanted to create something beyond the mortal. In L'elica, he could see the makings of it. At five feet, five inches tall, she was a slip of a thing, but she could knock down a man twice her size.

He wanted his new primes to be able to pick up a man and hurl him. And now he could see the path to it.

Darkness was the final key.

The stronger the concoction, the more powerful the resultant prime, like L'elica. But the powder and root atrophied in light, and the emerald drops were volatile. If exposed to light, the emerald drops burst into flame. And the stronger the batch, the more volatile the reaction.

The chemical bath and embalming fluid for the first primes had included all the requisite base ingredients plus one drop of the criminally expensive emerald drops. The resultant primes could not stand in daylight without bursting into flames, but they could mill about in a lantern-lit room, even stand right next to a lantern without any adverse effects.

With L'elica's chemical bath and embalming, N'ssag had taken a chance and included three emerald drops. That had made all the difference, but she was even more sensitive to light. She shied away from lanterns like they were bonfires.

In an effort to improve on the positive effects of her strength and intelligence, N'ssag had made a chemical bath where he'd added *five* drops of the precious emerald extract to the body tray. Back then, he'd still been working with two lanterns lit. As it turned out, that had been two lanterns too many.

Barely a moment after the fifth drop hit the tray and spread out, the chemicals exploded into flame, devouring the body he'd prepared. N'ssag had been blown back by the explosion and it had nearly set fire to his entire laboratory.

Now he stood over his latest attempt. The corpse of a strapping young mine worker who'd been knocked in the head with a falling rock lay in the body tray. The vinegar, *c'alynne* root, and *forsa* powder had all been swirled together in perfect proportions.

N'ssag had done away with all lanterns, and only guttering, shielded candles flickered, set at the furthest corners of the room. He pulled the bottle of emerald extract from his robes.

He could barely see it and, not for the first time, he cursed his weak Human eyes for needing light at all.

He uncorked the bottle and began to tip it, hoping he would be able to see clearly enough to know whether he had added three or four drops—

"Master," L'elica's voice came from behind him.

He almost dropped the bottle and thanked Nissra he didn't. If that bottle fell into the tray, the entire laboratory would erupt like a volcano.

"L'elica," he murmured, carefully tilting the bottle back upright and corking it. L'elica was a marvel. It had been painstaking to teach his other creations to call him "master," but L'elica had picked it up immediately. It made him feel like he ought to feel. This was the way the priests of Nissra *should* treat him.

He turned, but of course he couldn't see her. She could see him perfectly well, he knew. All the flesh renderings, original or prime, had spectacular night vision, L'elica most of all. "What did you learn?"

"She is trapped."

"Trapped? Rhenn is a woman running as part of a pentara in Baron V'endann's constricted little holdings. She hardly seems trapped."

"She is actually from somewhere else. They talked of traveling to other continents."

N'ssag's heart beat faster, and he set the bottle of emerald drops carefully on his work table. "Another continent?"

"Are there other continents, N'ssag?"

"Oh yes. They are mentioned in legends that date back before the Human-Giant Wars."

"But those are myths."

"Giants are real, my sweet. And so are the continents."

L'elica materialized from the darkness, standing by the slab where an array of body parts lay.

"What are they?" she asked.

"There are five..." N'ssag tried to recall. He had studied those ancient legends during his boyhood days among the priests of Kalistar. They had old tomes that no one seemed to want to read, but N'ssag had loved them because they talked of Giants and magic. They had talked of a time when mystical Thuroi connected all the continents.

"Pyranon," he said. "Is a land of fire and lava. Of sorcerer queens and giant bats. And Drakanon is a land where dragons roam the land."

"Dragons?"

"Yes, my sweet. And of course there is Lathranon, where lore unimaginable is kept. Each continent had something that made them special."

"And is Daemanon special?"

"You are the very proof of that, my dear. Daemanon bursts with life. It was where the Giants created every kind of life imaginable. Where there is the possibility of someone like you, created from Life Magic and darkness…"

N'ssag trailed off as he recalled the fifth continent, Noksonon. His heart began to race. "And Noksonon," he breathed.

"That!" L'elica said. "The tall mage who holds Rhenn captive mentioned that. He said something about her traveling back to Noksonon."

"She is from Noksonon," he mused. "A land of complete darkness."

"What do you mean?"

"There is no sun. Ever. The Giants cast a spell over the entire continent." He paced away from the tray then back. "L'elica, this could be the answer to my primes. If I could set up my laboratory in a place of unending night, how many drops of emerald extract might I put in the base solution? Eight? Ten? Oh, my sweet," N'ssag murmured. "This is the answer."

"To create more primes," she said.

By Nissra's Eyes! He could finally realize the true potential of his creations. The legends told of how the Giants had made provision for their Human servants to see in the dark, magical enhancements to their natural vision.

"In a land like that, I could see like you," N'ssag said.

"Yes."

"And think of how you would thrive there, L'elica. Think of how all my children would thrive there!"

"Yes, master."

"But first we must capture this Rhenn. You talked with her?"

"Yes, but not for long. She had a dagger that destroyed O'rsyyn, so I dared not get too close."

"O'rsyyn?"

"He went into her room before I climbed to the window. He attacked her."

"He tracked her from the battle?"

"He must have."

"That's more capable than I would have expected of O'rsyyn."

"I arrived in time to see the last of the fight. Her dagger... It did something to Orsyyn. She barely scratched him, and yet it took him apart."

"A magic dagger..." N'ssag mused, pulling at his lower lip. He'd wondered what would happen if one of his creatures encountered a magical weapon. "He came apart at the joints?"

"Yes, master."

Ah, of course. The magic dissolved the cohesive properties of the preparatory bath.

"Good to know."

"I wanted to kill her. She has slain four of my brothers now, but I did not interfere because... you told me to watch. To make your offer."

"That was well done, my sweet. Keep your fire burning. You will have your chance. We will even make her a prime when her usefulness is ended." Killing Rhenn and turning her into a prime was compelling. But a full memory return wasn't guaranteed. N'ssag needed Rhenn's faculties intact. He needed what she knew about Noksonon, about the great darkness, and N'ssag hadn't yet perfected keeping the memories when he did the life siphon.

With L'elica, he had succeeded in retaining her basic knowledge of decision making, learning, improving. She remembered language, social graces, and a high level of problem solving that his other primes lacked. Her memory of everything since her rebirth was impeccable, better even than N'ssag's, whereas the other primes tended to forget things after a week or so.

But he had stripped her of memories that might… get in the way. She could not remember her husband or her children. That had been relatively easy; he'd just ensured that anything past the age of sixteen or so had been obliterated in the transfer.

But with Rhenn, it would be more difficult. He couldn't just wipe out the last ten years of her memory. What if there was something important in there, about her kingdom, about Noksonon? No, he had to bring her back with full faculty.

Turning Rhenn into a prime would be premature.

"And she knows how to use this Thuros? How to reach Noksonon?" N'ssag asked.

L'elica shook her head. "No, master. That's why she's trapped. Nhevalos has something called a Plunnos he's keeping from her."

Curious.

"So she sees Nhevalos as her captor, not her savior."

"She hates him. I think she would have tried to kill him with the magic dagger if she could have managed it. But she was afraid of him."

"Oh… that is fine. That is very fine," N'ssag mused.

"I tried to take her with me, tried to convince her that you could help her leave him behind."

N'ssag grinned. L'elica had improvised. "You're a wonder, L'elica. That was well done. But she refused, I take it."

"Yes."

"I appreciate your innovation, and now we have the information that will make your second attempt work. Tell her we have a Plunnos. Tell her we can get her through her magical gateway."

"Do we have that, master?"

"No," he said. "But she has everything she needs to go home. She just doesn't know it yet. We will strip her of her knowledge, and then we will fill in the gaps."

"And go to Noksonon?"

"Yes, my sweet. We will go to Noksonon."

CHAPTER THIRTEEN

RHENN

The sun sank below the horizon as the sortie started up a small rise west of V'endann Keep. Twilight turned the fat leaves of the jungle into glistening, silver-and-gold lined plates. A sheen of light sweat covered Rhenn's body, but she was used to that now. The air cooled slightly as the sun vanished.

Water goblins had attacked a pair of carts on their way to V'endann Keep yesterday. Despite the solid routing A'vendyr's pentara—and three other pentaras—had given the goblins, they weren't getting the message. They'd been harassing the coastal villages almost every day, and A'vendyr and his new pentara had been sent out.

But Rhenn could barely concentrate on that.

The conversation yesterday with A'vendyr had been good. She'd felt like a queen again—reasonable, confident, in command—instead of a prisoner. She'd felt, for a brief moment, like there were alternatives to her hopeless captivity at Nhevalos's hands. She was getting through to the baron's son. She was changing his mind. She was moving events.

Rhenn had learned one unwavering thing about herself after being chased out of her own castle by Vamreth. She never, ever wanted to see herself as a victim again. She could be displaced, driven from her home, and chased into hiding, but she would stay strong—not give anyone the satisfaction of beating her down. Vamreth had killed her entire family and had wanted her to feel helpless, but she'd refused to give in to him or to those feelings.

She'd felt that if she'd cowered even once, if she'd believed for even one second that Vamreth had beaten her down, then it would actually have been true.

And now, under Nhevalos's thumb, she felt again like she had when she'd fled Vamreth as a frightened little girl. All the advantages she'd so carefully cultivated meant nothing next to the power of the Giant. Nhevalos was simply... better at everything. He wasn't just stronger. He was more experienced. He was a superior planner. He was faster. His skills seemed so many and so perfected that she couldn't conceive of the amount of time he'd taken to perfect them.

With Vamreth, Rhenn had seen her advantages immediately. She'd seen herself as the underdog waiting for her chance. Hungry. Powerful and hidden. Poised to strike.

With Nhevalos, she couldn't see any advantages, and it was driving her insane. In the past, there had always been something, some inspired idea she could grab to begin turning the contest in her favor.

But everything she tried seemed useless, like she was a mouse between the giant paws of a Kyolar. No matter which way she turned, no matter how brilliant her plan, she would always be within the Kyolar's paws. He could see every option she might take, anticipate every move. She was predictable.

She found herself dreaming of different circumstances, of how she might succeed if only a few things she lacked were within reach.

She daydreamed about the standing army of Usara, about her powerful friends: Lorelle with her superhuman Luminent abilities. Khyven with his miraculous ability to find a win, no matter what. Vohn with his keen insight and Slayter with his powerful magic. If they had been with her, she might put something together. She might find a way—

She glanced up to find that A'vendyr had raised his hand. The rest of the pentara stopped, and she almost bumped into J'alas. She shamefacedly halted, gritting her teeth as A'vendyr glared at her, annoyed.

Fantastic. Now she was mentally drifting. She wasn't paying attention to the moment, where every opportunity was to be found.

She could hear the water goblins now, and she wondered what victim they were devouring just behind the small rise. This area by the surf was hilly, but the jungle was no less dense. Rhenn had decided she could really come to like this strange kind of forest, this wet land. The humidity had been horrible at first, but she was coming to enjoy it. And the strange and wondrous large-leafed trees were actually quite beautiful. At first they'd seemed confining, but once she'd become accustomed to the way they felt—and alert to the dangers they hid—it almost felt safer in the jungle than outside it.

A'vendyr gave her a signal that indicated she should wait behind as the rear guard. It was a standard pentara procedure to leave one or two of their number behind when engaging a new force, so as to hide the full strength of the pentara, guard the retreat if necessary, and hold something in reserve. But usually this job fell to the second or third best warrior.

A'vendyr was breaking with protocol to show her he was displeased, ostensibly about her wandering attention, but she had to believe that some of it was motivated by their conversation the other day. She'd thought it had ended on a high note, but perhaps it had been a higher note for her than for him. She had been in command of the conversation, after all, had gotten what she'd wanted out of it. And A'vendyr had had nothing but time to reflect on the fact that he'd left getting nothing of what he'd wanted.

She gave him a frown and it was met with an implacable stare. She shrugged and made the hand signal that indicated she understood.

A'vendyr and the other three went up and over the rise as Rhenn slowed, creeping to the top to assess the field. As she slithered through the wet ferns to get a better view, something moved to her left. She froze.

The bloodsucker L'elica emerged from the darkness. She was a full thirty paces away, and there were so many trees between them that Rhenn would never have seen the bloodsucker if she hadn't stepped directly into Rhenn's line of sight.

Rhenn drew a breath to shout to A'vendyr.

L'elica held a finger up against her lips, and Rhenn hesitated.

"You wish a Plunnos." L'elica's soft voice floated across the distance, barely audible, but somehow Rhenn understood her perfectly. "Free yourself. I will take you to one." L'elica beckoned with a single finger.

Rhenn tensed, ready to leap over the rise and sprint toward A'vendyr and his pentara, to warn them of the danger in the jungle.

She hesitated.

Her mind, which had been spinning around at the total lack of options open to her, suddenly clunked into a single, unavoidable thought.

She could go with this monster.

It was insane, yes.

But it was also completely unpredictable. Even Nhevalos would never imagine she'd run off with a monster that had tried to kill her.

Water goblins squealed, and Rhenn peeked over the rise at her pentara. The goblins scattered as A'vendyr and his men fell upon them. Four V'endannian warriors. Six goblins, with half of those already in flight. Her pentara had this in hand—which A'vendyr had probably predicted when he'd left her behind. The pentara was fine.

Rhenn felt a tingling, frightening warmth spreading through her.

Senji's Teeth, I'm going to do this, she thought. *I'm actually going to do this.*

She crept back from the rise so the pentara wouldn't see her, and she stood up.

L'elica waited, eyes serious, as Rhenn drew her magic dagger and approached. When she was a half dozen feet away, she stopped, her gaze flicking to the dark trees all around. She didn't see any other bloodsuckers, but they were creatures of the night. *Would* she see them even if they were there?

"You have a Plunnos?" Rhenn asked.

"To open your gateway."

"You're lying," Rhenn said. "Why didn't you mention the Plunnos yesterday?"

"I did not know you needed it."

"You said you overheard my conversation. You knew."

"I did not know what a Plunnos was. But my master did."

"And he has one."

"Yes."

Rhenn prided herself on being able to detect a lie, but she couldn't read the bloodsucker. L'elica had an innocent face. She spoke plainly, sounded and looked sincere.

And she was a ruthless killer.

I want to believe her, Rhenn thought. *I want this to be true, that she has the means to get me home.*

That was the real danger. Rhenn wanted any option so badly she'd take this one, no matter how ridiculous, no matter how minuscule the chance for success.

"What does he want from me?"

"Information," L'elica said quickly. Maybe too quickly. She'd been waiting for that question. But did that mean she was lying?

"What could I possibly know that your master would want?"

"Noksonon," she said.

"He wants to know about my continent?"

L'elica nodded.

"Why?" Rhenn would never lead creatures like L'elica and her fellows back to her home. She'd rather die.

"Politics," L'elica said. "Like you, my master is caged by those in his order. He would rise above those who hold him down."

"And knowledge of Noksonon will help him to do that?"

"Knowledge of any kind helps him. My master seeks mastery over life and death itself."

Her comment from the previous day came back to Rhenn.

No. He wants you alive.

"He brought you back to life," Rhenn said.

"Yes."

That seemed true. Rhenn would swear it, and L'elica's serious, innocent face hadn't changed at all. By the bloodsucker's unchanging facial cues, Rhenn would judge everything else was also true.

"So I go with you, and your master asks me some questions about my homeland?"

"Yes."

"And in return, he gives me the Plunnos. And I go home."

L'elica nodded.

"And I'm not taking him or any of you bloodsuckers with me when I go?"

"Why would we go with you?" L'elica asked.

"To invade my kingdom."

Her brow wrinkled for the first time, as though she hadn't expected that. "No."

The commotion over the rise was subsiding. Rhenn's window to escape was closing.

L'elica seemed to come to the same conclusion. She held out one hand. "Escape. Help my master. Go home."

Rhenn flicked a glance over her shoulder.

By the five gods…

She looked back at L'elica. "Take me to your master."

L'elica nodded. "We must be quick."

"Oh, I can be quick." Quick to leap from the frying pan into the fire. Quick to lose all sanity.

L'elica ran into the jungle, and Rhenn followed. She thought about what Lorelle would think of this decision. She could see her friend in her mind's eye, throwing up her hands in a gesture of exasperation. She could hear Lorelle's voice in her head.

You can't make such reckless decisions, Rhenn! You're a queen. A queen has to remember the value of herself. You can't just rush into danger when the whim strikes you.

Except Rhenn wasn't a queen here. Her kingdom was one person: herself. She had to get out of here before anything Lorelle might say would apply. She had to risk everything, or she'd be here forever.

The bloodsucker never seemed to tire, leaping over ferns, weaving between thick-trunked trees. Rhenn was in prime physical condition, but after half an hour at that punishing pace, her lungs were on fire.

They'd left A'vendyr and his pentara so far behind they'd never catch up even if they did pick up their trail. Finally Rhenn lurched to a stop, gasping.

"L'elica!"

The bloodsucker stopped, turned. Rhenn bent over, hands on her knees, and sucked in the thick air. "Wait... I can't... keep your pace."

The bloodsucker's blond hair was windblown, but that was the only change in her. She wasn't breathing hard, didn't seem flush. The only change was that her face seemed more gaunt than before. That was damned eerie. It made the hairs on the back of Rhenn's neck stand on end.

You shouldn't be here, Rhenn. Lorelle's cautionary voice rose in the back of her mind. *You've dealt with many a monster, but you don't know this one. You don't know why it exists, how it works, or what its motivations are. You have jumped in over your head.*

"Rest yourself then," L'elica said. "This is as good a place as any for it."

A chill went up Rhenn's spine.

"As good a place as any for what?"

Rhenn felt the wisp of wind on the back of her neck a split second before the hidden bloodsucker struck. She almost had time to turn, almost had time to bring her dagger to bear.

But the thing pounced on her from behind and drove her to the ground. If Rhenn had been just a little less exhausted, she thought she might have been fast enough to throw the thing, might have given herself a chance to fight.

But wasn't and she didn't.

Her knees hit the ground. The bloodsucker's foot came down on her wrist, and Rhenn gasped at the pain. The magic dagger fell onto the grass. Strong hands clamped around her forehead and around her chest. Sharp teeth sank into her neck.

She gurgled a protest, but her arms suddenly became putty.

She felt the teeth drive deep, deeper, and her body went limp.

L'elica shouted something, a triumphant battle cry, but Rhenn couldn't make out the words.

The last thing she remembered was Lorelle. A hazy image of the Luminent hovered before her, as though she was actually here. Her beautiful sister spoke in her head.

I told you, Rhenn. I told you. Why don't you ever listen to me?

Chapter Fourteen

RHENN

Rhenn jolted awake. Vinegar pricked her nostrils and the cloying scent of decay hung heavily in the air. The stench made her want to gag.

Back at her little rebel camp in Usara, there had always been a practice fight going on, and when a fighter got their bell rung, Lorelle brought them back around using what she called "waking salts." It was a concoction of vile herbs sewed into easily ripped little packets. Once the packet was snapped beneath a groggy— or even unconscious—fighter, the acrid stench was like a knife to the brain.

This was like that, except overlaid with the smell of a two-day-old battlefield.

She sat up in the dark. Her first thought was that she was in a noktum without her amulet, but that illusion vanished and she remembered her predicament. She'd trusted that bloodsucker, and the bitch had done exactly what Rhenn should have expected. The whole thing had been an ambush.

Rhenn's sluggish brain awoke, and she tried to move. Manacles on her wrists and ankles clinked. Chains held her fast.

In her desperation to escape Nhevalos, she'd run headlong into a worse problem. In fact, she should be dead, except…

Come to that, why wasn't she dead?

No, he wants you alive.

A chill went up her back. What had once sounded positive now sounded insidious inside the echo chamber of her mind.

L'elica had said her master wanted information about Noksonon, but clearly she'd lied about everything just to get Rhenn under their power. What did her master *really* want? Rhenn guessed she was in some kind of basement. What foul magic simmered in this place?

She squinted against the dark and slowly realized there actually was a light source, a tiny one, as though it wasn't really meant to light anything. Was it a shielded candle? She couldn't tell. It was barely a glow twenty feet away, a soft yellow spot in the corner of the room. She twisted and spotted another one, then made a cursory inspection and realized there was a covered candle in each corner.

"I apologize for the manacles," a weaselly male voice said from directly behind her.

Rhenn jumped, then frowned at herself. That was not the first impression she wanted to give. She reined in her surprise, twisted about, and managed to see the man's silhouette.

"L'elica told me you are a lion in combat," the man said. "I, unfortunately, am not a lion. I was afraid if I didn't restrain you, you would hurt me upon waking."

He had that right. She was about done being abducted. She glanced past him, trying to force her eyes to adjust, but it became apparent her eyes were as adjusted as they were going to get.

"Hurt you? Why would I do that?" she asked.

The man gave a breathy little laugh. "L'elica didn't mention you were funny."

"You should see me when I have my sword. I'm like a palace jester I'm so funny."

Again, the breathy laugh, like he had the lungs of a chipmunk and couldn't quite get enough air. "I'm sure you are. Will you give me the opportunity to apologize?"

She tensed, but his footsteps moved away from her. She tried to follow him through the dark, but couldn't. She tracked him instead by his voice. "That is a powerful weapon you have."

"The dagger?"

"Yes."

"It does tricks, too. Want me to show you?"

He huffed his chipmunk laugh. "Perhaps in time."

"Where did you put that, by the way?"

"That, too, I will soon tell you."

"So we're just chatting until then?"

"I wanted to establish our relationship a little more concretely before… letting you free."

"Very well. Let's talk. What are you making in here? Rot sandwiches?"

He ignored her quip this time. "I'm excited to have a visitor. Someone who can appreciate what I'm trying to do here. Someone who can… understand. You'll soon see the necessity for the rather unique scents you are experiencing. And you'll become accustomed to them. I barely notice them anymore."

"That says a lot about you."

That pulled the chipmunk laugh again. "L'elica tells me you are a queen."

"L'elica seems to know a lot."

"My primes are very good at spying. They can see in the dark, you know. They lurk on rooftops, in shadows. Did you know the average person does not look up unless something calls their attention? Never. I've often wondered if it is a primal fear of some kind. Or if people are simply too self-involved."

"She was outside my window during my conversation with A'vendyr. She didn't leave," Rhenn guessed, and cursed herself for thinking that the bloodsucker would go away just because she'd finished talking.

How many stripes of a fool am I? Rhenn thought bitterly.

But she banished the self-recrimination. She couldn't afford to paralyze herself with such nonsense. She had to stay relaxed, fluid, to think her way out of this, to trust herself. She'd seen worse. This was just new. She had to assess the playing field and start working on how to get on top of the situation.

"But where are my manners?" the man said. "I imagine you can barely see. I have become accustomed to this low light, you see." He took one of the candles and held it up to a lamp. Light swelled in the room, and Rhenn took in her surroundings.

It was a mage's laboratory. Like Slayter's lab in the basement of the palace, except twisted into something that was half-laboratory and half-morgue. A long table—as long as the wall where the man stood—held rows and rows of glass bottles, vials, and beakers, all with different colors of liquids in them. There were six stone slab tables, exactly the size needed for a human body. Three of them had corpses on them, laying in steel trays filled with a sallow liquid. That was the source of the stench.

Rhenn also lay on one of the slabs, though not in a stench-filled metal tray, thank Senji. With the light, she could see old bloodstains beneath her, and she stiffened. It was all she could do to force herself not to recoil, not to try to thrash and get off when the chains would clearly not let her.

She swallowed hard, mastered herself, and forced herself to continue taking stock of the room. There were two covered windows high up. Yes, they were in a basement. She'd guessed that correctly. Why did mages prefer their labs underground?

The windows had been so meticulously covered that not a trace of light came through. A cage dangled from a thick chain in front of one of the windows, and it contained one of the bloodsuckers. Not L'elica, but Rhenn thought it might be one of the group that had first attacked A'vendyr's pentara.

She wondered if that was the one that had snuck up behind her and bitten her on the neck this last time. The bloodsucker was gaunt and thin, and he shuffled to the back of the cage as the light flared from the lamp. The cage rocked back and forth, the chain squeaking.

The man who'd spoken to Rhenn from the dark stood below the cage, and now she could see him clearly. He wore ratty black robes. The full-length cuffs were frayed, threads sticking out this way and that, and the elbows of the robe were patched. His hair was long with clumpy braids that didn't look intentional at all, more like he couldn't be bothered to cut his hair. He'd twisted those neglected locks together and tied them back to get them out of his face.

"Queen Rhenn, I am N'ssag," the man said. "And you and I have common purpose."

"That we both need a bath?" She raised her hand from the vile table, looked for somewhere to wipe it, then reluctantly set it back down.

This time, he smiled thinly. No breathy laugh. "No. We are bound by those who hold our freedom in their hands."

"I see."

"I offer you a bargain, my queen. You help free me, and I will help free you."

"Clearly you want me to be free." She held up one manacled hand.

"A temporary situation, as I have already told you. I simply wished to converse with you first, to open your eyes to what you don't yet see: we were meant to be allies."

A sarcastic quip leapt to her lips, but she held it. She'd risked her life to put herself in this stupid situation, she'd best see if there was any way to make an advantage out of it. Despite her predicament, the truth was: she was free of Nhevalos.

What this creepy little man was saying might actually be true. What if she *could* use him to get back to Noksonon?

"L'elica said you had a Plunnos," Rhenn said.

With his hands clasped together, N'ssag pressed his two index fingers against his lips. "More to the point: I know where one is reputed to be."

"Reputed?"

"Yes."

"And this helps me how?"

"You are a resourceful woman, and I am a man of knowledge. Together, we can obtain this Plunnos. Then you will no longer be under the thumb of the Giant who holds you prisoner."

Her eyebrows went up. "So you know what he is?"

"The Betrayer is known to anyone who has studied the histories of old. He has returned because we are on the cusp of the end of days."

She narrowed her eyes. "So you think some great war is coming as well?"

"Oh yes. Nissra's Order has been planning for it. But they are short sighted. They don't see what is clear, what obviously could help them in the upcoming conflict."

"I see. And they are missing...?"

"Me. What I can bring them. The strength I can wield on their behalf. They revile me, ignore me. But with your help, we could ensure that the Lords of old return, and we would be at their right hand. Not these insolent priests of Nissra. Do you see?"

"Ah, yes." What she saw was that N'ssag was obviously a loon. She began to think about how she might turn that to her advantage.

"The Betrayer confines you, traps you, twists you to his advantage. The priests of Nissra do the same to me. But you can escape him, punish him. And I can rise above these short-sighted, small minded men who hold me down. Together, we can deliver a victory to Nissra and usher in a new order that will last for thousands of years. The priests will bow to us then. Kings will bow to us. Nissra is lavish in her gratitude for those who serve truly."

Rhenn watched the zeal in the man's eyes. Good. There were ways to deal with maniacs. They were, often, easily manipulated if you dangled the object of their obsession in front of them. When she'd recruited followers to fight Vamreth, she'd spotted the Vamreth fanatics, like Duke Derinhalt, right away. Fanatics were powerful when pointed in a singular direction, but they weren't that great at outthinking manipulation.

Unfortunately, N'ssag seemed intelligent. She'd have to be careful.

"Who's Nissra?" she asked.

"Ah…" he said. "Nhevalos withholds from you, hides the truth from you. She is the great one. She has come to set things right in the world. She is a Giant like the Betrayer, but they are enemies."

So Nissra was exactly what Nhevalos was warning Rhenn about.

"And you want to see her win this upcoming war."

"She will crush Nhevalos, and you need never live under his thumb ever again."

But I'd have to live under Nissra's thumb then, she thought.

"You've piqued my interest," she said. "L'elica said you needed me because I know about the noktums."

"Yes."

"I'm all ears."

"You are a queen of darkness. I know all about Noksonon, about the spell that covers the continent, about how you live in absolute darkness. And how you can see there, how you can move there, how your Giants made it so their servants could work within the dark as though it were daylight to them." The man's dark eyes seemed to glow. "You want to leave Daemanon and return to your land of eternal night. I want to go with you."

So L'elica had lied about that, too. N'ssag *did* want access to Noksonon.

"Why?" Rhenn asked.

"It is essential for me to expand my work."

She flicked a glance around the laboratory. "Creating your bloodsuckers."

"'Bloodsuckers' is such an ugly name."

"What do you call them?"

"They are my primes. I have two different kinds of renderings. Some are plant renderings. That's where I started, but those are slow and stupid. My latest are rendered from the flesh of Humans. The earliest form of my flesh renderings were… inelegant. But my second form, like my dear L'elica, are so very close to human. My primes."

She hesitated, having a hard time calling the murderous creatures so benign a name. The bloodsuckers were corpses returned to life by some unholy magic concocted by N'ssag. And they were dyed-in-the-wool killers. "So you want to make more... primes."

"Yes."

"And darkness helps the process."

"It makes the binding more pure."

She resisted the urge to look at the dead bodies and kept the revulsion off her face. She was tap dancing on thin ice now.

The last thing she wanted to do was help this man create more bloodsuckers.

But if he actually could get her home, everything changed. She'd have resources, friends. And intelligent or no, N'ssag was just a man. She could deceive him. Manipulate him. Move him so that she could gain the advantage.

Hope flickered inside her. If he could really get her home, this might actually not have been as stupid a decision as it currently seemed.

"So let me get this straight," Rhenn said. "You get me a Plunnos. We go through the Thuros, and I show you how to navigate the noktums of my homeland."

"And we build an army to defeat Nhevalos, to destroy your nemesis, yes."

Build an army of bloodsuckers in Noksonon? Not on your life, she thought. Her flesh crawled at the very thought.

"Well?" N'ssag pressed. "Will you join me? Will you grasp this opportunity and become a queen not only of Noksonon, but of the entire world?"

These were her choices: to be a captive of an all-powerful, emotionless Giant who wanted to breed her. Or to partner with this reeking man who wanted to give the world over to *another* Giant. Rhenn bent her lips into her best charming smile and said the words she knew the sadistic fanatic would believe.

"And Nhevalos suffers?" she asked.

"He will burn in a torturous pit of Nissra's making from now until the end of days."

A *poetic* sadistic fanatic.

"What are we waiting for?"

N'ssag's grin bent his face in an unwholesome way. Just when she thought the man couldn't be any more repellent, he went and smiled at her.

"Partners, my queen?"

"Partners."

"Good. L'elica, if you will?"

Rhenn glanced to the right to find L'elica standing there in her powder blue dress with the dirt stains on it. As usual, the blond bloodsucker had no expression on her face. She raised a key and unlocked Rhenn's manacles. Rhenn pushed off the table, suppressing a shiver of relief at no longer sitting on old bloodstains.

"Thank you, my dear. You may leave," N'ssag said.

L'elica vanished into the shadows. There was a metal grinding, like unoiled hinges, and the bloodsucker was gone.

N'ssag crossed to Rhenn and extended his hand.

"I promise to aid you," he said.

"And I promise to aid you," she lied. She shook his hand; it was clammy and limp like a boneless fish.

"Excellent." He smiled in the dim light, and she imagined moss on his crooked, shadowed teeth.

He let go of her hand and moved to stand beneath the cage. The captive bloodsucker scuttled against the bars, watching N'ssag. "Now, my dear queen, we shall build our partnership. First, we must earn each others' trust. You're wary of me, and I of you. That is understandable. But I want us to move past that. I want you to know that when I give my word, I keep it."

"Master…" the bloodsucker said.

"This is G'elreg," N'ssag said.

"This one is sorry, master," G'elreg said.

N'ssag ignored him. "Rhenn, please believe that any discomfort you suffered at my hands was an accident. I gave specific orders that you were not to be harmed. G'elreg promised he would see my will done."

"This one is sorry, master. I was so hungry, and she was so juicy. So full of blood. Please…"

Rhenn felt a pit in her stomach, felt like something horrible was about to happen.

"I want you to know, my queen, that I take my promises seriously, and I take the promises others make to me equally seriously."

"Master, please—"

N'ssag yanked a cord attached to the thick curtains over the window. The curtains flew aside, and blinding light burned into the room.

G'elreg shrieked. He leapt at the bars as the light struck him. His shoulder exploded. His back erupted next, flesh spattering the cage and the wall. His head flew apart like a melon dashed against stone. In seconds, it was over. The remaining body parts quivered and continued to pop where they lay on the base of the cage.

"Senji's Eyes!" Rhenn gasped.

Flesh dropped from the cage, sizzling and splatting on the floor. The bits that fell into shadow, though, stopped burning.

N'ssag was spattered with gore, but he didn't seem to care. He turned to Rhenn, who couldn't wipe the horror from her face.

"I keep my promises, my queen," N'ssag said. "And those who break their promises to me face dire consequences."

Rhenn was no stranger to intimidation. This had been staged for her benefit. She knew all this, knew that N'ssag wanted to scare her and that she should resist, but it had been well planned. He'd surprised her, and her whole body shook.

"Your point is well taken," she said in what she hoped was a calm voice.

"Oh good." He smiled. "I can already tell we are going to be fast friends."

CHAPTER FIFTEEN

RHENN

o," N'ssag said. "Where shall we begin?"

Rhenn rubbed her wrists where the manacles had been. "My weapons."

"We have formed an alliance, my queen, and your first request is to arm yourself?"

"You say this as though you don't have your own weapons close at hand. L'elica in the shadows. Whatever manner of magic lies about in this place. You say I'm free, but I wonder if that is true? Are you just a different shade of Nhevalos?"

N'ssag licked his wet, wormy lips. Finally, he went to the drapes, pulled them closed, and secured them. The room plunged into darkness again. Rhenn had thought it was dark before, but after the bright sunlight, even the lamp N'ssag had lit seemed low and guttering.

"L'elica," N'ssag called to the dark.

The grating sound of the steel door came again, and though Rhenn could not see, she felt the blond bloodsucker's presence enter the laboratory.

"Be a dear and retrieve the queen's weapons for her."

"Master…" L'elica hesitated. "The dagger as well?"

"I have the dagger. And, yes. I will give it to her. She's right. She's our partner now. We will restore her to her full strength."

"Yes, master," L'elica said, but she didn't sound convinced. Rhenn's eyes were slowly readjusting to the darkness, so she listened hard as L'elica moved on the far side of the room. She couldn't quite hear where the bloodsucker was—

L'elica materialized next to her, carrying her sword, sheath, and belt. She also carried Rhenn's non-magical boot dagger, her non-magical waist dagger, and set them all down on the slab. She faded back out of sword range.

"That's a lot of weapons," N'ssag said.

"I like a lot of options." Rhenn strapped them on, feeling instantly more like herself. Now she would give herself decent odds of making it out of this hellhole alive if she chose to fight.

However, she was increasingly convinced she wouldn't have to do that. She felt N'ssag, as crazy as he was, was actually being honest. Which meant this could work.

N'ssag glided forward, holding the magic dagger with two hands as though it was some holy object. "This is powerful. Where did you get it?"

"A friend." She took the proffered weapon and strapped it on.

"Did he make it?" N'ssag asked.

"Partly."

"I see."

"Tell me more about this process of yours," she said. "Sunlight destroys your creatures."

"My primes."

"Your primes," she repeated. "Sunlight destroys them."

"Creating primes is best achieved in absolute dark. We can't attain absolute dark in Daemanon, not like the darkness you know. And even if we could, I couldn't work within absolute dark. I need to see, my queen. I need your ways. I need the artifacts your Giants created. I need an Amulet of Noksonon."

That took her aback. "How do you know about the Amulets of Noksonon?"

"Oh… I'm not one who spends… much time with people, my queen."

No kidding, she thought.

"I spend my time with books. I've read every single book I've ever seen. I've read ancient histories that talk of the other continents: Noksonon, Pyranon, Lathranon, and Drakanon. I know that Noksonon is covered with a grand spell of darkness. I know the Giants of Noksonon were called Noksonoi, and that they created magical amulets that allowed their underlings to see. I need this darkness, my queen. Do you know how powerful my primes could be if I created them in absolute darkness?"

No, I don't, she thought. *And I never want to find out.*

"Good. Then we're agreed," she said. "You find me a Plunnos, take me to the Thuros, and I'll put you in a noktum."

"For the greater glory of Nissra."

"For her greater glory," Rhenn repeated, trying to sound enthusiastic. "So, where is this Plunnos?"

"For that, my queen, we must take a journey. A journey to the ruins of an old Giant stronghold, called a nuraghi."

Rhenn thought of the castle inside the noktum, of the giant bats and Sleeths and Kyolars who protected it. "That's funny," she said. "That's exactly what we call them, too."

CHAPTER SIXTEEN

RHENN

T he nuraghi mounted a rise of craggy rock with a single pathway winding up to it on a raised road. Back and forth and back and forth, as though once there had been a gentle rise, but someone had poured acid on everything save the road. It jutted up like a ridge and was the only way to get to the front gate.

Behind the wall and the tall double doors, the nuraghi thrust up, a fortress that had once been grand and powerful, but had obviously been abandoned long ago. One great tower out of five had survived the centuries. The rest had crumbled to the ravages of time and the humid Daemanon weather. The stone that comprised everything—the crenelated walls, the collapsed towers, the still-intact wall that encircled it—was black, like this castle had been created in Noksonon and brought to this place.

It seemed to her like an ideal fortress for some baron or duke to make their stronghold—for Duke V'endann himself to have done—but it was clearly abandoned and had been for an age. Just like the nuraghis of Usara, no one wanted to live in this place.

Rhenn had been in a half dozen nuraghis before. During her younger years, before her rebellion had begun, she and Lorelle had traveled all over Usara looking for potential allies, and she'd visited every nuraghi she could, every nuraghi that had stood outside a noktum. They all had this feel. Forbidden. Like they were sacred graveyards and if anyone tried to inhabit them permanently, they would be assailed by ghosts that would break the mind.

She and Lorelle had stayed the night in a few nuraghis, but only one night each. One was enough. Rhenn herself had initially considered trying to make her own stronghold in one of these places—it certainly would have provided a kind of protection—but in the end, she had decided against it. For a rebel leader, morale was critical, and morale sank quickly inside those creepy stone walls.

If the Thuros was inside like N'ssag had promised, then this was also likely the place where Nhevalos had brought her through. She didn't remember any of this, of course. Nhevalos had done something to her the moment he'd taken her through those swirling lights. She remembered the blues, golds, greens, reds, and blacks, then the slithering of the liquid, as though it was passing over her flesh and through the organs of her body. She remembered seeing a glimpse of Lorelle's horrified, frozen face.

She remembered the Thuros room. The walls were made of huge, rough-cut, black stones. Nhevalos had turned with her on his shoulder, and she'd glimpsed an archway with a demon's head on its keystone. Then Nhevalos had said something to her in a soft voice, or more likely he'd recited a magical incantation.

That was all Rhenn remembered. The next thing she knew, she had awoken in her room at the baron's keep, and Nhevalos had told her how important she was, that he wanted to confide in her what was needed of her.

That she must give birth to a child, a Greatblood, for the upcoming war.

But if the Thuros was anywhere in this hot, humid land, it was in that ruined castle. She glanced back, wiping sweat from her brow.

Behind her, N'ssag struggled to keep up. Rhenn's first impression of the necromancer was that he was a vile miscreant who had somehow managed to thrive in the cracks of society. Rather like a cockroach. Since spending two days and nights on the road with him, her opinion of him had lowered considerably.

The man was an unending spewing of complaining and misery.

He complained about the trail. He complained about sleeping on the rocky ground. He complained about sleeping under the stars. He was slow, awkward, stumbling. He was completely unsuited to wilderness travel, or even to travel across a well-worn road.

He had insisted on a slow pace during the day, not only because he'd brought a donkey towing a small cart of his chemicals behind him, but also because he wanted to allow his "primes" the opportunity to catch up during the night. So what would have taken Rhenn a day and a half to reach the nuraghi had taken three, and she was about ready to pull her hair out. At least tonight he had agreed to continue traveling a little bit after the sun fell.

The man poured sweat, but he still insisted on wearing his greasy cloak and cowl. He panted as he pulled his horse to a stop. His donkey brayed pitifully and slowed as well. The narrow wagon behind it creaked as it rolled to a halt. N'ssag's pale skin looked waxy and wet in the moonlight. He contemplated the long, narrow pathway up to the nuraghi.

"Nissra be merciful," he breathed, and Rhenn forced herself to smile instead of rolling her eyes.

"You're going to have to guide that cart carefully up that," Rhenn noted. The raised pathway had once been wide enough for two horses to gallop abreast, but now there were sizable chunks missing all along the way. It was a chancy bet to assume the donkey would be able to navigate those with the thin cart.

"Yes… I believe you're… right," he huffed.

"There's no need for you to hike all the way up there, though," she said thoughtfully. "I could be up and back with the Plunnos before sunrise, I'd bet."

"Oh..." N'ssag huffed. "Yes... I see your point..."

"You can teach me how to read that map?" She'd seen him poring over a map by firelight as they had waited for his bloodsuckers to arrive. She'd caught a couple of the names on the map, and was certain it was of the nuraghi itself. Given half an hour alone with the map, she was sure she could figure it out herself, but she had to get it in hand first.

"Send you in alone... with the map?" N'ssag panted.

"If the Plunnos is where you say it is, I'll be in and out in a trice."

"Yes... I'm sure you're right." He made no move to procure the map. "But... I wish to see this place of magic... this place of Giants... for myself."

Rhenn checked her sigh. Their unspoken conversation told more than their words. With his prevaricating, he was trying to convince her that he trusted her, of course, but that he simply wanted to see things for himself.

"Suit yourself." She gave him a friendly chuck on the shoulder.

For her part, she acted breezy, trying to convince him that taking the Plunnos, opening the Thuros, and escaping home while leaving him behind wasn't *exactly* what she planned to do.

Neither of them was convinced, of course.

"How long is it going to take you to climb that?" She gazed at the thin, elevated walkway. It looked like something out of a painting.

"I'll... manage," he wheezed, looking resolutely upward. "My... primes will be here soon. They can... assist me."

No doubt they would. In fact, she wouldn't be surprised if L'elica showed up with a litter this time and they physically carried him to the top.

Rhenn wished she knew more about L'elica. Who was she? Why did she have such loyalty to N'ssag? Certainly she seemed like she had her own mind, thought her own thoughts. Why be loyal to this man? Because he'd brought her back to life?

Rhenn didn't think she'd be grateful if she died and N'ssag brought her back to life. It was a fate worse than death to be pulled back to the land of the living to serve such a vile creature. How could L'elica stand it?

Rhenn had tried to engage the bloodsucker in conversation the last two nights when she'd showed up just as the fire was about to die, but L'elica didn't seem interested in talking to Rhenn, almost as though she knew it was a plot to gain her trust and turn her on her master.

L'elica—and all the bloodsuckers—were a problem. Rhenn could have killed N'ssag a dozen different ways during the day if she'd wanted. Without his minions, he was practically helpless. Oh, she figured he probably had a smattering of poisoned weapons or magical knickknacks hidden in his moldy robes— Slayter always did—but magical knickknacks were useless against a fast dagger. That was another thing she'd learned about mages from Slayter. The mage could do just about anything, but it took time. His fastest spells couldn't be managed in even twice the time of a thrown blade.

Still, killing N'ssag did her no good. Not yet, anyway. Right now, he was her only path to the Plunnos. Of course, she was certain that by the time they arrived at N'ssag's hidden Plunnos, it would be dark and he'd be surrounded by his primes. That was a problem she'd been working on in her mind.

Rhenn had to find a way to circumvent the bloodsuckers, or at least to divide and conquer. She'd give herself good odds against L'elica and any two other bloodsuckers if it came to a fight, especially with E'maz's dagger. She wouldn't have to be accurate; she'd just have to scratch them to debilitate them.

But against six? Against a dozen? It was a desperate move with even the most advantageous circumstances. She hoped a viable plan presented itself before long.

She looked up at the winding road leading to the enormous double doors far at the top of the hill. For now, though, she simply had to walk the path and hope for a bit of luck.

She was due, wasn't she?

CHAPTER SEVENTEEN
RHENN

As they ascended, Rhenn marveled at the defensibility of this place. A handful of soldiers could hold it against an army ten times their size, because they wouldn't be able to attack except by the long, elevated roadway.

The closer they got to the gates, the more Rhenn's uneasiness grew—like someone was watching her. She kept looking over her shoulder, waiting for the bloodsuckers to appear, but they didn't. By the time she and N'ssag had hiked halfway up the raised road, she felt a constant prickle on the back of her neck. Were there yet defenders of this place? Were they watching from hiding?

Rhenn took to walking with the magic dagger clenched in her fist. N'ssag seemed to be oblivious, but that didn't surprise her. The man's combat senses were about as sharp as a polished stone.

N'ssag painstakingly guided his donkey and its cart slowly forward. Three quarters of the way up the roadway, when he seemed ready to collapse, the primes finally arrived. Rhenn saw them in the distance, running fast like a pack of dark wolves, covering tremendous ground. She'd learned that they didn't tire because of the magic with which they were imbued. N'ssag had proudly explained everything about his primes. They didn't eat and they didn't breathe. They sustained themselves on life force that was pulled into them, initially by N'ssag's own powers, and then after by taking the blood of another living creature into themselves. They could run as long as that life force was brimming, but without replenishment, they would slowly begin to look more and more like the corpses they had once been, before N'ssag had resurrected them.

They reached the base of the road and ran up. More than five minutes after Rhenn had spotted them, N'ssag, in the midst of his grunting, groaning, and complaining, finally noticed them when they were halfway up the road.

"Oh thank Nissra," he gasped.

The primes arrived, eerily calm, though every single one of them looked gaunt, even L'elica. Rhenn supposed running that fast for several hours in order to catch up took its toll. L'elica and Rhenn watched each other over the distance—Rhenn at the front of the procession, L'elica at the rear.

"You brought the litter?" he gasped. "This road is killing me. Just killing me."

"Yes, master," L'elica said.

He waved his hands impatiently. "Bring it. Bring it. By Nissra, I need a rest. Goodness knows I need a rest."

Four of the primes brought forward the poles and the canvas stretched between, creating a hammock that N'ssag fell into gratefully. Rhenn forced her lips to continue smiling, then turned and led the way upward. The waxy-faced, wormy-lipped necromancer disgusted her, but that was a hate she could tuck away. She simply had to keep telling herself that this was business. A few more steps, one single discovery, and Rhenn would be her own woman again, not a prisoner of some ancient Giant nor this wheezing, stinking man who thought the world owed him better than the dung-covered hill he'd made.

They reached the top of the roadway and the double doors. Rhenn pulled on the giant rung, but it didn't budge. The nuraghi in her noktum was a ruin like this one, but the gates, both into the courtyard and into the castle, had been broken, easily circumvented. This nuraghi had tumbling towers and broken stonework, but the outer wall was strong and thick, and so were the doors.

In the center of the double doors where the lock should have been, there was a slab of steel with an indented carving of the symbol of Daemanon.

She glanced around, then back at N'ssag. With the help of his primes, he levered himself out of the hammock and proceeded to limp the last dozen feet on his own.

Rhenn turned, looking up the length of the wall to see if there was any spot crumbling away, some path they could take that didn't go through those formidable doors. She couldn't see any. There was no visible way to get into the castle except this winding road.

The nuraghi perched on the top of a hundred foot cliff that tapered almost to the ground toward the back. But there appeared to be no other entrance, and strong, thick walls rose from rocky terrain at the back. A handful of soldiers might traverse that terrain to attack from the back, but not an army. Not without losing half their numbers to broken ankles and whatever hell the defenders could rain down on them from above.

"It needs a key. I don't suppose you brought one," Rhenn said.

"I have… everything… in hand…" N'ssag wheezed. L'elica held onto his arm, but her gaze never wavered from Rhenn.

"That's a relief." Rhenn turned away and rolled her eyes.

Rhenn had thought the uneasy feeling and the tingle on the back of her neck would vanish once the primes arrived and she could see them, but it hadn't. The longer it lingered, the more she was certain it wasn't coming from the primes. There was something in there, inside the nuraghi. Every time she was sure it was just her imagination, another spider crawled up her back. The first two times, she'd actually thought something was on her, but each time she'd smack at it, there was nothing there. She had to keep loosening her shoulders to banish the feeling.

"I have it... I have it here..." N'ssag wheezed and stepped toward her tenderly like his feet were bleeding. She backed up as though deferentially, but she forced herself not to wrinkle her nose. The man reeked of weeks-old body odor. She was astonished she hadn't noticed back in his laboratory, but she supposed even his reek would be overpowered by the stench of decay and vinegar that permeated his basement. She doubted he'd ever bathed in his life. She always stood at least three feet away from him, further if she could manage.

"How did you get a key to this nuraghi?" she asked.

"Oh..." he said. "It wasn't hard. I just..." He stopped in front of the enormous doors, put his hands on his knees and breathed for a time, then he straightened and withdrew a large, steel coin from his robes. Its large size reminded her of Nhevalos's Plunnos, but that was where the resemblance ended. This actually looked like a normal piece of steel. "I paid attention. I studied. Most don't know that you must have this particular... key to get inside. But I read up on it because... Well, because I read up on everything. And as... I came up with my plan to go to Noksonon, I located it."

"You just found it in the piles of your laboratory?"

He gave a wheezing laugh. "Oh no... No no... It belonged to Duke Soleff in Saritu'e'Mere."

"But no longer?"

"L'elica visited his apartments in the night."

"And stole it?"

N'ssag finally straightened. He was still breathing hard, but he was no longer gasping. "He should be grateful the key was all she took."

Rhenn glanced at L'elica, and the bloodsucker gazed back without emotion. L'elica was clearly the most powerful of the bloodsuckers, and the leader of the rest. For Rhenn's half-baked plan to work, L'elica would have to be the first to go. The death of their leader might spook the others.

Rhenn had no intention of holding back when it came to this combat. Once the Plunnos was in hand, she was going to put her magic dagger into L'elica's back. So far as Rhenn was concerned, there was no "fair" fight this time, not outnumbered a dozen to one.

The main problem was that L'elica seemed to be expecting exactly what Rhenn was thinking. Catching her off guard was going to be problematic.

The prickle of spider legs went up Rhenn's back again, and she looked sharply at the nuraghi.

"What?" N'ssag noticed the motion. "What is it?"

Rhenn considered telling N'ssag about it, but she didn't see any upside. If there was a danger inside, and Rhenn was getting some kind of early warning, perhaps it was better if N'ssag didn't know about it. Maybe whatever it was would kill him and Rhenn would escape with the map.

"Nothing," she said. "The nuraghi gives me an eerie feeling is all."

N'ssag grunted, stood on his tiptoes, and raised the thick coin over his head. The indented circle with the Daemanon symbol was seven feet up on the door, almost beyond his reach. With the tips of his fingers, he slipped the coin into the indentation.

A loud *ka-chunk* came from behind the doors, and the left door moved outward. It was only an inch, like something had been released and now the doors could swing open. L'elica pulled on one of the rungs and, surprisingly, the door moved easily.

A chill went up Rhenn's back. The doors were made of solid black iron. Hinges on a door that old should have been crusted with rust. And even if the hinges had been perfectly oiled, there was no way L'elica—even as strong as she was—could have pulled that twelve-foot-tall, foot-thick iron door open so easily.

N'ssag shuffled back behind L'elica even as he peered past the doors. Beyond stood a courtyard of smooth, flat stone. Nothing grew in there, though there were a hundred places—

patches of dirt by the castle walls, cracks between the flagstones—where weeds should have sprouted.

Twin fountains made of black stone rose on the left and right of a decorative stone pathway made of reddish stones. The path went straight from the gate to the steps at the base of the doors to the castle.

L'elica and the dozen other bloodsuckers moved inside. Rhenn waited until N'ssag gestured to her.

"Please, my queen. After you."

"I'll watch the rear."

"No one else is coming after us."

"Call it a habit."

"As you wish." He shuffled inside.

The hairs on the back of Rhenn's neck prickled as she followed the line of bloodsuckers and their master across the barren courtyard. As lush a place as Daemanon was, it was damned eerie to walk across a courtyard where nothing grew. Not a tree or a shrub or even a tiny lick of moss.

The feeling of being watched increased, and Rhenn checked the parapets along the castle. The nuraghi loomed over the courtyard with a hundred protected places where archers could unleash an attack. Once an army came up that raised road and through those double doors, there was nowhere for them to go. This courtyard was a killing box. Hemmed in by cliffs, walls, and castle, attackers would have to fight through or die.

She wondered now why this nuraghi had been built in the first place, and her mind drifted to the wars among Humans and Giants so long ago. This place was obviously built to stand off an army; it was the only reason to build a castle this way. The castle in the noktum by Usara's crown city was certainly formidable, and certainly capable of holding off an attack, but this was a castle made expressly for war. This had to have been some key strategic point that must be held at all costs.

But what was it defending?

A cold shiver went up her back. The Thuros. In an age where the continents were at war, what could be a more strategic asset than a doorway that connected continent to continent?

She glanced at the black, noktum-like stone all around and wondered if this had been some construct of the Noksonoi, the Giants of Noksonon. Had they somehow gotten the upper hand here in Daemanon long enough to build this castle? Had this been a Noksonoi foothold in Daemanon? A staging ground for military offensives?

"My queen," N'ssag called from a distance. She looked up from her reverie to see him all the way on the other side of the courtyard at the base of the enormous steps. The doors at the top looked like twins of the iron doors of the wall.

Rhenn jogged to catch up. Senji's Braid, she wanted to be out of here, but there was no way out except through.

She reached the steps, which were every bit as inconvenient as the steps in the noktum nuraghi, each one knee high, built for Giants.

She hiked up the steps as L'elica and her little band helped N'ssag up. Rhenn looked out over the killing box, imagining what a defender might feel as an army entered this trap. Exhilaration. The thrill of battle. The certainty of victory.

N'ssag stood on his tiptoes and fit the coin into the indentation on the second set of doors. Again, they shuddered like something behind had been released and again, L'elica pulled them open easily.

"Does anyone else feel that?" Rhenn finally had to ask. Suddenly it didn't seem as good an idea to conceal her intuitive warnings. Whatever force resided in this castle would likely kill them all which meant, at least for the moment, that she, N'ssag, and his primes were all on the same side.

L'elica looked at her with curiosity for the first time—a refreshing change from her usual implacable glare—but she didn't say anything.

"What is it?" N'ssag asked.

"The feeling that someone is watching us."

"I feel nothing."

"Well I feel something," Rhenn said.

"This is a place of great magic. Perhaps that is what you feel."

"I'm sure you're right, but this feels intentional. Like there's something that doesn't want us to be here. Something specific."

N'ssag peered into the dark. Beyond the doors, inside the nuraghi, it was as black as a shroud. "Nothing is without risk," he said, but his voice quivered. "Do you want to turn back?"

Rhenn grunted and moved inside. N'ssag's little band followed, creating a circle around him.

"No rear guard this time?" N'ssag asked.

"Hesitation is the cousin to cowardice," she murmured, drawing her sword.

"A noble sentiment. A brave queen," N'ssag said as he and his guard of bloodsuckers moved inside. The moonlight illuminated a square of mosaic on the floor, pieces of colored stone that had been put together to resemble the symbol of Noksonon, a golden sun with five golden rays being eaten by tentacles of obsidian.

Rhenn's heart beat faster. Why were the doors opened by Daemanon symbols, but the castle itself had been built with Noksonon symbols? What was this place?

The giant double doors slammed shut, plunging the room into darkness. Only a faint silver glow of moonlight emanated from somewhere to Rhenn's right.

"Noksssssononnn?" A voice tingled in Rhenn's mind.

"Rhenn!" N'ssag shrieked.

A monster lurched out of the pitch blackness.

CHAPTER EIGHTEEN

RHENN

Senji's Teeth," Rhenn hissed. She backed up, holding her sword and E'maz's dagger in front of her. N'ssag squealed like a pig somewhere in the darkness.

She couldn't see a thing, but that tingle on the back of her neck suddenly became a garrote around her neck, squeezing off her air. Something was in the room with them, something huge.

"Noksssssonooon?" it said again.

A wet thump sounded to her left, followed by the hiss of a bloodsucker. A second later, she heard another wet thump against steel, as though the monster had tossed the body across the room at the double doors.

The doors...

Rhenn spun toward where she'd thought the doors had been. The darkness disoriented her, but she tried to remember where they were. She cast about, but all she could see was that dull shaft of moonlight far down a hallway to her left.

Another wet thump, a scream. She felt something fly by her, so close her hair moved. The body crunched into the wall behind her.

The creature in the dark was throwing bloodsuckers. It was bodily throwing them.

She heard a bloodsucker hiss and growl, then the enormous thing howled like a chorus of twenty dogs. The howls turned into rumbling growls and another bloodsucker screamed.

Never mind the door, Rhenn thought. *The window will have to do.*

She didn't know what was outside that window, a ten-foot tumble or a hundred-foot death drop. All she knew was that it had to be a better chance than facing this monster.

She ran away from the melee toward that window.

Something caught her eye, low and gray and long like a dull silver spear laying on the ground. She skidded to a stop. The doors! It was the line of moonlight underneath the doors!

She sheathed her weapons and tried to get her fingers underneath the door, but it was too narrow. If she could just get the thing open, she could at least fight. In this absolute blackness, she was useless, like a blind man swinging wild. That was a pitiful way to defend or attack. She'd be dead in seconds.

"Rhenn!" N'ssag squealed. "Where are you? Where are you? Help me!"

She stood up and groped for a handle, found it. She pushed with all her strength. Her boots slipped on the cobblestones and she grunted with the effort.

The doors didn't budge.

"Rhenn!" N'ssag shouted.

"To the window!" she said, yanking her dagger and sword out again.

"What?"

"The window! Go to the moonlight!"

She plunged ahead toward that little slanted patch of light far away.

"Noksssssonooooon?" the voice said again. Each time it was the same insistent, curious tone. She bolted down the hallway. The fighting continued behind, but she thought she heard N'ssag's shuffle behind her. Another bloodsucker shrieked and thumped against the wall.

Rhenn burst into the moonlight. The window went all the way from the floor to ten feet up the tall wall, coming to a pointed arch in the center. Bubbled glass panes let the scant moonlight through, but it was enough to see by. Senji be praised, it was almost like sunlight by comparison.

And she reached it not a moment too soon. Soft, heavy footsteps thumped behind her as the creature pursued.

She raced past the light and spun around just as the creature came into the moonlight. The thing was a horror, and Rhenn stared up and up at it.

It stood on all fours with thick, powerful legs ending in dog paws that were as big around as wagon wheels. Its back was easily seven feet tall, and its belly was barely two feet off the ground. Its barrel-like body was strapped with thick muscles beneath short black fur.

It had toothy dog faces sticking out of its body everywhere: its ribs, its haunches, and the top of its back as though smaller dogs had started to grow out of the creature but stopped before emerging completely. Some of the dog snouts thrust out far enough to expose milky eyes. Some had only come out far enough to be noses, sniffing frantically at the air, and some were caught halfway between, just snapping jaws without anything but teeth and jowls.

The thing's actual head—or at least the head at its front—was like a giant bulldog, big and round with a jutting underbite and teeth as long as Rhenn's thigh. Its shoulders, however, didn't look like those of a dog or any other creature Rhenn had ever seen. Its thick, powerful legs rose up, connected to its trunk, but then continued upward past the neck. Bony bulges to either side of the bulldog's head led to arm-like appendages ending in bony, fleshy stumps that whipped about and struck the bloodsuckers. This was the source of the wet thumps. This was what had been hurling the bloodsuckers against the walls.

The beast squinted, blinking its huge, filmy eyes against the moonlight.

N'ssag's remaining bloodsuckers crawled over the enormous beast like mosquitos, ripping and biting. The bulldog head howled, and all the other mouths joined in.

"Rhenn, do something! Kill it!" N'ssag demanded, scuttling behind her.

She wanted to backhand the coward, but that beast was going to devour them if she didn't do something.

"It keeps saying 'Noksonon,'" she said. "Do you hear that?"

"What?"

"It keeps saying—"

"Nokssssssonooooon?" The word came again, and Rhenn looked up to find the bulldog's milky eyes fixed on her, except it hadn't spoken. In fact, there was no way that bulldog mouth could form words.

It was talking to her mind-to-mind.

"Yes!" she shouted, holding her hands up, weapons waving. "Yes, Noksonon!"

"What are you doing?" N'ssag asked. "Kill it! Don't bring it over here!"

"Shut up," she growled. "Make them stop attacking it for a second!"

"Get away," N'ssag said immediately. "L'elica, bring them over here."

One by one, the bloodsuckers leapt off the bleeding giant bulldog. The half-howling snouts went silent. The bony appendages stopped flailing, hovering fifteen feet in the air, fleshy clubs twitching like bug antennae.

"Noksonon!" Rhenn slowly came forward, holding her weapons high. As she neared, she saw the dried blood on its jowls and chin. Gobs of old blood matted its fur from its neck all the way down its chest.

"Nokssssonooon," it said in her mind.

"Yes. I'm from Noksonon."

"Hungry..." it said.

"We'll get you something to eat," she said. "Just calm down and stop attacking us."

"Hungry..." Thick ropes of saliva slid from its jowls, splattering on the floor.

"We'll get you food," she said in her most pacifying tone. The dagger suddenly grew so hot in her hand it was uncomfortable, as though warning her.

The thick-necked head plunged toward her, mouth open. Rhenn threw herself to the side, and the huge jaws crunched into the floor, throwing chips of stone and cracking one of those enormous teeth.

"Kill... Noksonon!"

Rhenn would surely have died right then had the dagger not given her that twinge of warning. She rolled to her feet and released any thoughts of a diplomatic solution.

Those last words had hammered into her brain like a strike, and it illuminated one thing for certain: this creature wasn't a Noksonon protector. It's sole purpose was to kill anything *from* Noksonon.

How it knew she was from Noksonon, she didn't know.

Rhenn popped to her feet and saw one of the fleshy clubs swinging down at her. With a cry, she leapt backward and the club hit the ground with a fleshy smack.

Her sword was already coming around in a high, tight arc. She chopped with all her might and severed the appendage at the joint.

All at once, the dog heads howled.

The creature was so vast they could pick at its thick hide all day long and only succeed in dying as it picked them off one by one.

But now that she'd seen it, she had a plan.

Rhenn took advantage of the Mouth Dog's pain, sidestepping forward and stretching into a deep lunge. She needed speed. She needed the element of surprise.

She needed this over quickly.

The lunge worked. The dog was still howling, the severed appendage spraying blood, as Rhenn thrust her sword into the dog's thick neck.

"Kill it!" N'ssag shouted, and the bloodsuckers leapt back into the fray.

Her sword went deep and stuck into something. The cartilage of the throat or maybe the bones in the spine. She didn't know. She didn't care.

The creature shuddered. Its howls turned to screams. It tried to back up, paws shuffling, but she leapt on it, leaving her sword buried to the hilt and using the pommel as a ladder rung. Grabbing a fistful of fur, she hauled herself upward. She went all in and bet the monster was lost in its pain rather focusing on her. She stepped on that enormous, jutting tooth—practically putting her foot in its mouth—and launched herself onto its head. She straddled the monster's neck like a horse.

The bulldog sensed its danger then, milky eyes rolling upward, trying to follow her. Too late.

It wanted an eyeful? She gave it an eyeful.

With a battle cry, she flipped E'maz's dagger in hand and brought it down with both fists onto that milky orb. It plunged deep and the entire giant dog literally jumped. Its thick, massive body went up in the air and came down. All the mouths screamed.

Rhenn held on with one hand and pushed deeper with the other as the dog shuddered and tried to throw her. Then L'elica was there, clinging to the bulldog's face and slamming her palm against Rhenn's elbow. The bloodsucker's formidable strength jammed the dagger, and Rhenn's forearm, deep into the eye socket, spearing the monster's brain.

A spike of pain hit Rhenn's mind.

"Noksssssonooon!" the Mouth Dog screamed, lighting her head afire.

Everything went black.

CHAPTER NINETEEN
RHENN

A sharp pain brought Rhenn around. She gasped, sat up and blinked in the thin moonlight. The bloody dog with all the mouths lay dead a dozen feet away from her, and L'elica hovered over her with a strange expression on her face. Was that admiration?

"Magnificent!" N'ssag crooned. He stood next to the dead dog with something in his hand. Was that a dagger? No. It was too thin. It was a spike with some kind of glowing ruby at the top. He had stabbed it into the giant dog, and now he yanked it free, blood dripping, as ecstatic as she'd ever seen him. He shuffled back and forth on his feet, looking at the dead monster and then back at Rhenn. "Oh yes... Oh yes..."

"Are you broken?" L'elica asked.

She felt woozy, but the disorientation faded. "How long was I out?"

"Moments only," the bloodsucker replied, holding out her hand. Rhenn hesitated a second, then grasped the bloodsucker's forearm. L'elica pulled her to her feet.

"Oh, my queen." N'ssag shuffled over to Rhenn. "You *are* a fighter, aren't you? L'elica described your prowess to me, but I didn't really believe it until I saw it for myself. How could I? You are magnificent!"

"Mmmm," Rhenn grunted. Once, praise from anyone would have lifted Rhenn's spirits, but as a rebel queen, sycophants far more talented than N'ssag had showered her with praise. And frankly, right now she wasn't in the mood to entertain the fiction that they were friends.

"We should keep moving," she said. "Who knows what else lies in this nuraghi."

"Mmm... Yes. So... focused. Yes, of course you are right." He pulled the map out of his robes and consulted it in the moonlight. "We must... That way." He pointed up the hallway, continuing in the direction they'd used to flee the monster.

N'ssag procured one of his understated lamps from the cart and lit it. The bloodsuckers all squinted and moved away. Only L'elica didn't shy away, but she narrowed her eyes and clenched her jaw.

"Is that cart really necessary?" Rhenn asked, not for the first time.

"Mmm... One never knows what one will... need."

"If there are more of those things in here, those wagon wheels are going to bring them right to us. That's probably what alerted that monster in the first place."

"Mmm..."

Rhenn glanced over at L'elica and thought she saw a glimpse of approval.

"Very well," N'ssag said. "We can... come back for it after we... Hmmm... Explore."

Rhenn nodded and started up the hallway. She counted the remaining bloodsuckers and realized they had lost three to the battle with the Mouth Dog. Only nine remained from the original dozen, and two of those were clearly injured. One had its left arm in a makeshift sling. One limped, barely able to keep up with even N'ssag's slow pace. Both of the injured ones kept looking at Rhenn hungrily, as though they could smell the blood pulsing in her veins.

Rhenn's odds had improved if she were to take this to a straight fight, but it was still a longshot to think she could fight all nine of them. Perhaps running into another monster would be a fortunate thing.

They did not, however.

They wound through the labyrinthine castle, sometimes going up stairs and oddly sometimes going back down stairs, as though there was no logical sense to the way the castle was built.

Finally, after most of an hour of crawling through the darkness and descending three stairways in a row, they came to a hallway without windows.

"Mmm... Yes. This is it," N'ssag said.

"This is what?"

"The third archway on the right, if I am correct."

"And if you aren't?"

"Mmm... Let's just... see what there is to see."

They moved to the archway. Like the others they'd seen in this place, it was nearly twenty feet tall, made for creatures that were far taller than Humans. There were no doors, as though this place was some kind of mausoleum. Sure enough, the moment they entered the room, Rhenn saw three sarcophagi lined side by side. She wondered if each one of the rooms in the hallway held corpses.

Each sarcophagus was enormous, sixteen feet long and six feet wide.

"Giants," she said.

"Yes..." N'ssag seemed to be salivating.

"Let me guess. The Plunnos is inside with the bodies."

"L'elica, if you would please. Let's start with the middle one," N'ssag said.

"This is what your books told you? To raid the coffins of Giants?"

"The Giants, my queen, were often buried with valuables, things that gave them power in life. Plunnoi were often among these artifacts."

"Often?"

"Yes."

"But not specifically. You don't know for certain that one of these contains a Plunnos."

"On the contrary, my queen. I did find an obscure passage that referred to the great Ventakos, one of the Daemanoi who wrested this castle away from the Noksonoi long ago. He was a great fighter, and it said that he collected many Plunnoi, but his favorite was a master Plunnoi that could take a traveler wherever they wanted to go in the world. This is what we're looking for."

"And the middle sarcophagus belongs to Ventakos?"

Instead of answering, N'ssag pulled a small book from his robes, opened it, flipped a few pages, then settled on a spot with a finger. He held the book under the light. There was an illustration on the yellowed parchment, a demon head similar to the Daemanon symbol, except this skull only had one horn and a snake grew from its fanged mouth, coiling up and around the horn, then facing the viewer.

N'ssag closed the book, reinserted it into his robes, then pointed at the sarcophagus. Rhenn squinted and she made out that same symbol carved into the stone.

"Ah," Rhenn said. "Safe bet."

N'ssag smiled his disgusting smile.

She took a deep breath and prepared herself. If there was a Plunnos in there, and if it was just like Nhevalos's, she could take it. She could make her stand in this place.

She glanced around, noting the items in the room. There wasn't much. The sarcophagi could be used as obstacles, to gain height advantage if she leapt upon them, to avoid if she didn't get that upper hand immediately. There were rotting tapestries, four of them. They were little more than rods with frayed patches of cloth dangling from them at this point, though. Folds of moldering cloth lay at the base of the walls beneath with counterweight rods in the pile. Those rods could be useful as weapons, too, should it come to that. She'd just have to be sure to dislodge the cloth first.

A basin stood to the far right of the doorway. For blood offerings? To cleanse one's hands before visiting the dead? She didn't know, but she didn't figure it would be useful in a fight.

Really what it would come down to were the bloodsuckers. Six of them currently struggled to lift the enormous lid of Ventakos's resting place. Two others stood guard at the door, looking outward.

Rhenn's gaze fell on L'elica. The bloodsucker watched her, eyes narrow as though Rhenn's thoughts were written all over her face. Rhenn gave a disarming grin. L'elica didn't smile back.

Rhenn turned away to watch the other bloodsuckers struggle with the lid. Damn. She was going to have to find a way to get behind L'elica, but that was looking to be impossible. If L'elica kept such a strict eye on Rhenn, she was never going to flank her.

Maybe now wasn't the right time.

The stone groaned and scraped, but the bloodsuckers pushed it off and it crashed onto the ground, cracking in two.

"Move away. Move away, you lot," N'ssag commanded, shuffling up the steps to the top of the dais. The thing was four feet tall, and N'ssag had to stand on his tiptoes to lean his body over and search. Rhenn started toward the sarcophagus, planning to take a look herself, but L'elica stepped forward, blocking her. The bloodsucker didn't say anything, but the message was clear.

Rhenn's anger flared. She wanted to fly into the bloodsucker's face and see if she could get the jump just by being unexpected, but she kept a chain on it. Yes, she was going to kill L'elica, but she had to see that Plunnos first. She had to be sure, otherwise the highly risky battle would be for nothing.

"Is it in there?" Rhenn asked over L'elica's shoulder.

"Ohhh…" N'ssag crooned to her. "Oh yes. The Plunnos and so much more." He raised his hand to show her. Even in the dim light, Rhenn recognized the four-inch coin. She felt its presence. That was a Plunnos. Except it had a different symbol than Nhevalos's on the side she could see. A pentagon with tiny gemstones at each point with the same colors that swirled on the Thuros: blue, gold, green, red, and black.

"You've seen one before?" N'ssag asked.

"That's a Plunnos all right," Rhenn replied.

"Ohhh... Let us test it." He shuffled down the steps and came toward her.

"I don't suppose you know where the Thuros room is," she said.

"Of course... Of course I do." The Plunnos vanished into his robes. He pulled out the map and held it under the lamp. "We must, of course, retrieve my cart now. Now that we know where we are. Now that we have the Plunnos."

"Of course," Rhenn said without enthusiasm.

"Oh, my queen. We are going to Noksonon."

"We are going to Noksonon," Rhenn said flatly.

CHAPTER TWENTY

RHENN

It took them another hour to retrace their steps, collect the wagon, and work their way to the Thuros room. N'ssag was quick at reading the map and navigating the castle. He seemed to have a knack for translating what was on a page into useful actions. She'd never seen anyone so talented at research except Slayter.

As they hiked through the creepy halls, Rhenn realized her sense of being watched had vanished. No spiders. No tingles. She no longer had the sense that someone was tracking her every move. She wondered if that feeling had come from the Mouth Dog, and now that it was dead, the feeling had also died.

She decided that when she got out of this mess, she was going to study history as hard as Slayter himself. There had been a war in this nuraghi long ago. She'd bet her life on it. Everything screamed defense, strategy, and battle. Rhenn would bet that Mouth Dog was some kind of guardian set here specifically to hunt anyone from Noksonon. That begged more than a few questions.

"There…" N'ssag breathed as they returned to the hallway with the moonlight. The donkey had been half devoured by the Mouth Dog, so three bloodsuckers detached it and hauled the cart along.

N'ssag led them back into the depths of the nuraghi, the cart creaking along behind them.

Soon, they approached a hallway with pointed arches, and Rhenn began to feel wisps of recognition. N'ssag led them to the third archway on the left, and as they entered, she beheld the Thuros, which stood on the far side of the room, just as she remembered. The five colors swirled lazily.

"Oh my…" N'ssag murmured.

A broken table, cracked down the middle, slumped in the corner just beyond the dais that led up to the Thuros. Debris from two chairs lay nearby a third that seemed completely unharmed. An old grandfather clock, its glass shattered and it hands missing, sat in the corner opposite the broken table.

Other than that, the room was empty.

Rhenn's heart began to race. Her time was up. She had to come up with a better plan right now, or take the risk of fighting all the primes—and L'elica—at once. In a moment, N'ssag was going to ask her to show him how to use the coin, ask her to lead him and his abominations into her homeland and set them loose upon her people.

She couldn't allow that. She had to make her stand.

"My queen," N'ssag said. "If you would do the honors. In all my studying, I have not found an instruction of how to use the Plunnos. Is there a secret incantation?"

She nodded and approached him.

"You heard Nhevalos say it?"

"Every word. He'd immobilized me, and all I could do was listen. So those words were burned into my memory forever," she lied. There had been no incantation. The Plunnos was the entirety of the process. Nhevalos had flicked it at the colors, it had bounced back into his hand, and the doorway had opened. He had mentioned that his Plunnos was "keyed to him," but she had to hope that was a lie, or that it wasn't true of all Plunnoi.

N'ssag pressed the Plunnos, warm and moist from being clutched in his sweaty hand, into hers.

The plan came together in an instant as she stepped up to the dais. L'elica followed, joining her but keeping a respectful distance from the Thuros. Rhenn glanced at the bloodsucker and smiled.

She drew a long breath, turning the coin over and over in her hand, then positioned it on her fist, thumb cocked below it.

She'd activate the portal, run through, then spin and flick the Plunnos back. If she was fast enough, only L'elica would follow her, and she'd lock the rest on this side without a Plunnos or a way to follow.

Then it would be just her and L'elica, and Rhenn was happy with that one-on-one fight.

Her heart beat faster, and she didn't know why she hadn't thought of this before. It was, really, the only way. It was perfect.

Speed was the key.

She stood before the swirling colors. She thought about telling N'ssag to prepare to come through. She thought about telling him to stand back in the case of a harmful backlash of magic. She thought about telling him to give her a moment to explore before following. She thought about telling some lie to give her just a fraction of a second more.

But she didn't say anything, afraid that her voice would betray her. She cleared her mind, imagined the Thuros room in Usara in intimate detail, then flicked the Plunnos at the colors. It hit the watery colors like they were a stone wall and bounced back directly into her palm. The colors slithered back toward the arch and revealed the room in Usara. Rhenn's heart thundered.

Home. She was almost home.

She leapt toward it.

Even as she did, she heard L'elica move behind her, leaping after, but Rhenn had a head start. She crossed the barrier, felt the liquid hit her. She twisted in mid-air.

The liquid slithered over her body, under her clothes, under her skin, and through her organs.

Then she was through, moving at the same speed as when she'd hit the colors. L'elica came through right after, but she was too late. Rhenn drew E'maz's dagger with her left hand even as she raised the Plunnos with her right. N'ssag stood on the other side. She expected to see surprise on his face, his mouth open in an "O" as he realized she'd betrayed him.

But there was no surprise. His eyes were narrow and his mouth pressed together in an angry line. He held something in his hand, a little piece of metal with a yellow stone atop it. He pushed it with his thumb. The yellow stone flashed.

Lightning shot into Rhenn's hand from the magic dagger. It lanced up her arm and into her chest, making her convulse. Her arm, already in motion to throw the Plunnos at the gate, twitched and the Plunnos pitched off to the side, clanging onto the ground in front of the dais.

L'elica pounced on Rhenn and for a critical second, Rhenn's limbs didn't work right because of whatever had hit her. L'elica's lips pulled back, revealing her fangs.

"No!" Rhenn gargled. L'elica's weight bore Rhenn to the ground, and her head slammed against the stones. That jolted her awake, knocking away whatever sorcery N'ssag had used on her. Rhenn brought her fist up to punch L'elica in the head—

The bloodsucker's teeth sank into Rhenn's neck, and the strength went from Rhenn's arm. Her fist splayed open and barely smacked the side of L'elica's shoulder.

L'elica took long, hungry gulps of blood, and Rhenn went limp. A fire lit in L'elica's eyes, but she pulled her bloody mouth away after three long sucks of blood. The color returned to her cheeks and her flesh filled with a rosy glow.

Rhenn was frozen as N'ssag shuffled through the Thuros.

"S-stop," Rhenn managed to mumble.

"Oh, my queen," N'ssag said with disappointment as he shivered at the effects of the Thuros, then shuffled down the steps of the dais to stand over her. The remaining bloodsuckers came through one by one and filed into the room behind him, all save two who remained on the other side of the Thuros. "I told

L'elica that you would stay true, that you wouldn't try to betray us. I told her, but she said you would do anything to bar us from what is rightly ours, this wonderful world of darkness where you live."

"D-didn't betray…"

"Oh, my queen. We both know that isn't true. You were trying to trap us on the far side and steal my Plunnos. I wanted to work with you. I really did. I envisioned us together. I would have made you my queen. We could have been lovers. We could have been partners that the priests of Nissra would have sung songs about until the end of time." He sighed. "But I see now that L'elica was right. I see now that you never had any intention of staying true to me. You only wanted to use me, to use my greatness for your own purposes, just like the priests of Nissra. But you will see, just as they will soon see. If you do not work with me willingly… you will work for me anyway."

"N'ssag… We… can talk."

"Oh we will, my queen. We will. But you will be far more compliant the next time we do."

Rhenn used all her strength to try to get her limbs to move, but she barely twitched a finger.

"L'elica my dear," N'ssag said. "Will you do the honors? Don't kill her. Not yet. I want her fresh for the rendering."

"R-rendering?" Rhenn gurgled.

"When you are reborn," N'ssag said. "You will not have any of this inconvenient resistance. You won't have to struggle anymore. You will be at peace. You will be my queen in all ways."

"No!"

L'elica crouched beside her, eyes glittering. Her bloody mouth descended to the slice in Rhenn's neck. She felt the teeth sink in again, but she couldn't stop it. She felt the mouth latch on. Her vision went blurry.

Then she felt nothing at all.

CHAPTER TWENTY-ONE

RHENN

Rhenn awoke naked in a bathtub filled with vinegar. The porcelain sides of the tub extended two feet up on either side of her, and she could see L'elica's and N'ssag's faces watching her over the rim.

"Oh... You are so lucky, my queen," N'ssag said.

With dawning horror, Rhenn realized this bath was a makeshift tray like the ones in N'ssag's laboratory. They'd stripped her down to her skin, and her arms and legs still didn't work.

Rhenn tried to take in her surroundings. The tub was Human sized.

"Where are we?" she asked.

"Isn't this nice?" N'ssag said. "L'elica found these rooms on the way down to the tombs. Servant's quarters, I believe. That's why the tubs fit a Human. I needed something to hold the chemicals of the rendering, you see."

"N'ssag, don't. This isn't necessary."

"Oh, I wish that was true. I didn't want to do this, but you've convinced me that you will never willingly help me."

"I will. I was!"

N'ssag shook his head in disappointment. "This is what I mean. You are very talented at lying. Perhaps you have fooled many others, but not me. I have watched the priests of Nissra lie to me for years. I suppose you didn't know how good I am at spotting lies, but now you do. At first, I had hoped you would come to see the truth. I had hoped you would see me as I should be seen, a great man on the cusp of coming into his own. I had hoped you would come to see how good we could be together, that you would appreciate me as a woman should... Did you think I didn't see how you recoiled from me?"

"You have me wrong. I don't—"

"Oh, I hoped. I hoped too hard." He waved it away like he was shooing a fly. "It doesn't matter now. After the rendering, you will not have any desire to lie to me anymore. You will want to please me in all things. You see, I instill a loyalty in all of my renderings when I put life into them. I color that life with a love for me. I have to, you see? My primes are stronger than me, deadlier, like you. But none of them would think of harming me."

"N'ssag—"

"You'll understand when we're through. You'll be happier. All of this conflict you have when you look at me, it will be gone."

She had to keep him talking. Already, some feeling was returning to her hand, but not enough to leap up and fight. She needed more time. "Whatever you want from me, I can give it to you." She tried to sound calm. Senji's Teeth, she tried. But lying here in the stinking liquid of one of N'ssag's corpses had unnerved her unlike anything before in her life. "I assure you, I can give it to you better as I am. There's no need for this."

N'ssag poured an entire bottle of something into the vinegar bathwater. He swirled it with a wooden spoon in his hand. "It would have been so much better if you had been able to love me... but that moment is over."

Rhenn sighed like they were two lovers having a spat and she was relenting. "Very well," she said. "I did lie to you. I... was afraid of what you might do to my kingdom. But I'm not lying now."

He paused, watching her.

"I thought you wanted to invade my kingdom with your primes, that you wanted to take it over."

"The world will soon be made up of only one kingdom, my queen. One I will form with you by my side."

"I see that now," she said. "I see it. Just… give me time. You've proven your power. You're right, I didn't see that before, but I see it now. You would be a worthy consort for a queen."

He watched her.

"Just… give me some time."

"I do not have time, my queen."

She drew a breath and tried to sell it. She tried with everything she had. "Very well then," she said as though considering the matter and coming to a conclusion. "I will do it. You and me. A kingdom. Together. If you want to start in Usara, then we start there."

N'ssag watched her, searching her eyes, then he smiled sadly. "Your desperation gives you away, my queen."

He put away his bottle and brought out another, poured it into the mix and swirled it again.

"N'ssag, you don't want to kill me. You don't want to… bring me back like this. My people will never follow a bloodsucker." Her throat constricted as she thought of herself like L'elica, like these other horrors. Alive, vaguely aware of herself as she had been. Never able to be what she once was. Living that way… Forever. "If you want to rule in Usara, take my hand now."

"They'll never know what you are. I've taken meticulous care to ensure my primes look just like living people. And you will be my crowning achievement. I am using a new process this time. An evolution that will begin with you. We will do this in complete darkness with L'elica as my eyes. We are going to try it, and you will be the strongest prime I've ever created. And… Heh…" He drew an excited breath. "Your corpse will be the freshest ever, because we won't be searching for someone already dead. We will create your new body by killing you now. You won't be dead for more than a minute before I begin the siphon."

"N'ssag—"

"And you will have the life force of the most formidable creature I've ever seen." He withdrew the spike with the red stone atop it, the one he'd pulled out of the Mouth Dog. The dusky ruby glowed a malevolent red. "My magic takes life from one creature and pours it into a dead body, but sometimes I need to store life force for a future time. That is what I did with the nuraghi monster. As it was dying, I took the last of its life."

She swallowed.

"Once I have put the life force of the giant dog into your corpse, you will bring me to Noksonon as a visiting dignitary. You will set me up with a kingdom inside the noktum and my primes will thrive."

"Yes," she said. "I will do all of that. Come. Let us do that."

He shook his head. "I understand you too well now, my queen. You are merely playing for time, and I cannot allow that. You *will* give me everything I need. Your knowledge. Your expertise. Your love. But you will do it under my command. Take comfort in the knowledge that you will still be you. Usually, I strip memories from my renderings. Their old lives. Their desires. Anything that isn't necessary for them to be good servants. L'elica had a family, you know, but she doesn't remember them. I'm not going to do that with you. I need the information in your head, so everything will stay." He smiled, and Rhenn wanted to throw up.

"N'ssag, please… For pity's sake, don't."

"I was wondering if you were going to beg. At the end. At the last." He took a tiny vial of dark green liquid out of his robes and held it like it was the most precious thing in the world. "I think part of me hoped for it. To see a queen beg. But I confess now, it's a little disappointing. It sullies you. But I will overcome my distaste."

"N'ssag—"

"Shhh." He patted her shoulder. "It will be all right. I know you think this is horrifying, but you'll see that you're wrong. You'll see soon enough. L'elica, would you please do the honors? It is time for her to die."

"N'ssag don't!"

L'elica reached in and cupped the back of Rhenn's head. The bloodsucker effortlessly pulled her body up from the vinegar solution and put her mouth to Rhenn's neck.

"Say goodbye to the land of the living, my queen," N'ssag said.

"I'll kill you!" Rhenn struggled to move, but only her fingers twitched. "I'll kill you!"

L'elica's teeth sank into Rhenn's neck, and there was no restraint this time. She gulped hungrily, and Rhenn's vision went blurry. She felt the very life being sucked out of her body, gulp after ravenous gulp.

"Oh yes…" N'ssag whispered.

Rhenn screamed, but no sound emerged. Her heart pounded so hard it felt like someone was hitting her in the chest with a sledge, so hard it felt like it was going to burst.

Thump! Thump! Thump!

Then it stopped.

Thump…

She opened her mouth wide, but she couldn't take a breath. Her vision faded to black. Rhenn was slipping down a well. She struggled mightily to hold herself up, but the walls were slick. She slipped, down… down… into darkness.

Then she felt nothing. Nothing to grab onto. Nothing to slip against.

And then she was no more.

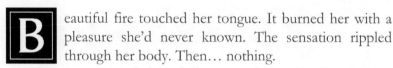

CHAPTER TWENTY-TWO

RHENN

Beautiful fire touched her tongue. It burned her with a pleasure she'd never known. The sensation rippled through her body. Then… nothing.

She was surrounded in darkness, and she felt like she was falling backward. Then, fire on her tongue. Delicious fire. A coppery, beautiful fire. She rose up from the dark, higher up. She still couldn't see anything, but she had the sensation of rising when the fire touched her tongue. Then… nothing.

Please, she thought. *Please, give me more.*

Another droplet of coppery fire touched her tongue. She rose. Please!

Another droplet. Then a drizzle.

Gods, yes!

Vaguely, she became aware of more than her tongue. She felt her jaw, her chin, her lips, her throat. They were all working, all trying to get more of the beautiful copper fire into her greedy mouth. Whatever that fire was, she needed more of it. She needed it desperately.

"Is she drinking?" came a voice. She felt like she should know that voice, but she couldn't place it. All she could think about was the fire.

"Yes," came another voice, and she was able to make a distinction. The first voice was male. The second female. Male... Female... These were attributions given to people. She, herself, was a person.

"Give her more," came the male voice.

The drizzle of fire became a small stream, and she licked and gulped every droplet she could.

"My apologies, my queen," the male voice said. "We did not have time to properly embalm you with the chemicals. But they are within L'elica's blood. They will find their way into you, too. You should feel honored. This is the first time we've done it this way. There are so many firsts this time."

With the stream of life-giving, blessed coppery fire flowing into her, she felt strength filling her body.

"I have given you the best of everything," the male voice said. "You took the entirety of the life of the dog, soaked it up like I've never seen a corpse do. You have taken blood from my strongest prime instead of the embalming fluid. You will be... magnificent."

Blood... The coppery fire was blood...

Horror awakened within her. She'd forgotten about fear; now it raced through her, mingling discordantly with the joy of the copper fire.

Other senses awakened then. She could do more than taste and hear. She could touch, smell, and...

She opened her eyes.

The room came into focus and she saw... everything. The broken wardrobe across the room. Five collapsed beds with brass head boards. The cracks in the ceiling, the rough texture of the black stone walls.

And that was just the background. The figures in the room were crisp shapes that glowed like ghosts. She kept gulping and licking at blood flowing into her mouth, and with her mouth locked on the wrist before her, she had to strain her eyes left and right to see everything. But even when she turned her vision one way, she was concretely aware of the figures outside her field of vision. She didn't just see people. She... felt them.

The closest two hovered over her. The male voice came from a man in the black cloak. His skin shone with an orange, natural glow, and she could feel the copper fire inside him, could see it glowing, tracing his veins like a crazy map.

The female voice came from the blond woman in the blue dress. She was different. The veins beneath her skin were barely noticeable, thin green lines along her arms and neck.

This woman's wrist was in her mouth. The stream of blood trickled from it, down... down... into her belly, lighting her up with exquisite joy.

Her...

Her belly. She... Her...

I have a name.

They all had names. All the people

Rhenn. My name is Rhenn, she thought, and she looked at the orange-glowing man, filled with delicious coppery fire. *That is N'ssag. And that is L'elica.*

More memories flooded into her. All of them, in a rush, filling her head, exploding into fire in her head.

L'elica had killed her; she'd sucked the blood from Rhenn's body and then given it back to her.

And N'ssag... He'd... brought her back from the dead.

Except she didn't feel dead. She wasn't a cold, decaying corpse. The blood lit her body on fire with exquisite pleasure. Every trickle that went down her throat was pure euphoria. She felt warm, strong. Her skin tingled with sensation. Her muscles felt powerful, like they could bend steel. It was as though everything she had been when she was alive had been... magnified.

A sun exploded in the room, erasing everything she could see. Rhenn hissed, shrinking against the back of the tub and turning her head away. She held up a hand against the miniature sun. Through the slicing rays of light that cut past her fingers, she saw that N'ssag had lit a lantern, the muted one that had barely illuminated anything before. Now it stabbed at Rhenn's eyes, blinded her, obliterated everything she could see except the faded figures of N'ssag and L'elica at the edge of the bathtub.

Then came the pain. The light ate at her skin. It was as though a thousand ants swarmed over her, biting her.

"S-stop..." she said.

"No no..." N'ssag said. "No, it's all right. I will keep it small." The burning sun diminished as he set it further away from her on a chair. That little distance made all the difference. The ants stopped biting. Her vision corrected, and she was able to see again.

"She's more sensitive to it," N'ssag said. "Did you see that, L'elica?"

L'elica watched Rhenn with no expression, but she held forth her dripping wrist, and Rhenn put her mouth to it again. The moment the blood touched her tongue, she sighed in joy. Vitality spread through her.

"It worked," N'ssag said. "Ah... Nissra be praised! It worked. Oh, L'elica, think of the primes we will be able to create together. Super primes. High primes. It will be glorious."

L'elica remained silent, as though she was deep in thought, but N'ssag didn't seem to notice.

"I think that should be enough," he said. "Don't deplete yourself, my sweet. The color is returning to her cheeks. You can stop now."

L'elica started to draw her wrist away from Rhenn's mouth—

Rhenn grabbed it, held it, brought it down and put her teeth to it. Her teeth...

Two of her front teeth were pointed and sharp as razors now. She ripped open a new slice high on L'elica's forearm and sucked greedily.

L'elica gasped and tried draw her hand away, but Rhenn held the bloodsucker firmly and drank more. With every passing second she felt stronger, felt the power in her limbs. So much power!

L'elica had seemed so strong before, but now she was like a rag doll that Rhenn could move at will. If she wanted to hold L'elica indefinitely, she could.

But a little voice in the back of her head whispered to her.

No… Not yet. Don't show them yet…

More of Rhenn's personality was returning all the time, and she began to think, not just react. N'ssag had killed her and brought her back. She was a bloodsucker now, just like L'elica.

But he'd also given her a new power. How much, she didn't know. But she suspected N'ssag didn't know, either. She had to use that advantage, but not right now. At the right time.

Wars were won from such decisions.

L'elica yanked her hand again, and Rhenn let her rip herself free, pretended she couldn't hold on. L'elica held her bleeding forearm, and as Rhenn watched, the vicious little wound slowly closed up.

The feeling of strength continued to rise within Rhenn, though, filling her as though the blood was still coming. She drew a breath and realized that, while she still could draw breath, she didn't need to. She didn't need air. All she needed was that coppery fire.

She also suspected food was beside the point as well, like it was for the other bloodsuckers. She felt she should lament that, but food had never made her feel like this, like she could uproot a tree and throw it. Eating food was like trying to move a sailboat by blowing on it. Drinking L'elica's blood was a hurricane.

Rhenn sat up and looked around the room with different purpose this time. Not discovery, but strategy. She saw the bloodsuckers; she saw/felt the blood inside them, rushing through their veins, the blood of the Mouth Dog. Something about that made her angry, like they had taken *her* blood. She felt their strength, too, saw it in the glow around their bodies: little green fires. But each one seemed like a candle next to L'elica.

Rhenn herself felt like a bonfire. N'ssag was right about one thing. Whatever he had attempted to achieve with his new "rendering," he'd succeeded.

She swore to make him regret it.

A slithering fear crept into her, and she recalled something he had said before he'd killed her. He'd told her that he would instill loyalty in her, that she would feel a desire to please him.

She didn't.

The only thing she felt was a desire to tear his throat out and drink him dry.

"How do you feel, my queen?" N'ssag asked, like she was his possession, like she was his pet.

A dozen things went through her mind—it seemed to think with uncommon clarity and speed now. She settled on one thought:

He needs to believe he's right, that I'm his slave. Until he feels safe. Until L'elica lowers her guard.

"I feel good," she said truthfully. She didn't know just how strong she really was. She hadn't really tested it. Could she overpower L'elica? Was she so much stronger than the other bloodsuckers? Or was she simply overconfident with her first rush of the coppery fire? She had to be careful, explore, experiment before committing. She had to make sure that when she made her move, it would be enough to escape.

"Stand up," N'ssag said as though he expected her to comply.

So she did. She rose from the chemical bath. The strong aroma of vinegar rose with her.

"Come here," N'ssag commanded, shuffling back a couple of steps.

She stepped out of the tub, but stopped there, not crossing the distance.

She felt nothing, no push to comply, no pain or punishment that she hadn't.

N'ssag wrinkled his brow. "I meant come over here." He pointed at the ground before him.

Rhenn forced herself not to smile. He thought he had control over her, but he didn't.

Her plan formed immediately.

"Of course." She strode over to him, stood exactly where he'd indicated.

N'ssag's brow smoothed.

...good that she is capitulating...

The words drifted into Rhenn's mind from somewhere, like a stray thought, but she recognized that it wasn't hers. The words had come from N'ssag. It sounded like him. It felt like him, like she had touched his thoughts with her fingers.

So exciting. I gave her the best of everything... She took all *the life of the dog, soaked it up like I've never seen a corpse do.*

N'ssag's thoughts floated to her, and she remembered the Mouth Dog, how it had pushed the word "Noksonon" into her mind.

N'ssag's magic was like a siphon, taking life from one creature and putting it into the dead. Had some of the Mouth Dog's attributes flowed into her with it? Had Rhenn just picked up some of the Mouth Dog's ability to communicate mind-to-mind?

She looked at the bloodsuckers who hung back, watching her balefully.

...hungry...

...hunt...

She looked at L'elica.

...stole my memories...

The thoughts were like autumn leaves drifting past on the wind, there and gone. Incomplete. Just bits of a far greater whole she couldn't quite hear.

"Good," N'ssag said. "That's good. Now tell me, my queen. On the other side of the Thuros, you led us to a room that was not pitch black. Dark, yes, but it was a normal dark. Was that the noktum?"

"No."

"Was the noktum close?"

"Very close." She spotted her travel-stained clothes several feet away from the tub, next to her pile of weapons. E'maz's magic dagger was there. If she could get to that, she gave herself very good odds of taking these bloodsuckers apart.

But now *she* was a bloodsucker, too. Would touching the magic dagger take *her* apart as well?

"Take us there," N'ssag said. "We're going to establish a new home in your land, my queen. Does that please you?"

"Very much," she lied, but with the same tone she'd told him everything else.

N'ssag smiled.

"May I get dressed first?" she asked.

N'ssag hesitated. His gaze roved over her nakedness with a hunger. "Yes. I... suppose you should. We'll have enough time for... We'll have plenty of time later, I suppose."

Rhenn moved past L'elica and N'ssag—giving the searing lantern a wide berth, and went to her pile of clothes.

N'ssag chuckled. "You realize you'll have no more need for modesty, my queen. In public, of course, but not around me."

"Oh," she said, like she was thinking about it, like she was understanding. But the truth was Rhenn didn't give a droplet of dung about modesty. She wanted her weapons. She'd wanted to put L'elica and most of the bloodsuckers on one side of the room and her on the other. Near the door. Near escape.

Quickly and efficiently, she put on her torn, filthy kilt and top and strapped on her weapons. Once everything was in place, she had to suppress a smile once more. She drew her sword and looked at it.

"You won't need that." N'ssag started toward her, heading for the door. "Put it away."

She said, "Yes, *master.*"

He caught the tone in her voice and snapped his head up, eyes wide. She had to give him credit for one thing: the man was smart. He added things up quickly.

"Rhenn!" he gasped.

She ran him through.

CHAPTER TWENTY-THREE

RHENN

'ssag wailed, stumbling away with her sword in his guts. It should have been a killing strike, but he'd twisted at the last second.

Rhenn yanked her sword out and the man sagged to his knees. She should have chopped his head off. If she'd been alive, she would have. But blood blossomed from his wound, and it mesmerized her. For a critical second, she longed for that blood, longed to leap on N'ssag and plunge her fangs into his stomach.

That hesitation took far too long.

L'elica slammed into her, driving her away from N'ssag and wrenching her sword from her grasp. The other bloodsuckers howled and leapt forward. The two behind howled as well, crouching to block the door, hands curled like claws.

Rhenn cursed her foolishness. She should have held the wrath from her voice for just a second longer! She could have killed him!

Now she could rely on her newfound power and try to finish all of the bloodsuckers right now, bet her untested strength, that she was enough to take on eight bloodsuckers *and* L'elica.

Or she could flee.

All of this flashed through Rhenn's hyperactive mind as she crashed into the ground with L'elica atop her. Rhenn's hands gripping the bloodsucker's wrists as L'elica's fingers drove at her face.

No. She couldn't get bogged down in this fight. There were simply too many unknowns. And if she failed, she would fall into N'ssag's power again. That was too horrifying to contemplate.

She hissed, brought her knee up into L'elica's groin so hard she propelled the bloodsucker up and over her head. L'elica crashed into the broken beds on the far side of the room. Rhenn leapt to her feet as the other bloodsuckers landed next to her.

They almost had her.

She spun and leapt at the two guards at the doorway, and she drew E'maz's dagger. The handle felt hot, but it didn't hurt her.

She barreled into the first, spearing his neck with her left hand as she slashed the other across the chest with the dagger.

The instant the blade cut flesh, the bloodsucker collapsed to the ground like its joints had turned to water. The fleshy pile of skin and bones howled pitifully.

Rhenn's left hand broke the neck of the other bloodsucker as she drove him into the doorjamb.

Then suddenly, she was free. She burst into the hallway. L'elica pursued, right behind her.

But Rhenn could fairly fly now. She'd never moved this fast in her life. The hallway became a blur as she shot down it, leapt up the dozen steps at the end and into the next hallway. She wended her way through the castle with perfect memory, dodging debris, working her way upward until she burst into the moonlit hallway where they'd killed the Mouth Dog. Its stinking corpse lay in a pool of congealing blood, but there was no coppery fire to it. She could not see the glowing traces of the Mouth Dog's veins. That was dead blood, not the gorgeous, fiery blood of the living. Dead blood was repulsive.

Rhenn remembered that the front doors had been impossible to open. She might force them open with her new strength, but if it didn't work, she'd be trapped. Instead, at a full sprint, she turned toward the window and leapt at it.

The thing shattered, spraying glass. She burst into the bright moonlight, and she saw everything in that breathless mid-air moment.

The crisp details of her new vision lit the distant wooded horizon with gorgeous clarity. Everything that should have been obscured by darkness was crisp and clear to her. The soft azure sky by the horizon, the trees ahead, the Giant's castle at her back like a mighty shield. The thick wall like stone arms encircling the courtyard, and the winding road, a brown ribbon leading to freedom.

But toward the moon, the light source, the sky became hazy and indistinct.

Rhenn fell then. The window had been more than two stories up, and she fell... fell...

She hit the flagstones. Her old mind told her she must surely break both legs, but though the impact jolted through her, her bones held.

She rolled, came to her feet. Her muscles flexed joyously, taking the strain and leaping into action, putting on a great burst of speed toward the wall and the road. Toward freedom.

She looked over her shoulder as she reached the gates. L'elica stood at the broken window, eyes wide.

Rhenn laughed as she shot through the gate and down the road.

Chapter Twenty-four

RHENN

henn ran into the night. Once she realized L'elica wasn't following her, nor were any of the other bloodsuckers, her current predicament began to sink in.

She was dead. Undead. She was a bloodsucker.

No. No no no.

She shoved down the thought of the horror she'd suddenly become. She had to think about something else, anything else. Yes. Her first priority was to get to safety. She made for the V'endann Barony.

Moonlight, apparently, did not hurt her, though it did obscure the crisp details of what lay in the dark, making anything lit by moonlight a little harder to see. But if sunlight now did to her what it had done to the bloodsucker in N'ssag's laboratory, then Rhenn had to be safely locked away somewhere by the time the sun rose.

Senji's Braid, N'ssag's lamplight alone had been excruciating.

She flew over the ground, feet pounding, legs churning as though her legs would never tire, and she finally reached the edge of the jungle. She knew this place. She and A'vendyr's pentara had come here once to search for water goblins. It had taken them six hours of jungle hiking to get here from the baron's keep. By her estimation, she had maybe five hours before the sky began to lighten. Maybe less.

Just run, she thought. *Run for your life.*

She leapt over and ducked under branches and kept running. She saw beasts in the jungle, birds sleeping in the trees.

After she'd been running for hours, a leopard spotted her, tracked her, stalked her. Then it positioned itself to attack, it hesitated, as though it had caught her scent and something was wrong.

She paused too, staring up at the leopard. She should have been gasping for breath, but her lungs no longer asked for air. She didn't feel a need for anything except…

Blood, she thought. *I want blood.*

"I was going to say copper fire," she murmured to the leopard, and it felt good to break the silence with her own voice. The leopard stared back at her with thin yellow eyes. She could see the blood in its body, too, a copper glow over the leopard's fine fur, a web of orange veins beneath its skin. She swallowed. She wanted that taste again, that unlimited vigor.

She found herself staring at the leopard, wishing it *would* attack.

The leopard must have sensed the shift in their relationship. The hunter was now the prey. It raised its furry, whiskered lips, baring its long teeth and letting out a breath. It turned and leapt away onto another tree.

Rhenn took an involuntary step after it, a primal part of her wanting to chase it down, grab it, sink her fangs into its neck.

"Stop it." She jerked her head away.

I'm not a bloodsucker, she thought. *I'm not.*

She continued her run. She didn't have time to stop, and she was close.

Rhenn's vigor, however, slowly began to fade. It wasn't a burn in her muscles, that familiar feeling she'd had so many times before: limbs feeling thicker, heavier, until they were simply spent. It was like her whole body was... becoming smaller.

When she'd begun her run, she'd felt like she could fly to the moon and back. Now she just felt weaker, slower. But there was no pain with it, only hunger.

She regretted not attacking the leopard.

"No," she whispered to herself. "No, I do not." She forced herself to ignore the urge to attack the many other creatures she could feel all around her.

Another hour of running and she could feel the sunrise coming. It was like she was standing on a turning clock hand and, when it struck the hour, she would burn alive.

She burst from the jungle and saw V'endann Keep across the long grasslands separating it from the trees. The moon hung low on the western horizon, as though warning her of the coming sunrise. The tall grass ruffled in a light wind, and it was quiet except for three creatures who huddled in the grass to her left.

Rhenn was so hungry, so afraid of the impending sunrise that at first she didn't pay attention to them. She'd been trying to ignore all living things altogether, because when she did think of them, all she could think of was blood. That sweet, invigorating coppery fire.

But she suddenly realized the creatures huddled in the long grass were moving closer. Like the leopard, they were hunting her.

She turned her attention on them just as they burst from hiding.

Water goblins.

They were all barely four-feet tall with squat, amphibious-looking skin, wet with sweat. One had a squid head, tentacles waving around its neck like a frayed scarf. The other had a rather human looking head with a big, pointed nose, Luminent-like ears, and a curly thatch of black hair. The third had enormous eyes over a long snout with barracuda teeth. Each bore crude weapons: a bone knife, a cudgel, and a crude spear with an iron head.

They looked like they'd seen battle recently. Dried blood smeared their clothes, and Barracuda had a dirty bandage wrapped around his arm.

Rhenn reached for her sword and realized it was missing.

Then the goblins were on her. She had a brief feeling that she should be frightened, that she should retreat, that she should draw a weapon.

But the water goblins were brimming with coppery fire.

The bone dagger stabbed at her from the right as the iron spear came at her from the other side. Squid-head came straight on with the cudgel. These three weren't amateurs. They knew how to fight together.

But they were just too slow.

Rhenn pivoted. The dagger slipped past her, missing by an inch as she reached out and caught the haft of the spear, stopping the point dead. The cudgel came down, but Rhenn leaned into her pivot, yanking the spear and pulling Barracuda into the path of the club. It thumped heavily on his head, and he dropped.

She leapt completely over Squid-head, landing on his back and sinking her fangs into his neck. Coppery fire burst into her mouth and she moaned. Bone Knife ran at her, trying to stab, but she kept her bite locked on Squid-head, gulping greedily as her body filled with euphoric fire. The water goblin in her grasp had gone limp, and she moved him in front of her like a shield.

Vigor flooded her body. She wanted to let her eyes roll back in her head and vanish into the glorious sensation. But she was vaguely aware that Bone Knife was still trying to kill her.

After the second time he unsuccessfully tried to stab Rhenn and stabbed his friend instead, she dropped the limp Squid-head and went after Bone Knife. Too late, he realized his mistake. He should have run when he had the chance.

He squealed, spun about, and tried to correct his error, but Rhenn's blood was high. The water goblin's veins burned like little lines of fire. With a mighty leap, she crossed the distance and landed on his back. He squealed again as she bore him to the ground and the air whooshed from his lungs.

She bit deep into his neck. The coppery fire flooded into her, and Bone Knife went limp. She sucked and sucked. She drained him dry, drained him until nothing else would come out. With a gasp, she raised her head, feeling like she could fly. Power vibrated through her.

She staggered back and stared at the three bodies. One unconscious. One staring sightlessly at the sky, paralyzed with whatever was in her saliva now. The last one, Bone Knife, was so drained of blood he was desiccated. He looked like a hundred-year-old corpse.

The euphoria slowly gave way to horror. Rhenn looked down at the blood splattered on her chest and arms.

"Senji save me…"

She turned and fled, sprinting across the field toward the dark and silent keep.

CHAPTER TWENTY-FIVE

E'MAZ

E'maz Undantel blinked sleepily, rising unexpectedly from a deep dream. At first, he didn't know why he woke. The sounds of his house were normal. Quiet. Every now and then, even as late at night as it was, he might hear the stamping or snorting of a horse from the stables two houses down, or wayward revelers, or mongrel dogs fighting for scraps.

He lived in the midst of the city, barely two blocks from the marketplace, five blocks from the keep. Random noises weren't uncommon.

But something unusual had brought him up from sleep, a solid sleep aided by about five ales which he'd drunk during the celebration tonight. Yesterday, over a hundred water goblins had tried to attack the keep—perhaps because of all the sorties Baron V'endann had been sending out—but one of A'vendyr's scouts had seen the force and returned with the news. It had given A'vendyr the time to set a trap for the goblins on the V'endann Fields in front of the keep.

The battle had been a rout of epic proportions. A hundred water goblins had died under V'endannian swords, and the baron had only lost nineteen warriors. Last night's celebration had been almost as epic as the battle. It would almost certainly continue tonight as well. E'maz had, of course, joined the celebration to honor the brave warriors who kept them safe, but it was hard to celebrate. He still mourned Rhenn. Nearly a week ago, she had vanished in a sortie looking for water goblins. Despite A'vendyr's best efforts to find her—E'maz had even joined the search party—they'd had no luck. Worse, there was evidence that it wasn't water goblins but bloodsuckers that had taken her. There probably wasn't much hope she was still alive. His fiery warrior woman, gone. E'maz was heartbroken. The ales he'd poured down his gullet tonight were actually a lament for Rhenn, not a celebration for the victory.

He laid back down. The noise that had awoken him had probably been some straggler, some reveler who had lost his way and had thumped the side of E'maz's house or something.

He began to drift back to sleep…

E'maz's eyes flew wide with the sensation of cold water spilling over his scalp.

No.

It wasn't a noise that had awoken him. It was silence. His house was dead silent. Not so much as a mouse scurried. Not so much as a moth fluttered. It was like every tiny creature in the house was holding its breath.

As if they were hoping some predator wouldn't notice them.

All of E'maz's muscles tensed as he pushed himself upright. His bedroom felt pregnant, heavy. Silent and… occupied.

Someone was here, in this room.

He peered intensely into the dark, ready for an attack. He had a sixteen-inch blade hanging on a clever hook just behind his headboard. It was the perfect length for fighting indoors. Long enough to give advantage over a common dagger, short enough that it didn't inhibit a fighter in tight quarters. E'maz had shaped it to fit his hand, and he was quite good with it.

Still trying to see what was out of place, he slid his hand around the side of the headboard—

"You won't need that," Rhenn's voice came from the dark. "I swear I'm not here to hurt you."

He leapt from the bed, forgetting about the dagger. "Rhenn!"

"You believe that, don't you?" she said softly.

He peered about the room. Was she behind the wardrobe? He squinted, trying to see if he could spot a silhouette. "Rhenn, where are you?"

"Tell me you believe me, what I just said. I would never hurt you, E'maz. I would never... Tell me you believe that." She sounded like she was on the verge of tears.

"Of course I believe it." He looked to the window. Cold moonlight shone in, but it was closed. Was she somehow outside? "Where are you?" He fumbled on his nightstand for his lamp.

"Don't," she said, and he felt a shift in the air, and he suddenly realized that her voice wasn't angled from some corner of the room. It was coming from above. He looked up just as she dropped from the thick, wooden rafters. She landed soundlessly, still half in shadow. "Please don't light that."

"What is going on?" he said. "We were all worried sick about you. Where have you been?"

She let out a sigh.

"Changing," she murmured.

"Changing..." He started toward her. "What do you—?"

He pulled up short as she stepped into the moonlight. Her hair was slick with grime and blood. It covered her face from the nose down. It was spattered across her front down to her navel.

"Gallantyr's Bones!" he exclaimed. "Rhenn, you're hurt. We have to—"

"I'm not hurt," she said. "But I need your help. Will you help me, E'maz?"

"Of course I will." He started toward her again.

"Don't." She held up a hand. "Don't touch me. I don't..." Again, her voice choked with emotion. "I don't want you to touch me like this. I would have... cleaned off, but I'm out of time."

"We'll get you clean," he said.

"No. You have to hide me. Now."

"Who is chasing you?"

She shook her head. "The sun. I don't have time. If you believe me. If you believe I would never hurt you, please hide me now."

The sun...

A chill went up E'maz's back.

"What happened...?" he murmured with numb lips. She'd been stolen by bloodsuckers. Her entire front was covered in blood like she'd been gorging at a pig trough full of it. She kept telling him she would never hurt him.

"Please," she said over a soft sob. "Please, E'maz. If you ever felt anything for me, please help me. I will answer every question. But it has to be tomorrow night or never."

E'maz felt like his head was floating above his body. She was telling him she was a bloodsucker. Somehow, they'd made her one of them. She was telling him she was a monster.

She watched his face from the shadows, tense, and he felt like he couldn't speak. He just looked at her, at her lovely body, at her lovely face, all splattered in gore.

Changing... she had said.

"Come with me," he said. "I have a root cellar."

She let out a little noise. He strode past her, and she followed at his heels. He went to the living room, moved a short table and threw off a rug, revealing a trapdoor with a rung cleverly sunk into the wood. He flipped it up, grabbed the rung, and pulled the door open. The root cellar was pitch black.

She moved past him, slithering into the dark doorway.

"Thank you." Her voice floated up from the darkness. "Please don't... Don't tell anyone. No one can know or..."

"I understand." Gently, he let the trapdoor descend.

He went to the basin in his washroom. He still had half a jug of water in there. He grabbed it, two towels and the basin itself, and returned to the trapdoor. He opened the door again, and she glanced up at him, apprehensive. He held out the half-pitcher of water.

"E'maz—"

"For cleaning. It isn't much. Better than nothing."

She took it, and he handed everything down to her gently. She took it all.

"Senji bless you, E'maz. Thank the gods for you."

"I'll see you tonight after sunset," he said.

"Thank you."

He closed the door, heart thundering, and stared out the window.

The sky began to lighten.

CHAPTER TWENTY-SIX

RHENN

When the sun fell the next night, Rhenn awoke feeling like a woman who had been split in two.

One side of her felt the thrill of the new power within herself, of everything she could do with this phenomenal strength. Before her transformation, she had been formidable. She had been a queen and a warrior, a nearly peerless swordswoman. But she'd still been taken captive by Nhevalos. She'd been shown what true helplessness was. In an effort to escape that helplessness, she'd run into N'ssag's arms, and he had been worse. He'd used her, humiliated her, then killed her.

But in bringing her back, he'd transformed her into something... remarkable. Not only had she escaped him, she'd torn through his bloodsuckers like a burning sword. The list of things she could do with this power kept growing and growing in her mind. She could lead her people through any danger. She could walk the noktum whenever and wherever she wanted.

And then there was the other side of herself.

This new power craved... blood. She knew she could not sustain her body on food. She couldn't even sustain it with the blood of an already dead creature. The Mouth Dog had shown her that. She had to kill to live. There was no other path, and it horrified her. Last night, she had gleefully ripped out those water goblins' throats, had gulped their blood in happy abandon.

She'd liked it. There had been no guilt, no conscience that she was tearing the life from one creature to take that life into herself.

How could she reconcile that? No matter how much good she might do with this strength, how could she ever justify... murder?

E'maz knocked on the trapdoor, and she jumped.

"Rhenn?" his voice came to her.

"Yes," she said. She longed to see E'maz, longed to throw herself into his arms and be the woman she'd once been to him. But she wasn't that woman anymore. Did she deserve to take such comfort from him? Did he deserve to be put at such risk? What if she couldn't control her thirst? What if it overtook her before she could get away from him? What if she did to him what she'd done to the water goblins?

And never mind the fact that, though she had wiped herself off as best as she could with the basin and rag he'd provided her, her body still had the vague scent of dead blood. Her clothes stank of it. She'd thrown them in the corner as far away from herself as she could.

"I didn't want to open the door until the sun was fully down, until twilight had turned to night," he said. "Are you all right to come out?"

"I am, but..."

He opened the hatch, and the light from the lanterns in the room stabbed at her eyes. She saw his glowing silhouette, crisply detailed in front, in the dark, and hazy along the edges from the light in the room.

"Will you come up?" he asked, clearly not able to find her in the dark.

"I don't want you to see me right now. I... I'm not wearing anything, and I can't put on my old clothes. I simply can't.

They're…" She shook her head. "You were very sweet to bring me the basin, but I'm still…"

"Of course," he said. "I have a warm bath ready for you. I have new clothes. The warrior's kilt you favor. I also have some normal dresses."

"You do?"

"I went to the market. I bought everything I thought you might need. I also have… food. Although…"

"Bless you, E'maz."

"Let's get you clean, then we can talk."

She wanted to cry at his kindness. He didn't know what sort of monster he'd welcomed into his house. How could he? *She* still didn't know. She had debated coming here at all, and part of her wished she hadn't. If she couldn't control her bloodlust… If she hurt E'maz, she couldn't live with herself.

The thought of attacking him like she'd attacked those water goblins made her stomach turn.

"I will… I will go into the den while you bathe and dress. I won't be able to see you from there. Will that be all right? You remember your way to the wash room?"

"I remember." Her throat caught, and she began to cry softly. "I'm sorry, E'maz. You don't deserve this. Maybe I shouldn't have come here—"

"Don't say such things. Of course you should have. We will work through this. You get yourself clean, then come find me in the den."

He stood.

"E'maz," she called.

"Yes?"

"Could you… please remove the lanterns? I don't need them to see, and they… The light hurts me."

He was silent for a long moment. "Of course," he said. His hazy silhouette moved away, and the light went with him.

Rhenn crept up the stepladder and into the dark house. The glow from the den was like a rising sun, but she went the other direction, toward the wash room. Just as he'd promised, a steaming bath stood in the corner, with three more pitchers lined against the wall, resting in braziers with glowing coals. Extra hot water. Bless him.

She sank into the clean water and reveled in the bath. Never in her life had a bath felt so good. Her hypersensitive skin luxuriated in the water in a way she'd never experienced before. She scrubbed and scrubbed and rinsed and rinsed until she was gloriously, completely clean.

As promised, there were three dresses, a male warrior's kilt and a homemade top—had E'maz made it himself?—similar to the one that lay stinking in the root cellar.

She put on one of the dresses, the lemon-yellow one. Rhenn didn't particularly like yellow, but she knew E'maz did.

She went down the hallway and into the den, entering hesitantly. She was used to striding into rooms with an air of command. But not tonight. Her entire life was nothing she was used to. Her very nature had changed, and she didn't want to seem threatening to E'maz. Not even for a second.

He sat in a chair next to the fireplace reading a book, a lamp on the table to his right. Thank Senji he hadn't started a fire. The very idea frightened her. If she'd been so sensitive to a mere lantern, what would a bonfire do to her?

The lantern's light dulled the details of E'maz, the hearth, the chair on the other side, and the table in the center of the room with another two chairs.

Her body still zinged with power from her water goblin feast. That vigor had lasted much longer than when she'd drunk from L'elica. Apparently if she didn't exert herself, none of her vitality was lost.

Her muscles were so strong that her body felt light as a feather. She wondered if this was how Lorelle felt. She placed each bare foot carefully on the ground. Her hypersensitive skin felt every grain in the wood floor. Each step was absolutely silent.

He hadn't seen her yet, hadn't heard her. She stood hesitantly in the doorway watching this good man who had helped her.

...cool the steel in double pails of water...

E'maz's voice spoke quietly in her head, like he was reciting something. The Mouth Dog's gift. She shifted uncomfortably, not wanting to spy on him.

E'maz caught the movement, subtle as it was, and looked up from his book. His eyes widened. She saw the coppery glow beneath his skin, could trace every one of his veins. She could *feel* his heart beat increase, even across the distance between them.

He stood up, and she watched his Adam's apple bob as he swallowed. "Rhenn... You..." He cleared his throat, and when he spoke again, the huskiness was gone. "Well, you look beautiful. You always do. But then, you know that."

"I don't know much of anything right now. Not much at all."

He went to the table, pulled out a chair for her. She went and sat in it. He took the one opposite her. "Tell me what happened."

So she told him. She told him everything. In their previous relationship, she'd simply enjoyed him. She hadn't told him anything because he hadn't needed to know anything except that she found him attractive. She'd stolen her moments of joy and kept him from anything else because he'd never been more than a pawn in her plan.

Now she told him everything, even about her life back in Usara. She told him who she'd been and how she'd gotten here. She told him about Lorelle, Khyven, even Vamreth. She told him about her abduction, and about her captivity here in Daemanon. She told him about her escape, about N'ssag, about her death and rebirth.

It took more than two hours from the precious night.

At the end of her tale, he sat back. He'd long since lit his pipe—a wide-bowled, stout thing—and pulled a draw from it. He slowly exhaled the smoke and said, "Gallantyr's Bones..."

"It's not fair," she agreed immediately. "Me coming here. It isn't. I've laid a pile of trouble at your doorstep, and you don't deserve it. No one knows I'm here. I can simply go, find somewhere else to be and no one would ever know. This doesn't have to be your problem, E'maz. It shouldn't be your problem."

"Shouldn't it now?"

"No."

He cocked his head and puffed his pipe. "I don't know what you believe, Rhenn, what your people believe. Where you come from, your ways are different, I'm sure. But in my land, a real man doesn't leave a woman without help when she needs it. And a real man especially doesn't do that when he's in love with her."

A lump formed in her throat. Senji's Mercy, he was just supposed to be a piece in her game. He was supposed to be fun, a treat for her amidst a life that was full of hardship. "You don't love me," she whispered. "You don't even know me."

He grinned around the stump of his pipe. "I think I'll decide who I do or don't love, if you don't mind."

"I manipulated you," she said. "To get you to make me that coin."

"Mmm. Yes. I spotted that. Don't think I didn't. You also came to me, though. Loved me. Don't think I didn't spot that, too." He pointed at her with the pipe stem.

"You're not mad? You should be furious."

"You mean about you manipulating me to give you something I'd have given you anyway? About the fact that you laid with me and joked with me and whispered in my ear and held me at night? Furious about that?"

"Yes."

"See, where I come from, we call that 'getting the better end of the deal.'"

She smiled. "I think we both got a nice deal."

He chuckled, and she felt safe. He wasn't going to spook, not from learning the truth of her manipulations, not from the fact that she was clearly not Human any longer. A warmth grew in her chest.

"So you're a queen…" he said.

"In another land, yes."

"And we've… You and I… I've…" He shook his head. "With a queen?"

She cracked a smile. "Queens are pretty much the same as other women."

"I hardly think that's true."

"Oh, it's true, believe me."

"Think I'll make my own mind up about what kind o' woman you are, if you don't mind." He rubbed his beard. "So, you need to get home. What's your plan, your majesty?"

"Don't."

"Don't what?"

"You know what you did. Don't call me 'your majesty.' I'm Rhenn to you. Now and always. Please."

"As you say."

"Thank you."

"So, you need to get home. What's the plan?"

She gave a rueful smile. "Well, the plan was long and complicated, and a colossal failure. So I don't know. All I know is that my people need me. I need to get back to them..." She trailed off. Was that even true anymore? Could she even be an effective ruler for Usara anymore? What kind of queen ruled only from the shadows, afraid of even the smallest ray of sunlight? "Or maybe... Maybe I don't need to go home anymore. Maybe it's over."

"What's over?"

"Me, ruling my kingdom. Me, and any of the dreams I had before..."

"I don't understand. What's changed?"

"What's changed?" She looked at him, tears in her eyes. "Don't patronize me, E'maz. You know what's changed. Look at me!"

"Oh, I have been. Been looking at you since you came out in that yellow dress. Fits you in all the right places. Can't stop looking at you, actually."

"That's not what I mean."

"Then what do you mean?"

"I can see the blood in your throat, E'maz. And I want to get at it. I want to tear your throat out and drink you dry. Did you know that?"

"Do you now?"

"Yes, I do. That's what *I* can't stop looking at."

"Then why haven't you?"

"Why haven't I...? Because I'm fighting it every single moment!"

"Yes, you are." He held her with a steady gaze, then repeated softly. "Yes, you are..."

What he was saying sunk in. "Yes. For now. But what about an hour from now? A day? What if I fail? What if my hunger slips loose and I attack you like I did those water goblins? What kind of queen is that?"

"The queen you are now."

"I can't fight this every single moment!"

He chuckled, his muscled belly bouncing.

"What's funny?"

"You? Can't fight? Every moment? I'm sorry, my love, but all I've ever seen you do is fight. That's where you live. That's your natural state. You say Nhevalos took you from your home, and you been fighting him ever since. Then you ran into the arms o' this N'ssag fellow, and you been fighting him. Then this Vamreth character, who took your kingdom when you were little, you fought him before. You said you were even using me to fight your fight. You have to wonder, Rhenn, what might happen to you if you ain't got nothing to fight against. You said you had peace in your kingdom for two months, then you were fightin' again. Kinda makes me wonder... If Nhevalos hadn't come along, what would you have found to fight then?"

"That's not true."

"Ain't it?"

"No."

"You sure? 'Cause now you got a fight. A big one. All the time. Now you don't have to be fightin' everyone. You got the fight inside. You ever think that's maybe what you needed?"

"To be a monster?"

"'Cept you ain't. Monster would have come back here, ripped my throat out, and drank me dry. You said so yourself."

"How can I be a queen like this?"

"You mean strong like you are? Smart like you are?"

"Stop it. I'm serious!"

"You think I ain't?"

The tears came then. She put her face in her hands and sobbed. Even now, she could feel the nearness of his blood, and she wanted it. She wanted that coppery fire he had inside. She *needed* it. How could she possibly fight that every waking hour?

Then his arms were around her, holding her.

"I don't have the strength for this," she whispered. "Not this."

"Oh, you do. Gods above, I don't think anyone else would, but you do."

She looked up at him, at this kind man. Senji's Spear, she wasn't sure if she could have held onto her sanity if she'd run to anyone except E'maz last night. Before last night, if anyone had asked her if E'maz was in love with her, she'd have said he loved a fiction she'd created for him. She'd stoked his desire, presented that desire to him and pulled him into her orbit. But maybe that wasn't true. Maybe he hadn't come because she'd seduced him. Maybe he was just this way and the two of them were actually compatible.

"E'maz…" She saw the coppery fire glowing beneath his skin. She was so close to his neck now. So close. Her mouth salivated. Her lips came closer… closer…

She turned them up and kissed him on the mouth. Senji's Mercy, it was the hardest thing she'd ever done. He kissed her back and she wrapped her arms around him. She tightened and tightened.

"Easy." He broke the kiss, his voice strained, and she realized she was hurting him.

"I'm sorry," she said, drawing away.

His arms tightened around *her* this time. "I didn't say go anywhere. Just go easy 'till you're used to all that new strength."

"I hurt you."

"I think I'll live."

"We shouldn't… do this."

He kissed her again. "We won't if you don't want to."

"That's not what I mean."

"Well let me show you what *I* mean." He gathered her into his strong arms and stood up.

"Is this really a good idea?"

"Is anything ever really a good idea?"

He carried her into the bedroom.

Chapter Twenty-seven

RHENN

Rhenn lay in E'maz's bed staring at the raftered ceiling. The big man slumbered next to her, tousled and trusting. He lay on his stomach, and she kept one hand on his broad, muscled back. The contact soothed her. Oddly, if she was touching him, feeling his warmth through her fingers, she didn't crave his blood as much.

She could still see it glowing beneath his skin. She still *wanted* it on her tongue, but he'd given her an alternative last night. He'd diverted her, pulled her into him, and it had been enough. It had not been the divine ecstasy of coppery fire lighting up her body, but it had been enough, a lifeline when she was drowning. He'd eased her fears and quieted her doubts. He'd proven to her that she could spend the entire night with him and not kill him.

Instead of *telling* her what she was, he'd risked his life to show her. And in the showing, now she could believe.

This new life wasn't a death sentence. Of course, she would never have chosen it, but she would never have chosen for Vamreth to kill her parents and take her kingdom, either. Yet there was no denying that event had shaped her into the woman—the queen—that she was.

E'maz had shown her that this transformation with its shocking gifts and its horrible price, was somehow the same. It was just a thing, just another burden. If she believed, fought, and found the right tools, she could bear it.

"I can bear it…" she breathed.

Now, in the quiet of the night, E'maz's question rose again in her mind.

What *was* the plan? How was she going to get home and put this entire horrible continent behind her?

It meant going back to L'elica. It meant getting that Plunnos. She cursed herself for not killing L'elica and all the rest at the nuraghi. Looking back, she believed she could have managed it. Her strength and speed were everything she'd initially assumed and more. She could have destroyed L'elica, could probably have killed them all and survived. Then she could have simply taken the Plunnos.

At least she'd killed N'ssag. She'd wanted to stab him through the heart, but taking him in the guts was almost the same. It wasn't an instant kill, but she'd seen enough wounds like that. N'ssag wouldn't last long. An hour, maybe more.

With N'ssag gone, the other bloodsuckers would turn to L'elica, of course. Where would she lead them? Would they return to N'ssag's laboratory? With N'ssag dead, would L'elica even care about the Plunnos anymore?

"It might still be there…" Rhenn murmured. The Plunnos might actually still be in that room in the nuraghi.

"Mmmm…" E'maz awoke, and she realized her hand on his back had begun to squeeze as she'd contemplated the possibility. "What is it?" he asked.

"I'm sorry," she said. "I didn't mean to wake you, but…"

"Tell me." He blinked and rose up onto one elbow.

"I think I have it. The plan."

"To get you home?"

"I killed him."

E'maz blinked, sorting through that scant bit of information. "N'ssag," he guessed.

"Yes. I killed him, so his blood…" She almost said bloodsuckers, but the word soured in her mouth. She was one of them now, and she refused for her defining trait to be that she sucked blood. "His *primes* are going to be without a leader. They might just leave his body there."

"Leaving the Plunnos behind."

"Yes."

"Then all there's left to do is retrieve it. We should go, yes?" he said. "Right now. Tonight."

"I can't. I barely made it when I had five hours and I ran at full speed. There's only four hours till sunrise. Maybe less."

"Then I'll rig up a box for you. Something where I can drive the cart during the day."

Rhenn paused as thoughts flashed through her mind. This presented a new dilemma. E'maz saw himself accompanying her, and maybe a part of her wanted him to. She didn't relish the idea of being alone, and if she got caught somewhere during daylight hours, having a protector for her hidden body—whether it be in a box or inside something else—could mean the difference between surviving and exploding in a fiery, spitting ball of flesh.

But having E'maz along also meant that he would be subjected to whatever trials she would face, be it N'ssag's primes come for revenge or some other creature wandering the nuraghi like the Mouth Dog.

In short, E'maz wasn't coming with her.

He stood. "I'll get started right away. Tonight. I could have it ready within a few hours. We travel tonight for the first leg of the journey, then you rest in the box as I drive the cart the rest of the way. By nightfall tomorrow, we could have you to the nuraghi. We could have you home."

She hated lying to him, but he'd never agree to stay behind. "Right," she said. "But don't start tonight, E'maz. Come back to sleep. Start in the morning while I'm in the cellar. Build it during the day. We can start the journey tomorrow night."

He paused, then nodded and laid back down.

She snuggled into him, putting her head on his chest.

"Rhenn," he said thoughtfully as he stared at the ceiling.

"Yes?"

"Are you sure he's dead?"

"N'ssag?"

"Yeah."

"I've seen a hundred wounds like that," she said. "He's gone."

"Mightn't they resurrect him? The primes? Like he did you?"

She shook her head. "They don't have the power. It's his personal magic that starts the siphon of life. No, trust me. N'ssag is a dead man."

CHAPTER TWENTY-EIGHT

N'SSAG

N'ssag was dying.

He was so weak now he could barely raise his head. Bloody bandages wrapped his waist, soaked red. L'elica had laid him in one of the rendering trays, and his life was slowly pouring into it.

The irony was not lost on him. He was going to become a corpse in the very tray where he had resurrected other corpses.

During the torturous two-night hell trek back from the nuraghi to his laboratory, he had commanded L'elica to find a live rabbit and bring it back to him. He wished he could have ripped its life force away to give to himself, to heal the hideous wound Rhenn had dealt him, but his magic didn't work that way. He could only give life from one thing that was alive to something that was dead. He wasn't a healer.

He had sucked the life from the rabbit, though, and poured it into the Keeping Rod. He had one last trick to try. He knew enough about life and death that he might be able to cast one last spell before he passed. As the last of his life drained out, he would activate the rod. He would activate his own power and try to start the siphon as he passed on. It was unlikely, but he might be able to do it. He'd have asked L'elica to begin concocting the chemical bath for his body, all save the emerald drops, in preparation, but they'd arrived at near dawn. There hadn't been time.

One of the drapes on the windows was drawn open. Light had already begun to pour in when L'elica laid him down. She'd been burned just getting back to the vault. She couldn't have stayed longer than that.

Still, chemical bath or no, if he felt he was starting to slip, he would jam the rod into himself and start the transfer. Perhaps he could come back in some form and salvage this mess.

He held the Keeping Rod tightly, waiting, and he thought of Rhenn. He'd given her everything, and the ungrateful bitch had stabbed her sword through his guts. If he hadn't sensed it a second before the attack, he'd have died right there in the nuraghi.

He still didn't know what had happened. Everything else had worked. Clearly, Rhenn was a magnificent prime, the first of what he was going to call his high primes, with a strength and speed that had outstripped even L'elica's. Rhenn had gone through his normal primes like a scythe through wheat. Nissra's Blood, that had been a sight to see. It would have been the best moment of his life if his guts hadn't been about to spill on the floor.

A knock sounded on the door. It jolted N'ssag, and that hurt. He groaned. The knock sounded again. He would have cursed at whoever it was, shouted at them to go away if speaking didn't hurt so much.

The latch clicked, and N'ssag realized with horror that the person was trying to come in.

"Go... away..." he whispered, and a fresh wave of agony rocked him.

The door, which L'elica had locked, suddenly unlocked, and it opened, shining bright sunlight into the laboratory.

"Ffff..." N'ssag said impotently. "Ffff..." But he couldn't form any of the words, and he couldn't raise his head. Any use of his stomach muscles sent agony through him. He had to conserve his strength for when L'elica returned, for when he made the attempt to bring himself back from the dead.

Ventat Obrey walked onto the landing that overlooked the sunken laboratory. His long cloak swept the floor and his cowl had been pushed back to reveal his slicked-back black hair. Even in the bright daylight, he still seemed cut from the night sky. He glanced impassively across the scene, seeming to inspect every slab, every tray, every wall, before his gaze fell upon N'ssag. That gaze burned into N'ssag's eyes, and he closed them.

"Report," Ventat said.

"I... am dying..."

Ventat seemed to digest that, and then he ignored it. "Where is the queen?"

"I... had her."

"Shall I presume she is the reason you're bleeding to death?"

"You... would presume correctly."

"So she escaped."

N'ssag coughed and tasted blood. He didn't answer.

Ventat descended the steps and walked over to the slab upon which N'ssag lay. He looked down, and N'ssag had forgotten how damned tall the man was.

"I do not accept failure."

"Well... kill me then..."

Ventat grunted. "I need you to follow through on your promise."

"Oh..." N'ssag coughed. "I... plan to, if I survive the day."

"What is your plan?"

"I... discovered that I..." He coughed and breathed for a moment. Talking took far too much energy.

"You discovered what?"

N'ssag tried to answer, but he could barely whisper. He wondered suddenly if this was the end.

Ventat sighed in annoyance. From a hidden pocket in his cloak, he withdrew an amulet with an emerald the size of a lime.

He leaned down, put the emerald on N'ssag's bloody bandage, and whispered a series of incomprehensible sounds. It sounded like a language, but it wasn't any language N'ssag had ever heard.

Suddenly, it felt like a twisted wheel made of blades was spinning into N'ssag's chest. He moaned. Dark spots appeared in his vision…

Then the pain lessened. The blades stopped cutting. The agony that had gripped N'ssag's entire body vanished.

He sucked in a breath and looked up at Ventat.

"What…? What did you do?"

"Where is Queen Rhenn?" Ventat asked.

N'ssag groped at his belly, and it didn't hurt to touch the area. The wet feeling in his lungs was gone, and as he ripped at the bloody bandages, he discovered the wound was also gone. He looked up at Ventat in wonder.

"You healed me."

"Yes."

"How… did you do that?"

"I do not have time to satisfy your sophomoric curiosity. Where is Queen Rhenn?"

"I… lost her. She stabbed me and ran into the night."

"And your… what did you call them? Your renderings?"

"My primes."

"Could your primes not catch her?"

N'ssag shook his head, sitting up and marveling at his wound, at the dawning realization that he wasn't going to die. "N-no, they couldn't."

"I thought they were faster than Humans."

"They are, but I transformed Rhenn."

"You had her. You did not kill her."

"I did. Then I brought her back as one of my own."

"Hmmm," said Ventat.

"I tried a new theory, and it worked. Mostly. I discovered that I was right. If I create my renderings in pitch darkness, their strength increases. Maybe twofold. Maybe more. She was… magnificent."

"But not under your control."

"That was the failure. I don't know why. I performed the same siphon with her as I have with others. She should have felt loyalty to me, should have complied with whatever I asked. But there were differences in the process. The failure could have come from a number of things. Or a combination of them. I was not in my laboratory, so the meticulous time and precision I take here I could not take there. She was in complete darkness, and I had L'elica be my eyes. Perhaps that affected the siphon. I didn't embalm Rhenn with the chemicals, only soaked her in them, and not for very long. I also took her right after she had died, moments only. She was the freshest corpse I'd ever rendered."

"You killed her, as I asked," Ventat conceded. "I did not tell you to bring her back."

"I expected to control her."

Ventat hesitated, as though considering. "What do you need to chase her down and eliminate her?"

"More primes, but I am limited by my equipment here, by the fact that I cannot see in the dark. The darker the room when I render, the more powerful the primes. But this time I won't make the mistake of taking such a fresh corpse. If I had to guess which of the altered variables was to blame, I'd say it was her nearness to life. That was why she was able to cling to her personality, to… deny me my right."

The man withdrew a chunk of onyx the size of a fist. It was a half-sphere set into a circle of gold with runes inscribed upon it. He set it down on the next slab over, which had no tray, and encircled the gold band with his finger. The runes glowed black, and then the sphere grew.

Wait… no.

The sphere wasn't growing. The dark was growing. Like the sphere was a condensed shadow that was expanding. N'ssag's eyes and mouth widened as darkness filled the laboratory like ink floating on air.

"What are you doing…?" N'ssag marveled.

"You said you needed darkness. I am giving you darkness."

The man was a more powerful mage than N'ssag had ever met. Even High Priest D'oreld didn't have this kind of power. Power over wounds and *also* over darkness?

"Who are you?"

"I am Ventat Obrey, servant of Lord Tovos and implementer of his will. He demanded that I use an underling from Daemanon to kill Queen Rhenn Laochodon. I chose you." Ventat glanced down at N'ssag with that implacable gaze. "I do not fail my master. And neither will you."

The darkness spread until it reached the walls. N'ssag involuntarily took a step back as it reached him, but he bumped up against the slab. The darkness caught up, flowed over him, and then he couldn't see. He couldn't see... anything. He might as well have been struck blind. Blessed Nissra, it was perfect, but...

"I can't see," N'ssag said. "I cannot work if I cannot see."

Ventat grabbed N'ssag's wrist and pressed something into his hand. A coin with a chain attached to it. An amulet. N'ssag fumbled with it, almost dropped it, then found the chain and raised it over his head. The pendant fell against his chest, but nothing happened.

"As with the Darkstone, you have to encircle the amulet with your finger. One finger in a clockwise motion," Ventat said.

N'ssag did as he was bid, and the room came into view in shades of gray. He could see!

"Is it still... dark?" N'ssag asked.

"You now have your own noktum," Ventat said. "It will fill whatever room you activate it in. If you activate it outside, it will make a cloud some thirty feet in diameter. Make your primes, necromancer. Make an army if you need. But bring me Queen Rhenn's head."

"Yes, Master Obrey."

"If you do not bring me her head this time, then I take yours and find someone else to do the job. Do we have an understanding?"

"Yes. Yes, of course."

"Good." The man strode to the staircase, and N'ssag watched, fondling the Amulet of Noksonon as Ventat climbed the steps, opened the door, and left. The sunlight did not intrude when he did. The darkness of his own personal noktum held it back.

N'ssag began to laugh.

CHAPTER TWENTY-NINE
L'ELICA

L'elica straightened after throwing the water goblin corpse on the pile. There was almost no room now, and she had to stand on a smaller pile of corpses to push the thing atop the eight-foot-tall pile against the wall. The vault was packed with water goblins corpses. It reeked of rotting fish, human decay, and dead blood. The first two scents didn't bother her, but L'elica couldn't stand the last. It was repulsive to all primes. The smell was so thick it was palpable. She felt stifled by it.

There were over a hundred water goblins stacked in fleshy, sliding piles, waiting for N'ssag to work his magic upon them. If she'd still been alive—if she'd still been Human—she was sure her back would have broken long before now. N'ssag had been sending her and the other primes out to gather all the dead on the V'endann Fields. Apparently while N'ssag and that bitch Rhenn had been traveling to the nuraghi, water goblins had attacked V'endann Keep in force.

They'd been slaughtered.

That had left the V'endann Fields ripe with material for N'ssag's renderings. L'elica and her fellows had been going out night after night, hauling corpses back, then going back out and hauling more. No one in the V'endann Barony had come to bury or burn those bodies yet. Instead the baron had ordered a five-day celebration.

The baron had buried his pentaran warriors, of course. They'd done that on the first night after the battle; it had apparently been worked into the celebration.

N'ssag had wanted those fresh Human corpses first, though, so he'd had L'elica and her fellows dig up those bodies while the revelers were singing and drinking, and then recreate the graves as though they'd been undisturbed. They'd worked from sunset to sunrise, but the going had been slow. They'd only managed to get a dozen of those warriors back to N'ssag that first night.

With his new noktum and his Amulet of Noksonon, N'ssag had started rendering them the moment L'elica and her fellows had brought them back. By the next night, instead of just the seven primes who'd survived the nuraghi and Rhenn's attack, they had a fresh new force to steal bodies. Ten of N'ssag's new "high primes" awoke, and they were quite effective. Stronger and faster even than L'elica, and entirely slaved to N'ssag's will. They had dug up the rest of the pentaran warriors and fixed the graves in half the time, then joined L'elica and the other primes in pulling water goblin corpses back to the laboratory.

Now all those corpses from the V'endann Fields were stuffed into the vault. There was barely enough room to move with only a thin, winding path between the metal door and the back of the room. The rest of the room was floor to ceiling corpses. L'elica's coffin—all of the coffins for the primes—were completely buried under bodies, and L'elica and her fellow primes had been forced to sleep in the single aisle, sandwiched in by the reek of the dead.

N'ssag had changed since Ventat Obrey had visited him days ago. When she'd left him that last night after the nuraghi, sunlight streaming into the laboratory, she had been sure she'd awaken to her master cold and dead. But the following night, she'd leapt from her coffin to find him completely healed. The mysterious mage Ventat Obrey, who'd started N'ssag on this path, had returned, healed him, given him a noktum for his laboratory, and left.

N'ssag had been working nonstop since then. If he had slept over the last four days, she hadn't seen it. His eyes were red-rimmed and sunken, but he didn't seem to need sleep. L'elica was certain it had everything to do with that emerald amulet Ventat Obrey had left with him. It glowed more with every day. It was as though N'ssag fed his lifeforce to his renderings, and the emerald fed lifeforce to him. He kept mixing his chemicals, preparing the baths, embalming the bodies, and bringing them back to life.

All of the pentaran warriors, and nearly twenty water goblins, were now rendered, but it was taking its toll on N'ssag.

She'd tried to talk to him, to get him to slow down, but N'ssag barely said anything to her anymore. Instead, he crooned over his "high primes," petting them as they stood in their stoic lines along the edges of the laboratory. N'ssag no longer seemed interested in L'elica. She had never questioned that N'ssag didn't talk with the previous primes, only gave them commands. They didn't speak much, only in simple sentences. They didn't think like she could. She was N'ssag's lieutenant because she'd retained some of her humanity. L'elica had simply been made... better. The previous primes couldn't lead in the field. They didn't improve. That was just the way of things. They weren't worth talking to, so N'ssag had always talked to her when he worked, ignoring the previous primes like they were inferior experiments, not worthy of his time.

Now she was the inferior experiment. Now N'ssag never seemed to have time for her.

T'sintu and B'eorg entered the back of the vault, hauling a corpse apiece behind them. They came in through the underground tunnel N'ssag had dug to allow his renderings to go out into the night and hunt without being seen. They each looked gaunt. None of them had fed yet tonight, and they'd expended energy for hours.

"Are these the last?" L'elica asked. Indeed, both the corpses looked barely viable for a resurrection. One was missing an arm. The other half its head.

T'sintu nodded.

"Go," L'elica said. "Hunt. The north side of the city tonight."

T'sintu and the others turned and headed immediately out the tunnel.

L'elica looked back at the door to the laboratory. N'ssag had his "high primes" now. The next step in the evolution of his renderings. That thought had settled into her over these last few backbreaking nights where she had been used as a worker instead of a leader and confidante.

When N'ssag had brought Rhenn back to life at the nuraghi, he'd achieved the purity he'd craved, but not the control. With his "high primes," he had fixed that problem. None of them had an ounce of rebellion in them. He'd stripped all of their memories and left only loyalty in their place. They were stronger, faster, more agile, and they didn't do the stupid things that the previous primes had.

N'ssag's words came back to her, words that he'd spoken to Rhenn just before she died.

I strip memories from my renderings. Their old lives. Their desires. Anything that isn't necessary for them to be good servants. L'elica had a family, you know, but she doesn't remember them...

And L'elica didn't.

N'ssag's words had hit her hard when he'd spoken them in the nuraghi, but so much happened afterward that she hadn't really thought about them until now.

L'elica had a family, you know, but she doesn't remember them...

It had stuck in her mind, and after these past nights of being treated like a common worker, she'd turned it over and over in her mind.

She'd had a family.

Who were they? What would it mean to have a family? The strongest connection she knew was her connection to N'ssag. Had she felt that for her family? Had she loved her husband and her children as she loved N'ssag? How could that even be possible?

She'd always felt complete before, certain of her place with N'ssag, certain of her purpose. But ever since Rhenn had stabbed a sword through N'ssag, ever since Ventat Obrey had given N'ssag the means to make his "high primes," L'elica was just an old tool past its usefulness, good only for carrying corpses that would soon surpass her in her master's esteem.

She felt a heavy pain in her belly, like her guts had been twisted, like she'd drunk dead blood.

Was this rage? Was she upset that N'ssag had stolen memories and never told her?

No. It wasn't that. Not really. She didn't care about this supposed previous family. She didn't know them. Whoever they were before, they were only a word now. They were no more important to her than these corpses. Family? Family was N'ssag. Family was her status among the previous primes. She'd lost both. Now N'ssag treated her just like all the rest of them, dirty and stupid. But she wasn't.

She told herself he was just tired. So much had happened so quickly and he simply didn't have time to talk.

She wound her way up the aisle bordered with water goblin corpses to the low stove hatch, the doorway to the laboratory. She opened it and slipped through.

Stepping from the normal dark of the vault into the eldritch dark of the noktum was like the difference between tasting the scent of blood on the air and gulping it in great, fiery gasps. L'elica felt immediately stronger, like the fibers of her muscles had thrown off unseen weights, like this was where she was meant to be.

In the noktum, not only did she feel better, she could see better as well. Though L'elica had always been able to see better at night than Humans, moonlight and even starlight tended to make shapes less distinct. Inside N'ssag's noktum, everything was crisp and clear and she had an infallible sense of objects in the space, almost like the noktum was an extension of her own body.

Cages with animals had been stacked in between all of the slabs. She could smell their excrement, their fear. Chickens, rabbits, even squirrels. A half dozen goats roamed freely about, bleating. All the animals seemed terrified, like they sensed their impending fate. Three goats had climbed the steps and stood next to the door, hoping that they would be released into the world again, that they would see sunlight again. The rabbits crouched in their cages, eyes wide, like if they could make themselves small enough, N'ssag would overlook them. The chickens cocked their heads left and right, sometimes pecking frantically at the cage.

They all seemed to sense that their lives were measured in hours.

L'elica had never seen the laboratory like this, jam packed with the materials for rendering and the renderings themselves. Every slab, every tray held a bath of N'ssag's embalming chemicals and a water goblin corpse. A half dozen reanimated goblins— better behaved than any water goblins in the history of the world—stood against the wall and awaited orders. All of the fallen pentaran warriors were here as well. N'ssag had brought all of them to life first. They stood straight along the wall closest to N'ssag like some quiet honor guard.

Among the warriors was V'osep. The newest. The strongest. V'osep had been the leader of his pentara. It was indicated on his sword harness, a little insignia L'elica had noted when she'd brought him in. She'd pointed this out to N'ssag in an effort to please him, and he had been pleased. For one brief instant he'd treated her like his lieutenant again. He'd smiled at her, talking about how he couldn't have done this without her. He'd made a special bath for V'osep, done a special kind of rendering that had allowed some of V'osep's memories to be retained, and when the pentaran leader awoke, he wasn't just a hawk-eyed slave like the rest. He gave counsel. He stayed close to N'ssag.

He stood in the place L'elica had once stood and acted like N'ssag's lieutenant.

"That... is that," N'ssag breathed, pouring eight emerald drops into the pan. That was more than twice what he'd given to L'elica. He'd just given twice as much power to a little water goblin with an octopus head. A sour taste filled her mouth.

She told herself that was the point. This was the next step in N'ssag's dream, and she should be happy for him. This was what he'd always wanted, what he'd always aspired to do.

But as she watched N'ssag smile wearily at V'osep like he used to smile at L'elica, her stomach twisted. V'osep was taking her place. He was moving into the spot that belonged to her.

She couldn't let that happen.

She glided over to the slab and came close to N'ssag, closer than V'osep. The "high prime" glanced at her and raised an eyebrow. For a moment, it seemed as though he would bar her advance.

L'elica almost bared her fangs at him. She'd like to see that. High prime or no, she would tear his face off.

"They are all gathered, master," L'elica said.

N'ssag started. "L'elica!" He hadn't realized she was there. Before, he'd always looked for her. He'd always anticipated her arrival. "I'm concentrating here."

"My apologies, master," she said. "I simply... I thought you'd want to know that there are no more viable bodies on the V'endann Fields."

"Good good..." N'ssag said dismissively. "I'm sure you did a competent job collecting corpses."

A competent job collecting corpses. But not standing by your side. Not giving you counsel about your plan.

"Is there anything else that I may—"

"No no." He waved her away. "Don't bother me. I was pouring the emerald drops, for Nissra's sake."

As if she didn't know. As if she would ever have done something to disrupt his preparation of a rendering, something she had helped him with so many times.

"Master—"

"Go sleep, L'elica."

Go sleep. The command he'd always slung at the previous primes, but never at her. Go sleep in the aisle among the water goblin corpses. In the filth like the other primes.

She glanced at V'osep, who stared steadily at her like she didn't belong here.

"I think you're right that Rhenn has run home, back to the barony," she said.

N'ssag seemed convinced Rhenn had returned to V'endann Keep, and he was determined to go get her. To kill her this time. L'elica had overheard him talking to V'osep. The pentara leader knew secret ways into the keep. N'ssag's unceasing renderings and his dependence on that glowing emerald amulet was all in an effort to create an army capable of overwhelming Baron V'endann and his defenses.

And Rhenn's death was only the beginning, just the first of what N'ssag seemed to crave in this upcoming battle...

She knew he now envisioned his army of high primes growing. With every battle they won, there would be more corpses, and with every new corpse, there would be a new recruit. It would build and build and build upon itself like a great tidal wave that would crash over the entire continent of Daemanon. They would all be fresh, N'ssag had crooned to V'osep. They would all be birthed inside his noktum, more high primes to go forth and take over the world.

"I would help you, master, with your plan," L'elica said.

"You would help me?" N'ssag turned to her. His eyes were red-rimmed, his cheeks sunken. She wondered if he had eaten anything at all these past days. "I don't have time for this, L'elica. I told you what you can do to help me. I don't appreciate this insubordination."

"I don't need the rest, master..." She trailed off, glancing over at V'osep, who looked at her like she was a rat that had crawled up on the dinner table. "I belong at your side."

"Do you see what I am doing here? I'm single-handedly trying to create an army. Or I was until you interrupted me. Now I am taking precious time to explain my orders to you. Should I have to do that?" He paused as though waiting for an answer, but when she opened her mouth to speak, he interrupted her. "No. I should not. When I give you an order, I simply wish you to follow it. I don't need you for this. How can you possibly help me with this?"

Again, she glanced at V'osep, but the twisting in her guts prevented her from speaking.

"I don't know what's become of you." N'ssag waved at her. "But you used to try to be presentable when you came to see me. Just look at you."

She glanced down at herself. Her blue summer dress, the only clothing she'd ever known, was practically black with grime. It was torn in several places all the way up to her hips, revealing her bare and grimy legs. The body of the dress was also torn, revealing dirty patches of flesh along her ribs and collarbone. Her neck and shoulders were smeared with the dead blood of water goblins.

For the first time, she felt shame. Futilely, she lifted the torn parts of her dress as though she could put them back into place, but they just fell back, lank and useless.

"I didn't…"

"Did you ever think to maybe clean yourself up before you come before me?" N'ssag asked. "Did you ever think maybe it disgusts me to see you like this?"

L'elica's face crumpled, and she tried to swallow, but she couldn't. It was like a mouthful of dead blood was in her mouth, and she couldn't force it down her throat.

"I… was doing what you asked me to do."

"Yes, well now you're not. I told you go sleep. Go." He turned back to his work. L'elica looked up into the disdainful eyes of V'osep.

Trying vainly to swallow the lump in her throat, she turned and shuffled away, holding the scraps of her dignity—and her dress—to her chest.

CHAPTER THIRTY

E'MAZ

E'maz finished the half hitch on the fourth and final rope that secured the box to the wagon. Sweat beaded on his chest and his arms. He'd spent a furious morning and midday in the forge, but he had Rhenn's box finished.

The outside looked like a common farmer's box, perhaps meant for carrying cabbages or some other produce, but inside the wooden facade was a casket of welded steel. If what Rhenn had said was true, he couldn't afford to have even a single ray of sunlight come through. Wood was too flexible, so he'd gone with steel, with padding and cloth to line it. The thing was airtight except for the vent he'd created in the bottom, which he'd offset with a second plate and then covered with cloth. No light would enter the box. Not even a flicker. He was exhausted now, but the deed was done.

Now he just needed to visit the stables. He kept two draft horses there for when he needed to travel to Saritu'e'Mere and bring back iron and other supplies for the forge. Compared to his usual haul, a thin steel casket with Rhenn inside would be a light load.

He turned to go and pulled up short.

Standing in the street by the door to his forge was none other than the son of the baron, A'vendyr V'endann. The pentaran leader wore his fighting kilt and the X harness he favored for his sword.

Rhenn had told E'maz everything about Nhevalos's schemes, including the fact that Nhevalos wanted to have Rhenn bed this man, then carry his baby. It was one of the reasons Rhenn had courted E'maz. Apparently A'vendyr had been willing to go along with the plan. He had, in fact, reprimanded her for her dalliance with E'maz.

E'maz had never really thought much of Baron V'endann, but he'd never really had that much use for nobles in general, considering his past. His mother had hated the nobility. She'd claimed their family had once been of a royal line. Mother had liked to say that grandmother had descended from the kings of Pelinon themselves. She'd told stories about how grandmother had been drummed out of the court at Pelinon by scheming, backstabbing nobles. So she had hated nobles, hated them all.

To be fair, E'maz's mother had been a bitter woman, too enamored of fanciful stories and strong drink. As a child he'd believed her tales, but as he'd grown he'd seen them as the necessary padding for the poor life his mother had lived. Still, her tales had instilled a healthy skepticism for all things "royal."

"Never trust a noble," Mother had said, and E'maz didn't. Not out of hand.

However, while he'd never liked the baron, he'd always liked A'vendyr. E'maz had made the man's blade, after all, as well as two others for his pentara, including Rhenn's. A'vendyr was always courteous, always asked for things in a reasonable timeframe—which most nobles did not—and he paid on time.

A'vendyr showing up here, now, was decidedly inconvenient. And possibly suspicious. Although, perhaps all A'vendyr wanted to do was place an order for a new dagger or some such.

"My lord," E'maz said, leaving the cart behind as though it didn't matter. He strode toward the front door of his business.

"E'maz," A'vendyr said. "How are you?"

"I am well, my lord. Congratulations on your recent victory." A'vendyr had been instrumental in the routing of the water goblins. "The people chant your name at the celebrations."

"My thanks," A'vendyr said.

"I imagine you've got a few nicks in your blade. If that's what you're about, I'm happy to sharpen those out for you. Take me no time at all."

"No, actually. Well, actually yes. I do have a few, and that would be most welcome, but…"

E'maz waited, then said, "If you're wanting a new blade or some such, my lord, I'd be happy to help you with that as well. Though that will take some days."

"I… Well, actually, no. I've come to see how you are."

A cool prickle went up E'maz's back. This would be the first time A'vendyr had come to see E'maz just to "see how he was."

"My lord?"

"I… I saw you at the first celebration. But last night, you left early."

"I was tired, my lord."

"Of course. I just thought…" A'vendyr hung his head, then brought it up and held E'maz's gaze. "I just wanted to tell you that I… I knew about you and Rhenn. I was told. And I'm sorry. She was under my protection. It's my fault she's gone. And I'm sorry."

E'maz felt like he was on dangerous ground now. A professional exchange, he could handle. But he wasn't a liar or a manipulator like the nobles at court. Intrigue was not his game. He had big secrets and no training in how to hide them. Rhenn was hidden at his house right now. He had a casket he'd made for her sitting on a cart in plain sight upon the cobblestoned road.

New sweat broke out on the back of his neck.

"My thanks, my lord. I… I miss her." He tried to make his voice sound sad, but he feared he sounded completely stupid.

He was sure A'vendyr would notice, but the man just kept talking.

"If I'd known what was waiting for her in that jungle, I'd never have left her behind to guard the rear. Please believe that."

"I do, my lord."

"She was..." A'vendyr paused. "Exceptional. As a tactician. With a blade. With a sharpened tongue, for that matter."

E'maz forced a laugh, and A'vendyr smiled.

"At any rate, I... I invite you to sit at our table tonight. We would be honored if you would join us."

E'maz doubted the baron would be honored, but A'vendyr sounded sincere.

"I would like that, my lord," E'maz lied. "I will... Well, I will do as you suggest. I will... I'll see you there." Every word felt like clumsy curds falling from his mouth and splatting with insincerity.

"Good. That's settled." A'vendyr extended his hand. E'maz clasped it, and the handshake was strong. E'maz had always thought he could tell a lot about a man from his handshake, and A'vendyr's was good.

"I look forward to it, my lord. Thank you for the honor."

A'vendyr turned to go, but his gaze caught on the box and the wagon. "What have you got there? Looks like a cabbage box."

"Ah, no," E'maz said, then threw out the first lie that flew into his mind. "Hinges. I'm going to... Saritu'e'Mere to... take their scrap hinges."

E'maz recoiled inside himself at the poorness of the lie.

"Hinges. Really?" A'vendyr seemed as confused as he ought to, considering the story. Except for the casket E'maz had just crafted, he hadn't worked on a hinge in years. That was for lesser blacksmiths. He was a weapons smith, and a highly paid one.

Gallantyr's Bones, he wasn't cut out for this kind of thing!

"It's a good deal on... the hinges. Otherwise I wouldn't bother." He could feel the heat on his face.

"Ah." A'vendyr paused, and E'maz could see him trying to puzzle it out, then the baron's son shrugged. "When do you set out?"

"A day or two. After the celebrations, of course."

"Did you apply for an escort?"

"Didn't see the need, really. I think you may have cleared the roads for a year, my lord."

"All right then," A'vendyr said. "Best of luck. See you tonight."

"Yes, my lord."

The baron's son walked away, and E'maz wanted to sink into the ground. He hurried off to the stables.

CHAPTER THIRTY-ONE

E'MAZ

E'maz stood at the front door of his house, looking up the street. The wagon and the horses were ready just outside, but with every passing minute, a foreboding grew in his belly.

An hour ago, just as he'd promised, he'd had the wagon ready and the horses hitched when day turned to night and Rhenn rose from the cellar. She'd put on the kilt he'd bought her—he'd burned the bloody ones at his forge—as well as the custom top he'd made for her. She'd had her weapons strapped on, including the magic dagger E'maz had given her. He'd brought her a replacement sword for the one she'd lost at the nuraghi, of course. It wasn't customized to her hand, like the previous blade he'd made her, but Rhenn could have made magic with any sword before her transformation. Now she could probably wield a two-handed sword with one hand.

"You ready?" he had asked.

"Almost," she'd said. "There's one more thing I need to do."

"Where are we going?"

"Not we, just me. I'm sneaking into the palace."

"What?"

"Nhevalos had a map of the nuraghi. We're going to need that."

"I'll go with you."

She'd shook her head and pointed a finger that touched his chest. "You… are not very sneaky E'maz Undantel. Me, I'm like the night."

He'd shaken his head. "I don't like this, you being out of my sight."

"I know."

"If anyone recognizes you, they're going to stop you."

"They're never even going to see me."

"What about Nhevalos?"

"I thought you said he hasn't been around for days," she had said.

"I thought you said he was a *Giant*. Which means he could be around and we'd never know it."

She'd moved close to him, pressing her lovely body to his, and kissed him. "I'll be right back." And she'd vanished into the night.

She'd been gone far too long. He knew how long it took to walk to the palace and back. Even without Rhenn's new fleet-footed nature, she should have been back fifteen minutes ago. If everything went well.

Clearly it hadn't.

He was going to have to go in there, and he'd get caught up in the celebration. He had to have something to apologize for the fact that he hadn't been there at the beginning, like he'd promised.

Damn Rhenn and her overconfidence.

He went back inside to grab a jeweled dagger as a gift for the baron—

And stopped in the entryway. There, on the ground, was a carefully folded piece of paper, meant for him to see. His heart sank as he picked it up, opened it, and read it.

My beloved E'maz,

Please forgive me. For everything you've done for me, the last thing you deserve is for me to lie to you. You have been perfect. The perfect gentleman. The perfect lover. The perfect friend. I cannot express how dear you are to me, and that is the very reason I cannot take you with me. There are dangers you can't imagine. I couldn't bear the thought that you might be hurt because of me. I simply couldn't bear it.

Please understand. Please trust me. I will return tomorrow night.

Yours,

-Rhenn

E'maz crumpled the note in his fist, and he saw the entire thing for what it was. She'd allowed him to make the wagon so he could convince himself that she'd wanted him to come along. But that had never been her plan.

Well, he knew the way to the nuraghi. He might not be able to catch her in his slow wagon, but he might catch her astride a single horse. She might need help and he'd be damned if he was going to just sit here and wait when she needed him.

He grabbed a bridle and a saddle from his back room and headed out into the street to unhook one of his horses—

He pulled up short as he saw the three figures in the shadows. They all wore X harnesses. Warriors of a pentara.

"A'vendyr!" E'maz said as the baron's son stepped into the lamplight.

"Hinges?" A'vendyr said, nodding at the cart and horses.

E'maz was caught red-handed. He didn't know what to say. He just wasn't a talented liar. Not like Rhenn. No doubt *she* could talk her way out of this situation.

E'maz dropped the saddle and bridle to free up his hands. He clenched them into fists. The other two warriors spread out, flanking him.

"You're going to fight us now, E'maz? What's going on?"

"You tell me, showing up outside my house with two of your warriors. What should I expect?"

"Drop the act. You're not good at it, E'maz. Where is she?"

"Who?" he said stupidly.

"When you didn't show up at the celebration, I sent someone to find you. You should have counted on that, friend. He saw Rhenn, saw her kissing you, then running off into the night."

E'maz opened his mouth, but nothing came out.

"I cared for her, too, as a comrade if nothing else," A'vendyr said, and this time there was an edge to his voice. "You didn't think I deserved to know she was alive? Did you think you were the only one who suffered at the thought of her death?"

E'maz swallowed. "I… She told me she didn't want you to know she'd returned."

"Why?"

"I…"

"What's the wagon for, E'maz?"

E'maz clacked his mouth shut.

"Where did she go?"

Face burning with shame, E'maz shook his head.

"We're not enemies, E'maz. At least, I didn't think we were." A'vendyr nodded his head and one of the pentara went into E'maz's house. E'maz stepped forward to stop the warrior, but two others blocked his path. Where had the new one come from? All of A'vendyr's pentara was here, all save Rhenn.

The two warriors didn't touch E'maz, but they looked ready to. He hesitated as the man who'd entered his house found the crumpled note and picked it up.

"Put that down!" he snarled. He tried to bull his way past, but the two warriors grabbed his arms. He tried to throw them off and succeeded with one, pitching him to the ground with a mighty shove—

He never saw the punch. It cracked across his jaw and stars burst in his vision. His knees hit the cobblestones, and he fell on all fours, trying to shake off the punch as the whole world spun.

He looked up to see A'vendyr shaking out his fingers. "It doesn't have to go this way, E'maz. We're on the same side. Just tell me what's happening. Is she a spy? Is that why you can't tell me? Who is she spying for?"

"She's not a spy."

"Then why not tell me?"

"Because she told me not to," he slurred through a split lip that felt like it was swelling to monstrous proportions.

"Note says she's coming back tomorrow. It's in her handwriting," the warrior with the crumpled piece of paper said.

"Tell me where she is, and we can sort this out tonight. Peacefully," A'vendyr said.

"No," E'maz growled.

A'vendyr's lips tightened and he nodded at his warriors. "Then we do it the hard way." All three approached.

E'maz fought them, but not very well and not very long.

CHAPTER THIRTY-TWO

RHENN

Rhenn approached the nuraghi cautiously. The winding road led up to the stout, impenetrable walls. The crumbling towers jutted at the sky like broken teeth. The moonlight laid a hazy blur over its silhouette, but she could see the detail in the darkened spots, even at this distance.

It had only been three days since she'd fled this place. Three days. It seemed like a lifetime, like everything had happened in between. Her attempt to fool N'ssag, her brief escape home, her death, and the desperate battle where she'd gutted that bastard and had run for her life all seemed like a hazy dream.

Now that she was here, she didn't want to be here at all. She wished she was back in E'maz's arms, safe and warm and hidden. Loved.

She looked down at her hands. They looked exactly like the hands she knew, but they weren't. Just like everything else about her. E'maz had still looked at her like she was the woman she'd been before; he'd still desired her like he'd done before. But was she actually the same? Was her old personality simply some parasite that clung to the new horror she'd become, refusing to let go?

Did she have a right to return to Usara? How would her kingdom benefit from having a bloodsucking queen?

She tried to banish the thoughts. She was here now. She should at least see what there was to see. Were the bloodsuckers still in there, L'elica and her brood, clustered around the corpse of N'ssag like pups around their dead mother? Would they spring upon her instantly when she appeared, driven with the need to end the woman who'd killed their master? Was she walking right back into the battle she had fled?

She drew her new sword and started up the road.

The gates remained open, and the courtyard was silent. She felt for that sensation that someone was watching her, but it was gone. Even the vague feeling that she didn't belong here—that sensation that every nuraghi emanated—was gone.

At first it was a relief, but as she made her way up to the thick double doors of the castle—which stood open this time— she wondered if the more welcoming feel of the nuraghi wasn't because the monsters were gone...

...but that she was now one of them.

Again, she shook off the thought and walked across the courtyard and into the castle.

The corpse of the Mouth Dog remained where it had fallen. She gave it a wide berth, wrinkling her nose at the disgusting smell of its long-dead blood. Senji's Teeth, the stink!

Glass littered the floor from the shattered window that had been her escape. Shards of it dotted the pool of congealed blood, and a single footprint pressed into it. With the crisp clarity of her new sight, she actually recognized the size and shape of the shoe. L'elica. This was where she'd stepped as she'd raced to catch Rhenn.

She saw no other footprints.

Rhenn prepared herself, holding her sword in one hand and E'maz's magic dagger in the other. If she ran into L'elica and her horde of primes, the fight was going to go differently this time.

She understood her strengths now. She longed for that fight because one way or another, it would be settled forever.

She ghosted through the halls until she arrived at the place where she had been "reborn." A chill scampered up her spine as she approached. The prime whose neck she'd broken lay where she'd felled him, crumpled against the hallway just outside the door. The one she'd stabbed with the dagger lay in a mass of flesh and bones, just as when he'd died as well.

She crept forward and entered the room sword first, ready for battle.

Nothing.

She put her back against the wall, scanning the shadows of the ceiling. L'elica liked to attack from above. Then her gaze flicked over the broken bed, chairs, clock…

And finally came to rest on the bathtub where N'ssag had killed her.

Nothing.

Wherever L'elica and her brood were, they weren't here.

Rhenn relaxed her guard, though she did not sheathe her weapons, and walked to the place where she'd gutted N'ssag. There was a notable bloodstain on the floor, but no body. She moved to the tub and saw her own blood darkening the pool of chemicals that half-filled the bathtub. She remembered her panic, her final helpless plea to N'ssag before he ruthlessly—excitedly—took her life.

There were only a few hours left before sunrise, so Rhenn left the horrible room and searched other areas of the nuraghi. She started with the tomb of the Giants, but the sarcophagus with the body of Ventakos held no further treasures, no other Plunnoi.

She tried to lift the enormous stone lids from the other two sarcophagi, but she couldn't budge them. It had taken all of L'elica's primes to throw the first one to the ground, but even with her new power, Rhenn simply didn't have the strength by herself. She struggled for an hour, pushing, pulling. She'd even pounded and pried at the thing with a length of rusted iron that had once been a giant sconce, but she couldn't break it, couldn't lift it, couldn't get inside.

Dejected, she searched the rest of the castle. She found a room filled with mirrors in the same hallway as the Thuros room. She found an enormous, grand throne room with tall, stained glass windows. In that place, with its monolithic stairway on the far side leading up to a Giant-sized throne, she'd felt that morning wasn't far off. The stained glass windows that flanked the enormous hall glowed with moonlight, but she felt the sun coming like it was clawing its way up the horizon, eager to catch her.

She'd have to stay the day here, deep in the nuraghi. She'd have to wait out the sun. She'd known that's how it was going to go. There simply wasn't enough time for her to run all the way here, then all the way back to V'endann Keep in one night. Not after all that searching.

Reluctantly, she retreated from the throne room into the bowels of the castle, back to the tombs of the dead Giants, deep down where the sun couldn't reach her.

Though she was deep underground, completely away from any sunlight, she still felt the sun rise. It was like a thrill of fear in her heart, followed by a lethargy. Daytime pulled at her, made her want to descend into that dreamless, inert state to which she'd succumbed in E'maz's root cellar.

But this was not E'maz's cellar. There was no safety here. There might still be protectors wandering about the castle. She couldn't allow herself to "sleep."

So she wrestled with the sarcophagi lids, still having no luck. But her exertions finally brought the hunger. Her body ached for the coppery fire. If there had been a single living creature in this subterranean castle, she'd have fed immediately.

After pacing the room, she finally decided to conserve what vitality she had. She sat down in the corner.

The day moved on, and as Rhenn waited, she thought about the room where she'd been "reborn." She thought about the fight, remembered the moment she'd stabbed N'ssag. She'd felt the sword go into him. Saw his face, the surprise, the pain.

She'd stabbed him through the guts. A gut wound. A large one. Plenty of blood. He was a dead man…

But she hadn't *seen* him die. She hadn't watched the light leave his eyes. Despite what she'd assured E'maz, despite what she wanted to believe, she didn't actually *see* N'ssag die.

During the long day, doubt flowered inside her. She hadn't wanted to face the idea that N'ssag had survived, but having come here, having seen the room where the body was *not*, she couldn't help herself.

Of course, the most likely explanation was that L'elica had taken the body with her. Her precious master.

But what if N'ssag hadn't fallen to his knees and bled out? What if he'd hung on? L'elica would have tried to take him back to Saritu'e'Mere. But that could never have worked. The man had barely made that journey when he was fully healthy. It would surely have killed him.

Wouldn't it?

Her heart beat faster. The truth was… she didn't know. She'd stabbed him. He'd been alive when she'd left him. His body wasn't here. And he was a mage. That was what she really knew.

Mages had a number of tricks. What if he'd been able to cling to life long enough to… to what? To stay alive.

What if he was still alive?

A chill scampered up her back. She had longed for a fight with L'elica—with all the bloodsuckers. She wanted to hack and slash at them. But the idea of facing N'ssag, of seeing that wormy-lipped, sallow-skinned face… It paralyzed her.

She realized now that she'd assumed N'ssag was dead because she *wanted* him to be dead, because she couldn't stomach the idea that the man who had captured her, dominated her, made her beg, and then killed her… She couldn't stand the idea that he was still out there. Because if he'd done all those things once, he could surely do them again.

The thought of facing N'ssag again turned her bowels to water.

It was irrational. She knew that. She had enough strength she could rip him in half. He was no fighter.

But he was a mage. Everything—her entire transformation—had been orchestrated by him. What if he had simply forgotten to place his loyalty spell on her? What if he could have fixed his error, but she'd stabbed him so quickly he hadn't had time? What if the next time she saw him, he simply snapped his fingers and she turned into his perfect little obedient slave, just like L'elica?

Rhenn didn't know anything about this magic N'ssag had wrought. The seeds of her own downfall could be rushing through her veins right now, just waiting for N'ssag to trigger them. She was his creature, after all! She was exactly what he'd made her to be—

Calm yourself, she thought. *He's not here, and if he was, you'd kill him.*

But her heart continued pounding. If N'ssag was alive, then her road home went through him. She'd have to face him, or give up the notion of returning to Usara forever. If he was alive, he had the Plunnos.

She would have to face him again.

She stared at the wall, arms clasped around her knees, and set her mind to working on more useful things than the horror of being captured by N'ssag again.

If N'ssag had escaped, what would he do next?

He would go to Saritu'e'Mere. That was certain. He would return to the safety of his laboratory.

Imagining that he could heal himself, he would transform his own injury and fear into anger, determination. What would he do next?

The answer popped into her mind instantly. He would search for her, of course. She was his prize, the next evolution of his renderings, his "queen." N'ssag would still want to get to Noksonon, but more than that, he would want her back. What frightened her the most—his reclamation and domination of her—was also her greatest advantage. It made him predictable. N'ssag's gaze had burned with desire every time he'd looked at her. "My queen" this and "my queen" that. Obsession had radiated from him like heat.

Yes. That's exactly what he'd do. He'd come looking for her—

Her thoughts came to a dead stop. He'd come looking for her… She frantically took that knowledge a step further. Where would he look for her? Where would he start?

V'endann Keep.

There was no other place. Just as Rhenn was certain that N'ssag, injured and scared, would return to Saritu'e'Mere, so too would he assume that Rhenn, injured and scared, would return to V'endann Keep.

L'elica had listened to Rhenn's conversation with Nhevalos, her conversation with A'vendyr as well. What if L'elica had shadowed Rhenn at other times, too? What if L'elica knew about E'maz?

He was in danger. N'ssag would come after Rhenn, and that would lead him to E'maz.

She jumped to her feet and sprinted from the room. She raced up the steps at the end of the hall and down the next, but as she approached the stairway that went up to the part of the nuraghi with windows, she slowed.

Light.

Those steps went upward into a blinding, burning brightness. When she looked at it, it felt like ants were crawling on her eyeballs. With a gasp, she retreated back down the hallway and crouched against the wall, hugging her legs to her chest.

She couldn't face that sunlight, couldn't get to E'maz until night fell. So she crouched there, helpless, her body craving blood, her mind alight with fear. She cursed herself for not seeing this, for not anticipating this. She should have stayed with him!

Please, she thought. *Please be safe, E'maz. By all the gods, please let me not be too late.*

CHAPTER THIRTY-THREE

RHENN

ight fell, and Rhenn burst from the nuraghi like a bird in flight, running with all of her superhuman effort down that winding road and toward the jungle.

A frightened herd of deer burst into a sprint as she shot across the grasslands, and her bloodlust flared. She could see the veins glowing beneath their fur. She chased them, leaping into the air and landing upon the back of the one at the rear of the herd. It stumbled and went down.

She ripped into its neck and fed. The blood coursed into her, filled her up. She gulped and gulped and let the coppery fire burn through her.

Slowly, the euphoria passed, and she came back to her senses. She didn't know how long she had crouched upon her kill, her eyes rolled up into her head in ecstasy. She jerked from the desiccated corpse and wiped shamefully at her face. Blood covered her chin, and she tried to make sure it didn't stain her clothes this time.

But now she was brimming with energy, so she left her shame and the dead deer behind. She shot through the jungle like an arrow in flight. She didn't look up, didn't focus on anything else except dodging branches and leaping fallen logs until, after hours of exertion, she came to the V'endann Fields. She plunged across the tall grasslands until she reached the shadow of the great wall.

The tall walls had a pillar every twenty feet or so, and they stuck out about two feet from the wall proper. In the corner where a pillar and the wall met, several bricks were missing along both the wall and the pillar, easy handholds for someone who could jump ten feet straight up in the air. Quietly, she clambered up like a squirrel, topped the wall, and dropped down the other side.

The streets were quiet. It was a full three hours before sunrise, so she wasn't worried about the sun, but if N'ssag had somehow survived, if he'd sent his primes to wreak vengeance upon her, they would target E'maz.

She ran through the streets until she reached his house. She paused in the dark alley across the street and assessed. From the outside, everything looked fine. The cart E'maz had made for her was still parked on the cobblestone street, though the draft horses were gone.

Quietly, she crossed the street and entered the house. The chairs were quiet next to the hearth, and no lanterns burned in the den. Everything seemed all right. E'maz would be asleep at this time. She saw no signs of struggle, no blood on the floor.

Silently, she moved into the bedroom, checking every corner for anyone who might be skulking. Nothing. There was no sign that a prime had been in this place.

But neither was there a sign of E'maz. The bed was empty.

New worries began to form. He wouldn't have tried to chase her, would he? If so, he would probably have taken the eastern road, rather than run through the jungle. Was it possible they'd crossed paths in the night? Was he out there, right now, alone and vulnerable?

The thought of E'maz out on the road riding through water goblin territory with N'ssag's primes potentially looking for him made her queasy.

"E'maz?" she called softly. No response.

She searched the rest of the house. She even checked the root cellar, though he'd have no reason to go down there except when she was here. She turned and went back into the den...

And stopped.

A'vendyr stood outside on the street just beyond the door she'd left open.

"He's not here," A'vendyr said.

She couldn't find her voice. She'd come ready to kill a host of primes if she had to. But she hadn't expected A'vendyr. This wasn't the plan. She wasn't ready to try to explain her current condition to anyone except E'maz.

"Where is he?" she asked.

"That's all you have to say? We lost you, Rhenn. We thought you were drained by bloodsuckers and left to rot somewhere in the jungle. Yet here you are, back from the dead and not a word to anyone. Did our... Did we mean so little to you?" The man sounded genuinely aggrieved.

"It's not that," she said. "Is E'maz safe?"

"Why would I hurt him?"

Anger kindled in her chest. "That's not an answer."

"You feel like I owe you answers? You, who let us believe you were dead and now skulk around the city at night. What happened, Rhenn?"

"Tell me where E'maz is," she growled.

"Or what? What will you do? Will you fight me?"

"If I have to. Did you take him to the palace?"

"Yes."

"Why?"

"Because he's harboring you, hiding you, and that makes no sense at all. Which, in turn, makes me suspicious. Worse, he won't talk about you because you told him not to. Why, Rhenn?"

"Why should you care?"

"Why should I...?" He threw his hands up in the air. "Because I am my father's son. Because he rules here and, by extension, so do I. Because everything that happens in V'endann is my business."

"Let E'maz go. He has nothing to do with this."

"What's 'this?'"

Rhenn's heart hurt. He wasn't going to let it go. And if he didn't let it go, if he didn't give E'maz back willingly, she was going to have to take him by force.

And then what? What kind of life would E'maz have if she broke him out of prison like he was actually guilty of something? She had to use diplomacy here.

"Very well," she said. "I'll tell you, but it has to be tomorrow. For tonight, just set E'maz free, and then I'll come to you tomorrow night and explain it all."

"Like you came back to us after the bloodsuckers snatched you? Like that?"

"Be reasonable, A'vendyr. This is… complicated."

"It's complicated? Like the fact that you're now a bloodsucker?"

Her heart stopped. "Why would you say something like that?" she blustered.

"Because we watched you, Rhenn. We have been watching for you. We saw you when you kissed E'maz. We saw you leave. The way you clung to the shadows. Your speed. Your silence. The way you went up and over the wall to avoid the guards at the gates. You move like them. And since you've returned, you haven't been spotted in the daylight. I think E'maz has been hiding you, protecting you from the sun. That's what the box is for, isn't it?"

She swallowed hard. "It's not what you think."

"Then tell me what it is."

"I told you. I will. But it has to be tomorrow night."

"Because there's only a little time before sunrise."

Rhenn didn't say anything.

A'vendyr threw a cluster of chains through the doorway. It splayed out on the floor before her, and she saw that it was four manacles chained together. "Put those on, and then we will talk."

She looked at the manacles, then back at him. "Don't make it like this," she murmured. "Please."

"Put them on. Show me that you're not an enemy to the barony."

"You're a fool if you think I'm putting those on."

"Then you are an enemy of the barony."

Her anger boiled over. "I'm already your prisoner. I have been since I arrived here." She gestured at the manacles. "And this is just the latest, crudest way of showing it. I'll die before I put those on."

She started toward him, stepping over the manacles.

"Rhenn," he warned. He was clearly wary as she stalked him. "Don't."

"Tell me where E'maz is."

She reached the doorway, and A'vendyr drew his sword.

"You'll never have a chance to use that." She stepped into the street.

"I hope not," he said.

Rhenn's head jerked to the side, spotting the three warriors on her left and to her right at the last instant. She crouched, but something heavy fell on her from above, and suddenly she was tangled. Thick rope lines surrounded her. They'd thrown a net from the roof!

The six warriors leapt forward, grabbing strands of the net, wrestling with her arms, and bearing her to the ground. She fought, but the net fought back at every turn. She couldn't bring her great strength to bear. The pentaran warriors were ready. She wasn't.

Straining faces came into her view as she twisted and struggled. Then she saw A'vendyr. His hand came down with the pommel of his sword. The strike hit her solidly in the temple.

Everything went black.

CHAPTER THIRTY-FOUR

RHENN

Rhenn awoke as cold bars hit her back and she rolled into a wall. No, not a wall. More bars. They'd put her into a cage. She flipped to her feet, blinking, as the door slammed shut. Rhenn had been knocked out before, and coming around had always been a groggy, slow process.

Not this time.

Her mind came awake in an instant, and her body was ready to act. She leapt at the gate.

"Watch her!"

"She's awake!"

She almost made it. She slammed against the door, throwing the two warriors back. One fell backward, the second slid away, his boots scraping on the cobblestones, but the third managed to hang on. The door didn't swing wide, but opened a little.

Rhenn squeezed the upper part of her body through and was about to use all of her strength to shove the door wide—

A cudgel came down on her head, and the abrupt darkness fell on her again.

● ● ●

She awoke an instant later, her body sprawled across the cage as the warriors loaded it onto E'maz's wagon. The box E'maz had made for her had been shoved to the back to make room. The warriors had brought horses but hadn't hitched them up yet.

The first time they'd knocked her out, she could only have been out a few moments. This time, even less, and as before, she awoke with full clarity.

She bared her teeth.

"Look at her!"

"A'vendyr, her teeth are pointed!"

"Quiet," A'vendyr commanded.

"A'vendyr," Rhenn said. "Stop this. What are you doing?"

"What I should have done from the beginning," he said. "I am taking control of this situation."

"By putting me in a cage? I'm one of your pentara!"

He hesitated, then shook his head. "Rhenn was a part of my pentara. I don't know exactly what you are."

"I'm still Rhenn!"

"That's what we're going to find out."

That sounded ominous, and panic bubbled to the surface. She was in a cage, out in the open. The sunrise was coming.

"Be reasonable," she said. "Do you think you need to put me in a cage?"

"You have fangs, Rhenn."

"Let's talk about this reasonably."

"Is that what you were preparing to do when you came through the door? Talk?"

"Yes."

"I know what someone looks like when they're preparing to attack." A'vendyr shook his head. "I came to find my friend, my comrade. Then you charged me."

"You were going to trap me in a cage no matter what I did. That net was ready long before I came at you."

"In case you did something crazy, like charge at me."

Rhenn bowed her head and gripped the bars so tightly her knuckles turned white.

They got the horses hitched up and the wagon jerked as it started forward.

"A'vendyr, you have to let me out of here."

He didn't say anything, just walked ahead of the slow moving wagon.

"If you keep me in here... If even one bit of sunlight touches me, I'll die."

A'vendyr hesitated, his head half turning as though he'd look at her, and it gave her hope. He wasn't completely dedicated to this path. He might be turned from it if she could just find the right words.

"If you're going to kill me, give me the sword. The sunlight..." She couldn't finish the sentence, envisioning her body ripping itself apart in popping strips of flesh like the hapless G'elreg.

A'vendyr glanced back, and again she saw reluctance in his eyes. "The baron will decide what is to be done with you."

The cart trundled on, and they wound their way up the main road to the keep's gate. Rhenn's heart pounded as she felt her helplessness. Again. Over and over, this seemed to be her lot. From the hands of one person who controlled her to another.

And she was more vulnerable now than ever before.

Before her transformation, she would simply have lounged in this cage, pretending like it didn't bother her. She would have thrown her enemies off balance by her nonchalance. Rhenn had never really been afraid of death, not since she and Lorelle had grown to womanhood together. She knew that death was coming for her. One couldn't be a rebel or a queen, either one, without expecting death to live close by.

But that was just a normal death. She'd envisioned herself dying in combat, a worthy end for a warrior.

But to feel her body tear itself apart... If the sun rose and hit her, there would be no chance to wield her sword. No chance to charm or seduce the sun. She would simply explode in burning strips of flesh.

She tried to master her fear of it. She tried to face it like she'd faced a hundred other possible deaths, countless times in the past, but she just couldn't. G'elreg's destruction kept rising in her mind. His scream. The blood. The fire.

She gripped the bars and closed her eyes, tried to shut the image away. She had to get ahold of herself. The frightened lost their self-control, and by doing so they also lost any hope to think clearly, to help themselves. She couldn't be that person.

So she pretended to be the person she'd once been. Uncaring, reckless, a self that didn't have a clock ticking in the back of her mind, telling her that there was barely an hour before the sun would rip her apart.

The keep doors opened and they trundled inside, up the corridors with the narrow cart. When it could go no further, four of A'vendyr's warriors picked up the cage and carried it into a room on the left. Rhenn considered reaching out of the bars, grabbing an arm and breaking it. Maybe even hauling an arm inside the cage and tearing into it with her fangs, but that was the bloodlust talking. She had to play this differently. She had to be… patient.

She examined the room. There was a bed, neatly made, a small table with two chairs, and a wardrobe. A guest room. This was the place where visiting nobility would stay when they visited the keep. She took all of that in at a glance, but she settled on the open window last. When the sun rose, there was nowhere in this room that would be safe.

They put her in the corner against the outside wall, below and to the left of the window.

"We need the truth," A'vendyr said. "If you'd have come to me first, I could have helped you."

"Or you would have put me in a cage. Just like this."

"I didn't force this. You did."

"By visiting E'maz. By doing nothing at all to you."

"By being a threat."

"How am I a threat? I hadn't attacked anyone until you attacked me."

"You're a bloodsucker. What you *are* is a threat. And because you and E'maz are so tightlipped about what is going on here, I'm forced to assume the worst."

"I am more than willing to talk."

"Now you are. Now is too late for me to do anything for you. The baron knows about you, and he has given orders. That's the end of it."

Rhenn swallowed. She'd never liked the baron, and the baron had never liked her. He'd hated that she'd become part of A'vendyr's pentara. He'd hated that she ran around the keep in her shameless kilt. Before now, she'd always reveled in making him angry as she'd flaunted her rejection of his backward customs. It had only been Nhevalos, no doubt, that had kept the baron in check, and she'd enjoyed straining that relationship.

Now she wished she hadn't tried so hard to alienate the baron.

"If I'm a prisoner, why aren't I in a prison cell?" She'd seen the prisons below the keep. Those cells didn't have windows.

A'vendyr seemed to read her mind. He glanced at the window, then back at her.

"If you let that light touch me, I'm dead," she said. "You won't be able to question a burnt pile of flesh."

"I'm going right now to alert the baron to your presence. He'll come before the sun rises."

"You're making a mistake, A'vendyr."

He hesitated, then he turned on his heel and left. His retinue followed him.

Rhenn looked balefully at the open window, the night breeze blowing in. It chilled her, and goosebumps raised on her skin at the thought of what was coming. G'elreg had been fully exposed to direct sunlight. Could she survive a room filled with sunlight if she wasn't in its direct path?

She doubted it. Her reaction to mild lantern light had been so strong, so painful, that she had to believe even the reflection of direct sunlight would utterly destroy her.

She waited a few excruciating minutes after A'vendyr had left—and she meticulously listened for motion outside the door—before she reached outside the bars and grabbed hold of the lock. She was strong now, stronger than she'd ever imagined possible. The question was: was she strong enough to snap steel?

Angling the padlock up and over, she braced it against the hasp in the door and settled her nerves.

She jammed it as hard as she could, trying to snap the bolt. She pushed so hard the metal squeaked, so hard it cut into her hand.

It didn't snap. It didn't even bend.

She tried over and over and over, twisting, jamming, trying to break the lock. She tried until her hands bled, until red trickled down her wrist. Finally she pulled her ravaged hand back inside the cage and cradled it against her chest.

Damn it.

As she watched, the wounds on her palms slowly healed. She could feel the copper fire rushing to that place, recreating her flesh as it used to be. It took less than a minute, and she was completely healed.

Hanging her head, she gripped the bars and waited for her fate to arrive.

CHAPTER THIRTY-FIVE

RHENN

Baron V'endann entered the room with two attendants and two royal guards. He looked nothing like his son. A'vendyr was tall, strapping, with well-muscled arms and an upper body reminiscent of Khyven's ridiculously broad shoulders. The baron, on the other hand, had narrow shoulders and a short, pudgy neck that gave the impression he had no neck at all, just a torso that became a head, with arms sticking out from the sides. The baron wasn't obese, but if he had ever been athletic, any evidence of that had faded long ago under a good layer of pudge that spoke to his lavish eating and drinking.

He entered the room looking like he'd dressed hastily. His doublet was off-kilter, and the laces on the sleeves of the billowing shirt beneath were undone, drooping almost to the floor. Part of his belly showed on his left side.

His ire was equally exposed. His piggy eyes took in the room, finally coming to rest on Rhenn's cage.

"That's her?"

"Yes, father," A'vendyr said.

"Well someone get some light in here. I can't even see her!"

One of the attendants brought forward a very strong lamp and shone it in Rhenn's direction. The light stabbed at her eyes, and she recoiled, moving quickly to the back of the cage.

"It doesn't look like her," the baron said.

"Father, please…"

The baron gathered himself up. A smug smirk tugged at the corners of his mouth and he squinted at her. "She doesn't seem the same at all, does she?"

"Father, she—"

"It's like all the arrogance has been drained out of her." The baron approached the cage and leaned over, having to put his hands on his knees so his belly didn't overbalance him. "It's hard to strut when you're stuffed in a cage isn't it, dear?"

"Father, please," A'vendyr said. "I think the prudent thing—"

"Quiet. The prudent thing is to follow the edicts of the prophet, and that's exactly what I plan to do. He came here to honor us and to honor her. We listened. She, like the feckless slut she is, chose to spurn what was given, to spurn us and our ways, and to throw the blessing of the prophet in his face."

"That's not what happened," A'vendyr said.

"Shut your mouth, boy. I know what happened. Nhevalos told me exactly what happened just before he left."

Rhenn held up a hand against the light. "Nhevalos is gone?"

"Give me that lantern," the baron commanded. The attendant passed it over, and the baron approached her cage, bringing the killing light with him.

Her eyeballs already felt like fire ants were crawling on them, but now her skin heated as the light came closer, like she had her face next to a glowing hot stove. She couldn't see anything in front of herself. Not the baron or the cage or the floor. Just that ferocious ball of golden fire.

She hissed and pressed herself against the back of the cage, trying to block the light with both her hands. Her forearms began to smoke.

"Father, you're hurting her! Stop it!"

"Why are you defending her? Look at her! She's chosen her side. That's why Nhevalos revoked his blessing."

"He... what?" A'vendyr said.

"The prophet fights monsters of the dark. He has no need for a slattern who throws herself into the hands of the enemy. Nhevalos's last words to me were that Rhenn was no longer to be your consort. She's not his chosen anymore. And I can tell you I've never heard gladder news."

"Where did he go?" Rhenn gasped. Her throat rasped, parched from the light and the heat.

"Shut up, slut. We don't answer your questions anymore. We honored you because the prophet told us to. Thankfully we have been released from that obligation. You are no longer an honored guest in this keep. The only question is, what are you? A spy?"

Rhenn huddled into herself. Every part of her exposed skin—her neck, her arms, and her legs that weren't covered by the kilt—began to blister.

The burning sun bobbled and retreated suddenly. Rhenn gasped in relief, blinking gummy eyes and trying to focus on something, anything, in the room. The bars of her prison came into focus first, then the floor, then the pudgy form of the baron who stared incredulously at his son.

A'vendyr had taken the lamp away from his father and shielded it behind his body. He spoke in an emotionless voice. "Do you wish me to kill her, father? Tell me, and I'll run her through with a sword. But not like this."

Tense silence fell in the room. The baron's guards went completely still, as though readying themselves should the baron order them to attack his own son.

The baron fumed silently.

"The lamp light is burning her. Is that what you wish?" A'vendyr asked. "Do you wish to torture her to death?"

The baron's face went beet red. "You still *want* her, don't you? You want this Nissra-be-damned monster in your bed! Come to your senses, boy. You're smitten with a phantom. The slut you knew as Rhenn is gone. That thing is all that remains."

The baron spun on his heel and started for the door.

"What are your orders, father?" A'vendyr called after.

"She's to stay there. Right there. Don't you let her out of that cage," he flung the order over his shoulder.

"May I please move her cage to a room that won't have sunlight—"

"No!" The baron left the room.

A'vendyr stood there for a long moment as the baron's retinue filed out after him, leaving him alone with Rhenn. A'vendyr sighed, then put out the lantern. The room plunged into blessed darkness and Rhenn slumped against the back of the cage.

A'vendyr went to the window and drew the curtains, blocking out the moonlight completely. They were made of a thick, red velvet, and they did a good job of shutting out any trace of light. The room came into even better focus.

He left, but then returned a moment later carrying the curtains—and curtain rod—from the next room over. He tossed one side of the rod up onto the wide hook attached above the window, then the other side of the rod onto the left. He spread the curtains out, blocking off the seam on the left side of the window, then the seam in the middle.

"That ought to be enough," he said.

"You're not going to let me out of this cage, are you?" she asked.

"I was given orders."

"And you always follow orders."

"You know I do."

"Set me free, A'vendyr. I promise you, all I want to do is leave your barony and never come back. That's all I've *ever* wanted to do. I'm no threat to you. Do you really think I am?"

He sighed. "I don't know what to think. My father's not wrong. You're one of them now. You can't bear the light. And I'm guessing you... That you also..." He gestured at the bloodstain on her top. "You sound like Rhenn. You even look like her. But are you? You see my dilemma."

She gave a mirthless chuckle. "*Your* dilemma…"

He stared at the floor.

"Thank you," she said softly.

He looked up.

"For the curtains. For… stopping your father. I'm grateful."

He let out a breath, seemed about to say something, then didn't. He went to door, looked back at her, then he turned and left.

Somewhere outside, Rhenn felt the sunrise coming.

CHAPTER THIRTY-SIX

RHENN

Rhenn's heart raced as she waited for the sunrise, waited to see if the curtains would be enough. Soon, heat radiated from the thick fabric, but A'vendyr's meticulous work paid off. No streams of light got through the double layer on her side of the window where the cage lay. On the far side, however, a thin slice of killing light illuminated the edge of the curtain, and a fierce flare lined the bottom where it brushed the floor.

Thankfully, it wasn't enough to hurt her. She imagined to a normal person, the room would seem so dark they could barely see, that the lines of light would be barely noticeable. But she felt them like she'd have felt bright sunlight on her shoulders. Hot, but not painful.

That's how she spent the day, shifting uncomfortably. She wondered if the baron would come to see her again, to taunt her, but he didn't. Neither did A'vendyr.

The day seemed to last forever, but eventually the piercing lines along the bottom and far side of the curtains softened and the heat receded, the almost uncomfortable warmth faded from her skin, and she breathed a sigh of relief.

Less than an hour into that blessed night, a man opened the door and came into the room. His hooded candle illuminated him, softly blurring the left side of his face until he set it down, closed the door, and turned to face her.

With the candle at his back, she could see him clearly. It wasn't the baron or A'vendyr. In fact, this man didn't even seem V'endannian.

He was pale skinned, not like the bronzed V'endannians. His hair was long and black and he had piercing hazel eyes. He dressed more like an Usaran than a V'endannian, with long, loose, gray pants, a thick belt, a blousy shirt with billowing sleeves and a black cloak hanging from his shoulders. He had to be sweating inside that ensemble, but he didn't show it. No sweat on his forehead. No look of discomfort.

He approached her cage without the slightest pause, and his face was grim. Everyone, including the baron, had approached her with trumped-up courage or cautious hesitation. This man didn't seem afraid of her at all.

He crouched next to the cage, looking her in the eye.

"You're Rhenn Laochodon?" he said in a deep baritone.

"That's right."

"Do you know who I am?"

"Cage inspector?"

He didn't crack a smile. "I'm a Guardian of Pelinon. My name is Kell Duranti."

She *did* know what a Guardian was, actually, and it took her aback. Everyone in V'endann and beyond knew who the Guardians were. They were the voice and the hands of the king of Pelinon. The barony of V'endann was the northernmost holding of that enormous kingdom. There were only thirteen Guardians in all the land, and they apparently made judgements and dispensed the king's justice wherever they went.

"Well Kell, I should report to you that I'm being held against my will."

The man didn't blink, didn't do anything.

"Are you here to restore my rights and set me free?" Rhenn asked.

"Hmmm," he grunted.

"Then why are you here?"

"I was in Saritu'e'Mere when I heard about the water goblin attack on this barony. Water goblins don't usually attack defensible structures as large as V'endann Keep. It piqued my interest, so I came to get more information for King Stevan, just in case this is a sign of things to come from the water goblins."

"I see."

"But I was in Saritu'e'Mere because of you."

"Me?"

"Rather, those like you. Baron V'endann calls them bloodsuckers."

"Unfortunately, I may have coined that term," she said.

"And now you're one of them."

The statement stung, but it was stinging less and less every time she heard it. "Well, sometimes the wheelbarrow of life is full of apples." She shrugged. "And sometimes horse manure."

"Hmmm," he grunted. "You seem mostly like a normal person."

"Thank you. So do you."

Still, no smile. Clearly not a man to be charmed.

"The baron wanted to kill you. I requested that he not."

"I'm inclined to say 'thank you' but I get the feeling the moment I do, I'm going to regret it."

"The king needs to study you and those like you."

"Called that, didn't I?"

"I'm leaving in the morning. I'll be taking you with me."

"Listen," she said, gripping the bars. "I don't belong here. I was brought to this place against my will. I am a queen where I come from, and I've been stolen from my kingdom. I don't want to go south with you. I want to go home. Help me."

"Baron V'endann mentioned something of this," the man said without batting an eyelash. "You came from far away?"

"Noksonon."

"Hmmm," he grunted. "Is it an island of Gael?"

"No, it's another land, through the Thuros."

He narrowed his eyes. "What's a Thuros?"

"A gateway that goes between continents."

"So... from Pelinon to the islands?"

"No. Not here. Not on Daemanon. It's... It's entirely different than here."

"I see. And you get there through a magical doorway."

"Yes."

"These provincials are easily convinced of such things, aren't they? You'll find I'm not the same. They also claim some prophet brought you to them."

"He did."

"But you weren't a bloodsucker at the time."

"No."

"Who turned you into a bloodsucker? Was it also this prophet fellow?"

"Nhevalos."

"Of course. Is he in this with you?"

"Look, you get six strong warriors to go with me to the nuraghi, and we can unearth another Plunnos. I'll *show* you that it works. I'll take you to Noksonon."

"Hepreth's Nuraghi is off limits to any but the king's personnel. You and I are going south, and the king can decide what to do with you. I hear your friend constructed a coffin expressly to help you travel during the day. We'll use that."

"Where is E'maz?"

"I believe the baron has him in prison. Aiding and abetting the enemy."

"He had nothing to do with this. All he did was... I forced him to comply."

"Hmmm," Kell grunted. "He left you during the daytime to build that rather extensive box, and he was forced to do this?"

"I manipulated him. Please set him free. Please."

"He refuses to tell his baron anything about you, even now. Even though we have you in custody, even though we've explained to him what you are. Seems he already knew. That right there is enough for him to be in prison. That sounds like collusion with a murderer."

"I haven't murdered anyone!"

"The baron says that you and your kind have been killing people in the villages throughout the barony."

"Not me... There were others."

"How many others, would you say?"

"About a dozen. Less now. I killed three of them when I escaped."

"Escaped? From whom?"

"The necromancer—the one who's turning corpses into bloodsuckers. His name is N'ssag. He's a priest of the order of Nissra."

"Is he now?" Kell raised an eyebrow, the first sign of emotion she'd seen on that craggy face. "King Stevan will be quite interested to know that—"

A distant shout arose outside the window. Then another.

Kell Duranti stood with a fluid economy of motion that surprised her. He went to the door, where he paused and picked up his candle. "It's been educational talking with you, Rhenn Laochodon. I will see you in the morning."

"What's happening?" she asked. "What's going on?"

He didn't reply, simply swept out the door and closed it behind him.

The shouts came louder outside, more frequent. The first two had been far off, like someone had shouted all the way from the wall surrounding the keep.

Then came other sounds. Swords clashing, shields smashing, people running, orders being shouted. Rhenn had known those sounds all her life.

War had come to V'endann.

CHAPTER THIRTY-SEVEN
RHENN

T he sounds increased, and the desperation of the shouts grew. The whole city seemed to be in turmoil, and Rhenn wondered if the water goblins had rallied to attack V'endann Keep a second time. But she couldn't see a thing from her position in the corner.

It went all night long.

The fact that it never quieted, that dozens of water goblins never streamed into her room, seemed a good sign. The defenders were holding off the attack.

Then, close to sunrise, the fighting stopped. A great silence fell over the city. She listened hard, trying to determine who had failed, the attackers or the defenders.

The door to her room banged open and the baron entered in a fury, a dozen bloody and bedraggled guards at his back, swords dripping.

"What did you do?" the baron growled. "What did you do!"

He held that bright lantern and shone it in her corner, blinding her, and she scrambled to the back of the cage.

"What happened?" she asked.

"The bloodsuckers! You brought them here. You're a spy for *them!*"

"Tell me what happened." Her body burned, and she tried to protect her eyes from the blinding light. "I don't know what you're talking about!"

"You are a plague upon my lands, you thing of the night," he said. "You were from the first moment."

If she squinted below her upheld hands, she could just make out the silhouette of his boots at the edge of her cage. Everything else was overwhelming golden fire.

"Kell Duranti suggested that it was all a scam. You and your imposter Nhevalos. All to make us let our guard down so you could do exactly this."

"Do what?" she screamed at him.

"Enough, I don't know why I'm even talking to you." He continued, but it sounded like he was speaking to someone behind him, someone else in the room. "It's not like this dead creature has a soul. Kill her."

She heard swords ringing as they cleared scabbards.

"A'vendyr!" she shouted, hoping he was somewhere in the room. "I don't know what's happening. It wasn't me!"

"He's not here, slattern. He's not going to save you this time."

Rhenn pressed herself against the back of the cage, trying to see where the swords would come, but she couldn't. She couldn't see anything except the thin view of approaching boots.

She tensed, waiting for her death—

"Wait," the baron said. "Wait, no. No, not the sword."

Her cage jerked, and she fought to keep her balance.

"Well don't just stand there, you idiots."

Swords sheathed, and the cage jerked again, this time profoundly. Steel scraped against stone as they pushed her out of the corner. The lantern light passed behind her, and she could finally see something. If she stared directly away from the light, she could see the fuzzy outline of the door. Based how far they'd taken her, she was in the exact center of the room.

"Yes. There. Perfect," the baron said.

The lamplight moved around her, toward the door, and she turned away from it. Now she could see the baron's silhouette against the curtains. He was indistinct, a rumpled doublet and those silly, pointed shoes. He reached up and yanked both curtains down. The rings popped and one of the hooks actually tore from the wall. The curtains thumped to the ground, revealing the tall window looking out at the eastern horizon. It was still night, and she saw the sky and the stars with better clarity than anything in the room.

"This is what you fear, isn't it?" the baron said. "The coming of the sun. The coming of justice. Well, my only regret is that I don't get to see it happen. I suppose I'll just have to satisfy myself with the thought of it, of how you'll suffer."

He strode around her cage.

"V'endann," she called. "V'endann!"

The bright light left the room, as did the baron and his retinue. The door closed, and the room plunged into blessed darkness.

She turned around, staring at the naked window, staring out at the darkened eastern horizon. The moment the sun came up, it would shine directly on her. Maybe for a moment, the direct sunlight would go over her head. But even that would likely kill her. And if not, the sun would climb higher in the sky with every second, and its rays would climb over the edge of the window, descending lower and lower until she was completely exposed.

Rhenn swallowed, unable to look away from the window, from the coming of her death.

CHAPTER THIRTY-EIGHT

RHENN

It was only a few moments before she heard the baron at the door again. The latch rattling, the door opening. Rhenn spun in her cage, ready to shield herself from the intense light of his lantern...

But there was no lantern and no baron.

L'elica slipped inside the room, a sledge hammer gripped in her right hand.

Doom spread over Rhenn's scalp like ice water. N'ssag's most powerful prime had come back for revenge. Rhenn tried to think of options, tried to think of what she could do trapped inside this cage, but it was the same dilemma all over again. L'elica could stab at her just like the baron's men had been about to do.

Except the bloodsucker wasn't wielding a sword. She held a hammer. She did have a sword pushed through her belt, though.

Rhenn narrowed her eyes in recognition. That was Rhenn's sword! The one she'd shoved through N'ssag's guts.

L'elica didn't fly at the cage, though. Instead, she just stood there, staring at Rhenn. The bloodsucker looked... different, and at first glance Rhenn couldn't figure out how.

L'elica wore a dark blue dress, different than the faded, stained blue dress she'd worn before.

And yet, it was more than just the dress. It was…

She'd taken a bath. Her usually dirty arms were scrubbed clean. Her blond hair shone like she'd washed it. Two pouches on straps hung crosswise over her body from each shoulder. She wore a dagger belt around her waist and Rhenn's sword. She wore little half-boots, the kind a lady of the court might wear to impress the other ladies.

She took a step toward Rhenn's cage.

"N'ssag isn't dead, is he?" Rhenn asked, playing for time, trying to think of something she might do to stop the inevitable. At the very least, perhaps she could keep L'elica talking long enough to have the sun rise on both of them. Rhenn would die, but maybe she could take L'elica with her.

The bloodsucker crossed from the door to Rhenn's cage.

This is it, Rhenn thought. *After everything, this is how I die.*

But L'elica set the hammer down and leaned the long handle against Rhenn's cage. She didn't draw the sword. Instead, she deftly managed the blade, adjusted her dress, and knelt on the floor.

L'elica reached into her pouch, withdrew the Plunnos N'ssag had taken off the dead Giant. She held it out with a trembling hand.

Stunned, Rhenn stared at the proffered coin. L'elica reached into the bars of the cage, and for some reason Rhenn couldn't explain, she allowed the woman to touch her. L'elica took Rhenn's wrist gently, and then pressed the Plunnos into her hand.

"Help me," L'elica said softly.

A number of questions raced through Rhenn's mind, but she couldn't settle on any one of them. She just stared at the Plunnos, then back at L'elica.

Tears slid down the cheeks of the undead woman, though her face remained as expressionless as ever.

Rhenn finally managed to open her mouth. "What do you want?"

"I will set you free," L'elica said. "I'll set you free. And then you help me."

Rhenn glanced at the sledgehammer. By Senji's Stars, was this a rescue?

"After I set you free," L'elica said. "You will take me with you to Noksonon. You agree… to take me. Not to betray me. To put me in one of your noktums. If you do that, you'll never see me again."

"No," Rhenn said. They'd been through this before. She would not open up her homeland to the horrors created by N'ssag.

"You'll die if you don't," L'elica said.

"I'd rather die than let N'ssag loose on Noksonon."

L'elica shook her head. "Not N'ssag. Just me."

"What?"

"Just me."

"So N'ssag *is* dead?"

"No. He lives."

Rhenn tried to figure out what the woman was saying, and then it hit her. "You've broken faith with N'ssag?"

"Yes."

"That's a lie."

L'elica hesitated, looked down at her knees. "I've come to find…" she said, but not like she was answering Rhenn's statement. "My entire life is a lie. Everything. This…" She fingered the new dress she wore. "Me."

Rhenn narrowed her eyes.

"I don't know what I was before he made me," L'elica said. "I didn't care before, because… I was everything to him before, and now I am nothing. An experiment. I thought he and I were forever… But I am just a tool he created, now chipped and worn. An old, battered hammer beyond its usefulness…. I am no longer his chosen. So now I must care what I was before… this. It is all that occupies my mind."

"What did he do?" Rhenn murmured.

"I disgust him now. I am old. Dirty. He sees me like he used to see the primes birthed before me. Now I am nothing to him, and I wonder what I was before. I wonder what I can be after. I should be able to be something, shouldn't I? I cannot accept becoming one of the older primes. An unthinking brute, stupid and dirty and good only for the lowest tasks. I cannot."

"He's created new primes..." Rhenn murmured. "Like... Like me."

She nodded. "He calls them 'high primes.' And yes, they are like you. Faster, stronger, except he wiped their memories. They are utterly loyal because they know nothing different. Just like me. Just like I used to be."

Rhenn narrowed her eyes. It was a good lie, because it was believable. N'ssag saw himself as the center of everything important about the world. His excitement about "his next breakthrough" was everything to him. It made sense that he would continue to have new favorites with his new successes.

But the believability of the lie was what made her distrust it the most. This was exactly the kind of thing N'ssag might try.

"You're saying he cast you aside," Rhenn said.

"I left before he could."

Senji's Teeth, she was good. She seemed sincere. "I don't believe you."

L'elica's head came up like she didn't understand what Rhenn had just said. "You must. If you don't, we both die here. The sun will rise in moments."

"Except I'm already dead, aren't I? *You* saw to that," Rhenn said. "You sucked the blood from my body until my heart stopped beating! Then you pushed your poison blood into me until it started beating again, filling me with this unholy need to drink blood! It doesn't matter to me whether you're lying to help N'ssag, or whether you're genuine, I'd rather burn alive than help you!"

"I understand that you have no reason to trust me," L'elica said. "Just as I have no reason to trust you. But together, we might survive. You want to go home; I have what you need. I want to escape N'ssag forever; you are what I have. And the two of us only have so much time. He has created an army. Nearly a hundred and fifty high primes."

Rhenn's eyes grew wide. That was why the baron had been furious. That was why he'd left her here to die in the sunlight. "That's what attacked V'endann tonight!"

"Tomorrow night, he will return, and there will be no place for us to run. He is coming here for you."

"What... stopped them?" Rhenn asked.

"N'ssag didn't expect Baron V'endann's people to hold out so long. He didn't expect to fight a Guardian. The man's magic was formidable. So N'ssag had to pull out before he had succeeded. One more hour, and the keep would have fallen, but he had to flee the dawn."

"The dead..." Rhenn remembered the Fields of V'endann, littered with goblin bodies. "He turned the dead water goblins into..."

"Into high primes."

"Why..." She began to say, but then she knew why. "Why here? Just vengeance against me?"

"Yes, he wants to kill you, but more than that he wants bodies. Now that he has an army, he doesn't just want a provincial barony. He wants to create an army that can take Saritu'e'Mere. All of Pelinon, even. He wants to cover the continent with his high primes and rule. And..."

"And what?"

"He can do it. Given enough time."

Rhenn saw the horror of it. "The people of the barony. As they fall, as their army is depleted..."

"N'ssag's grows," L'elica finished.

Rhenn thought about it in stunned stupefaction. An army that could resurrect the dead would only get stronger with every battle, while its enemies would get weaker.

She began to think of what she could do to save Baron V'endann's people, to somehow shield them from this evil...

And then she stopped. Why? Why should she care about this backwater little barony. They'd belittled her, shamed her, corralled her, and tried to force her to marry A'vendyr. They'd hunted her, caged her, and then at the utmost end, they'd tried to kill her. She owed them nothing.

"Let's go," Rhenn said.

L'elica shook her head. "You must promise me, Queen Rhenn—on your kingdom, on your crown—that you will fulfill your part of the bargain after I fulfill mine." She touched the hammer's handle.

They locked gazes. They both knew that Rhenn was faster and stronger than L'elica, not to mention that Rhenn knew how to use that sword at the bloodsucker's hip. Once the cage was open, Rhenn would have all the advantages.

She thought about telling L'elica exactly what she wanted to hear and then killing her anyway. But Rhenn had never made a deal she'd gone back on before, not until N'ssag.

It was as though Senji herself had taken notice of that lie, that lack of honor. Rhenn had never been very religious, but she wondered if her transformation was Senji's punishment for a queen who went back on her word.

She set her intention, set her commitment, and she spoke.

"Very well, L'elica. I will give you what you ask for. But know this. The moment you try to double-cross me, our deal is done. And once we cross into Noksonon, once I put you in the noktum, you will go as far away from my kingdom and my people as you can. I never want to see you again. And if you ever hurt any of mine, I'll stake you to the ground in the Night Ring and let the sunrise have you."

"Agreed," L'elica said without hesitation.

"In addition, you follow my lead to the Thuros, understand? I don't go where you tell me. You go where I tell you. If you break with any of these conditions, I'll feast on every last drop of your blood like you feasted on mine."

They stared at each other, and neither flinched.

"I believe you, Queen of Noksonon."

"I am Queen of *Usara*."

L'elica picked up the hammer and brought it crashing down on the lock. It took three hits, and the lock broke. L'elica opened the door and stepped back. Rhenn emerged and finally stood up to her full height. The two watched each other. Slowly, L'elica drew Rhenn's sword and passed it over.

She took it and sheathed it through her belt.

"We have one stop to make before we leave," Rhenn said.

"We have twenty minutes until sunrise, Rhenn. We have to get away from here—"

"You follow my lead, remember? Not the other way around."

L'elica pressed her lips together, but she didn't argue.

They ran soundlessly out of the room. Rhenn took them up the hall, down a stairway, down another hall, then down another stairway. Every doorway they passed hung open, belongings scattered on the floor as though hastily packed. There wasn't a single person left in the keep.

Rhenn ignored the remnants and went deeper, down to the prison. The thick wooden door to the guard room was ajar, and she pushed past it. The room was empty. Half-eaten chicken lay on wooden plates. Half-drunk ale rested in abandoned mugs. All the weapons on the walls had been taken. She looked hastily for a key ring, but couldn't find one. Still, the far door that led to the cells was open, and she slipped through.

"What are we looking for?" L'elica asked.

Rhenn was going to snap back at her that they were looking for E'maz, but her heart sank as she stepped into the aisle between the cells. Every cell door was open, and the key ring lay on the floor halfway up the hall.

"They let the prisoners out..." she murmured, stunned.

"You're looking for your lover," L'elica said.

Rhenn whirled. "You know him?"

"Yes. He had a big beard. Big shoulders and arms. A blacksmith."

"Yes! Did you see him?"

L'elica hesitated.

"What is it? You saw him."

"Rhenn, I am sorry."

"No..." She felt sick to her stomach. "No, he was here. In the cells. They said they put him in prison."

"I saw him when N'ssag's forces reached the keep. He was on the wall with a sword, fighting alongside the V'endann warriors. They… The high primes took him. He fell. Three of them pulled him off the wall, and he fell."

"Gods damn it!" Rhenn lashed out with the sword. It sparked on the bars. She fell to her knees and slammed her fists against the stone floor.

"I… am sorry," L'elica said.

Rhenn just hunched into herself, clenching her bloody fists. She thought about pursuing N'ssag. She considered forgetting about Noksonon altogether and making the rest of her life about finding N'ssag and finishing the job she should have finished back at the nuraghi.

Rhenn shoved herself upright. She started for the door when L'elica stopped her.

Rhenn dislodged the bloodsucker's grip. She wanted to kill someone, and L'elica would be just fine. The woman deserved it. Wasn't she just as much to blame for E'maz's death as N'ssag?

But Rhenn had made a promise. And she wasn't going to break her promise again. Not ever.

"Don't touch me…" Rhenn said through her teeth.

"You cannot go that way," L'elica said.

"I told you. We follow my lead—"

"The sun is rising. There are no windows in this place. We are safe here. Where will you go that will be safer than here?"

"Maybe I deserve to burn."

"Maybe we both do. But I spent the last few days wondering what I wanted. Once N'ssag cast me down with the other primes, I realized I wanted more than what he could give me. I want a better life, Queen Rhenn. Perhaps, for the first time, a real life. I want something more than what he decreed for me." L'elica paused. "Don't you?"

L'elica was right. N'ssag had defined both their lives with his heinous magic. He had gutted them and replaced them with his handiwork. He was keeping them in his palm even now, moving them in relation to his ambitions, and she wasn't going to allow that anymore.

It was time to wipe the muck of this backwards barony and this entire misbegotten continent from her feet and go home.

"Very well." Rhenn walked into one of the open cells. It was dark and strangely peaceful. "You stay over there. I don't want you anywhere near me."

L'elica paused, then she faded back, out of sight.

Rhenn knelt in the cell and put the point of her sword—the sword E'maz had made for her when she'd first come here—onto the flagstones. She rested her head against the pommel.

"I'm sorry, E'maz," Rhenn said. "I… I'm so sorry."

She hadn't prayed to her patron goddess for anything since she'd been a child, but she prayed now. She prayed for E'maz's soul. She prayed for a better life for him in the beyond, better than he'd been allowed here.

Senji, take his soul to you, she thought. *If I ever did anything right in your eyes, take E'maz gently into your halls. Treat him with the honor he deserves. He was a good man.*

CHAPTER THIRTY-NINE

RHENN

The time passed slowly, but L'elica had been right. The keep had been evacuated. Not a single person came down to the cells. Not a single sound echoed anywhere.

She and L'elica paced the dark cells. They were the longest hours Rhenn had ever known. Finally, after everything, she had the Plunnos. All she had to do now was make it back to the nuraghi, and she could go home. And with E'maz dead, she wanted to go home so badly her teeth ached. She wanted to be away from this cesspool.

She fantasized about seeing Lorelle. Blessed, lovely Lorelle. It was always her sister's voice that spoke in the back of Rhenn's mind whenever she was about to do something reckless. But just the sound of her voice reminded Rhenn that she was loved without judgement by at least one person. Lorelle's harangues had always been welcome.

She thought of Slayter. Distracted, impossible to keep on point, and yet always the one with the right answer. She still didn't understand the man's magic or how his mind worked, but he could create the miraculous. Without him, there would have been no victory against Vamreth.

She thought of stalwart Vohn, his biting comments that made him seem like he always saw the dark side of every situation. Yet he was always the first to see the best in a person. He'd seen it in Khyven.

And Khyven... The missing piece who'd almost single-handedly destroyed her rebellion... and then single-handedly saved it. Khyven the Giant-killer. Khyven the fountain of the impossible.

She missed them. By Senji's Grace, she missed them so much. She wondered if her real passion to return to Usara wasn't because of her duty to her people, but because she missed her family.

Whatever the reason, Rhenn didn't belong here. The very fabric of this place didn't suit her. It never had. N'ssag wasn't her villain. This wasn't her kingdom. Let the baron, the Guardians, the King of Pelinon deal with the horrors they had unearthed. Rhenn had her own horrors to deal with back in Usara.

These dark thoughts occupied her during the interminable day, but as it drew to a close, both Rhenn and L'elica could feel it. The blood that pumped in their veins seemed to know, seemed to itch as the night came.

"Will N'ssag return here?" Rhenn asked, speaking to L'elica for the first time during their long wait. She wondered if they would emerge from their protective dungeon into the open night only to find an army of high primes waiting for them.

"He will go where Baron V'endann has taken his people. Do you know where that might be? Is there a safe hold somewhere nearby?"

Rhenn shook her head. "Nothing for miles. The keep is the safest place in this area. The nearest bastion of civilization is Saritu'e'Mere. Would the Guardian Kell Duranti have taken them there?"

"I do not know what a Guardian would do," L'elica said. "But the sun has set. It's time for us to leave."

Rhenn tried to ignore the fact that with the night came hunger. She wanted to feed. Her body had healed the burns inflicted by the baron at an amazing rate, but it had depleted her energy as well.

She clenched her teeth, and they left the prison without another word.

They left the deserted keep, the deserted city, and began their journey through the jungle. They ran hard. L'elica could not keep up with Rhenn's fastest pace, so Rhenn slowed to match the woman. Rhenn's hunger grew with the exertion, and she kept her eyes keen for some kind of prey she could feed upon. But it was L'elica who spotted the herd of deer just at the edge of the jungle.

So they hunted. They took down one apiece, fed, and started the run again.

They made remarkable time, and the towers of the nuraghi hove into view when only half the night was gone.

Rhenn slowed as they approached. The nuraghi was not as she'd left it. The stout front gate had been completely torn down. "What happened here?" she murmured.

They sprinted up the raised, winding road, and the answer became all too clear. Corpses of V'endannians littered the courtyard and blood was splattered everywhere. A few of N'ssag's water goblin high primes also lay among the dead, bodies dismembered or burnt.

"They came here," Rhenn murmured. "During the day. They retreated here." Her imagination went wild with the possibility. The nuraghi, of course! It was the only other place within a day's travel that afforded better protection than the keep.

If they hadn't been harried by the high primes during the day, even the slow movers could probably have made it during a twelve-hour span. And those who were more fleet-footed could have arrived here more quickly. She scanned the parapets of the wall and saw evidence that they'd reinforced it, had prepared for an attack.

Apparently even that had not been enough to stand against the high primes.

"Senji's Blood," Rhenn murmured as she walked among the dead.

"We are in great danger here," L'elica said. "I do not think the battle is ended."

Rhenn glanced at the castle door, also broken and hanging on its hinges. They had retreated. There might be survivors inside the nuraghi, still fighting the bloodsuckers.

"They slaughtered them," Rhenn murmured.

"What do you care?" L'elica asked.

"What do I...?" Rhenn turned toward the blond woman.

"You said they imprisoned you. Tortured you. Left you to the sunlight—"

"I didn't want to see them die."

"Why not?"

"Because..." Because Humans were good and bloodsuckers were bad. "This is..." Rhenn said. "This is a great evil, L'elica."

"Evil? What is evil?"

"Us..." Rhenn murmured. "We are. All of us... bloodsuckers."

L'elica's eyes narrowed. "Why?"

"Because we suck blood to stay alive! Because we were created by the worst person I've ever met."

L'elica's jaw muscles worked. "How do you know this? How do you know that we are the evil ones, and not the baron?"

"Because N'ssag is rapacious and the baron is just... ignorant. Frightened."

L'elica shook her head. "I don't see the difference. Both of them want to kill you. Why are we the evil ones? Humans kill. They don't just drink the blood of others; they tear their bodies apart and eat the flesh."

Rhenn couldn't argue with that.

L'elica squinted up at the nuraghi. "I don't want to be evil..." she murmured.

Rhenn glanced sideways at the bloodsucker, and for the first time Rhenn considered what it must have been like for L'elica to wake up to this life. To know only that N'ssag had brought her back and to feel an unswerving loyalty to him for that. To believe that this was what life was like: chasing, hunting Humans, feeding on the glorious coppery fire.

Rhenn felt so confused. She closed her eyes and pressed the palms of her hands to her brows.

"He's here for you," L'elica said softly.

Rhenn opened her eyes. "N'ssag?"

"Not him alone. A powerful mage named Ventat Obrey is driving him. Ventat works for someone even more powerful than himself. He supplied N'ssag with the noktum, gave him the ability to see within it. It is because of Ventat Obrey that N'ssag has his high primes. That mage wants you dead. He was sent for that purpose alone."

Nhevalos's words floated in her head. *You stand in the center of a storm, Rhenn Laochodon … and these events will spin around you like blades.*

"If you want to stop them, you cannot beat them through combat. Not without a hundred high primes of your own. But you can deny them both their prize. You."

"I just… run away?"

L'elica gestured at the nuraghi. "Will you run into this battle, then? Run in and die? What will that serve? But if you are not to be found—if you return to your land—N'ssag will lose his prize. Ventat Obrey will kill him for it. He swore as much. N'ssag already failed him once."

L'elica was right. It was the right decision in every way.

This isn't my fight, Rhenn reminded herself. *Even if I could change the outcome by charging in to help, this was never my battle! I don't belong here. I was stolen and taken to this place against my will!*

"Let's go," she said.

"Quietly," L'elica said. "We must avoid detection."

"I can be quiet." Rhenn led the way into the nuraghi, past the cracked and open double doors, checking every corner for N'ssag's high primes. She saw none.

Including the shadow that detached itself from the eaves directly overhead and silently ran across the roof.

CHAPTER FORTY

RHENN

henn quietly led the way up the corridors. She knew exactly where the Thuros room was and the quickest way there.

They both kept an eye out for N'ssag's high primes, but neither she nor L'elica saw any. At one point, Rhenn heard the sounds of battle, but it came from down a corridor to the left, toward the enormous throne room she'd seen the last time she'd been here.

Rhenn gave a significant look back at L'elica, who glanced tensely to the left. There was still a battle. That meant there were survivors, but the blond woman had been right. If they were to stop N'ssag's plan—not to mention the hopes of whoever this Ventat Obrey was—they had to get out of here. The best outcome would be if N'ssag simply couldn't find Rhenn, didn't know she was at V'endann Keep, didn't know that she'd come to the nuraghi during this battle.

They nodded together, jogged down the right-hand hallway, and arrived in the Thuros room.

The colors of the Thuros swirled, eternally waiting for those who knew its secrets. Rhenn pulled the Plunnos from her pocket and stepped onto the dais. She could hardly believe it. She was here at last, yet she hesitated, turning the giant coin over and over in her hand.

Rhenn had dreamed of returning home since she had been abducted, of seeing her friends again, but now that she was here, everything had changed. She was a bloodsucker. Would even Lorelle receive her as a friend? Luminents believed in the sanctity of life. Lorelle had never killed anyone in her life, even throughout all of the battles they'd shared together. How could a Luminent condone that Rhenn now had to feed upon the living?

"Why do you hesitate?" L'elica asked. "Work the portal."

"I just…" Rhenn began.

"We are not safe here, Rhenn. It is sheer luck we made it this far. We shouldn't linger."

"You're right. Of course you're right." Rhenn flipped the coin at the swirling colors. It struck and bounced back directly into her hand. She thought of home. Of the basement beneath her father's study. Her study.

The swirling colors retreated toward the stone arch of the Thuros. The basement room appeared beyond.

A hiss rose behind them, and L'elica spun, crouching.

A high prime slunk into the room, followed by another, and then another.

"They found us," L'elica said. "Go! We must go now!"

Rhenn charged into the open portal with L'elica right behind her. The oozing feeling slid over her body and through it. She and L'elica landed on the dais on the other side.

"My queen!" a breathy voice called after her.

Rhenn spun, arm raised to throw the Plunnos and shut the gateway, to cut off her kingdom from this hellish place. But she froze.

Beyond the Thuros and across the room, N'ssag stood in the doorway. His greasy ponytail hung down across his face like he had been running. Breathing hard, he held his ruby-topped rod in his hand. The ruby glowed, and the sharpened end was slick with blood that dripped onto the ground.

"Don't…" he said. "Be hasty. Don't be so hasty."

"Close the portal," L'elica demanded.

Rhenn was about to throw the Plunnos when two high primes dragged someone else into view behind N'ssag. The muscled man hung limp between the powerful high primes, his curly hair lank in his eyes and bearded face downcast.

"E'maz!" Rhenn yelled.

He raised his head at her voice. One eye was swollen shut. His left cheek was bruised and he had a cut from brow to chin. His tunic was stained red. There were two puncture wounds high on his right side, like he'd been shot with arrows.

N'ssag had stabbed him with that damned rod!

"This is your lover, yes?" N'ssag said, moving to E'maz's side.

"Rhenn, close it!" L'elica said.

"You told me he was dead!"

"I thought he was. I saw him fall!"

"Let him go," Rhenn said to N'ssag, approaching the portal.

"Oh I will… Of course I will, my queen. But you see… we have unfinished business, you and I. If we can just… finish it. Then I will let him go." N'ssag beckoned for her to come back through the Thuros.

Rhenn's heart hammered. "Give him to me."

"Yes…" N'ssag said. "Yes… I will. Of course I will. Just… come back through."

"Rhenn, close the——"

N'ssag stabbed E'maz in the side, deep. He cried out and drooped in the grips of his tormentors. The ruby glowed brighter.

Rhenn screamed and leapt through the portal.

"Rhenn no!" L'elica shouted.

But all Rhenn could see was that insidious rod sticking out of E'maz's side. All she could see was his blood as N'ssag yanked it out. She landed on the dais on the Daemanon side and drew her sword.

"I'll kill you!" She leapt at N'ssag.

Something hard slammed into her sword arm, and her strike went wild. Her sword clanged to the ground, slid across the stones. Someone had hit her from behind!

Rhenn whirled to find that two of the high primes had somehow crept across the room and positioned themselves on either side of the Thuros. They'd attacked the moment she'd come through.

She slammed a fist into the face of the one on the left and kicked at the knee of the one on the right. Her fist landed solidly, blasting the creature back, but her kick missed. The bloodsucker clambered up her, grabbed her right arm and sank its teeth into her.

She punched, but another high prime caught her left arm.

"No!" she shouted.

Then L'elica was there. She slammed into the bloodsucker who had bitten Rhenn's arm, tearing him free. The teeth took flesh, and Rhenn shouted through the pain.

She spun, but two more high primes slammed into her before she could orient. Then another. And another.

She kicked and punched and fought, but she'd lost her leverage. They were *all* as strong as she was. Keening like a wildcat, she struggled as they lifted her off the ground and slammed her back down. Each had a different limb, and they pulled, spread-eagled her on the ground.

Rhenn craned her neck wildly, looking for a weapon, something to turn the battle.

All she saw was L'elica, held similarly against the ground, blood leaking from slashes across her face, except there were only two high primes on her, one with both her arms, the other with both her legs. They seemed sufficient to hold her.

N'ssag smiled as he crossed from the captive E'maz to Rhenn.

"Ooohhh," he said. "Oh, you are beautiful, my queen. Oh, the things I wish we had the time for…" He pushed aside his voluminous cloak and drew a dagger from his waist. She recognized it as E'maz's magic dagger.

"You remember this, I think," he said. "I found it at the baron's keep. Such powerful magic inside. I do love it so. It tends to undo my creations. I think you remember that."

"I'm going to kill you…" She seethed.

N'ssag chuckled. "No, I was foolish enough to give you one chance, back when I hadn't yet perfected my new process. No more chances." He glanced at L'elica. "Oh, my sweet. My dear, traitorous L'elica. You broke my heart. I gave you everything. Everything. And you betray me? Your fate will be the worst, I think. I will slice you with this dagger until you stop moving. You see, I'm very interested in its properties, in what it does to my primes. Clearly, I cannot afford to destroy my useful primes. But the two of you, yes. I believe in taking responsibility for one's actions. I made you. I will unmake you both."

"Better do it quick or—"

"Or what? Or what, my queen?" He shook his head and brought the tip of the dagger up to her eye. She turned her head away, but one of the high primes grabbed it and forced it back. "No, I've seen through your act, my queen. The way you swagger into a room. The way you command those around you. You pretend you have an army at your back, but you don't. You have no one and nothing. A lone, pitiful woman with delusions of power. This is my kingdom, not yours—"

A retching sound came from behind Rhenn, like someone was vomiting.

"Oh," someone said, as though trying to talk while they were still throwing up. "That is… That is just fascinating. Those people are dead. All of them, except maybe the greasy one. They're *dead!* How are you doing that?"

Rhenn wrenched her head.

Slayter stood in the archway, eyes glowing with interest as he wiped vomit from his chin. A dark cloak unfurled behind him, slithering back to reveal a woman who looked like a Luminent except with midnight skin and hair, all save one glowing blond lock at her brow. The cloak retreated behind her body, and Khyven the Unkillable stepped around her.

He walked through the Thuros, eyes narrowing. Slayter followed, his shoulders jumping as he shivered at the sensation, and the black-skinned Luminent came last.

Khyven smiled his charming smile, the one that seemed friendly. The one that meant he was ready to kill.

"That's our friend you've got there." He pointed at N'ssag with his sword. "I suggest you let her go."

CHAPTER FORTY-ONE

RHENN

Rhenn gasped. She'd never been so glad to see anyone in her life.

N'ssag's eyes went wide. He seemed to comprehend everything in a flash. These were Rhenn's friends. Warriors from her kingdom. These were, in fact, the army he'd just said she didn't have.

He raised the dagger to stab her in the chest, but Khyven was faster. The man was ridiculously fast. In the time it took N'ssag to raise the dagger high enough to get a good strike, Khyven drew his own dagger and threw.

The weapon stuck in N'ssag's shoulder, and he screamed, dropping the magic dagger. It fell point first into the hand of the high prime who held Rhenn's head. The high prime shrieked, body jerking. It shuddered and stumbled away, like its joints could no longer hold its bones together.

The bloodsucker to her left shied back, surprised, and Rhenn viciously yanked her left arm free. With a shout, she punched the high prime to her right with all her might. She felt his face bones snap. He let go with a howl.

Then Khyven was there, sword flashing. The two high primes holding her legs leapt up to fight. Too late. One lost an arm to Khyven's blade, though the second managed to dance back out of range, moving in a blur.

"This one!" Slayter said triumphantly.

Thunder boomed and lightning forked through the room. It was so bright it blinded her. Three high primes shrieked. Rhenn smelled burnt flesh.

"Oh! That's *very* effective," Slayter said.

She could only hear his voice. She couldn't see anything yet, her eyesight still recovering from his light show.

"Protect me, my primes!" N'ssag shouted in high pitched panic. "Protect me!"

Still blind, Rhenn crouched, waiting for an attack. Instead, a gentle hand touched her shoulder, light as a feather.

"I've got you, sister. I've got you."

"Lorelle!" Where had she come from? Rhenn reached up and clasped her hand.

"They're fleeing," Khyven said, sounding satisfied. "Quick bastards, aren't they?"

Rhenn still couldn't see, but Lorelle helped her up by the arm.

"I can walk," Rhenn said. "I just can't see." But her vision was already beginning to return. "Lorelle" resolved in her sight. Lorelle's voice was coming from the black-skinned Luminent.

"Lorelle?" Rhenn blinked, astonished.

Lorelle's mouth crooked in a half-smile. "I've been through some... changes."

Now Rhenn could see Lorelle's familiar features in that dark face. "Senji's Spear! That's... That's... Yes, a change. How—?"

"Time for stories later, I think," Khyven said. "I assume there are more of those things out there?" He pointed at L'elica with his bloody sword. She had risen and stood at a distance, giving wary glances to Khyven, then Slayter, then back to Khyven. "On our side or not?"

"She's with me. She and—" Rhenn spun around as she remembered. "E'maz!" The bright swelters in her vision were receding, and she saw him crumpled on the ground before the doorway. She leapt to him, gently gathered his big body in her arms. She stood up, lifting him easily.

"Rhenn…" Lorelle gasped.

Rhenn never would have been able to lift someone E'maz's size. Not before. Not when she'd been… Human.

"Um… You mentioned changes. Me, too." She tried to sound like her casual self.

"We are going home, everyone," Khyven said, still staring at the doorway Slayter had limped to. "Let's discuss all this later."

"Oh look, there's more of them," Slayter said, leaning his head out the doorway. "I think there's a whole army of them in this place." He glanced up at the ceiling and the walls, as though distracted by the very stone. "Is this a nuraghi?"

"Slayter, get to the Thuros," Khyven commanded.

The mage backed away from the doorway. "A Daemanon nuraghi…" he said wonderingly. "Do you know how much—"

Khyven grabbed the mage's arm and pushed him toward the dais. "Thuros first. Speculate after. Why don't you go back and see what you can do about healing Rhenn's friend." Khyven put himself between the door and the Thuros.

"Oh yes. Spells for Life Magic. I've created several things in preparation for Vohn's—"

"Slayter!"

"Through the Thuros, yes." He stepped up the dais and followed Rhenn, E'maz, Lorelle, and L'elica through the magic portal. Khyven waited until they were all through, then sprinted after, leaping the three steps and plunging through the portal.

Rhenn set the limp E'maz on the floor, stood up, and flicked the Plunnos at the gateway. The portal receded, then vanished, becoming swirling colors once more. Rhenn dropped the coin and fell to her knees next to E'maz. He wasn't moving, but she could see the blood beneath his skin. Still moving. Still flowing, though sluggishly.

Khyven hovered near. "Lorelle, can you—"

But Lorelle already had her medicine kit out. She pulled a vial of purple liquid, looked at it in the light of her blond lock—

which was glowing fiercely—and nodded.

"Lift his head and pour this into his mouth," she said to Rhenn, handing it over. "Khyven, stop standing there looking grim and make yourself useful. Cut his tunic off."

Khyven drew a dagger, stooped and, with one deft motion, slit E'maz's tunic up the middle without touching flesh. He gently flipped open the flaps, exposing the three horrible holes in E'maz's side.

Rhenn poured half the bottle into E'maz's mouth, and E'maz jerked, opened his eyes. He drew a shuddering breath. He blinked, looking like he had no idea where he was, then he focused on Rhenn.

"Rhenn..." He smiled. "Selestina's Light, I thought they'd killed you..."

"I'm fine, E'maz, just hold still—"

"This next," Lorelle interrupted, handing Rhenn a vial of red liquid. "On the wounds. Right over the top. It's going to sting."

Rhenn poured the vial over the wounds in E'maz's side. A white foam appeared, and E'maz hissed. The trickling blood slowed to the barest ooze.

"You're next, Slayter," Lorelle said, casting about and finding him staring at the swirling Thuros, his head cocked. "Slayter? You better not be thinking about that stupid Daemanon nuraghi."

Slayter started, looked at her, then said, "No, I was just thinking about—"

"I don't care," Lorelle said. "The wounds. Heal them."

"That's what I was thinking about! I was just trying to remember..." He snapped his fingers. "Ah! Yes." He opened his cylinder, clicked through his clay disks, stopped, backed up, then clicked through a few more. Finally, he extracted one. "This is the one," he said emphatically. "This is the good one."

"You need a quicker system for that," Khyven murmured.

"A quicker...?" Slayter shot him a reproachful glance. "Well, life must be nice when you only have two options to choose from. Let's see, should I use my sword this time? Or should I use my dagger? Sword? Or dagger. I just can't decide."

"Slayter—"

"It's not so easy for some of us!"

"I'm sorry."

Slayter knelt by E'maz, awkwardly managing his prosthetic leg. Khyven took hold of his arm to balance him, but the mage shook him off and muttered, "a better system..." Then he turned a smile toward E'maz. "You're going to like this spell. It's exhilarating."

The mage produced his decorative metal scraper and scraped the last line on the clay coin. It glowed a fierce orange, and he snapped it in two. The glow reached out from the broken pieces like octopus tendrils, touching the holes in E'maz's side. They spread over the wounds like a glowing blanket.

"Oh!" E'maz gasped.

"I told you. This'll heal the flesh, knit things up. It's got an anesthetic, euphoric quality. Feels like quaffing four beers at once. Of course, four beers wouldn't do anything for Khyven." He shot a narrow-eyed glance at the big man, who held his hands up in surrender. "But feels pretty good for the rest of us."

When the orange glow faded, the wounds were, miraculously, gone.

"That does... feel better," E'maz said.

But he still looked deathly pale. His speech was so soft it was almost slurred, and his eyes remained half-lidded. Rhenn glanced at Lorelle. "Is that right? Should he look like that?"

"It... he should be fine," Lorelle said, but her voice told Rhenn immediately that something was wrong.

Slayter cocked his head and looked at E'maz as though he was an equation that didn't balance.

Lorelle glanced up. "Slayter what is it?"

"Hmmm. That's curious. I wonder if this is—"

"Slayter, what's happening? Why isn't he better?" Rhenn demanded. Even as she said it, E'maz sank back, no longer able to hold himself up. Rhenn cradled him.

"It's good to see you, Rhenn," E'maz murmured. "I didn't think I'd see you again..."

"It's going to be fine," Rhenn said, but fear crawled up her back like a spider. If Lorelle or Slayter couldn't solve this... Was E'maz going to die?

"Slayter—"

"A moment," Slayter said, clicking through his disks. Khyven stayed grimly silent and no banter flew between the two. Slayter found the disk he was looking for and carved the final line in the clay. It flared to life, orange light flying up from it more dramatically than before. The light descended again and settled on E'maz's belly for a moment. Then it flowed away, forming the shape of a funnel that reached about a foot away from E'maz's body. The thin part of the funnel bent and narrowed into a trickle of liquid light that gathered in a pool on the cobblestones.

"Fascinating..." Slayter said.

"What is that?" Rhenn demanded.

"I wonder if this is why that Life Mage could bring back the—"

"Slayter!" Lorelle barked.

"It's his vitality..." Slayter said. "His, uh... His life force. It's draining out onto the floor."

A spike of fear plunged into Rhenn's heart. "Well, stop it."

The mage's eyes flicked to the glowing ooze pooling on the stones, then sinking into the cracks. He glanced back at E'maz, mouth open, and blinked. Slayter's brow furrowed, and for the first time he looked like he didn't know what to do.

"I... I don't know this magic," he said. "I need time to research it..."

"We don't have time," Khyven said.

Slayter glanced at Khyven. "I..." He hesitated. "All right. All right. Uh, Khyven give me your dagger."

Khyven's dagger appeared in his hand. He flipped it about and handed the hilt to Slayter. "What are you going to do?"

"Only thing I can think of." He stabbed the tip into his palm.

Lorelle winced. "Slayter, what are you doing—"

"Shhhh." Slayter's eyes burned with intensity. Carefully, meticulously, he carved a symbol into his own flesh. His eyes tightened and he began to hum as he did it. The humming became a shout as he finished. Blood dripped from his hand. Light flared, and this time it was red.

Slayter gasped and slapped his bloody palm on the floor where the orange light pooled.

The red light grew, shaped like a larger version of Slayter's own hand. The fingers grasped at the last of E'maz's glowing life force, as though trying to stop it, cup it, catch it.

"Do it," Slayter growled. "Do it!"

But the fading life force slipped through Slayter's magical fingers. The orange light slithered into the pool, then through the cracks in the floor, and it was gone.

"Rhenn, I…" He shook his head. "It didn't work. I don't… "

"There's got to be something we can do," Khyven said. "Can't we, I don't know, put a plug in it?"

Slayter swallowed, and he looked ill. "I don't have the plug."

"So make it up!"

The mage's shoulders slumped. "I'm sorry, Rhenn. I'm sorry. If I had time. Just a little time, but he's…" He glanced at Rhenn, mouth open, brow creased. He looked like a little lost boy, but he spoke softly, firmly. "If you have something to say to him, you should say it."

"What does that mean?" Rhenn said.

"Talk to him, Rhenn," Lorelle said.

"Oh Senji, no…" Rhenn turned to E'maz, tears brimming in her eyes.

"Didn't work, huh?" E'maz said, but he smiled. "Your friend… He brews quite a cocktail. That was… nice. Not as nice… as seeing you, though."

Rhenn's tears spilled over, streaking down her cheeks. She grasped E'maz's big, callused hand. "I'm sorry. I dragged you into this."

"There you go… taking the credit for everything again." He drew a long, difficult breath.

"It's my fault."

"Stop. We chose each other, Rhenn. People do that, you know. Not everybody dances..." He coughed, wincing. "...dances to your tune... It's still... funny you don't see that. You didn't just choose me. I chose you. You can't... bear the burden of everything just because you think you're smarter than everyone else."

Rhenn couldn't speak. All she could do was cry.

"I love you, Rhenn. More than I ever loved anything before. You... surprised me. You do that. Never met... anyone like you. You... bring people together in the strangest ways. Just by... being close to them. I think you actually convinced A'vendyr that... putting women in pentaras was the natural thing to do. That's a gift... changing people's minds like that. Not just... changing them. Changing them to something better. I swear you could convince a fish to follow you onto land. I wish... I wish our two peoples could have actually met, could have..." He trailed off and closed his eyes. "Don't stop, my love..."

"E'maz!" Rhenn cried.

His eyelids flickered. "Love you, Rhenn. Don't stop."

"E'maz!"

His eyes closed, and he let out a long breath. The orange funnel coming from his side faded, like the last of the orange light was flowing from him and draining away. The flow stopped. The stream stopped. The pool trickled into the floor, and it was gone.

Rhenn flung herself over him, holding him tightly as she felt the last of the life leave him.

CHAPTER FORTY-TWO

RHENN

henn didn't know how long she cried over E'maz's body, but no one disturbed her. The Thuros was closed.

They were safe.

At long last, she was safe. She could take a breath and not worry about the danger. She could grieve. For E'maz. For the horrors she'd endured. She let it all out over E'maz's body. This genuinely good man had been cut down by N'ssag's evil.

Except it hadn't been N'ssag, had it?

It had been a man named Ventat Obrey who had given N'ssag all the materials he'd needed to destroy the V'endann Barony, and E'maz along with it.

Don't stop...

She raised her tear-streaked face and glanced at the Thuros, then looked around at her assembled friends. Her plan formed in an instant. For the first time in a long time, she knew exactly what she ought to do. She knew how she could best use this newfound power she'd been given.

And it wasn't as Queen of Usara.

"Thank you..." she said to her friends. "Thank you all for coming for me."

"Well, that's what we do," Khyven said with his lopsided smile.

"How did you know?"

Khyven had his arms crossed over his chest. One finger rose from that muscled arm and pointed at Slayter. Rhenn glanced at the mage.

"Oh, well. It was actually rather simple, really. I don't know why I didn't think of it before. I really should have. I feel bad about that. After you came through the first time, I was alerted—"

"You knew when I first came through?"

"Sure. But I had assumed that if you came through, you'd stay. But you popped through then right back through. I wasn't quick enough, so clearly I had to come up with something else—"

"Slayter," Lorelle said. "Just answer her question."

"Oh, I laid a trigger spell over the room. It has to do with movement lines, which are kind of like imaginary lines based on a very specific motion of the air to complete the inscribing. In this case, the entire room is the 'clay coin.' So you could have a dozen people walk in this room, moving the air about and nothing would happen. You could even have someone walk up to the Thuros and nothing would happen. But the moment somebody walks out of the Thuros, it completes the movement line and the spell activates, telling me that someone had just come through. But this time, I paired it with an alert to Lorelle, so she could come get me. With her fancy cloak. That's how we got here so fast."

"Well, thank you."

"It's good to have you back, your majesty," Slayter said.

"It's... good to be back." Her heart sank a little, because Rhenn wasn't staying. She was going back to Daemanon. She'd fled, believing L'elica because she'd wanted to believe, because she'd wanted to be back home so badly she could convince herself that the best way to fight this horrendous evil was to flee. But that had been a lie, and E'maz had paid the price. How many more E'maz's were, even now, dying?

Rhenn knew she couldn't stop N'ssag's army. But maybe, just maybe, if she snuck back through and hunted the necromancer himself, she could kill him. She could end the source of all of this poison. And then he'd never come to Noksonon. He'd never do here what he'd done in Daemanon. The V'endann Barony would be the only casualty to this evil.

She knew her friends would go with her if she asked them, but she wasn't going to allow that. Her last act as Queen of Usara was going to be protecting them. She wasn't about to sacrifice her family on a one-way trip. Let them have their lives as they were meant to be, and maybe Rhenn could hold the darkness back just a little while with her sacrifice.

More of Nhevalos's words came back to her: *You will not fall because I will not allow it…*

There was gritty satisfaction to that. This one time, that Giant bastard was going to be wrong.

"My friends, this is L'elica." Rhenn pointed at the woman, standing far away by the double-locked gate of the noktum. She'd seen where she wanted to go, seen what was promised to her. No doubt L'elica could also feel the presence of the noktum just as Rhenn now felt it.

L'elica had been a true companion at the last. She didn't have to leap back through the Thuros to Rhenn's aid, but she had.

"This woman is my friend L'elica," Rhenn continued. "Without her, I'd have died on Daemanon. She's the only reason I made it this far, and I made a promise to her. She lives in the darkness, and I promised to give her safe passage into the noktum."

"That's well done." Khyven gave L'elica a half smile, and he pulled the chain of a necklace up and out of his tunic. Attached were two keys. He walked over and opened both gates with them. "Thank you, L'elica."

L'elica glanced at the two open gates, then turned her gaze on Rhenn. "You kept your promise." She sounded surprised.

"I did. And I always will. I have broken my last promise. Be sure you keep yours."

L'elica nodded. "You are... honorable. Thank you."

"Thank you."

L'elica stepped up to the tentacles, then looked over her shoulder.

"There are predators in there larger than you," Rhenn said. "But if you're careful, I think you'll flourish."

The bloodsucker nodded, then stepped forward and let the tentacles take her. They pulled her in, and she was gone. Khyven locked the gates behind her.

"Now is it time for the stories?" Slayter asked.

"A mug of ale first, I think," Lorelle said.

"Four mugs for me, apparently." Khyven winked at Slayter.

"I'll just have wine," the mage replied.

Rhenn forced the tears not to come again. It sounded so wonderful, but that was no longer her life. She didn't drink ale. Or wine. She drank blood. That golden vision no longer belonged to her. Carnage. Death. Those were hers, and she would deal them until she had no strength left.

But she would deal them to the right person.

"Sounds amazing," Rhenn said. "But I wonder if... I wonder if you all could all give me just a second here, with..." She glanced at E'maz.

The three of them paused for the length of a heartbeat, then Khyven said, "Of course."

"Wait for me in the study?" Rhenn asked. "I'll be right up."

Lorelle gave her a soulful look, as though she saw right through Rhenn's facade, but she turned with the others, opened the little door to the stairs while they all filed through, and closed it behind them.

Once Rhenn heard their footsteps fade, she rose, went to the discarded Plunnos, and picked it up. She ascended the dais to stand before the Thuros and drew a deep breath.

Maybe she could save a few V'endannians in the bargain, if she hurried.

She raised the Plunnos—

A knot of shadows formed on the right side of the Thuros. It unfolded and unfolded, growing larger until Lorelle stood there, her floating cloak flowing behind her as if on some invisible wind.

"You didn't think that was going to work, did you?" Lorelle asked softly.

"Lorelle..." Rhenn swallowed and took an involuntary step away from the Thuros, bringing the coin behind her back. "I was... just..."

"Going back through the Thuros," Khyven said. Rhenn spun and the big man left the stairway silently. "Which, frankly, I like."

Slayter followed Khyven out the door.

"Are we going back to Daemanon?" He seemed excited.

"Looks like it," Khyven said. "You're geared up for a war?"

Slayter patted his cylinder that kept his spells. The hand he'd carved up for E'maz was tightly bound with a white cloth. "Ready, sir knight."

Khyven smiled at Rhenn.

Rhenn cleared her throat. "What battle?"

"Please." Khyven gestured at her tattered, blood-smeared clothes. "The one you left."

"We're going with you," Lorelle said.

"Nobody is going anywhere." Rhenn frowned. "I asked if I could... have some time alone with E'maz. And I was—"

"Lying to us to protect us." Khyven turned a smile on Lorelle and, to Rhenn's stunned surprise, her Luminent friend returned it warmly. "We already learned that lesson. We don't do that anymore."

"We have a new rule," Lorelle said. "What one does, the others do. We're a family."

"I've never had a family before," Slayter said. "I must say I rather like it."

"Tell us about this battle of yours," Khyven said.

"You're staying here," Rhenn commanded. "That's a royal command."

"Yeah... I don't think so." Khyven uncrossed his arms and loosened his shoulders like he was preparing to go into a bout. "I have this pesky aversion to royal commands."

"I will die before I let you go through that Thuros again," Lorelle said. "Without me."

"Better said." Khyven pointed at Lorelle. "She's more poetic than I am."

"This is going to be amazing." Slayter rubbed his hands together.

"You're not going!" Rhenn said. "You don't know what's on the other side."

"Oh, I think we know a little of what's on the other side." Khyven fingered the bloody cloth that dangled from his belt, the one he'd used to clean his blade.

"You were going to go alone. And based on what I've seen so far of your opponents, that means you don't plan to survive." Lorelle shook her head. "And that is unacceptable."

"True," Slayter said.

"Again, pure poetry," Khyven added.

"I..." Rhenn's voice caught in her throat. What they didn't know—what she couldn't tell them—was that she already hadn't survived. N'ssag had killed her; they just didn't know yet.

Khyven drew a dagger, tested its edge, then flipped it easily, catching the handle.

"You don't understand. I *have* to return," Rhenn said softly. "You don't. E'maz is dead because of me, and the man who made him that way—"

"Is that creepy guy with the greasy ponytail and ruby rod?" Khyven asked.

"E'maz is dead because I loved him. Because I pulled him into my world and—"

"E'maz is dead because Mr. Green Teeth stuck him in the side with his ruby stick," Khyven said. "You didn't do that."

"I did."

Khyven's irreverent posture eased, and he spoke gently. "I understand you believe that. But we heard E'maz's words, too."

Rhenn shook her head. She didn't want to talk about E'maz. She just wanted them to go away and let her do what needed to be done. She needed them to be safe. "There are other things you don't know…" she trailed off. She couldn't bear to tell them what she'd become. Let them at least remember her the way she once was. Her voice broke. "Just let me go."

"Not on your life," Khyven said softly.

"Please…" Rhenn fought a sob.

"You've been through something," Khyven said. "That's clear. We all saw it from the first moment. We don't care. Whatever it is, we're going to work through it together."

"Khyven—"

"Rhenn, you taught me what it was to have a family again. At first, I didn't understand what that meant, and I almost threw it away. That's never happening again. My family doesn't go into danger without me. Ever."

"Poetry," Lorelle agreed, and winked at Khyven. Khyven shot her a fond glance.

"Did you know I did the calculations after we faced the Zek Roaches, the Nox, and Tovos," Slayter interrupted. "Facing a Giant with just the three of us should have been impossible. But you know what? He's stuck in a dragon cave. With a Dragon Chain!"

"You faced a Giant?" Hope kindled in Rhenn's heart.

"It's a story," Khyven said.

"But this, that I'm heading into, it's a hopeless battle…" Rhenn said. "It's already lost."

"Oh… I doubt that." Khyven idly tested the dagger his thumb again.

"They might be dead even now."

"The others like E'maz?" Khyven asked.

"Yes."

"Guess we shouldn't stand here, then."

"Khyven—"

"Tick tock tick tock."

"You are a stubborn man."

Khyven glanced at Lorelle. "See how I get all the blame? This was your idea, but I get the blame."

"You're larger," Lorelle said. "Odds say more things are going to hit you."

Khyven looked back to Rhenn. "You've got a war with impossible odds on the other side of that Thuros, and you don't want to give me a part of it?"

"Khyven—"

"Are you just afraid I'll show you up?"

Rhenn gave a half-sob and half-laugh.

"You're not getting rid of us," Lorelle said softly.

Rhenn hung her head. Her conscience railed against their stubbornness, but beneath that, her heart felt warm.

"You're all crazy," she murmured.

Khyven laughed.

"Crazy is subjective, did you know that?" Slayter said. "Once, for an entire month, I studied different social circles in Usara. Nobles. Field workers. Everything in between. What is crazy in one social group is not crazy in another. So the word crazy doesn't really mean what you think it means. It's all—"

Khyven put a gentle hand on Slayter's shoulder, interrupting him. "I think we have a war to win. Rhenn?"

She looked into his eyes, and he nodded. She turned to the Thuros and raised the Giant's coin, then glanced back to them.

"Thank you." She flicked the Plunnos at the swirling colors.

CHAPTER FORTY-THREE
RHENN

R henn plunged into the Thuros. The invisible oil slid over her and through her. She emerged onto the dais of Hepreth's Nuraghi. Khyven came after, landing lightly and moving into a protective position in front of her. Slayter came next, tripped on his robes, and fell onto his hands and knees. Lorelle followed, her forbidding cloak trailing behind her like a liquid flag of darkness, touching and joining with every patch of shadow. She dipped gracefully and helped the mage to his feet.

Slayter stood up, tapped a blue ring on his finger, and a phosphorescent light glowed. Surprisingly, the magical light didn't hurt Rhenn. She suddenly realized that the light from Lorelle's magical lock of hair hadn't hurt her either.

Glad she didn't have to reveal her shame at this particular moment, Rhenn turned her attention to the room. The Thuros room was empty save the high prime corpses they'd left behind. Slayter snatched a disk from his cylinder, concentrated, and snapped it. Orange light glowed about the corpses.

"Oh, this is a fascinating spell. Their borrowed life force is slowly draining from their bodies, just like E'maz's. Except it's taking longer, which means it was retained by something." He went to the nearest body as he fumbled through his pouches.

"Slayter…" Lorelle murmured "Vohn says to stop wasting your magic. We've got a battle to win."

"Ah…" He seemed to think about that, looking wistfully at the corpses, then touched the fingertips of his hands together impatiently. "Of course."

"Vohn?" Rhenn asked. "Where's Vohn?"

"He's the cloak," Khyven said.

"He's a *cloak?*"

"He's *not* the cloak." Lorelle gave Khyven a reproachful glance. "He's inside the cloak. He's actually… Well, he's actually the Dark. But he can 'see' through the cloak."

A smile bent Rhenn's lips, and for an instant, she felt a little more like her old self. "Well, now we *have* to survive this because I need to hear the story."

"It's a story." Khyven grinned. "Let's find the bad guys first—"

"Uh," Slayter said. "If the living dead things are the bad guys, they've found us."

Rhenn spun to see figure after figure slink into the room, shoulders rounded, faces gaunt, fangs bared. The first thought that came to her was that they were too late, that Baron V'endann, A'vendyr and all their people were already dead.

"I guess we start here," Lorelle said.

"Better to get to it," Khyven agreed, moving wide and raising his sword to draw attention.

Rhenn carefully stowed the Plunnos and picked up E'maz's magic dagger from the floor. "No need to pull any punches with these fellows. Let's take them apart."

"You don't want to keep one alive for questioning?" Khyven asked.

"*I* want to keep one alive for questioning," Slayter said, clicking through his spells. "Just think of what we could learn with—"

"Slayter!" Khyven and Lorelle said in unison.

The bloodsuckers attacked.

CHAPTER FORTY-FOUR

RHENN

Rhenn got one glimpse of Khyven sliding to the side as the high prime flew at him. Both combatants blurred as they charged. The bloodsucker grabbed for his face, but he turned sideways. The creature's jagged fingernails slashed by his neck, just missing.

Khyven's sword did not.

Steel flashed and the bloodsucker's head rolled across the ground in a splatter of blood.

Rhenn readied herself for the second bloodsucker as it launched, but a patch of darkness unfurled over the bloodsucker. It was Lorelle, descending with that cloak of hers like she could fly. It swirled around the high prime, seeming to suck it inside. It grew smaller, thinner, like it was being pushed through a tube. The creature shrieked, and then it was gone.

Lorelle landed on her feet next to Rhenn. The Luminent had one eye squinched shut like she'd swallowed a rock.

"That was unpleasant," she said.

"What *was* that?" Rhenn asked.

"I sent him through the cloak, but he didn't quite go. Not sure what happened to him, actually."

"Ha!" Slayter snapped one of his disks. "This one!" Orange light flared in his hand. A barrier comprised of the same orange light formed over the doorway to the room, separating them from the bloodsuckers. Four more had slipped through the doorway before Slayter's spell took effect, but about a dozen rammed up against the orange barrier.

With howls of rage, the four inside attacked. Khyven spun at the nearest, feinting high and spinning low. The thing's claws went over his head and Khyven chopped its leg off mid-thigh. It shrieked and tumbled into the corner.

The second flew at Rhenn and Lorelle.

"I'll set him up." Lorelle flew at the bloodsucker, her light Luminent body more gravity defying than Rhenn remembered. Her cloak flared out, engulfing the high prime, but this time Lorelle spun in mid-air and ejected the bloodsucker so that he faced the doorway.

Rhenn lunged.

The thing was fast. It reoriented itself before its feet even hit the floor and lashed out with its arm. But Rhenn was ready and even faster. She caught the high prime's arm on her sword, severing it, then closed the distance and brought herself face-to-face with it. She stabbed hard with E'maz's dagger, up and under its ribcage.

Its eyes flew wide. Its mouth stretched inhumanly long, and its silent scream lasted half a second.

Then its body fell apart. Forearms went limp at the elbows. Upper arms detached from the shoulders. The head detached from its neck, legs from its hips. Each component clung with stretching bits of flesh, then the whole body collapsed in a bloody mess on the floor.

The third bloodsucker leapt at Khyven and the fourth at Slayter, who had knelt next to the high prime Khyven had decapitated.

"Slayter!" Rhenn shouted. The mage seemed oblivious to the danger, and he was too far away for her to reach him—

But Khyven was there. He yanked his sword from his last foe, stabbed his new attacker with his dagger as it came down on him from above, and stretched long, kicking Slayter's bloodsucker in the hip. The powerful kick shoved the prime past the mage. Its grasping hands only touched the hood on the mage's robes.

Rhenn sprinted. Lorelle leapt into the air. Khyven charged.

They converged on Slayter's bloodsucker at the same time. It fought. It died.

"Slayter!" Khyven barked.

"Wait wait…" Slayter held up a hand to silence them. He pulled out a thin dagger with no cross guard. It's pommel was an emerald the size of an egg, and Slayter palmed it. He stuck the thin blade into the top of the bloodsucker's neck stump. The emerald glowed green.

Slayter looked up, his eyes alight. "Oh wow. Did you know—"

"No, I don't want to know," Khyven growled. "Slayter, that thing almost killed you!"

The mage looked around like he wasn't sure where he was. He glanced at the now-dead bloodsucker. "Oh. Well, you got it."

Khyven raised his hands incredulously and turned to Lorelle, who shook her head.

"We need to make an agreement," Khyven said. "You can't do your research projects in the middle of a Senji-be-damned battle!"

"So… so… so I did a spell on this fellow here…"

"Get up." Khyven took the mage's arm and lifted him to his feet.

Slayter put up his hands, warding off Khyven. "No no. Remember when I said they were sensitive to light and that something was keeping life in their bodies longer than E'maz's? Well, I think I figured out the reason. This Life Mage—this necromancer—is doing something to the bodies to help them retain the life force in a way that our bodies don't. Like some kind of embalming. And Khyven, it's volatile. I think that this chemical, whatever it is, you'd have to store it in absolute dark because—"

Khyven crouched next to Slayter and jerked a finger over his shoulder. "There are people who could be dying right now. I need you to focus and put your mind on helping us save them."

Slayter blinked. "Yes. Oh... Yes, of course, Khyven. That's... sort of what I'm talking about. The blood... the embalming..." He glanced around at the sour looks everyone was giving him. "But... All right. I see your point. We should hurry." He stood up, looked reluctantly at his headless corpse, turned and looked at the slathering wall of bloodsuckers held behind his orange energy field.

He gave a vague grin at his handiwork, then his eyes rolled up in his head and he toppled over.

Khyven caught him and held him upright. "Damn it, Slayter! How much magic have you used?"

"It's been... a little bit." Slayter smiled weakly. "But I... I've got this." He pulled out a small steel vial, fumbled to uncork it.

"Slayter, no." Lorelle stopped his wrist.

"What is that?" Rhenn asked.

"A concoction of his," Lorelle said. "Primarily an extract of kadenza leaves. It's not good."

Slayter looked up at Lorelle. "You would give your life to help these people."

"Slayter—"

He looked at Khyven. "You would give your life for these people. And you." He turned to Rhenn. "Do I have any right to hold back when I can do something?"

"You could die," Lorelle said.

Slayter gently took her hand from his wrist. "I'll rest after."

Lorelle pressed her lips together, but she didn't stop the mage as he downed the vial. Slayter's eyes flew open, his whole body shivered, and he shook his head. A grin spread across his face, and he turned to the doorway. Lorelle took a step back, but her gaze never left the suddenly energized mage.

"Release it on my command," Khyven said, striding toward the frenzied bloodsuckers like it was no big deal. Senji's Teeth,

Rhenn loved that man. Vohn had been right. With Khyven around, the impossible *did* seem possible.

She joined him. "Everybody ready?" she asked.

"It would be nice to have your Mavric iron sword right about now," Slayter said to Khyven.

"It was in your workshop. Rhenn would have been gone by then."

"Did you name it yet?" Slayter asked.

"No."

"You should name it. And carry it. Why don't you carry it?"

"Things happened too fast," Khyven said.

"Which is why you should carry it."

"The thing is creepy."

"It's not creepy. It's magical."

"Same thing."

"I'm pretty sure it's bonding with you."

"What?"

"Certain magic swords bond with their wielder."

Khyven looked horrified. "Oh good. That's not creepy at all."

"You'd have it now if you just—"

"Shut up, Slayter. Release the thing."

"Renalgon's Force Wall."

"What?"

"It's not a thing. It's Renalgon's Force Wall."

"Release it!"

"Yes, sir knight."

Slayter closed his eyes in concentration.

Rhenn said, "Wait!"

One by one, the bloodsuckers on the other side of the energy field turned and ran into the darkness. In seconds, they were all gone.

Khyven opened his mouth, seemingly about to say something, but closed it again. He turned to Rhenn. "What's that about?"

"I don't know."

"They were summoned," Lorelle murmured.

"V'endann," Rhenn murmured.

"V'endann?"

"He's the baron. His people are the ones we're trying to save."

"Release it, Slayter," Rhenn said.

The orange light flickered and faded. Not a single bloodsucker charged from the darkness.

Khyven inched forward, sword up. He peeked out, looking both ways, then glanced back at them. "Gone."

"Wherever they went," Lorelle said. "That's where we need to go."

"I know where they went," Rhenn said.

"We follow you, your majesty." Khyven bowed.

Rhenn shot down the passageway with her friends behind her.

CHAPTER FORTY-FIVE

RHENN

You hold yourself in reserve," Khyven said to Slayter as the mage limped along. It was easy to forget that Slayter had only one leg until he started running. He had mastered Vohn's prosthetic so well that until this moment, Rhenn had forgotten about it.

They moved up the hallway, and Rhenn tried to keep herself between the eager Khyven and the slower Slayter. Lorelle resolutely matched her pace to the mage, taking rear-guard and protecting him should something come from behind.

Slayter slowed even more as they passed a room with a broken door, then he stopped altogether. He poked his head inside.

"Do you see that?" he asked no one in particular. "Mirrors."

"We can't stay here, Slayter," Lorelle said.

"What is it?" Rhenn skidded to a halt and called back.

"Nothing. He's just having a moment." Lorelle grabbed the mage's arm and propelled him forward.

"Did you know that Rauvelos has a mirror room almost exactly like that in his castle?" Slayter asked. "Do I know its purpose? No, I do not."

"Neither do I," Lorelle said.

"That doesn't drive you crazy?"

"No." Lorelle grabbed his shoulder again and pointed down the hallway as Slayter paused again, looking like he might go back to the room.

"I detected no magic, here or at Rauvelos's castle," Slayter said. "They're just normal mirrors. Why would a giant raven need so many mirrors?"

"Preening?" Lorelle said.

Slayter seemed to consider that seriously, and Lorelle shook her head. She hurried him forward to the archway where Khyven had already disappeared from view.

Rhenn turned the corner into the gigantic audience chamber from another age. The ceiling had to be a hundred feet tall, broken through in a couple of places where the stars shone down. The walls were tall and thin with arched windows like a church. On the far side, two giant staircases—with steps as tall as Rhenn's waist—lined the edges of the wall, then moved to converge at a great landing where they joined a double-wide staircase. Those steps went directly up to what must have been the royal box of whatever ruler had presided over this long-dead nuraghi. The fight concentrated there.

Dead bodies, both water goblin bloodsuckers and V'endannian warriors, littered the floor leading up to the dual staircases.

"Senji's mercy," Rhenn murmured. They'd fled here with hundreds, but from what she could tell, most of those lay dead on the floor. Active fighting still raged at the top in the royal box. Somehow, the survivors had barricaded themselves into that top room. It was a fine choice for a last stand. The bloodsuckers could not attack from above as the box butted right up against the ceiling. But from what Rhenn could tell, there was no way out except back down that wide, tall staircase.

And the bloodsuckers swarmed all over it.

There could be no more than a few dozen people from the barony remaining, if they weren't all being drained of life at this very moment.

"There's the battle," Khyven said.

"Senji, I had hoped..." Rhenn murmured.

"Are these your dead?" Khyven gestured at the bodies.

"Yes, but..."

"All right then," he said, and he sprinted toward the base of the steps.

"Khyven!" she called after him, then she cursed and followed. He leapt up the overlarge steps one huge lunge at a time. She could have kept pace with him, but she didn't want to leave the others behind. "Don't get separated!"

"We're the cavalry," Khyven called back, vaulting step after step. "Let's be the cavalry."

"Damn it," Rhenn cursed, looking back. Slayter and Lorelle finally reached the first step. The mage was already winded. He looked up at the intimidating staircase, then he let out a breath and clambered to the top of the first step.

"Go," Lorelle said to Rhenn. "Help Khyven. We're right behind you."

Khyven reached the landing where the two staircases became one, and he roared a challenge at the bloodsuckers. There had to be two dozen of them, and none of them human. Apparently N'ssag's "honor guard" of undead V'endann warriors were elsewhere. Some of the water goblins had tentacles. One had an alligator's head. One had the taloned forearms of an eagle. Half of the throng didn't even pause in their efforts to attack the royal box. But the other half whirled around, looking down the steps as Khyven took them in mighty leaps.

"Come on!" Khyven shouted, waving his sword and trying to draw them toward himself, away from the defenders.

That group keened and launched themselves down the steps, tentacles slapping, alligator heads snapping, claws scraping. For a moment, Rhenn could see movement behind the makeshift barricade of chairs, tables, and debris at the top. Some of V'endann's people were still alive!

Her heart leapt and she pounded up the stairs with her newfound strength. She made the landing where the stairs came together just as Khyven reached his opponents. He angled to the side of the stair, using the tall wall to guard his right flank. A dozen water goblins swarmed over him, and Rhenn lost sight of him.

It looked like Khyven had been completely overwhelmed. She shouted and charged toward them.

Blood and bodies flew as Khyven's sword flashed above the throng. He emerged from the pile, spinning, with two of the water goblins clinging to his back. The first gripped his steel shoulder plate, snapping its fangs at the air, trying to get to his neck. The second had its claws tangled in Khyven's mail shirt, swinging out as Khyven spun. Miraculously, there wasn't a scratch on the man. He just kept moving and slashing as though this was an orchestrated dance, as though the water goblins were jumping intentionally into the path of his deadly blade.

As he emerged from the goblin pile, four corpses lay in his wake.

Rhenn caught up, sword drawn, and threw herself into the fray.

Khyven, still turning, stepped toward her and led one of the goblins into her waiting strike. The dozen that had attacked him were down to half that, and with a roar, Khyven leapt back into them, this time with Rhenn on his right side. Rhenn came in close, wrapped an elbow around one of them and ended it with a vicious neck twist. She disengaged and leapt up and over the second, landing on its back and burying E'maz's dagger in its neck. The thing fell apart, its entire body going limp and crashing to the steps like a bag of bones.

Khyven stopped the next goblin, spearing it through the head. Rhenn parried a sword strike and slashed another goblin across the belly with her sword.

Rhenn's bloodlust sang through her, the need for violence, for the copper fire to course into her mouth and throughout her body. She'd used so much energy to come this far.

The remaining two water goblins bolted around Khyven and down the stairs. With remarkable speed, he spun and threw his leg out. The nearest goblin tripped and slammed his face into the stone. Rhenn leapt after it, hungry.

Khyven came out of his spin, dagger in hand, and flung it at the lone goblin who'd escaped.

The blade caught it directly in the back of the skull. It went limp in mid-air, hit the stairs, and flopped to the landing with a bone-crunching finality.

Rhenn pounced on the last goblin. Her bloodlust to suck the still-flowing blood from its body almost overwhelmed her. It was all she could do to stop herself. She was starving, but she couldn't let Khyven know what she was. She couldn't bear that shame right now.

Instead, she poked it with E'maz's dagger and it collapsed.

"Come on." Rhenn surged up the stairs. The other dozen goblins had finally broken through the barrier of the royal box. She and Khyven arrived in time to see the ragged remains of A'vendyr's and B'elsin's pentaras—a total of six fighting men between them—struggling for their lives against the dozen bloodsuckers who'd broken through. Behind the V'endann warriors were Baron V'endann, his twelve-year-old daughter, and more than a dozen others from the V'endann household.

Senji's Spear… Hundreds had fled here. Was this scattered group all that remained?

Khyven roared a challenge and charged.

The surprised goblins turned, realizing their fellows had not finished off the interlopers.

"Don't let up!" Khyven roared. "Finish it!"

Two goblins went down as Rhenn charged alongside Khyven. He took one. She the other. The warriors of the pentaras saw that help had come, and they took heart, redoubling their attacks.

Four goblins turned to face Rhenn and Khyven. He killed two with a wicked back-and-forth slash of his blade. She stabbed one with the dagger, swept the knee of the last, and took its head with her sword.

The remaining eight goblins were now trapped inside the royal box. They tried to flee, but Khyven stood in the hole they'd made, arms wide as though to collect them should they bolt. The pentara and Rhenn's party converged.

The goblins fought like cornered rats. But Khyven and Rhenn did not relent, and the warriors of the pentara found their second wind.

Every last goblin bloodsucker died on cold steel.

A'vendyr, covered with blood, and one of the remaining pentara warriors, stared openly at Khyven.

"This is Khyven the Unkillable," Rhenn said. "The friend I mentioned."

The baron's son went to the edge of the royal box and looked incredulously down at the dozen dead bloodsuckers on the stairs.

"Told you you'd like him," Rhenn said.

Now that Rhenn wasn't in the midst of a battle, she assessed the survivors and realized the royal box had an antechamber filled with more people than she'd originally assumed. Between the royal box and its antechamber, she estimated more than fifty of the baron's people were still alive.

Baron V'endann bustled forward. He'd lost his heavily embroidered cloak, and his fancy doublet was spattered with blood.

"You," he said, shaking with rage. "You bitch."

Khyven's eyes narrowed and he stepped in front of the baron as he cleaned his bloody sword on the rag stuffed into his belt.

"That's Queen Bitch to you," he rumbled.

"Father." A'vendyr came forward, hands up. "She just saved our lives. Please—"

"Stand out of my way, brute," the baron growled, looking up at Khyven. "I am the ruler here. Stand aside or—"

"Father, please," A'vendyr said.

"Listen to your boy." Khyven put his chest—which was at eye level for the baron—in the man's face. He sheathed his sword with a long, intentional movement. "You'll live longer."

"They were looking for you." The baron pointed around Khyven at Rhenn. "The bloodsuckers asked for you. They attacked us because of *you*."

Rhenn wished she could refute that.

"They would have come sooner or later," she said.

"So you *did* know!" the baron said. "And you did nothing to warn us!"

"I tried to help you. You locked me in a cage and left me for dead," she said.

"He did what?" Khyven glanced over his shoulder, giving that charming grin that almost always preceded violence.

Rhenn realized that Khyven might actually kill the baron if she didn't calm this situation down. "Baron V'endann, we can assign blame later. Right now, we must escape."

"I'm not going anywhere with you!"

"Good," Khyven said. "Go back to your little room and die."

"Khyven please." Rhenn held up a hand. "Stand down—"

"I'll stand down when he shows the proper respect. Otherwise I suggest we leave these fools to the brilliant leadership of this puffed-up ingrate."

"Shut your mouth!" the baron demanded. Khyven stepped forward, forcing the baron to stumble backward. Rhenn put a hand on his arm.

A'vendyr turned his pacifying gesture on Khyven. "Please. My father is in the grips of battle shock. He doesn't know what he's saying. We are grateful to you. Where do you suggest we go?"

"Back through the Thuros," Rhenn said.

"The what?" A'vendyr said.

"The magical portal. The one that goes to my kingdom."

"On Noksonon?" the baron blurted.

"You'll be safe there," she said.

"We're not going to Noksonon," Baron V'endann snarled. "We're not following you anywhere!"

"You'd rather stay here and die?" A'vendyr asked.

"I'd rather—"

"Oh… good…" Slayter panted. He limped into view at the opening of the barricade, breathless. "I was afraid… there was another staircase. Did you know that—?"

"Not now, Slayter," Khyven said.

"Actually, you'll want to listen to him this time." Lorelle materialized from the dark behind Slayter, her cloak unfurling around her. The baron, A'vendyr, and everyone behind them stared at the black-skinned Luminent, mouths open. "The battle's not done."

"There's... more," Slayter agreed, huffing. "They're... coming. But no... necromancer yet."

Rhenn stepped toward him and looked down at the vast audience chamber below. A half dozen bloodsuckers—resurrected V'endann warriors, not water goblins—came through the giant archway with N'ssag shuffling in the middle of them. He held something that looked like a golden harp, a U-shaped piece of metal that glittered in the starlight.

"*There* he is," Slayter said, sounding excited again as though he'd been waiting for N'ssag to appear. "What's he holding?"

"That's only six," Khyven said. "I can take six."

"Wait," Rhenn said. She'd never seen that golden harp before, and she didn't know what it meant.

"What *is* that?" Slayter's eyes glowed with curiosity, clearly focused on the same thing Rhenn was focused on.

"I don't know."

"There's a *lot* of magic down there," Slayter said. "Can you feel it?"

"Am I the one who feels magic?" Khyven asked.

"If you'd bonded with the sword, I bet you would."

"Stop it with the sword."

"I'm just saying you should carry it."

"Slayter!"

The mage held up a clay coin, scratched the final line on it with his scratcher. It glowed orange. He breathed deeply and closed his eyes like he was savoring it. The orange glow swelled in his fist, then he opened his eyes and snapped the clay coin.

Below, each of the approaching bloodsuckers glowed orange. The harp in N'ssag's arms burned with an orange fire.

But that was nothing compared to the miniature orange sun that grew in the hallway on the far side of the throne room.

Thuds shook the floor. The orange sun in the doorway grew brighter. Something was coming. Something magical.

"Whatever it is," Rhenn murmured. "It's big."

"Your necromancer—"

"N'ssag," Rhenn interjected.

"Your necromancer N'ssag has resurrected something that required a lot of magic…" Slayter murmured.

"Something big?" Khyven said.

"Something big," Slayter echoed.

"Don't tell me," Khyven said.

An enormous creature staggered through the archway. Its long-dead, gray skin was falling off its bones. Massive muscles bulged and strips of flesh hung from great rents in its body. It was naked except for patches of rotting clothing clinging to its shoulders and hips. Its eyes flared with the orange light Slayter had made.

"That's a Giant," Slayter said.

CHAPTER FORTY-SIX

RHENN

hyven's bloody fist tightened around his sword. "There's still only six of them."

"And a Giant," Slayter reminded him.

"And one Giant."

A second Giant shuffled through the doorway, eyes glowing orange. And a third.

"Three Giants," Slayter corrected.

"Sometimes, you could say nothing," Khyven said through his teeth. "Have you ever tried just saying nothing?"

Slayter glanced at Khyven like he didn't understand the question.

Suddenly, Rhenn remembered the Guardian, the supposed protector of the Kingdom of Pelinon. They could use a Guardian right about now. Where was the man? She spun to A'vendyr. "What happened to that Guardian fellow? Kell something."

"Kell Duranti."

"Didn't he lead you here?"

A'vendyr looked grim. "He did. He brought us to the nuraghi, let us in. He helped us fortify it against the bloodsuckers. He used powerful magics to secure it, and it would have worked but..."

"What happened to him?"

"A powerful mage showed up. They fought."

A chill went up Rhenn's spine. Another mage. Ventat Obrey. L'elica had mentioned N'ssag's benefactor was a powerful mage. "Did Kell Duranti fall?"

"I don't know. Their battle destroyed the gates, and then Kell went after the man. They crashed through the wall of the castle, and... then the bloodsuckers attacked. We had to flee. I don't know what happened to Kell Duranti after that. What kind of man can match a Guardian, Rhenn?"

"A powerful one," she said. She wondered where the battle had taken them. She wondered which of them had prevailed in the end. But one thing was for certain, they couldn't rely on the power of the Guardian Kell Duranti for this battle.

Slayter, who had been staring at the undead Giants during the entire exchange, suddenly spoke. "They're dead. So they probably can't use magic. That's a good thing at least."

The lead Giant stopped thirty feet into the room, standing in the midst of the corpses, bloodsuckers and V'endannians alike. He leaned back his head and opened his mouth wide, extending his huge, rotted arms outward. Half of the Giant's face had fallen away, and his jawbone and teeth in the left side were exposed in a sinister smile. Rhenn thought she felt something, like a ripple through the air.

"Or maybe they can..." Slayter murmured. "Oh wow..."

"Wow?" Khyven responded. "What's wow?"

The corpses around the Giant stirred, then sat up, got to their hands and knees, and shuffled to a standing position. N'ssag hunched over the golden harp, trembling like he was concentrating on keeping his body from flying apart.

The Giant groaned, shaking the walls with his thunderous, animalistic voice.

The entire room of corpses turned and faced the stairs.

"Well I was wrong," Slayter said. "They *can* do magic. And if they can do magic, the odds of us being able to defeat them drop to about—"

"Lorelle," Khyven said. "Can you use your cloak to get us back to the Thuros?"

She glanced at him. "The four of us. Yes."

"No, all of us." He gestured at the baron and his people clustered in the shadows. A few of them had come forward enough to see into the room, to see what was coming for them.

She looked pained, then shook her head. "I'm sorry, Khyven. I don't think so. Maybe over the course of an hour."

"We don't have an hour. I'd give us five minutes."

Lorelle shook her head.

"Go," Rhenn murmured. "The three of you go. I'll stay."

Khyven loosened his big shoulders. "Nah."

"We're not leaving you, Rhenn," Lorelle said. "Live together. Die together."

"Besides, I thought I was going to die long before now, choking underneath the boot of some greasy Ringer," Khyven said. "This is much better. I mean, how many people get to say they died fighting three Giants?"

"No one, technically," Slayter said. "No people would say that. I mean, people who died fighting a Giant. Because you'd be dead, so you really couldn't talk anymore—"

Khyven chuckled and shook his head.

Slayter held his finger up. "Unless you were *those* dead. Some of them can talk."

"Let's get to it." Khyven swung his sword to the left and right of his body.

"Actually, I had an idea," Slayter said. "You know what I said about those chemicals?"

"No," Khyven said.

"No?"

"You say a lot of things. Most of them I don't understand."

"Oh, well, the embalming chemicals for the corpses. They are extremely volatile. To sunlight. Is what I said. If I had sunlight, we could really do something here. Just a little bit of sunlight, even."

Rhenn swallowed. "The sun won't rise for another couple of hours."

"This battle will be over in seconds," Khyven said.

"I have a flash spell," Slayter said. "It might be enough to slow some of them down so we could get by. Maybe we could lure them to the Thuros, open it to the dragon's lair and shove them into the noktum."

"And set Tovos free?" Khyven asked.

"Maybe these Giants and that Giant will kill each other."

"Because that's likely?"

"We're not luring them anywhere," Lorelle said. "That archway is the only way out of here. The moment we go down there, they'll swarm us."

"We are not taking them back to Noksonon," Rhenn said. "Not anywhere on Noksonon. Slayter, your sunlight spell sounds like the best option. Can you… focus it?"

"Not really."

"Then we can't use it. The sunlight will hurt Rhenn," Lorelle said matter-of-factly.

"Oh, I had thought of that," Slayter said. "You'll have to lend her your cloak, of course. It'll protect her if she huddles into it."

"Wait! Why would you think I…?" Rhenn looked at Lorelle, then at Khyven. Each of them looked back steadily.

"It's all right," Lorelle said softly. "We've all gone through… changes."

"You know!"

"Slayter told us." Khyven put a hand on Rhenn's shoulder. "Did you really think we would care?"

"When did you… When?" Rhenn asked.

"Oh, the moment we came into the Thuros room," Slayter said. "The dead and the living give off very different auras."

Rhenn didn't know what to say. "Lorelle, I…"

Lorelle shook her head gently, as though telling Rhenn she didn't have to explain anything. Rhenn swallowed.

"We don't always get to play the part we want," Khyven said. "All we can do is play the part we get. You're family."

Lorelle unclasped her cloak, handed it to Rhenn. "We all have our weaknesses. It's about time you had one."

Rhenn couldn't speak over the lump in her throat. She cleared her throat and said. "I thought..." She swallowed. "I thought ale was my weakness."

Lorelle smiled. "All right, two."

Tears brimmed in Rhenn's eyes. "And making reckless choices."

"So three."

Rhenn hugged her sister, and Lorelle hugged her back tightly.

"If I didn't have to go into battle right this second, I'd be crying," she said.

"I think we've all earned a good cry," Khyven said. "After the fight, maybe?"

"After the fight," Rhenn whispered into Lorelle's midnight hair.

"If I cup my hands around the spell I might actually be able to direct it..." Slayter murmured. "I could—" He stopped talking abruptly, which was something Slayter never did unless someone cut him off. He stared at the slowly advancing army of the dead, and his eyes went wide.

"Slayter?" Rhenn said.

He stood stock still like he'd been frozen with a spell, then he came back to life suddenly and whirled to Lorelle. "Take me to the mirror room!"

"What?" she said.

"The mirror room. Teleport us there."

"What about Rhenn?" Rhenn had the cloak in hand, had been about ready to put it on.

"Why the mirror room?" Rhenn asked.

"No time. The Plunnos, your majesty. Give me the Plunnos."

Rhenn hesitated.

"There's no time. Trust me."

She pulled the Plunnos out of its pouch and handed it to him. He inspected both sides, and a big smile spread across his face. "Yes."

"Slayter, what is—"

"I've worked it out. We only have a limited number of seconds. Keep them busy. Fight, Khyven. Fight, and I'll be back."

"With what?" Rhenn asked.

Slayter spun to Lorelle. "Quickly, or there's no way we can save all these people."

Lorelle swirled her cloak around herself and Slayter. The cloak enveloped them, balled up, and seemed to fall back into the darkness.

They vanished.

"See?" Khyven held his free hand and the hand with his sword out, palms up. "I never understand what he's saying. I think Slayter lives in an entirely different world than the rest of us. All I got from that is that he wants us to fight. You?"

She slashed her bloody sword a few times like Khyven had done. "That's what I heard."

"Good," Khyven said. "That, I understand."

Rhenn grinned. "Simple."

"Straightforward."

The undead Giants lumbered across the wide, checkered marble floor. They had almost reached the base of the divided stairway.

Rhenn turned to Baron V'endann and his subjects.

"This is the last stand. I don't care if you know how to fight or not, pick up a weapon. Swords and daggers if you have them. A stick, a rock if you don't. If you don't fight for your life, we all die here."

They stared back at her in paralyzed silence.

A'vendyr nodded.

"We fight together," she said. "Or we die together. All of us!"

"Yes!" Everyone except the baron and his daughter responded this time. Those two just looked on in wide-eyed disbelief.

Rhenn turned to face the undead army. The Giants had made it to the stairway, and a horde of water goblin bloodsuckers flowed around them, howling and leaping up the steps.

"What's the strategy, your majesty?" Khyven asked.

"Take this." She offered him E'maz's dagger.

He looked at it, reluctant. "Rhenn, that's your—"

"I know what it is. Look, this royal box is a death trap, but it's also the most defensible position we have. Slayter says to play for time, so we're going to trust him. We'll make this last as long as we can."

"This magic dagger rips them apart," Khyven said. "You should keep it. We protect the queen—"

She shook her head. "We protect everyone. We're all living or dying here. Either we're all making it, or we're all dead. You'll use the dagger to its best advantage."

"It's not going to matter up here—"

"You're not staying up here. You're going down there. Just you. Scare the hell out of them, Khyven. Slow them down. Then get your ass back up here."

His eyes widened, and then he gave that charming smile. "I see." He sheathed his own dagger and she slapped the handle of E'maz's dagger into his hand.

"Go, Khyven. And don't die."

"How many of them do you want?"

"Get me a dozen."

"It's good to have goals." He charged down the steps.

Rhenn took a deep breath, hoping their faith wasn't misplaced in Slayter, hoping she hadn't just sent Khyven to his death.

CHAPTER FORTY-SEVEN

SLAYTER

The idea hit Slayter like a lightning bolt. He stared at the slowly advancing army of the dead, and his eyes went wide. Yes. It was the only way. It was the only possible way for them to all survive.

Slayter knew many things, even more than anyone guessed. His friends acknowledged him as intelligent, for certain, but they didn't really understand. How could they? To Slayter, it was as though the entire world was filled with pieces of information that could be connected together to understand things. Of course, everyone did this. It was how one came to conclusions. Connect information, make a decision. But the difference was that most people had a dozen bits of information—at most—to put together at a given moment.

Slayter had hundreds.

It was the reason he frustrated his friends. They didn't see all the pieces, so they always assumed he was daydreaming. He never told them that he was at once equally frustrated with them for not knowing what he knew, for not understanding what he understood. But it wasn't their fault. They simply didn't have enough pieces.

So there were many things he knew.

Slayter knew he was surrounded by heroes. It was why he had chosen Rhenn in the first place, all those years ago. Every single person around him right now would give their lives in this fight. And he knew they would all die.

Unless, of course, he could pull off this idea. He needed the mirrors from the mirror room. He needed the Thuros. He needed speed.

He whirled on Lorelle.

"Take me to the mirror room!"

"What?" she said.

"The mirror room. Teleport us there."

"What about Rhenn?"

"Why the mirror room?" Rhenn asked.

"No time." He held out his hand. Every second they wasted the chance he could pull this off went down. "The Plunnos, your majesty. Give me the Plunnos."

Rhenn hesitated.

"There's no time. Trust me."

She gave it to him, and he checked it. "Yes."

"Slayter, what is—"

"I've worked it out. We only have a limited number of seconds. Keep them busy. Fight, Khyven. Fight, and I'll be back."

"With what?" Rhenn asked.

She wanted to know the entire plan, but his choices had dwindled to one, and he could tell her, or he could act.

Slayter knew that every second was going to count, and he couldn't afford to waste even one. Based on how quickly Khyven, Rhenn, and Lorelle had dispatched twenty-three bloodsuckers in the audience hall—adding in the villagers and considering their collective fighting skills based on the one hundred and forty two of the V'endannians that lay dead on the floor of that room, and of course subtracting Lorelle from the combat equation because she was with him, and further knowing that Rhenn's party wasn't just facing twenty-three water goblin bloodsuckers this time, but one-hundred-and-two walking corpses, twenty-seven Human and goblin bloodsuckers, and three Giants—Slayter calculated his friends would last between seven and fourteen minutes before they were overwhelmed.

Slayter knew that, with Lorelle's help, he could get the mirrors set in the right place in eleven minutes if things went smoothly, twenty-one minutes if there were minor difficulties.

He wasn't exactly sure about that one because there could be unanticipated impediments to removing the mirrors from the wall. They might break. He and Lorelle might struggle to find objects to position them in the hallway correctly. If everything went easily, he'd have three minutes to spare. If it went poorly, his friends would be dead seven minutes before he could finish.

Slayter also knew that if anyone ever tried to enter his laboratory without permission—assuming it wasn't one of his friends—not only would they see an empty room, but they would be taken with the notion that it was the most boring room imaginable with nothing whatsoever of value. And once they left, they would be slowly taken with colorful diseases. Sudden cleft-tongue syndrome. Itchy scalp affliction, as though a hundred fire ants were crawling underneath their hair. Angled foot malady, where every time they tried to put their foot on the ground, it would turn as though the ground were forty-five degrees to the right or left. Cross-eyed infirmity. Nefarious invisible turtle affliction, where the victim would see turtle heads poking out from every single nook and cranny that could possibly fit a turtle head.

Slayter knew that the spell he'd created for bringing his friend Vohn back from the Dark required another component that he hadn't been able to master yet. Once that spell was perfected, he'd need to be able to heal Vohn's body instantly after with a second spell. And Slayter wasn't particularly good at healing spells.

Slayter knew that in this nuraghi alone, there were likely to be between five hundred and two thousand rats.

Slayter knew that there were almost innumerable different types of Plunnoi, and that the one he carried was a master Plunnos, capable of going to any of the many Thuroi in all five continents.

Slayter knew he had to run from the mirror room to the Thuros room with all haste, but that if he moved too fast, he would trip, so he would have to remember to walk slower than he wanted to so as not to jeopardize his plan by adding the extra time to pick himself up off the ground.

Slayter knew his plan would work if he was physically competent enough. Unfortunately, aside from deft and precise fingers, Slayter had never been physically competent at anything, an annoying ability that people like Khyven took for granted every single day.

Slayter knew that the undead Giants on the throne room floor were unimaginably powerful.

Slayter knew that Rhenn, who had fascinatingly been killed and brought back from the dead, had apparently retained all of her personality. She acted and talked like the woman he had known with the exception of a sadness and reluctance that could easily be attributed to anyone who had undergone extreme trauma.

Slayter knew that this begged the question: what would those undead Giants retain? They looked much deader than Rhenn, but did the length of death matter? According to the legends, Giants had been capable of working all five streams of magic while someone like Slayter could only work one. And that undead Giant had worked a great spell to bring back all the other corpses. So it further begged another question: what more could those Giants do?

Since Slayter did not have a definitive answer to that question, he could not figure this into any of his calculations. So he didn't.

Slayter knew this could be a problem.

All of this went through his mind in the time it took him to turn to Lorelle.

"Quickly," Slayter said. "Or there's no way we can save all these people."

Lorelle wrapped her cloak around him, and the last he saw of Rhenn was her concerned frown. Slayter was pulled down a long, thin tube. It squeezed his guts, felt like it was going to break his bones, felt like it was going to crack his head.

And then he was standing in the shadows of the mirror room. His bones were unbroken, his head uncracked. But his guts rebelled against the horrible experience. They rippled in traumatic spasms. He fell to his knees and threw up.

"Slayter..." Lorelle took his arm. He shook his head, because he knew that if she jostled him, he'd have to throw up again.

Lorelle was quite attuned to the emotional states of others, so she didn't touch him, and he managed to keep the vomiting to just once.

He swallowed the acid taste and waited three seconds, then held out his hand and she helped him to his feet.

"We'll need seventeen mirrors." He wiped his sleeve across his mouth and tried not to smell the vomit. "We can reach twenty one of them without magic. So that's good. The larger they are, the better they're going to work. So we have to try not to break them."

They set to work removing the mirrors from the walls. They were fixed with iron bars attached to circular plates with some kind of adhesive. After the first two broke, Lorelle got a look at what was making them stick, put together something from her magnificent healing kit, applied it to the adhesive with a little eye dropper, and the next fifteen came off smoothly.

That took seven minutes. His friends might already be dead.

"Come on!" Slayter carried four of the mirrors. He and Lorelle placed them in the hallway exactly as Slayter had envisioned in his mind. One here at this corner, then another on the far side, then two here. Then they ran back and got more mirrors. Then three there, four there, and so on. Miraculously, they didn't run into any bloodsuckers. This necromancer N'ssag had obviously brought all of his fighters to the main room.

Slayter knew that this was a mistake on N'ssag's part, and it was one more piece of information Slayter could log in the back of his mind in case he ever faced N'ssag one on one.

Lorelle and Slayter finally got the mirrors set and made it to the Thuros room.

That took them five more minutes.

Limping, he ran up the steps of the dais and pulled out Rhenn's Plunnos. This was the part he wasn't sure about. This was the part he hadn't calculated because he had never used a Plunnos before. But then, if he couldn't make the Thuros work, they were all dead anyway.

Slayter knew as much as any Human about Thuroi and Plunnoi, which was to say, precious little. But he thought this should work. This really ought to work.

He held the giant coin in his hand and envisioned the Thuros he wanted. He'd never been there himself, never even met anyone who had. He'd only seen a rendering of it in an old book. But Slayter knew the name of the place.

He hoped that would be enough.

He opened his eyes and threw the Plunnos at the swirling gateway.

CHAPTER FORTY-EIGHT

KHYVEN

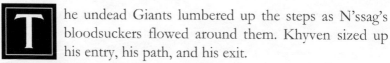

The undead Giants lumbered up the steps as N'ssag's bloodsuckers flowed around them. Khyven sized up his entry, his path, and his exit.

Get me a dozen. Rhenn's words echoed in his mind.

The blue wind swirled out from him. It had been changing ever since his trip to the Great Noktum. It didn't just point out possible weaknesses in his opponents or their deadly attacks. It gave Khyven what seemed like possibilities of all kinds. Not just how to attack, but how to... act.

This new development was frightening and invigorating at the same time. Khyven didn't exactly like the idea of allowing magic to do his thinking for him, didn't want to depend on something outside of himself to make his decisions. But at the same time it felt like his best self was slipping secrets to him about how to become better.

And now that he was pretty sure he was actually going to die, he didn't give a rip about whether it was risky to grow his dependence on the blue wind. Today, it was certainly more risky *not* to.

Three ambitious water goblins raced up the steps to brace him, ranging out ahead of the army of living corpses the undead Giant had raised. N'ssag's "high primes" and the Giant's undead seemed markedly different. The bloodsuckers were fast and strong, and they made strategic decisions. The Giant's living corpses were slow and apparently not intelligent at all. They moved up the stairs slowly, one at a time. Khyven figured that, one on one, the walking corpses would hardly pose a threat. But then, there were hundreds of them. Even the most lunk-headed soldiers could do damage if there were enough of them. That's why armies worked. Even Khyven's arm would falter after fighting that many, even if they came one a time and were as slow as molasses.

But I'm not going to be here that long, he thought. *I'm just going to scare the hell out of them. I'm going to get me a dozen.*

The first goblin, who had a human-ish face with tentacles for hair, jumped eight feet into the air, no doubt hoping to surprise Khyven as it attacked from above. The creature was only four feet tall, but it carried a human-sized sword longer than it was. The blue wind showed the coming of that blade, which the goblin intended to bring down in a two-handed strike on Khyven's skull.

The second goblin, who had a giant nose and pointed ears, wielded two daggers—one of crude iron and one of fine steel. He scuttled low like a cockroach, going for Khyven's legs. The blue wind showed a curved attack that would hamstring him.

The third goblin, a turtle-beaked fellow with big eyes, opened that beak and squawked fearsomely, no doubt trying to spook Khyven before running him through the gut with that spear he carried.

Good to know.

Khyven danced with the blue wind.

He leapt straight up above the hamstringing strike into the path of the sword, blocking it with his own blade. The contact sparked. Khyven leaned over in mid-air and rolled over Turtle Beak's spear.

Two Daggers, the goblin going for Khyven's legs, hissed as he hit only air. Squid Hair grunted as Khyven's powerful block—and the goblin's own momentum—shoved his own sword back into its face, denting its forehead and slicing off a tentacle.

Khyven sailed just over Turtle Beak, he dragged Rhenn's magic dagger across the side of the goblin's neck. The goblin collapsed like a meat sack. Khyven landed deftly on the steps to find Two Daggers already closing again. Khyven stop thrust with his sword, skewering the charging goblin through the eye.

Two Daggers said, "K-k-k…"

And collapsed.

The blue wind lashed out, and Khyven danced around it, moving to the right of Squid Hair's follow-up strike. The goblin had recovered lightning fast from his bleeding head wound.

Khyven blocked Squid Hair's strike, leaned incautiously forward and nicked Squid Hair's knee with the magic dagger. Khyven would never have exposed his neck like that for such a weak strike, but he'd seen that magical dagger in action. He didn't need a kill strike. He just needed to draw blood.

The goblin's knee went soft, he squealed, and he crashed to the ground. Squid Hair's sword bounced down the stairs. Khyven rose, lunged, and finished the goblin with a quick neck stab.

All told, the little fight had taken six seconds, and the other bloodsuckers—Humans by the look of them—weren't coming nearly so fast. There were ten of them, and they approached in formation.

Ten to one. Khyven had the blue wind, but he knew it wasn't a guarantee of success. He'd learned that when Vamreth's knights had attacked Rhenn's camp. It didn't matter if you knew where all the strikes were coming from if there were too many strikes for two arms to parry. Khyven had to bring the fight to them, surprise them, attack the flank, break up their formation.

He had to—

The blue wind rushed past him, pointing with a frantic, vibrating arrow as it blew back up the stairs. Khyven glanced over his shoulder, but there were no enemies. What did that mean—?

Something grabbed him then, like some giant, invisible hand had wrapped around his waist. He couldn't see his attacker, but he hacked left and right with his sword.

The invisible force lifted him straight up in the air, over the advancing bloodsuckers, over the advancing undead army, in an arc toward the wall with the tall, stained glass windows. It hurled him at the base of the stones.

"Senji's Teeth!" Khyven cursed, hurling his sword away to keep from impaling himself and flinging his arms up over his head.

He hit the stones like a bird in flight.

Intense pain shot through him.

Then he knew no more.

CHAPTER FORTY-NINE

KHYVEN

Khyven awoke with a start. It felt like a boulder rested on his chest, making it hard to breathe. His entire body felt like it had been beaten with clubs. His ears rang. His blurry vision slowly came into focus.

A dozen undead corpses held him fast, and his peril hammered home instantly. The blue wind whirled around him, agitated, showing every angle of his danger like an array of blue spears pointed at him. He jerked quickly, trying to dislodge his right arm. He'd lost his sword and Rhenn's magic dagger, but if he could just reach the dagger on his hip, he might do something.

He ripped his arm free from the grasp of the corpse on his right, but only for a second. Three other living corpses piled on before he could grapple with the weapon at his waist. The sheer weight of them bore Khyven's arm back to the ground.

He growled.

The hunched necromancer, N'ssag, shuffled forward, gripping a sickle of gold that looked like a stringless harp. N'ssag might have crawled out of a coffin himself, just like all his playthings. His robes were torn and dirty, even moldy. His skin had a pallor that said he'd not seen the sun in years, and he looked like he scrubbed his long, tangled hair with horse dung.

"N'ssag," Khyven said.

"You know me." N'ssag seemed pleased. "And you must be Khyven the Unkillable. Rhenn told me all about you."

"I doubt that."

"Oh, but you shouldn't. We were allies, she and I."

"Uh huh."

One of the undead Giants loomed over the necromancer. Its milky, sunken eyes slid inside its sockets, and it swayed like it didn't quite have its balance.

Khyven concentrated on the blue wind, hoping for something he could use to get free, to get the upper hand, but there seemed to be nothing. Or at least nothing he understood. Dark blue stripes flowed over the golden harp in N'ssag's hand. Clearly, the harp was important, but Khyven wasn't sure how. Or what he was supposed to do with that information.

The wrist of one of the undead holding Khyven was close enough to bite, but there wasn't a dark blue funnel there, which either meant doing that wouldn't be enough, or it wouldn't do anything at all.

Never mind the fact that sticking a dead man's wrist between his teeth made him want to vomit.

One of the hard lessons Khyven had learned in the Night Ring was that sometimes it was best to wait. When there were no options, conserving strength and waiting for a precious moment might present an opportunity.

So he waited. And hated it. He tried to calm himself.

N'ssag convulsively gripped the stringless harp. "She is valuable, did you know?"

"Rhenn?"

"My queen is so valuable."

"*Your* queen."

"Oh yes."

"The way you say that is really creepy."

N'ssag ignored the comment and his eyes sparkled with interest. "Do you know why?"

"Why she's important?"

"Yes."

At first, Khyven had thought N'ssag's question was rhetorical, but it wasn't. This was a question N'ssag didn't know the answer to. The interest in the man's eyes was palpable. He was practically salivating to find out whatever made Rhenn "important," and he thought Khyven could give it to him.

That was an advantage. A gift of time. As long as Khyven had something N'ssag wanted—and the necromancer thought Khyven would give it—the necromancer wouldn't kill him. Khyven had to stretch that out.

"I do, actually," Khyven said, and as he did, he realized that, by Senji's Teeth, he actually *did* know.

Just before Rhenn showed up, Slayter had been talking about Greatbloods and Giantkillers. Night and day. Every time Khyven had turned around, Slayter wouldn't shut up about Greatbloods and Giantkillers. His obsession had sparked from what had happened in the Great Noktum.

After they'd returned home from the Great Noktum, Khyven, Lorelle, Vohn, and Slayter had put together all of their various stories and had come to four conclusions.

First, the Giant Tovos had sent Zaith to seduce Lorelle because he'd hoped she could lead him to Rhenn.

Second, Tovos wanted Rhenn because he thought she was a weapon against Giants.

Third, Tovos was wrong about Rhenn; he had likely been fooled by Nhevalos, who'd stolen Rhenn and left behind the cryptic statement, "I'm sorry. He lived, and that means things will move quickly now."

Finally, Khyven and his friends had all agreed that the "he" in that statement referred to Khyven himself. That, alongside Zaith's statement of, "*You're* the one. *You're* the Greatblood. It's not the queen. The Betrayer fooled Him. *You're* the one he wants!" convinced them all that Khyven was this so-called Greatblood. He was the "Giantkiller" which, it would make sense, Giants like Tovos—or any other Giants for that matter—hated.

In short, Rhenn wasn't the Giantkiller but Tovos, and all of his minions, thought she was. It was Khyven, and it probably had everything to do with the blue wind, though he'd be damned if he knew how that was supposed to defeat Giants. He'd met Tovos, and even with the blue wind, Khyven's first encounter with the Giant had almost been disastrous. Tovos had simply snapped his fingers and immobilized Khyven.

In their second encounter with Tovos, it had taken Khyven, Slayter, Vohn, Lorelle, a Mavric iron sword, and a Dragon Chain to defeat the Giant. And even at that, it had been a very near thing. If that battle had lasted even a second longer—or if the Dragon Chain hadn't contained Tovos's magic—that fight would have gone very differently.

Zaith had warned Khyven not to let on what he could do, not to give Tovos any reason to think that he was hunting incorrectly for Rhenn. That ignorance was a protection for Khyven—and undoubtedly a part of Nhevalos's plan.

And now here Khyven was in the clutches of yet another villain who had control of *three* Giants and who seemed to be searching for the same thing Tovos had wanted.

All of this flew through Khyven's mind as the pungent necromancer leaned forward. For a fleeting instant, Khyven wondered if this was how Slayter felt, being so smart all the time.

"Tell me why she is so important, Khyven the Unkillable," N'ssag said. "And I will spare you."

"So… if I throw Rhenn under your knife, you'll let me go?"

"Precisely."

Khyven laughed. He didn't mean to; it just slipped out.

He had affected laughter many times in the past, but this one was genuine. Save his life to put Rhenn in danger?

Once, he would have. Senji's Spear, he'd have done just about anything to save his own neck. He *had* done just about anything. He'd killed and lied, schemed and hidden. He'd done it for so long he'd forgotten who he really was.

Rhenn, Lorelle, and Vohn had brought him back from that place, had given him a reason to fight aside from saving his own skin. He'd happily give his life for any of them.

"I realize that brutes like you rely solely on arrogance and the strength of your arms, but please tell me... You don't actually think you're unkillable because people call you that, do you?" N'ssag asked.

Khyven's grin widened. "You're not very good at this, are you? Intimidating people. You haven't had much practice, is what I mean."

N'ssag's eyes flashed, and behind him the Giant rumbled like it was somehow linked to N'ssag's emotions.

"Oh, I'm sure I can do better," N'ssag murmured. "You realize I don't need you. All I need is Rhenn. If you know the information I need, and you don't tell me, I'll just break your bones until you do."

The living corpse on Khyven's right grappled with his little finger. Khyven clenched his fist, made the creature fight for it, but eventually the thing pried his pinky up... and then back. The bone snapped, and Khyven grunted.

"Nice," he breathed. "I... broke four fingers my first two months in the Night Ring. You want to impress me, better break an entire arm."

"Is that what you'd rather?"

"Or my neck."

N'ssag narrowed his eyes in frustration. "You're really not going to tell me, are you?"

Khyven chuckled. "No, I'm really not."

"Does your life mean so little to you?"

"So much, actually."

N'ssag looked confused at that. "How could it benefit you? Either I'm going to break you until you're worthless or I'm going to slit your throat and bring you back as one of my own—"

The sounds of battle, which had been a din in the background, suddenly seemed closer. N'ssag looked up, and then looked surprised. Khyven desperately wanted to know what was going on, but he couldn't see past the living corpses and the towering Giant. And he wasn't about to give N'ssag the satisfaction of asking.

"Well, that's a surprise," N'ssag said.

"The smell? Your smell? It's finally getting to you?" Khyven asked.

N'ssag's lips tightened, then he looked over the shoulders of his undead. "I think your queen is trying to save you. Isn't that backward? Shouldn't you be saving her?"

"She's not good at sticking to plans. Especially her own plans," Khyven said sourly. "Well, N'ssag. Better get cracking."

"I'm beginning to think you *want* me to break your arm, Khyven," N'ssag said. "So I'm not going to. How about I just bring your queen to you, and then she can watch while I ask her the same questions I asked you? Except this time I'll just remove your body parts in front of her."

"She'll die before she let's you take her—"

Snarls and yells rose in the air. The bloodsucker honor guard parted, and half a dozen walking corpses came forward, a struggling Rhenn gripped between them.

They slammed her down on the marble floor next to Khyven and held her pinned just like he was pinned.

"That didn't go well," Rhenn growled.

"Because you didn't stick to the plan," Khyven said.

"The plan went sideways."

"Because you didn't stick to the plan."

"Shut up."

"Yes, your majesty."

"So… my queen," N'ssag said, clutching that stringless harp spasmodically. "You dodged my questions so disarmingly when we were friends. Now I'm afraid I'm going to have to be more pointed. Why does Nhevalos want you?"

"I have great legs," Rhenn said through her split and bleeding lips.

N'ssag's eyes flashed and he turned to Khyven. "Slit his throat," he commanded.

"N'ssag—" Rhenn began, but he cut her off.

"No, my queen! No. You've killed my children. You scoff at my magic. And when I give you the greatest of all gifts, you spurn me. No, you made me suffer for my largesse. It's time you suffered."

Khyven took a deep breath and let his body go limp as one of the bloodsucker honor guard drew a dagger and went around behind his head.

The euphoria sang through him, and the blue wind whipped about him like a twitching cat's tail. He'd have one chance. Just one. When the bloodsucker moved behind him, he'd yank his right and left arms with all his might. If he could break free from even one of them, he'd get a dagger this time.

The bloodsucker drew his knife.

Khyven yanked—

The living corpses yanked back, hard, as though they'd expected him to do that.

Damn.

Khyven clenched his teeth as the bloodsucker leaned over him, upside down in Khyven's view. The dagger descended to his neck—

The dagger jerked away as the bloodsucker twitched upright, swatting at something on his temple.

A dart fell next to Khyven's head. A blowgun dart. Lorelle's dart.

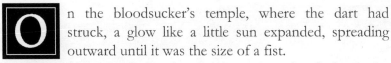

CHAPTER FIFTY

KHYVEN

O n the bloodsucker's temple, where the dart had struck, a glow like a little sun expanded, spreading outward until it was the size of a fist.

Rhenn gasped, turning her head away as the flesh on the right side of her face bubbled.

But that was nothing compared to the reaction of the bloodsucker who'd been hit. He jerked and screamed as the flesh peeled off his face like shingles in a hurricane. Blood sprayed and bones erupted from its cheek and skull.

"Senji's Teeth!" Khyven exclaimed as the gore rained down on him.

The body collapsed, falling right next to Khyven's head. The nearby living corpses—all the ones holding Khyven and Rhenn—twitched. They didn't seem as violently affected by the light, but their grips went slack for an instant.

With a powerful motion, Khyven yanked his arms free, grabbed the dagger at his waist, and surged to his feet, kicking one of Rhenn's assailants away. She folded in half, kicking both legs upward and nearly taking another's head off. Khyven spun, about to slash at the nearest living corpse—

"No, my love," Lorelle murmured in his ear from behind. "Just fall back."

Her cloak unfurled behind them, encompassing him and Rhenn. Instead of attacking, Khyven simply fell backward.

"No!" N'ssag shouted. The Giant roared overhead, and all of Khyven's hairs stood on end—

Then he was sliding into that horrible tunnel that got narrower and narrower until he felt like he was squeezing through a piece of straw.

He shouted, and then it was over. He stood at the threshold of the tall archway—the only escape from the throne room. Between them and the steps they'd climbed to save Baron V'endann and his people stood the army of living corpses, the bloodsucker honor guard, the three Giants, and N'ssag himself, who was casting about wildly trying to find out where they were.

Khyven clenched his stomach and demanded that it stop trying to flip itself inside out. Slowly, painfully, the urge to vomit subsided. Rhenn leaned one hand against the archway, head down, huffing as though she was trying to do the same thing. Like Khyven, she managed to keep her stomach settled.

"No," Rhenn huffed. "Lorelle... we need to save the baron... and his people. Take us up... to the throne room."

"This had to happen first," Lorelle said. "Slayter told me I had to bring you here. He said that by his calculations you'd be dead in the next thirty seconds."

"That's frighteningly accurate," Khyven murmured.

"He's frighteningly smart," Lorelle said.

"Where is he?" Rhenn asked.

"Halfway between the Thuros room and here, I'd guess," she said.

"With mirrors?"

"It's a story."

"Maybe we should hide," Rhenn said. N'ssag was looking everywhere around the throne room except at their archway. It was a miracle he hadn't spotted them yet.

"No," Lorelle said. "Slayter said to get you, and then for us to all stand here in the archway. To attract attention."

"Attention? We want to lure them here?" Rhenn asked.

"Yes."

"Well, that's not going to be hard."

N'ssag saw them, and he shouted in triumph. The three Giants turned. The bloodsuckers shrieked and leapt forward. The rest of the living corpses shuffled toward them.

"We've got about five seconds. And we don't have any weapons." Rhenn clenched and unclenched her fists.

"I have a dagger," Khyven said.

Rhenn glanced at him and gave him an expression like they were about to ride into battle with a toothpick. "Great."

"Take this. You're going to need it." Lorelle unclasped the cloak from her shoulders, wrapped it around Rhenn, and flipped the cowl up over her head. "I'm sorry about the dart. I just didn't have time to do it better."

"It's fine." Rhenn touched the burned side of her face, which was already starting to heal, and she vanished from Khyven's view except for her nose.

The bloodsuckers were almost on them. The Giants lumbered forward, one long step at a time, just ahead of the living corpses.

The entire hallway behind Khyven suddenly filled with a blinding light. A silhouette, dark against the light, limped toward them.

"Slayter!"

"See?" The mage breathed hard, carrying a mirror three feet in diameter. "I told you!"

"You didn't tell us anything," Khyven yelled down the hallway, shielding his eyes. "What did you do?"

Khyven checked on Rhenn. She had ducked behind the wall, the noktum cloak wrapped protectively around her, head to toe.

"The Thuros," Slayter huffed. "I opened it to another Thuros that's right by the Lux. I read about it. Pure sunlight. Bang."

The bloodsuckers arrived, shrieking as they jumped high in the air, flying down on Khyven and Rhenn. Only as they came down did they realize the hallway had suddenly filled with light. Khyven sidestepped the first attacker, and the bloodsucker stumbled into the light-filled hallway. He popped like a blood blister.

Only a spray of red remained on the wall where he'd been.

"No!" N'ssag yelled across the room. "Turn around! Come back!"

The bloodsuckers tried to stop. The Giants tried to stop. But the living corpses still lumbered forward stupidly, shambling ever closer to the archway.

"Get back!" Slayter finally arrived, holding a three-foot by two-foot length of mirror in his hands. "Get out of my way!" He angled the mirror, catching the blinding light coming down the hallway and sending it into the audience chamber.

The beam cut through the darkness and N'ssag's high primes like a fiery sword. The bloodsuckers exploded, spraying blood everywhere. When the beam hit the shambling undead, though, it only seemed to stun them. Slayter focused on the chest of the nearest Giant. The beam hit it dead center and its ribcage blew outward, showering the floor with rotting organs and entrails.

He passed the beam over the second Giant, blowing its leg off as he huffed, trying to recover his breath and steady the beam at the same time. He finally focused it on the Giant's head, which exploded.

"Here..." The panting Slayter beckoned to Khyven, who looked wide-eyed at the carnage the beam had caused. "Take it. I... can't breathe... Just... point it at anything that moves..."

Khyven grabbed the mirror and raked it through the room. He aimed first at the bloodsuckers, who scattered like roaches, frantically scrambling for any bit of cover from the deadly beam. N'ssag screamed at his creations to run even as he did the same. But the room, which had been a trap for his enemies moments ago, was now that same trap for them.

The final Giant strode behind N'ssag and picked him up in its huge hands. They reached the windows, which began ten feet off the ground and rose upward to the top of the crumbling ceiling. The Giant thrust N'ssag at the stained glass window.

"No! Not like that," he shrieked. "Not like—ahhhhh!"

N'ssag threw his hands up in front of his face as his body shattered the glass. The Giant forced the screaming necromancer through the jagged glass even as Khyven caught the Giant with the beam.

The angle and the distance made the beam go wide, covering the Giant's entire body with sunlight. The thing blew apart all at once. Legs and arms fell amidst a rain of rotting meat. Guts covered the broken window.

At that instant, all of the corpses the Giant had brought to life fell to the ground like marionettes with their strings cut. They did not get up again.

N'ssag was gone. Only bloodstains remained on the window's jagged glass.

"I'll get him," Lorelle said.

"I'll go with you," Rhenn said from within the cloak's protection.

Khyven was about to protest, but he saw the sense of that. The only thing left were a handful of fleeing bloodsuckers, and Khyven and Slayter would do better mopping up if they could fill this room with light without worrying about Rhenn.

Rhenn opened the cloak for Lorelle, who slid into its embrace like it was part of her body. The darkness condensed, enveloped them both, and they were gone.

"Khyven and I will just stay here," Slayter huffed.

"I don't think I'll ever get used to that cloak," Khyven said.

"I don't like throwing up." Slayter made a face, then he brightened and pointed at the sizzling remains of the huge corpses. "Giants. We should search them."

"Search them?" Khyven wrinkled his nose.

"They might have something on them," Slayter said as he limped toward the nearest Giant corpse.

Propping the mirror against the archway so that it cut a significant beam into the room, Khyven sighed and followed, staying alert for any last desperate attacks.

CHAPTER FIFTY-ONE

N'SSAG

N'ssag staggered down the craggy slope behind the keep, holding his tattered cloak together and wincing with every step. A light rain had begun, and the ground was slick. He slipped and caught himself with a low tree branch, slipped again and just about rammed his head into another. Each movement pulled at the slices on his body, and he whimpered.

The underside of his left leg and butt burned like fire. Every time he took a step, daggers of agony shot through him. The meat between his shoulder blade and his spine felt like it had been laid open to the bone, and his left arm barely worked. The Giant had smashed the window with N'ssag's own body in an effort to comply with N'ssag's command to help him escape. Some of the glass hadn't broken when the Giant shoved N'ssag through, and it had cut him deeply.

He cried openly as he limped into the dark, clutching the golden sickle to his chest with what meager strength remained to his left arm. He used his stronger arm to help him stay on his feet.

They're going to kill me, he thought. *They're going to catch me, and they're going to kill me.*

He slipped and went down, crying in anguish when he sat down hard. He almost blacked out from the pain, and when he came to his senses he realized he was sliding down a slope. He slipped and tumbled into the dark, picking up speed.

"No," he whimpered. He flailed, trying to catch something, and the golden sickle flew off into the dark. He reached for it, and a rock hit him right in the slice on the back of his leg. He gagged on the pain. Dark spots appeared in his vision, and he almost passed out. With a sob, he flipped to his right side as he slid faster and faster.

He could hear rushing water ahead, and to his horror he realized he was headed straight for a river.

Nissra preserve me! he prayed.

He went over a small drop-off and landed awkwardly on his feet. For a moment, he just stood there, blinking, then he tried to scramble out of the gathering stream that sluiced past him, but his feet went out from under him. The water took him again, and he continued his slide. He could see the next drop-off ahead, and it looked much larger than the first. There was nothing he could see beyond it except air. Nothing he could hear except the rushing of water.

I'm going to die, he thought. *I'm going to die!*

He grabbed fistfuls of mud, but everything was so slick he simply could not hold on. Just as he neared the drop-off, though, his cloak pulled tight, choking him.

The water churned over him. The cloak tugged at him, like the branch it snagged on was whipping in the wind, yanking back on him cruelly. After every yank, he tried to grab a breath, but water poured over his face and mouth.

He coughed, reaching up, tying to grab the cloak, trying to gain some purchase so he could control his spinning movement. He reached up and—

And touched someone's hand.

Spluttering, coughing, N'ssag raised his head. His cloak hadn't been caught on a branch or a rock. Someone had grabbed it!

The man was tall, wide in the shoulders, and the cowl of his black cloak hung low over his face against the rain.

Khyven! It was Khyven the Unkillable!

The man hauled remorselessly on the cloak, choking and yanking N'ssag from the water.

"No!" N'ssag whimpered, patting at his belt. He had a small knife there. He fumbled it out of the little sheath—

The man knocked the dagger away. It clinked against a stone, plopped into the water, and was gone.

"Don't be stupid," the man said, and it wasn't Khyven the Unkillable's voice at all. In fact, N'ssag knew that voice. He peered up into the dark, into the fierce and angry gaze of Ventat Obrey.

"Ventat!"

"Shut your mouth, N'ssag," Ventat hissed. "They're out here, looking for you, but we have an advantage. They won't come here to start. They wouldn't imagine that you'd purposely throw yourself into a river leading over a cliff."

"It wasn't... on purpose." N'ssag blinked against the rain and licked his lips.

"Really?" Ventat said with frosty sarcasm.

N'ssag hung his head.

"Honestly, I would let you die," Ventat said. "But you've done something tonight that makes me think you could be an asset to my lord."

"Thank you."

"Now listen. They're chasing you," Ventat said. "And they're going to catch you unless you do exactly as I say."

"Y-yes."

"Come with me." He stood up and hauled N'ssag to his feet. His arms were incredibly strong.

"Where are we going?"

Ventat grabbed N'ssag's robes and pulled him up, eye-to-eye. The yank sent a hot wave of pain through N'ssag's left shoulder, and he gasped. "Listen necromancer, that Luminent has a noktum cloak. She can teleport around like a jumping thergi, and the only reason she hasn't stuck a dagger into you yet is because she doesn't know where you are. That will change when she hears your senseless chatter. So shut your mouth and follow me. Understand?"

"Yes, I—"

"Don't speak, just nod."

N'ssag nodded.

"Now keep up, and don't fall. We're going back into the nuraghi."

N'ssag wanted to ask why in Nissra's name they were going back to the nuraghi, but he realized that he'd already be dead without Ventat's help.

He bowed his head against the rain and followed.

True to his word, Ventat wended his way through the forest and back to the ruined castle of the Giants. N'ssag kept looking over his shoulder, waiting for Rhenn's "Luminent" to appear, but she didn't.

Finally, carefully, they climbed up a portion of the wall where there was a crack in the wall just large enough for a person. With Ventat's help, N'ssag climbed up and squeezed through the crack into a hallway. Ventat led, working his way through the castle like he knew it intimately. In short order, they came to the Thuros room.

The Thuros was open to a blinding light. It filled the entire hallway with intense daylight like a noonday desert.

"What…?" N'ssag said.

Ventat turned and made a fist with his hand, thumb sticking out, and jerked it across his throat.

N'ssag didn't need a translator for that.

Shut up!

The man shielded his eyes from the light and walked up the dais. He pulled a Plunnos from his pocket and threw it at the archway. The moment the coin hit, it bounced back, and the light winked out. Instead, between the purple afterimages on the back of N'ssag's eyes, he could see a room beyond the archway with wooden furniture, stone floors and walls, and a high ceiling.

The man grabbed N'ssag's arm and yanked him through.

Goo slithered around and through N'ssag's body as he crossed the threshold. He gasped as he stepped out onto a similar dais in the stone room with the wooden furniture.

Ventat flicked the coin at the threshold again, and the room of the nuraghi vanished. Swirling colors replaced it: blue, gold, green, red, and black.

N'ssag looked at his benefactor, and the man's angry-eyed gaze held his.

"All right," he said. "Now, we talk."

"Where are we?"

"In the castle of my Lord Tovos."

"Who is Tovos—?"

"This is where I ask you questions, necromancer, and you shut up. Or I kill you."

N'ssag swallowed.

"You took on a task for me, and you spectacularly failed. I was going to kill you. Then I was going to let you die at the hands of those Usarans. Then you did something unexpected. You brought those Giants back to life." Ventat's thick, black eyebrows hung low over his black eyes. "Could you do it again?"

"Y-yes," N'ssag stammered.

"Good. I require your help, and you're going to give it to me. Or we're back to our previous state of association."

"Our previous state?"

"Where you spectacularly failed me and I kill you."

"O-oh. Of course."

"Are we clear about that?"

"Yes." The fiery pain of N'ssag's leg grew now that his heart had stopped beating so fast. It felt like his leg was slowly being squeezed between two uneven pieces of iron.

"Lord Tovos has gone missing," Ventat said. "We are going to find him. You are going to put all of your resources into this."

N'ssag clenched his teeth as he thought of his laboratory, as he thought of his precious army that Rhenn and her friends had just destroyed. "I have very few resources to help you at the moment."

"In the Great Noktum, we have no end of resources for someone like you," he said.

"What is it, precisely, that you want?"

"We're in the midst of a secret war, necromancer, and whether you know it or not, tonight you've chosen a side. You are going to create another army of undead to find him. We are going to search every corner of the Great Noktum until we find what has become of my master. Then he is going to lead us. He is going to bring a war down on those Lightlanders like they've never seen before."

"If you want an army of my high primes. I will need bodies," N'ssag said.

"Bodies..." Ventat echoed in a low voice. "The dragon Jai'ketakos had recently provided an entire city of Nox bodies. They await your ministrations."

"I will need darkness," N'ssag said.

"You will need darkness..." Ventat echoed, and he began to laugh.

Chapter Fifty-two

RHENN

Rhenn and Lorelle searched the darkness, but they couldn't find N'ssag. It should have been simple. He wasn't a woodsman. The man could barely walk a line without tripping, and Lorelle and Rhenn worked the dark like they'd been born to it, and they worked the forest because they *had* been born to it. They flew through the rain and the woods together, searching the edge of the forest near the nuraghi and within. Rhenn spotted tracks that went into the lush trees, but they were already faded. As the rain came down harder, they were quickly being washed away. It became almost impossible to find places where a person might have passed.

"How could he be so fast?" Rhenn asked, frustrated. Did he have some kind of teleportation artifact? Something that would hide him, maybe? She *had* to find him.

"I can't hear a thing in this rain." Lorelle squinted against the heavier and heavier water droplets.

"I don't understand it." Frustration welled up within her at the thought of losing the necromancer. They'd achieved a great victory tonight, but it would all be soured if the cause of all of this carnage escaped justice.

"Maybe he drowned." Lorelle held a forearm up, wincing at the rain like a cat.

Rhenn felt a deep foreboding. Nhevalos's words rose in her mind about the forces moving in the world. The fact that N'ssag had mysteriously disappeared so quickly and completely... What if he had help? What if something else, some powerful force like Nhevalos himself, had spirited N'ssag away?

Rhenn's keen night vision spotted a wide leaf at the edge of a steep slope. The leaf had been torn in half. Her heart beat faster.

"What if he fell?" she murmured. *That* sounded like N'ssag. Rhenn moved to the edge and peered through the falling rain. Sure enough, a dozen feet down the hill was a broken tree limb, low hanging, just above a small stream of water created by the deluge.

"Come on!" Rhenn jumped down the slope. She slid with little streams of water, jumping lightly left and right to catch her balance. It was slick, and even an athletic person might have had a hard time keeping their feet. But Rhenn's new strength and inhuman agility was easily a match for the terrain. Lorelle stayed right behind her, leaping nimbly along the same path.

The rushing of water became louder, and Rhenn pulled up short at a small drop-off. The water cascaded over, hit the ground and kept going. A short distance beyond that was big drop-off. Rhenn hopped down lightly and found the impact point of another body. She smelled blood.

"He was here," she murmured. A smear of blood marked a cluster of tangled leaves and there was a five-pointed mark in the mud made from a clawing hand. N'ssag had tried to catch himself, failed.

"He kept going." Rhenn slipped and hopped all the way to the next drop-off. A true waterfall shot over the edge into a fifty foot drop where it joined a raging river below.

Lorelle pulled up next to Rhenn, breathing hard. Rhenn had expended so much energy that she felt hollow, like her skin was tight against her bones. It had been far too long since she'd fed. She glanced at her friend and could see the veins of coppery fire beneath her midnight skin. She saw the blood rushing, and she wanted it. Senji's Teeth, she wanted that euphoria trickling on her tongue. She wanted to reach out and put a hand on Lorelle's slender neck, feel the pulse of that coppery fire—

She jerked her gaze away.

"Is everything all right?" Lorelle asked.

"I... We have to keep moving."

Lorelle put a hand on Rhenn's bare forearm, and the touch was like lightning. She wanted to sink her teeth into that dark wrist.

Rhenn spun away. "Don't touch me!" She scrambled back, putting at least six feet between herself and her friend.

Lorelle's eyes went wide. "Rhenn, I'm sorry. I didn't mean—"

"Just don't touch me right now."

Lorelle held Rhenn's gaze for a long moment, then nodded. "Of course, sister," she said softly. As though nothing had happened, Lorelle turned back to the rainy expanse before them. "Do you think he fell?"

Rhenn forced herself to focus on the chase again. At first, she examined the drop-off, but then she turned and looked a little further upstream for something, anything.

"There." She moved a half dozen paces up and saw the quickly fading mark of a boot heel, sunk so deep in the mud either the person was very heavy or very clumsy. N'ssag. Rhenn leapt to stand next to the footprints...

And found two sets. Two different boot prints. N'ssag's and someone with larger feet. "Somebody helped him. Somebody else was here."

Two different types of boots, and they angled back up the slope...

Toward the nuraghi.

"They went back." Rhenn cursed. Of *course* they'd doubled back. She was imagining all manner of magical escapes, but she'd overlooked the most obvious. The Thuros! Where else could they go except into a river? There was absolutely nothing else for miles. N'ssag would have known he could never outrun them, not one of his superhuman high primes and a Luminent with a teleportation cloak.

"The Thuros," Rhenn breathed.

"You think he went through the gateway? I thought you had the Plunnos."

"He had one, too. And probably more, since he unearthed those Giants. Who knows what he found in their crypts. Lorelle, can you teleport us there?"

But Lorelle was already wrapping Rhenn in her cloak. The gut-wrenching effect took hold.

They stood outside the doorway of the Thuros room. Rhenn prepared herself for the blinding light, but it was gone.

"The light…" Rhenn murmured.

"Come on!" Lorelle said, leaping around the corner and into the room.

N'ssag and another figure in a black cloak stood on the dais. Beyond them through the open Thuros was a room Rhenn had never seen before, but it was clearly inside a noktum. That absolute darkness was intimately familiar to her now since she'd become what she was. The room was made of midnight black stones and it had ornately carved furniture made of some dark, polished wood.

Without a word, she leapt forward, Lorelle matching pace—

The Thuros closed, the swirling colors returning just as Rhenn reached it. She slammed her hands against the now-solid magical barrier.

"No!" she wailed. "No!" She collapsed to her knees.

N'ssag had finally made it to Noksonon.

CHAPTER FIFTY-THREE
RHENN

Rhenn knelt there cursing herself, cursing her failure. That madman was in Noksonon, maybe in Usara itself, and there was nothing she could do about it. Slayter had the Plunnos. By the time she could get it from him and give chase, even if she could somehow get the Thuros to open up to that same place, she was weak. And N'ssag had a new ally she knew nothing about. It would be foolish to give chase without a plan. She could be walking right into a trap.

They'd lost him. For now, N'ssag was free.

"We'll come back. We'll find him," Lorelle assured her. Rhenn felt her friend coming closer, felt the heat of the coppery fire within her.

And beyond that, behind Lorelle, behind the wall of the room and the walls of the nuraghi, she felt the sun coming, too. It was almost sunrise. It wouldn't be long now.

"Come on," Rhenn said. "Let's get back."

Lorelle unfurled her cloak, and Rhenn stepped into the sweet darkness. Her guts wrenched and suddenly they stood in the throne room.

Fighting the urge to vomit, Rhenn blinked away the aftereffects and looked out over the carnage.

Water dripped prodigiously through the holes of the tall ceiling, making it seem like the storm was actually inside the nuraghi. The throne room was filled only with wet corpses. It didn't seem completely real. She'd seen too many faces among those dead bodies that she knew from the V'endann Keep. Those same faces, those same friends, had been pulled up like puppets to dance to N'ssag's tune.

Rhenn turned her gaze upward at the stairway where the survivors had slowly begun to creep down the steps. She wended her way through the carnage and met the survivors on the landing where the first two staircases met.

There were barely fifty left alive from the several hundreds who had fled here from the baron's keep, and they all milled uncertainly around Baron V'endann, who seemed to have lost his ability to respond. He just kept looking and looking at the carnage like he couldn't believe what had happened.

"The immediate threat is over," Rhenn said to A'vendyr, whose right arm was in a makeshift sling. He hesitated, then nodded at her.

She was relieved that he was alive—relieved that any of them still lived. He had comported himself well in the fight. He'd been a true warrior, but now that the immediate danger was done, it was hard not to remember everything he'd done to her back at the keep. Her capture. Her imprisonment. A'vendyr had stood by while his father had nearly killed her. Whatever sense of friendship she might have felt for him was gone. She just wanted to be away from this entire continent.

But she was facing him as a queen now, not a prisoner, and a queen couldn't afford the luxury of a tantrum. She had to approach it like a diplomat.

"Thank you, Rhenn." A'vendyr extended his hand. "My father will not say it—he will blame you for all of this—but I know you could have left us to die. I'm grateful."

Despite her fatigue, despite the frightening changes that had befallen her, this was a moment to create relations with

V'endann, and possibly even the kingdom of Pelinon. So she shook his hand, all the while looking at the glowing copper veins in his neck, all the while wanting to drain him dry.

My life has become a continuous war, she thought. That wasn't what she wanted, wasn't what she would have chosen, but…

Khyven's recent words echoed in her mind.

We don't always get to play the part we want. All we can do is play the part we get.

"I would help you with this, if I could," she said to A'vendyr. "But I can't stay. Know that the fight is over, though. The bloodsuckers are dead or run off. The necromancer is gone. The best thing to do now is to bury your dead, then make your way back to the keep, salvage what you can, and get things operating there again. You are going to have a lot of refugees returning to see what remains. Best to be there for them, let them know that the barony lives on and that it will function again."

He nodded. "I see now that… We should never have tried to force you to be here in the first place. The prophet was wrong. I wish… I wish I'd seen it sooner."

"I wish you had, too. We could have… been friends, A'vendyr."

"I hope we still can be."

She let out a weary breath. "Perhaps."

"It's difficult." He drew a shaky breath. "Your coming has made me question everything I ever knew. Everything I ever believed in."

"Maybe that's a good thing," Rhenn said.

He nodded ruefully. "Maybe it is."

Khyven approached from a group he'd been reassuring, and he stood next to A'vendyr like a taller, wider, stronger version of the strapping V'endannian warrior.

"You couldn't find him," Khyven guessed. "N'ssag."

"We had difficulty tracking him through the rain," Rhenn said. "He actually doubled back to the nuraghi. We caught up with him in the Thuros room right as the light went out. He used it. Went through."

"I thought we had the Plunnos," Khyven said.

"There are more than one. And he had a friend, too."

"Not one of his creatures?" Khyven asked.

"No. Someone tall with a cloak," Rhenn said. "Not V'endannian. He was dressed like a Usaran. That's all we glimpsed before they went through and closed the portal. I fear it might be this mage, this... Ventat Obrey. A'vendyr said the man was here, fought one of Daemanon's Guardians."

"We have to go," Lorelle said. "We need to be back through the Thuros before sunrise."

Rhenn gave her a grateful glance and nodded. "Where's Slayter?"

"On the other side of the little half-wall."

They walked down the steps from the landing and turned the corner.

Slayter had his arms elbow deep in the chest cavity of one of the Giant corpses.

"Senji's Vomit, Slayter," Rhenn said. "Yuck!"

The mage looked up, pulled his dripping hands out of the entrails.

"I found two Plunnoi on them. One is a master Plunnos," he said.

"Well... great job, I suppose." Rhenn made a face. "But stop. We have to go."

Reluctantly, Slayter looked down at the Giant's corpse, then shrugged. He shook his hands at the ground, spraying viscera, then wiped them on his robes.

Khyven wrinkled his nose. "Even I think that's gross."

"Is there anything you won't do to satiate your curiosity?" Lorelle asked.

Slayter looked up at her, blinked like it wasn't a rhetorical question. "Like what?"

"Like stick your hands in rotting guts," Khyven said.

"Well, you just never know what you might find. It could be useful."

"Come on," Rhenn said.

They said their final goodbyes to A'vendyr and his people and went quickly to the Thuros room. The mesmerizing colors, which Rhenn dreamed about for so long now seemed like a dangerous promise instead. With the Plunnoi resurfacing, anything could come through those swirling lights. That gateway meant the world was a lot larger—and more deadly—than it had been before.

She flicked her Plunnos at the colors and thought of the basement room in her palace. It appeared.

Yes, there are new threats, she thought. *And we will meet them. We will be ready for them.*

And maybe, in this breath before whatever was going to come, she could enjoy the moment.

She looked back at the faces of her family. Khyven's steady gaze was already on her, confident, a guardian who wasn't going to let any harm come to her—to any of them—if he could help it. Lorelle stood next to him, eyes filled with a quiet concern, and behind her Slayter turned the bony, severed finger of a Giant over and over in his slick hands, studying it like it was talking to him.

She cracked a smile. Yes, there were many threats in the world. And she'd taken many scars, some so deep she didn't know if she'd ever heal from them, but she was still herself. E'maz had been right about that. Despite all that had happened, she was still Rhenn Laochodon. Her horrible adventure was over, and whether or not a hundred more were lining up to take its place, she was done with Daemanon. She turned back to the archway.

And, at long last, Rhenn went home.

CHAPTER FIFTY-FOUR

RHENN

Rhenn could not find her sword. Everything in the palace seemed upside down since she'd returned three days ago, since she'd tried to reclaim the reins of command while being completely unable to walk around in the daylight.

They were explaining it as a disease she had caught while visiting Imprevar—which was the cover story Lord Harpinjur and Vohn had invented to explain her abduction. This fabricated disease made Rhenn ridiculously sensitive to light, so for now she was holding all of her audiences in candle-lit rooms after the sun went down.

The story was holding, but there was going to be a time limit. They'd have to think of something better before long. Also, the candle-lit rooms were a little bit of torture for Rhenn. If they lit the lights too brightly, she could barely see. If they made them too dim, nobody else could see. She'd put in a request to Slayter to see if he could come up with a magical light that didn't burn her, but he'd been busy in his laboratory for three days straight. She knew he was feverishly working on how to extricate Vohn from the Dark, so she suffered the itchy eyes and throbbing headaches that came with the meetings.

After defeating Vamreth, she had enjoyed her royal duties. She'd taken easily to being queen, like the part of her that was born to rule was finally happy. She'd even enjoyed the trumped-up finery. But now every part seemed a chore. Being the center of attention while she had to hide at the same time was painful.

And so tonight she, Khyven, Lorelle, and Vohn were going to do something distinctly different. An adventure where she could unleash her new abilities.

A village in the south of Usara had been attacked, so they were going hunting. The little town of Duart had been utterly destroyed by noktum creatures, its people massacred. This had never happened as long as Rhenn had been alive. The noktum was highly dangerous, of course, but only for those who went into its dark embrace without protection. Only rarely did a single noktum creature leave the Dark to claim a victim. They never came out in force, and Rhenn had never heard of them attacking an entire village. It was a mystery, and she longed to get to the bottom of it.

But more than that, she longed to throw off her constant, careful restraint.

Tonight, she could leave behind the candle-headaches and her battle to keep from tearing at the necks of her nobles, alight with the lines of copper fire. Tonight, she would run through the noktum and maybe find some beast that looked evil enough that she wouldn't feel quite so horrible when she fed on it.

Senji's Boots, where the hell was her sword?

She'd left it right against the wall there; she was sure of it. But it was gone.

A knock sounded on the door. That would be Lorelle.

"It's open," Rhenn said.

Lorelle slipped inside the room, her cloak following her like a floating blanket of shadows. "You don't look ready," she said.

Rhenn hurled a pillow across the room in frustration. She just wanted out of the castle for a moment. Was that so much to ask? Something uncomplicated? Where was her sword?

"I can't find my sword."

"No?"

Rhenn detected the amused tone and turned. "You took it?"

"What makes you think that?"

"Because you sound suspicious."

"It wasn't me."

"You're lying."

Lorelle raised her eyebrows. "I? Lie?"

Rhenn narrowed her eyes. "Who has it?"

"Slayter."

"Why does Slayter have my sword?"

"Come find out." Lorelle turned and led the way.

They descended the five stairways down to the basement of the palace where Slayter kept his laboratory.

Rhenn knocked on the thick, iron bound door.

No answer.

They knocked again, louder.

"Yes yes yes," Slayter said impatiently from inside.

"I'm guessing that's our invitation," Lorelle said.

Rhenn pushed the door open.

Slayter stood over a round pan about two feet wide and six inches deep. It was filled with a dark liquid. He had a staff in the corner that gave off a blue glow that didn't burn Rhenn's eyes.

Interesting. *That* was what she needed in her audience chamber!

"Slayter, did you take my—"

"Quiet quiet," he murmured, holding a vial of some kind of blue liquid over the pan of chemicals. He dripped a few drops into the mixture. "All right," he murmured, and Rhenn was pretty sure he wasn't talking to her. He went across the room to where a hooded lantern burned. He carried the lantern back to the pan. "Just a moment. Just a moment."

He brought the lantern over the mixture, then removed the shield. Rhenn looked away, blinded, but she heard a pop and sizzle. The bright light vanished, and she blinked away the afterimages.

Slayter stood forlornly over the pan.

"Didn't work?" Lorelle guessed.

He sighed. "I think I've figured everything else out, but I'm pretty sure I don't have the right drops."

"What are you doing?" Rhenn asked.

"Trying to recreate N'ssag's formula."

"What?" Rhenn felt a spike of fear. "Why?"

Slayter looked up, seemingly surprised at the question. "Because I need to know. We all need to know."

"Why would you want to know how to make bloodsuckers?"

"Well, aside from the fact that it's good to know how our enemies gain their strength, I'm curious. Such knowledge could be put to many other uses than making bloodsuckers. The preservative qualities are amazing. It might help bring Vohn back, keep him in stasis long enough to give his body time to heal."

"Oh."

"I've worked out a little of what N'ssag did. He's a Life Mage of impressive abilities. I imagine he's one of the top magic users in all of Daemanon to do what he's done, so I'm studying up on Life Magic."

"Well, I don't want to disturb you. I just came to get my—"

"Yes, I've got your sword," Slayter interrupted as though reading her mind.

Rhenn glanced flatly at Lorelle, who just smiled. "Excellent. May I please have it back?"

"Took me a moment, but I think I got it just right." He brought Rhenn's sword up from behind his stone table, and he'd added a giant ruby to the pommel. It was affixed to the bottom with thin strips of steel that looped up and over the ruby, securing it in place.

"Slayter..." Rhenn said, and she fought the emotion that welled up within her. E'maz had made that sword for her. It was one of his only gifts to her, one of the only things she had left of him. She didn't want a ruby on it. She wanted it exactly the way it had been.

She fought her disappointment. Slayter was, no doubt, trying to do something nice for her, but it hurt to see the changes.

"Slayter, that was... balanced for my hand. You add too much weight to the end and it disrupts that balance—"

Slayter waved her argument away. "I thought of that. There are spells in and around the ruby. It and the steel bands weigh nothing. You'll see. Pick it up." He indicated the sword, and she took the handle, lifted it.

The entire sword was actually much lighter than it had been, still perfectly balanced. It moved like a dream.

"Thank you. It's pretty, but I'd like you to take the gem off. I want it the way E'maz made it. Surely you can understand that. Besides, rubies make me think of..." She trailed off. They made her think of the spike that N'ssag had stabbed into E'maz over and over, that had drained away his life force.

"Of the stick that N'ssag used?" Slayter put his finger right on that particular sore spot.

"Yes..."

"That's because it's the best stone for this kind of spell."

A chill went up Rhenn's back. "What spell?"

"Lorelle was telling me that, um, you were struggling with your new... abilities. The sunlight. Sucking blood—"

"Slayter..." Lorelle admonished.

"Oh, sorry." He looked apologetically at Rhenn. "Sorry. Not sucking blood. That's insensitive." He glanced at Lorelle for affirmation. She rolled her eyes. "The, uh, the removing of another's life force and making it your own."

"Just get to the point," Lorelle said softly.

"Right. Right. Well, I can't, um, I can't make it permanent. But if you spin the ruby—it's free floating inside the bands—if you spin it, it'll slowly turn back to its original position. The more you spin it, the longer it takes. And, for that time, you can be in the sunlight without burning. Like, five minutes, maybe."

"What?" Rhenn felt light-headed. "What are you saying? I can stand in the sunlight again?"

"For five minutes. Maybe. But you better be in the dark again when the ruby stops spinning. Oh, and don't drop the sword, or..." He chuckled, made an exploding gesture with his hands.

"Slayter," Lorelle admonished.

"Sorry. Don't drop the sword. It would be bad."

"Slayter... I don't know what to say. This is... this is an amazing gift."

"Oh, there's more. The bloodsuck..." He stopped himself, flicking a glance at Lorelle. "The... transfer of another's life force thing. That's what the ruby does. You see... Well, you know why you have to take the liquid that has the life force of—"

"Senji's Teeth, Slayter," Rhenn said. "Just call it blood."

"Right. Well, you have to consume living blood. We know this. But do you know why? It's because your body doesn't perpetuate itself anymore. It doesn't... remain alive unless you put more life into it. Because it died. But it was resurrected almost perfectly. Your heart beats. You're warm. You're just like a living person except you can't keep yourself alive. That's what the blood is. It contains lifeforce, and you have to replace that because your body doesn't do that through food anymore. You stay alive because you keep putting new life into yourself. But you *are* alive. Just... differently. You've been infused with a Life Magic that craves replenishment just like Lorelle and I crave food. So it's really the same principle. We—me and Lorelle—our living bodies process the food and turn it into life force—"

"I know what eating is, Slayter," Rhenn said.

"Well, you can't pull lifeforce from food anymore. I mean, you can eat it. Your body will digest it, just like a normal living person. And you'll eliminate your bowels just the same as you ever do, it'll look and probably smell the same—"

Rhenn made a face. "Slayter..."

"Ah. Apologies. The point is that you can't transform food into lifeforce anymore. Your body is purer. It requires a purer form of life force than food: blood. Now here's the interesting thing I discovered: N'ssag's stick was purer still. It took the lifeforce from E'maz's blood and stored it as energy in the ruby.

Then he could redirect it wherever he wished."

"Yes." Rhenn nodded. "He used that same stick when he brought me back. I was given the life force of a Mouth Dog."

"Exactly..." Slayter stopped, looked up. "A Mouth Dog? What's a Mouth Dog?"

"I'll tell you later."

Slayter looked disappointed. "Anyway, well, that's what this does."

Rhenn looked at the sword, then back at Slayter. "The sword?"

"You stab the sword into someone, and it sucks their life out." He nodded enthusiastically. "I put a little needle on the very end of the pommel. Just a short one. It will only go about a quarter of an inch into your palm. When that needle touches your blood, it will transfer the lifeforce into you. No need to drink blood."

"Transfer? Another person's life force?"

He held his hands out, smiling. "You don't have to bite anyone." He seemed particularly satisfied with himself.

"You're saying I can stab this sword into someone and steal their life force?"

"You have to, you know, stab the needle into your hand after. But yes." He grinned. "You don't have to, you know, feed anymore. And the best thing is, this should be a purer transfer. You should be able to go double the length of time you did before, between, you know, feeding. Maybe more."

"Slayter, I can't... I can't stab someone with this," she murmured.

"I'm not saying use it on a *friend*," Slayter said. "Chase down a deer with it. Anything living will work. I didn't mean go 'round slaughtering the countryside."

Rhenn frowned.

"You deserved better than you got, Rhenn," Lorelle murmured. "This will make it easier."

"I still have to kill things to live."

"Well, we all do, really," Slayter said. "Animals. Plants. This is just more direct."

"And insidious," Rhenn murmured.

"Insidious?" Slayter creased his brow. "I don't know that it's—"

"I'm sorry, Slayter. I just have a lot to..." She trailed off. "Thank you."

"I'll work on improving it," he said. "It's theoretically possible you could pull life force straight from plants, if that would make you feel better. Or maybe from just everything at once all around you, just a little bit from every living thing around you such that no one would know. But I haven't gotten there yet. I've mostly been focused on getting Vohn back. I'll try harder—"

She stepped forward and hugged him. "I didn't mean to be ungrateful. It's an incredible gift."

He stiffened in the embrace, patted her awkwardly on the back. "My pleasure, your majesty."

She ruffled his bright red hair. "Your majesty?"

"If we're done," Slayter said as though his mind had already moved on. "I have work I need to get back to." He turned back to his pan of chemicals.

"I think we are dismissed." Rhenn looked at Lorelle.

"Let's go poke Khyven in the finger with your new sword," Lorelle said as they headed out the door. "See if we can calm him down."

"Don't even joke about that."

"Just a little bit?"

"What's gotten into you?"

"I'm all dark now," Lorelle said.

Rhenn laughed as they left Slayter's laboratory and closed the door.

CHAPTER FIFTY-FIVE

SLAYTER

layter knew that Shalure would be in his laboratory. He opened the door and saw her in the corner on what he was beginning to think of as her chair.

She sat near the tall bookshelves with the room's single window in the foot-thick stone wall behind her. It only looked out onto another hallway. There was no natural light in the laboratory; it was too far beneath the palace. Of course, Shalure had already lit the lamps. Polite girl.

She greeted him with a graceful flicker of her fingers.

Good morning.

He gestured back.

I trust you are doing well. The sun was exceptionally red this morning, wasn't it? I stood on my balcony for nearly half an hour cataloging the different hues. Did you know that most people can't see all the hues of a sunrise?

She smiled at the long response.

No, she gestured. *I didn't know that.*

Clearly, she liked it when anyone spoke to her in the hand language Lorelle had taught her, and was still seemingly grateful that Slayter had taken an interest.

When he had first seen her and Lorelle talking with their hands, during one of their meetings in the Queen's Room, he'd been curious. So he'd asked to borrow the book. By the time the meeting was over, he'd memorized it, in between Rhenn's questions about the Great Noktum and Khyven's rather clumsily veiled attempts to learn about his own magic, something he'd finally taken an interest in.

The next morning Slayter had mastered the symbols with his hands.

In most physical endeavors, he was inept. He tripped at least twice daily. If Khyven asked him to leap over a barrel, Slayter would undoubtedly fall on his face. He had never focused much attention on even attempting to be athletic.

However, he *had* focused enormous energy and thought on making his fingers do exactly what he wanted them to do in every given moment. Line Mages needed precise lines. Fingers made lines. The better the lines, the better the Line Magic. It was a mathematical certitude. So finger dexterity was not an area where Slayter could accommodate his physical shortcomings. Because of this, his fingers were more deft and agile than those of even the ridiculously talented Khyven the Unkillable.

So mastering Lorelle's hand language had been relatively easy, and the next day when he'd seen Shalure and talked to her fluently, she'd been stunned. That had been three weeks ago, just after Rhenn had returned.

Since then, Shalure had taken to loitering in Slayter's laboratory.

As a general rule, he didn't like other people in his laboratory unless he had something specific to show them. Of course, when he'd been an apprentice, he'd been forced to work with others. And when he'd become Vamreth's court mage, he'd been forced to train apprentices. Or at least to try.

Every time had been tedious.

The truth was most people simply couldn't see magic at work, and those who could inevitably fumbled with the basics like a pig at a dinner table, flopping about with their cloven hooves. At best his apprentices, and even his former masters, had stared over his shoulder trying to comprehend what he was doing as he worked with line work or potions, like they could understand if they could just get close enough. Which was ridiculous. And they didn't. They never did.

Tedious.

But Shalure didn't have another place to be and Slayter considered, of the two evils of having someone in his laboratory and Shalure feeling ostracized, tolerating her was the lesser of those two evils. After all, she'd once lived in the north, the daughter of a baron with all the privilege and power to go with her station. Then she'd been Khyven's paramour. And then, of course, Vamreth's cat's-paw. But that was all done. Those avenues were shut. She couldn't—or wouldn't—go back to her father's holdings. Khyven was with Lorelle now. And Vamreth was dead.

From what Slayter could tell, the poor thing had no other friends or family, just their group. Clearly, she needed a friend. Normally, it would likely have been Rhenn. But with Rhenn's transformation and trying to reintegrate into her routine as queen, she was far too busy to take on new friends. Lorelle treated Shalure like a student. Khyven clearly felt awkward when she was around...

Which was a mystery, actually. Slayter simply didn't understand that. He knew it had something to do with the fact that Khyven and Shalure had been physically intimate with each other, and that now Khyven was physically intimate with Lorelle, but... Why?

Slayter knew this situation wasn't rare. Khyven and Shalure weren't the only ones to tiptoe around each other after grappling beneath the sheets and then doing away with that activity. He'd seen other nobles about the palace exhibit exactly this same behavior. He just didn't understand why. Did the person with which you'd been physically intimate fundamentally change after you stopped the act of copulation? He couldn't perceive it. Khyven was the same. Shalure was the same. But somehow they couldn't be in a room together without getting fidgety, avoiding eye contact and, in Khyven's case, sometimes blushing.

Slayter had thought about this odd behavior for a long time, and he had come to the only sensible conclusion.

It made no sense.

What *did* make sense, and was of particular relevance to Slayter, was that Shalure's sudden vacuum of potential friendship had made him a target. She had floated toward him like a feather toward the ground. If Vohn had been here, it would have gone differently. Slayter calculated an eighty-nine percent chance she'd have latched onto Vohn instead.

But Vohn wasn't here.

So when Slayter had picked up her hand language, she'd made his laboratory her new place, and Slayter her new friend.

The interesting thing was that he didn't find her tedious. In fact, he found her interesting. Spurned by Khyven, mutilated by Vamreth, she had found the strength to stand up into a new role. It was undefined as yet, but the grit was there. He saw it in her eyes every time he looked at her. She was going to be something new, she just didn't know what it was yet. And Slayter was highly interested to see what that was going to be.

She tapped the spine of a book to her right. Krudonae's *Life Basics: The Foundation of Zomajea.* A question. So polite.

He nodded, and she gently slid the old volume off the shelf, opened it up on her lap, and began reading. She took exceptionally good care of everything she touched. Another reason he didn't mind her being here.

Slayter set about the day's task. Every day's task. He laid out a new clay disk on his stone grinding table next to his spell scratcher and a pestle and mortar. She didn't ask him what he was working on. She knew, and Shalure didn't ask inane questions. She had a lively mind behind her mute mouth. Always watching. Always categorizing. Never asking a question when her brain could answer it for her. Always putting her knowledge to good use.

Refreshing girl. Fascinating girl.

He'd love to engage with her more, but for one of the rare moments in his life, he felt the pinch of time.

Slayter hadn't brought Vohn back yet.

After the discovery of the bloodsuckers and the Daemanon mage N'ssag, Slayter had assumed he'd have a dozen new paths to that goal.

Vohn's body had dematerialized almost exactly at the moment of death. His ability to do that was a rare racial trait held by a few Shadowvar, and Vohn had used it to save his own life. But once he reincorporated, all the wounds he'd sustained in the Great Noktum would also return. He'd die a second later.

Slayter had to stretch that second into ten.

He had concocted some healing spells, but each one of them required the normal focus, the breaking of a clay coin, and the pushing of Line Magic into the intended recipient. In other words, it required ten seconds to do it correctly. That was ten times too long. Of course, a living body was unpredictable. People had been brought back from worse than what Vohn had endured. Some people had been brought back to life after being dead for longer than ten seconds. Slayter figured that with his current resources, he had a sixty percent chance to bring Vohn back regardless, if he attempted the spell right now.

Sixty percent, though, was unacceptable. Slayter required a one hundred percent chance, and he had not found the way yet—

The door banged open like a bull had butted it, smashing into the wall and startling him. Khyven stood there, filling the frame like a portent of doom. He held a piece of paper.

"That was loud." Slayter winced. He knew it was a waste of time to try to stop people from being what they were, and even more futile to stop Khyven from being what he was, so Slayter didn't bother to request that Khyven not slam open doors in his laboratory.

"Have you seen Lorelle?"

Slayter squinted his eyes, envisioned a pair of bull's horns on Khyven's head. He could almost see them.

"Slayter!"

"Yes?"

"Lorelle!"

"What about Lorelle?"

Khyven crumpled the paper as his hand curled into a fist. Yes, Slayter could definitely see the bull's horns now. He wondered if he would ever be able to see anything else when he looked at Khyven—

"Senji's Teeth, Slayter, have you seen her?"

"I went straight from my balcony to here this morning. I've seen Shalure." He pointed a thumb over his shoulder.

Khyven looked at the corner, spotted Shalure, did an awkward blink, then avoided eye contact. He looked back at Slayter. "What?"

"I didn't see Lorelle. I saw Shalure."

"Why is that important?" Khyven winced at the words, then held up a pacifying hand to Shalure, still without looking at her. "I meant no offense, Shalure. It's not that... I didn't mean that you aren't important, it's just that Lorelle is missing."

"Lorelle is missing?" Slayter raised his eyebrows.

"That's what I said!"

"You asked if I—"

"Slayter!" Khyven's face reddened further, and he looked like he wanted to pick Slayter up by the neck and shake him.

Slayter's gaze flicked to the paper in his hand and he focused on filling in the blanks in Khyven's irrational behavior. "She left you a note. She went somewhere and left you a note."

"We all agreed we weren't going off on quests without the entire group."

"We did." Slayter held out his hand. Khyven crossed the room and gave him the crumpled paper. Slayter smoothed it out, glanced at it.

Went with Vohn. Nokte Murosa. No time. Back soon.

"Interesting."

"Interest—no, it's not interesting! We agreed we weren't separating. Rhenn and Lorelle, they said... All of us agreed we weren't running off solo anymore."

"Clearly she had no time to tell you." Slayter pointed at the paper. "That's what this line—"

Khyven brushed Slayter's finger aside. "I know what it says."

It finally occurred to Slayter what Khyven was actually asking. Why couldn't people just say what they meant? "You want me to find her."

Khyven rolled his eyes like Slayter was being the ridiculous one.

"I can find them. I made sure of it after our adventure into the Great Noktum."

Khyven's fierce gaze softened into satisfaction. "Good. That was well done."

"Ever since Lorelle vanished with the Nox, I took samples from each of you like Rauvelos suggested. I can find you whenever I need to."

Khyven's satisfaction wrinkled. His brows creased. "You did what?"

"Hair samples." Slayter pulled a pouch from his robes, opened it. He withdrew a lock of Lorelle's ebony hair, picked three strands from it and laid them on the stone table, and put the rest back into the pouch.

Khyven self-consciously patted his head. "You took my hair?"

"Not just yours—"

"When?"

"Do you want me to find Lorelle, or do you want me to tell you the story?"

"You can't just go taking people's hair for magic."

Slayter squinted. That was a fallacious statement. Clearly he could. Slayter tried to suss out the real meaning. "You mean 'shouldn't?'"

"Yes, I mean 'shouldn't!' Slayter, you—"

The door banged open again. Why did everyone feel the need to bang open his door?

Lorelle stepped into the room. She was slightly stooped, and the hand she held on the door had left a bloodstain.

"Lorelle!" Khyven leapt to her, but she warded him off.

"I know how to do it." She looked past Khyven to Slayter. "Or rather, Vohn does."

"You're bleeding," Khyven said.

"Like you've never bled before."

"You said you weren't going off alone."

"I was with Vohn."

"That's not the—"

"Khyven." She gave him a stern glance. Slayter had noticed Lorelle's stern glances had elevated since she'd become... dark. "The wound is fine. It can wait, but we only have so much time for Vohn. Let's get Slayter working then tend the wound."

Khyven's lips pressed into a thin line, but he nodded once.

With a deft gesture, she whipped the noktum cloak from her shoulders and tossed it at Slayter. It glided across the distance like a bird, then settled around Slayter's shoulders.

"We must be quick," Vohn spoke in his mind as the cowl rose and covered Slayter's head. *"I have learned much of late."*

"What was in Nokte Murosa?"

"A powerful mage named Ksara. She needed help, but that's another story. The noktum is alive, Slayter. It's sentient."

"You mean the way it connected to Lorelle? Like a craving-level sentience?"

"I mean that three Giants gave their lives to create that continent-covering spell. They're discorporate, like I am, except they don't have bodies waiting for them. They are the noktum. One of them wishes for me to bond with the Dark permanently. She'll never let you reconstitute my body if she can help it. But right now, at this moment, she is distracted. We have to move quickly."

"I haven't figured out how to keep you alive long enough to effect my spell."

"You won't need to. I can. Ksara showed me how."

"How?"

"With the Dark itself. But if we wait too long, Paralos will reawaken. She will find me. She will stop the Dark from helping me. Please, Slayter. Make your preparations now."

"They're ready. If you can keep yourself from dying for ten seconds, they're ready."

"*Do it!*"

Slayter nodded. If his friend said he could keep himself alive, he could. And if not, well…

Worry was a waste of time and energy. Slayter believed it was a much more constructive use of one's resources to concoct backup plans and pivot quickly.

Slayter knew of one certain backup plan. Or as close to certain as there was. He could bring Vohn back from the dead if he should happen to die. Slayter was almost one hundred percent certain he could recreate what N'ssag had used to make his bloodsuckers.

Of course, then Vohn would suck blood to live, so it wasn't ideal, but if there was no other choice…

Slayter took the cloak from his shoulders, placed it over the stone table, cleared away the pestle and mortar, and picked three clay coins from the shelf on the pillar nearby. He let them roll between his fingers as he prepared himself.

Khyven and Lorelle, who had seen Slayter cast complicated spells before, stood back, waiting. Shalure drifted closer, but he heard her footfalls stop about four feet behind him.

Slayter cleared his mind of everything. The laboratory fell away. Khyven, Lorelle, and Shalure fell away. The light from the lanterns dimmed in his vision, and even the stone table seemed to fade. All he could see was the cloak and the three disks he had painstakingly carved rolling between his fingers. He set the second and third disks down next to the cloak and held the first gently with his fingertips.

"Are you certain?" Slayter asked one last time, though his mind was already drifting into the spell.

"*I am,*" Vohn said.

Slayter drew a smooth breath, felt the magic in the clay, in his soul, in the elements and life and emotions all around him. The lines of the incomplete symbol on the clay disk began to glow orange. He picked up his spell scratcher, focused his gaze on the disk, and finished the final line. Orange light flared, and he felt the power rush through his body, into the disk, building up, building the pressure. It was like forcing an ocean of joy into a thimble.

The clay disk trembled, desperate to release the magic. Slayter held it... held it... until it contained every bit of magic he would need.

He lifted the disk and snapped it in two.

Orange flared in the room, plunging into the cloak, then coming back out swirling and settling on the stone table. At first, it simply looked like a blob of orange, then it swirled faster and faster like a hurricane trapped by some invisible walls that surrounded the table.

The orange light flared again, then vanished.

Vohn's body lay there, his arms and legs limp. That horrible arrow sticking up from his chest.

This was the critical moment. Slayter knew he could bring Vohn's body back from the Dark. The doubt lay in Slayter's ability to throw Vohn into stasis in time. This was the moment where his friend could die if Slayter couldn't do what he'd promised.

Slayter's mind hovered over the risks, but his fingers leapt to the task, smoothly picking up the second disk.

It was tricky attempting two spells at once. The diffraction of attention could cause both spells to fail. Quick succession was better, more powerful, though it required precise dexterity. Slayter snapped the second disk.

Orange light flared, half as brightly as the first spell. This disk didn't have to hold as much. It just needed to be quick.

A part of Slayter's mind kept meticulous track of the time. Seven seconds had passed. That was faster than he had anticipated. And it was six more seconds than Vohn's body could wait.

If Vohn's special trick didn't work...

That's when Slayter saw a line of shadow, like a tentacle from the noktum, flowing from the cloak to Vohn's chest where the black-feathered arrow stuck up like an unholy flag. Vohn's miracle assistance, no doubt.

"Pull out the arrow... Pull out the arrow... Pull out the arrow..."

Slayter had been so focused on his spell that he hadn't realized Vohn had been talking to him. The voice was getting weaker.

"Pull it out... Now..." Vohn said, and then his voice faded away.

Slayter yanked on the arrow, but it didn't come out. In every envisioning he'd done of this moment, the arrow had come out with one tug. But it was stuck. It was jammed into bone. It had gone through Vohn's heart into his ribcage.

Slayter had not counted on that.

Panic trickled into his mind, broke his concentration. He tugged again. The arrow did not budge. His focus fragmented. The magic began to retreat. He could see the table. He could see the walls of the laboratory. He could—

Khyven's big hand closed over Slayter's gently, carefully. The strength in those fingers compressed Slayter's hand excruciatingly over the arrow like a vice. Khyven yanked once, hard.

The arrow jerked free.

Then Khyven's hand was gone. Khyven was gone.

But Slayter's focus was still broken. He couldn't hear Vohn's voice anymore. He raised his hand, and it shook. He couldn't feel the magic. This was the part of the spell that Slayter was the worst at. Healing. He'd never been much interested in healing. He'd really only begun studying it because Khyven became a part of the group. There were always more bloody injuries around Khyven.

Slayter realized his thoughts were wandering. He realized he'd lost track of the time. He realized he'd lost track of his spell. He was failing. He was going to lose his friend—

A soft hand touched the back of his, and he glanced over. It wasn't Khyven this time. It was Shalure. She wasn't looking at him, though. She was looking directly at the hole over Vohn's heart, as though to guide his gaze.

He looked back at Vohn. There was still blood leaking from that wound. That meant Vohn was still alive.

Slayter's focus snapped back into place, and his fingers snapped the third disk.

The magic rushed into the wound, and it was more than Slayter expected, more than there should be. It was as though Shalure's touch had... funneled more magic through both of them.

For a long moment, Vohn's body glowed bright orange with light ribbons of red as well, but he didn't move.

Then his chest expanded, and Vohn gasped. He drew a shuddering breath, coughed, and drew another breath.

The magic rushed out of Slayter, taking almost every ounce of his strength. He sagged against the stone table. This exhaustion was nothing new. It came every time he used all the magic he could muster.

He heard a thump to his right and blinked to see that Shalure had collapsed to the floor.

Fascinating... he thought. That was a classic response for a first-time magic user. He would have to... Well, he would have to explore that later.

As Khyven knelt next to Shalure, Slayter felt Lorelle's warm grip on his shoulders, holding him up.

"You did it," she said, and there was a smile in her voice.

"Yes. It did... work. Do you know what he did? He held his heart together with pure darkness. He stopped his death with darkness."

"Yes, I know. That was what he learned from Ksara. She held herself together in a similar fashion."

"Fascinating."

Vohn groaned. He tried to sit up, and Lorelle left Slayter to help him. He groaned again, squinched one eye shut and focused the other on Slayter.

"You... couldn't make a healing spell that healed it all the way?"

"I'm not very good at healing," Slayter said.

"That's all you have to say?" Vohn grunted.

"I could say more." Slayter was already feeling better. His vigor came back quickly. "Did you know that Shalure has magic talent? I should have spotted that."

Vohn groaned again. "Senji's Patience, I should have stayed in the Dark."

Lorelle chuckled, glanced over at Khyven. "Is Shalure all right?"

"She's breathing. I… I don't know. What happened?"

"She helped with the spell," Slayter said. "She doesn't know how to draw from everything, though. So she took straight from her own life force. She's been reading Krudonae's scribbles. He was a fair hand at explaining obscurities, but he forgets some of the basics. Ironic, really, since his book is called—"

"Is she going to be all right, Slayter?"

"Oh, yes. She just needs sleep."

Khyven gave a sigh of relief. "Very well. Good."

"So… I have to live with this pain forever?" Vohn groused.

"No," Lorelle said. "We will get you patched up."

"No, I mean listening to Slayter prattle on. That pain."

Lorelle chuckled.

Slayter looked at his friend. He went around to the other side of the table, stood on his tiptoes and put Vohn's horned head gently between his fingers. He leaned over, careful not to jostle him, and kissed him on the forehead.

Slayter wasn't sure exactly why he did that; he only knew he wanted to. "I missed you, Vohn. I am glad you're back."

Vohn blinked. And for once, he didn't have anything to say.

Epilogue
RAUVELOS

Rauvelos was the steward of the Usaran Noktum.

The Humans and other mortal races that scuttled across the land thought they knew what Usara actually was. They saw it as a Human kingdom, something ruled by Humans back to the beginning of recorded time. In fact, their memories were so short they believed the Laochodon royal line was the only line that had ever ruled in Usara, aside from the recent usurper Vamreth. It was ludicrous from Rauvelos's perspective, but Humans barely thought in terms of decades. They never thought in terms of millennia.

Triada had been around for eight hundred years, created and ruled by Humans. Imprevar was barely a kingdom, having only existed for four hundred years. The ignorant Humans who ruled those places looked at Usara as their equal.

But Usara was ancient, and its history held more than a Human mind could comprehend. It had not been created by Humans, and it had only been ruled by them for seventeen hundred years. It was once the domain of Lord Nhevalos, and in those days Usara had extended all the way from the eastern tip of the claw to Imprevar's western shores, from the North Ocean to the southern tip of Triada.

Rauvelos had been born into that kingdom, a place of eternal night, a place where Lord Nhevalos had reigned supreme. That was before the Lux had broken the darkness apart. That was before Nhevalos had gone into his one-hundred year retreat, vanishing from the lands after the Purging of Iliut San where ten thousand Humans had perished beneath Harkandos's laughter.

That was before Nhevalos had returned and told the Noksonoi Lords they must free their Human slaves. That was before the Noksonoi Lords rose up and destroyed his kingdom, before they'd labeled him the Betrayer.

Rauvelos had not agreed with all of Nhevalos's wild notions about Humans. Perhaps even now, he still did not. But Rauvelos knew two things. The first thing he knew was power. He had grown up seeing the effortless way Nhevalos had ruled his realm, and he would never place a bet against his lord. There was no one smarter, more cunning, or more ruthless on any continent.

The second thing Rauvelos knew was loyalty. He had only ever served one master, and he planned to serve only one master until his bones and feathers sifted into the dirt.

Rauvelos was a part of Nhevalos's legend. He did not require his own legend and he never had. Nhevalos had taken hold of the forces arrayed against him and, with his incomparable will, had bent those forces into a shape of his desire.

For many years after the attack, the Noksonoi had thought Nhevalos dead. It was Rauvelos who found him, who nursed him back to health.

It was Rauvelos who had stayed by his side in those early days as Nhevalos plotted his rebellion. It was Rauvelos who had led Nhevalos's armies against the other Noksonoi in the Human-Giant War. And it was Rauvelos who had been put in charge of his master's tattered kingdom afterward, a steward over a barren land as his lord went out into the world to seed his plans.

Rauvelos had believed in his lord. He had bled for his lord. In Nhevalos's absence, Rauvelos had lived and breathed the life of his domain. There was no one who knew his lord or his lord's lands better.

And so, of course, Rauvelos sensed his master's return instantly. He felt the crossing of Nhevalos's life force from the realm of the Lightlanders to his domain. For the next half an hour, Rauvelos tracked his master's progress as the Kyolars and the Sleeths realized who it was and spread the word.

By the time Nhevalos walked through the broken gates, almost every creature in the noktum had gathered at the wall and Rauvelos stood at the window of Nhevalos's throne room, looking down at him.

The form his lord had chosen was short like a Human, and he strode across the cobblestones like one of them. But he exuded all the power of a master in his domain. He reached the center of the courtyard and looked up, directly at Rauvelos.

Nhevalos vanished and reappeared behind Rauvelos in the throne room. Rauvelos turned and bowed until his beak touched the floor.

"That is not necessary, old friend," Nhevalos said. "You need not bow to me."

"I made my choice long ago," Rauvelos said, and he rose to his full height, which put him looking down at Nhevalos again. He didn't like that, but he understood the need for Nhevalos to retain Human form. It was part of his mastery, part of his plan. It was one of many things that set him apart from the rest of the Noksonoi, and why he would always defeat them. Nhevalos would do anything—absolutely anything—for his vision. Even if it meant looking, acting, and living like a Human.

"You've done well here," Nhevalos said, walking around his throne as though he dared not come too close to it.

"I've done only what you asked me to do, master."

"I've been gone for a thousand years."

"As you say."

"I gave you no instructions regarding Khyven or his group."

"I sensed your hand upon him."

"Did you? I wonder if others may feel the same."

"I doubt it, my lord. I know your mind unlike any other."

"How did you guess?"

"He used Lore Magic in that odd fashion you were trying to perfect. And he was... lucky."

"And the others?" Nhevalos asked.

"They amused me."

"I had intended to let the Luminent die," Nhevalos said.

"I wondered about that. But it played out interestingly enough, and to your liking, I assume."

"It did."

"I assumed you did not want me to invade Tovos's realm. Not yet."

"Wise."

"But it was clear to me that I was not going to stop Khyven and his friends from walking into the Great Noktum. Not short of eating their legs, anyway. I assumed that if Khyven was your sword, facing Tovos might sharpen him."

"A gamble."

"Sometimes I cannot help myself."

Nhevalos fell silent, then looked up at Rauvelos. "I left you for ten centuries. You have the right to be angry."

"I am not angry, master."

"Indeed."

"Is it time to re-invoke the glory of Usara?" Rauvelos asked.

Again, his master went quiet.

"You do not intend to re-invoke the glory of Usara ever, do you?" Rauvelos asked.

"It is not for the Noksonoi to rule these lands. That includes me."

"You do not wish for these Humans to expand the Usaran kingdom to what it once was? They could rule it, if that served your purpose."

"We are not building an empire."

"What are we doing then, master?"

"Stopping one."

"I see."

"The pieces are in place. I only hope that they are strong enough to do what needs doing. Some things are impossible to tell."

"They faced Tovos and lived," Rauvelos said. "That was impossible. I am beginning to enjoy tallying the things Khyven does that are supposed to be impossible."

"The tests are almost at an end. Then the real contest will begin."

"What can I do to prepare, master?"

"You've done all. More than I had expected, everything I hoped. You've stewarded the most important pieces on the board."

"You had planned to use Khyven and the queen, but not the rest?" Rauvelos asked.

"I plan to use them all now. They have... exceeded my expectations. The group dynamics are... unexpected. An oversight on my part, perhaps. We Noksonoi do not work well in groups, so sometimes these things are hard to see."

"I agree, master."

"But my oversight can be useful."

"Queen Rhennaria is still your choice to lead the Human armies?"

"She is."

"Will her effectiveness in that role diminish now that she is... something new? Or was that part of your plan?"

Nhevalos moved to stand beside Rauvelos and stared down at the courtyard, but he didn't answer the question.

Rauvelos continued in another direction. "Will they follow her? She's more a creature of the noktum now than she is Human."

"That is precisely the reason they will follow her. In the days to come, they will not have a choice."

"Ah."

Together, he and his lord surveyed what was left of Nhevalos's kingdom. Rauvelos wondered if, at long last, the noktum would be restored to its original grandeur.

"And her baby?" Rauvelos asked. "Will it play a part, too?"

"Everyone plays a part," Nhevalos said. "Everyone."

INTERLUDE

KHYVEN

Khyven stepped down the last few steps and into the Thuros room, deep in the bowels of the palace. He'd snuck away from the party and, strangely, had followed his feet here. The Thuros glowed without illuminating anything. Blue, gold, green, red, and black swirled like colors on a lake.

He simply hadn't been able to stay upstairs. The party had been boring. And cold. Rhenn held this particular ball half-outside on the royal courtyard. In the snow. The early spring storm had blanketed the kingdom of Usara in a foot of white, but Rhenn had made the most of it of course. The moonlight ball, she'd called it.

Rhenn had started a new tradition of almost nightly galas, regular events where the nobles who wished to remain in the queen's good graces could see her, talk to her, build their cases with her. But two parties in a year was plenty for Khyven. One a month was simply ridiculous.

Lorelle, Khyven, and Lord Harpinjur had ensured the spreading of the rumors that the queen had taken a liking to galas upon return from her supposed travels to Imprevar. Over the months, Queen Rhenn had become a lover of the night, dance, and drink. It was a plausible affectation of an eccentric personality, and Rhenn played to it.

After all, it wasn't a difficult pivot for her to make. She had always loved drink and dance, a wink and a promise and, if the rumors from her rebel camp had been true, a turning of the sheets or two when the mood struck her. So it was in keeping with her old personality.

But Rhenn wasn't the same woman she'd once been. It wasn't just her new need for blood, either. What she'd gone through in Daemanon had stripped away her carefree veneer. Of course, Khyven knew that facade had always hidden a driven, calculating soul, but Rhenn's had also always been a happy one. A part of that light had died with her paramour, E'maz. Khyven hadn't known E'maz, not even a little bit, and he wondered what had happened, just how close the two of them had become.

He thought about his own happy ending, about how he'd never met anyone like Lorelle, and since the moment that she'd bonded with him, his life had never been the same.

Back in the Night Ring, he'd *thought* he'd known what he wanted, but now he was certain. He knew what he was. He was here to serve, not to acquire riches or titles or power or prestige, but to pit his abilities against the foes of his friends, against anyone who would threaten his family or what they were trying to do. He wasn't a killer anymore. He was a protector. A guardian.

Yes, Rhenn had changed. But they'd all changed. They'd changed as though it was building to something.

He looked down at his hands. Large, callused, competent... He could wield any weapon with the skills he'd built with the Old Man, with Nhevaz, and then in the Night Ring. But as good as he was with the instruments of killing, that's not what was special about him in the end.

"What you did requires more than training to fight... It requires magic."

Lorelle had said that to him during their first real conversation. Magic. Khyven's magic. She'd been right, and now that magic was changing. He didn't just see opportunities in battle. The blue wind was starting to tell him how to effect greater change. How to set up longer and longer sequences of events that allowed him to navigate danger and come out unscathed. The battle in Daemanon had proven that.

And so Khyven had come away from the party to think. He'd had to be clever about it to escape without Lorelle growing suspicious. Through their connection, Khyven could always sense when she was near, and he was sure she could sense the same about him. So he'd slipped away when she was engaged with another Luminent who had come to Usara.

Under Rhenn's rule, more strangers were coming in. Vamreth had always despised Shadowvar, Taur-Els, and Luminents. He'd discouraged trade and interaction with them, preferring to deal only with Humans. Over the last six months since Rhenn had been queen—the two months that Khyven had been asleep, the month Rhenn had been in Daemanon, and the three after she'd returned—she had done everything she could to encourage travelers to bring their business to Usara, and the kingdom was thriving.

He gazed at the Thuros, his feelings mixed.

So why this? Why come here?

Because the blue wind had beckoned him. Little wisps had threaded away from the party, and he had to know.

But the fact of the matter was: he didn't like this place. It was here he'd discovered his brother Nhevaz was someone else entirely. It was here where he'd almost died with the Helm of Darkness on his head. It was here that Rhenn had been abducted. It was here where her paramour had died. This very floor.

It was an ugly room, and it had only brought danger to his friends.

Khyven curled his fingers in and let his hands lower to his sides.

When he'd realized that this was where he was going, he'd

made a detour to his room to arm himself. Typically he only carried a dagger at Rhenn's galas. Lorelle liked to dance, and dancing with a sword was awkward at best. But when the blue wind was talking, Khyven knew that being armed to the teeth was the prudent course.

So he had his sword, the sword Slayter kept saying he should bond with, the Mavric iron blade that had killed Gohver. It didn't hurt Khyven anymore, didn't burn him, although it did speak from time to time, little whispers about what it wanted to do...

It didn't say anything now, though.

He stared at the Thuros's swirling colors, and he was fully prepared for something to happen.

And something did.

The blue wind rushed up the steps in a gust. The transformation of its nature wasn't always clear to Khyven now except when it came to the familiar life-and-death nuances of battle. So he wasn't certain what that was supposed to indicate.

But he *was* certain about one thing. He wasn't about to charge up those shallow steps and try to go through the Thuros without alerting his friends. Separating the group was a mistake they'd made a number of times now.

In fact, as the swirling colors began to melt away toward the sides of the arch, revealing a stone room beyond, Khyven was tempted to return to the stairs. Now he felt a little angry at himself that he'd come here alone, and he wondered if the blue wind had the ability to deceive him, to dampen his better sense.

So he might have been well advised to run. It was probably the prudent course.

But who was he trying to fool? He'd learned in the Night Ring there was rarely benefit to running, especially when you were outnumbered, because that's exactly what everyone expected. And he'd learned from Slayter, strangely enough, that running sometimes kept you from learning important information. So Khyven stayed. He watched.

Nhevaz came through the portal.

Nhevaz. Nhevalos. Rauvelos's master. Rhenn's abductor. And possibly the person responsible for every horrible thing in

Khyven's life.

No. Khyven wasn't going anywhere. Not until he had some answers.

Nhevaz was taller. Of course he'd always been taller than Khyven, but he was clearly growing. He was over seven feet tall now. Slayter had said the Giants of old could be as tall as fifteen feet. Was Nhevaz reverting to his normal state?

"Khyven," Nhevaz acknowledged as casually as he might have done back in the Old Man's camp.

Khyven slowly, dramatically, drew the Mavric iron sword. He didn't really want to kill Nhevaz. He wanted answers. But things didn't always go to plan, and Nhevaz was damned fast.

Nhevaz's hand rested on the pommel of his own sword. It was a relaxed gesture, and if it were any other swordsman, Khyven would have had the advantage. If it were any other swordsman, Khyven could lunge up those shallow steps in the blink of an eye and skewer his opponent while he was still fumbling to draw the thing.

But this was Nhevaz.

"Are you certain that's the first thing you'd like to test?" Nhevaz asked.

"Go ahead. Tempt me." Khyven set up a slow walk along the perimeter of the dais, his blade hovering at waist level, seemingly casual. This relaxed, draw-your-opponent-in tactic wasn't something Nhevaz had taught him. Khyven had learned it in the Night Ring.

The blue wind swirled around Nhevaz's feet like it didn't know exactly what to do.

Some help.

"You have learned much since last we met," Nhevaz said.

"'Since last we met'? Is that what you call it? You tricking me? You pretending to be Vex the Victorious and fighting for King Vamreth? You stealing my friend and turning her into a bloodsucker?"

"I didn't do that."

"No, you just kidnapped her and left her to a mage that

ripped her life out and turned it upside down."

Nhevaz didn't say anything to that.

"Are you here to kidnap *me* now?" Khyven asked. "Because that's not going to go the way you want it to."

"I'm here to help you."

"That sounds nice. The child I was would have believed you. I know better."

"Do you?"

"You're damned right. I know who to protect now. And I know who to kill." He pointed his sword at Nhevaz.

"Then you still know almost nothing."

"Yes. Try that. Insult my intelligence. I'm sure that's going to help you with whatever plan you have, Nhevalos the Betrayer. Yes, I know who you really are. The name suits you. So no, there won't be any more mystical brotherly advice. You're *not* my brother. You're a liar and a manipulator. Slayter told me everything."

"Did he?"

"Ancient Giant. Slayer of countless people. Master of that carnivorous raven Rauvelos in your castle. Schemer. Betrayer."

"Hmm."

"And the one who hurt my friend." Khyven almost leapt up the steps. Almost. He didn't like waiting. He liked pushing the action, setting the terms, forcing others to dance to his dance. But he could hear Vohn's quiet voice in the back of his head, almost as though the Shadowvar was here.

Not everything is solved with a fight, Khyven. By Senji, you've got to remember that or you're going to get us all killed.

So Khyven held back. He waited. He forced the stretching tension in his arms and chest to ease.

"You have come through your fire. Now it's time to use your power for what it was meant to do."

Khyven shook his head. "Look at what you did to Rhenn. The sun will kill her. She'll never see another sunset, another sunrise."

"Yes. Let's look at her. She is the queen of what will become the most powerful kingdom on Noksonon. Now she is a woman who can see in the Dark, can move through the Dark with ease."

Khyven narrowed his eyes and he felt a chill. "What are you saying?"

"The Dark is coming. War is coming. Rhenn has the power to lead her people, to lead all the people of Noksonon."

A premonition blew through the center of Khyven's chest like a cold breeze. Rhenn had told him everything Nhevaz had told her. "The Dark... over Usara?"

"Over everything."

"This is part of your war?"

"Everyone's war. The Eldroi will not stop at one continent. You can no longer afford your ignorance."

Khyven bared his teeth, stepping toward the dais. Forget diplomacy.

Surprisingly, Nhevaz stepped back. At first Khyven thought it was a retreat, but Nhevaz's long arm reached behind himself toward the portal, and Khyven saw the coin in his fingers. It tapped the plane between the archway, and the background shifted.

Now it was a large chamber of sharp-cut black stone with thick pillars widely spaced. Inlaid silver runes in a language Khyven had never seen before covered the pillars and adorned an arched doorway thirty yards distant.

A pitched battle of short, muscled soldiers roared beyond.

The defenders wore thick, heavily flanged and spiked plate mail of black adorned with gold and silver. Their helms varied from individual to individual, but they fought in small groups, and those groups wore matching cloaks with distinct standards upon them.

The attackers, on the other hand, all wore blocky, matching plate mail of dark gray and identical helms adorned with short, curling horns of black. Khyven recognized the symbol of Daemanon—a green, horned demon's head—decorating breastplates, shields, and standards.

Thick axes rose and fell. Shields clashed. Bearded men

screamed in fury and pain as they bled and died. The clash of steel reverberated through the Thuros like high-pitched thunder as more warriors pushed through that distant archway.

"It begins," Nhevalos said.

"What is this?"

"Daemanon. The Thuros Kraken'Suur, nestled within the depths of the Delver nuraghi Jul'Torai. The Wergoi are already moving on Deihmankos's command. Their mission is to secure all Thuroi." He looked at Khyven, who had stopped his advance and stood at the base of the dais. "I want you to come with me."

"No."

"There is someone you must meet." Nhevaz flipped the coin—the Plunnos—at Khyven. Reflexively, he caught it.

"I give you the key," Nhevaz said. "All you need do is flip it against the threshold and think of this place. It will bring you back."

Khyven wouldn't have believed Nhevaz except he'd just seen him use it. He clenched the coin, then glanced at the entrance to the stairway that led back up to the palace, back to his friends. Slayter had a spell on this Thuros. He should have sensed its usage like he had when Rhenn had come through. He should have been here by now. Him and the rest of them.

"I've disabled your mage's spells," Nhevaz said, as though reading his mind. "Come with me, Khyven."

Khyven looked back through the portal. Now he saw a man, a Human, fighting alongside the "Delvers." He was the same size, the same build as Khyven.

"There he is," Nhevaz said.

There was something eerily familiar about the Human fighter. The blue wind swirled past Nhevaz and through the Thuros, circling the fighter.

"Who is that?"

"Come with me. I will show you."

Khyven looked down at the Plunnos gripped in his fist. He gave one last glance to the stairway, then leapt up the steps and through the Thuros. Nhevaz followed languidly, like he wasn't in a hurry.

Khyven half-expected the Thuros to flicker and return to the swirling colors, but the portal back to Usara stayed open.

The fight continued to rage. A few had noticed the two of them, and it seemed that none knew exactly what to make of them. Aside from their armor and the demon-head standard, Khyven couldn't tell the difference between the Delvers and the Wergoi—they both seemed short and burly.

Nhevaz knelt, put his knuckles to the ground, and whispered something.

The flagstone floor shook. The attacking half of the short, armored warriors suddenly fell through the ground up to their necks. The ground solidified, and the warriors—Khyven guessed the Wergoi—were all imprisoned.

The raw display of magic stunned Khyven. Nhevaz stood again, and one of the Delvers turned. He had a blocky nose and a mix of fiery red, orange, and gray-streaked hair that spread out from his scalp in a wiry mane. His unbraided beard seemed to have a life of its own, and his armor was done in the same style of his people, with one difference. It also bore the Daemanon symbol etched into the collar ring, except not quite the same as the symbol on the attacking army's standard. It was that same demon's head, but transfixed by a Delver sword.

"Lord Nhevalos." The Delver fell to one knee. "I thank you for your assistance, but that was unnecessary. I beg you save your magic."

"I did not do it for you, Thorfyll. I have come for the Guardian Rellen."

Thorfyll glanced at Khyven, and then a glimmer of recognition widened his eyes. His taciturn expression softened to… What was that? Surprise?

"Is this him?" Thorfyll asked.

But the Human behind Thorfyll, suddenly bereft of enemies—all of whom struggled helplessly, half-buried in the floor—turned toward Nhevaz and Khyven. He strode closer. A tiny black dragon with green eyes rode the man's shoulder, its tail coiled about his neck.

As he neared, that eerie sense of familiarity grew. The man was probably about ten years Khyven's senior, but he had the same dark hair, the same wide set to his shoulders.

"Thorfyll. What's... Is this who I think it is?" the man asked, absently reaching up to stroke the chin of the dragon on his shoulder.

"Rellen," Thorfyll said. "This is Lord Nhevalos of the Noksonoi."

Rellen's brows crouched low over his eyes.

"The one who loosed Nissra upon my kingdom?" His voice simmered, and his eyes seemed to glow with anger. "Nhevalos the Betrayer—"

"Mind your tongue, Guardian," Thorfyll warned.

Rellen seemed ready to ignore the Delver. His hand twitched like he wanted to draw his sword, and Khyven decided he liked this Rellen.

Rellen flicked a glance to Khyven. "And who is this?"

Nhevaz ignored Rellen's question and turned instead to Khyven.

"Khyven, meet Rellen of Corsia," Nhevaz said. "Your brother..."

INCENDIUS

BONUS SHORT STORY

T he moment the betrothal celebration began, a stifling heat grew in Kaela's chest, squeezing her lungs until it felt like she was suffocating. No one seemed to notice. Mugs clink and ale flowed. The smoke from the fireplace hung in a haze above the shifting bodies and the dancers in the center of the room. The musicians flogged their instruments, but it sounded like a chaos of dissonance. Surrounded by Mother, Father, all of Kaela's relatives, and the Vyndholm Clan, she felt trapped.

The notion of escape grew in her head until it was irresistible, until something inside her burst, and a cool thrill spilled throughout her body.

She could escape, if she wanted to.

Father laughed with Duke Vyndholm, and the Duke's son—her betrothed—smiled charmingly at Mother. Kaela stepped backward, and no one noticed. The thrill grew, tingling through her. It almost seemed magical that no one noticed as she took another step back, then another, then made for the southern archway. People looked at her, but it was almost as though they looked through her, as though a princess escaping her own betrothal party was perfectly normal to them. No one stopped her.

She stepped into the hallway and left the stifling heat and attention behind, then immediately ducked into a servants' corridor.

It seemed odd to her—only for a moment—that she so desperately needed to escape the celebration. Maerlond seemed a nice enough fellow, and marrying the Duke of Vyndholm's son was her duty. Kaela had always done her duty.

She ducked down one servants' corridor after another, startling the men and women bringing trays of food the other direction. She had never explored the servants' corridors before, even as a girl, but she quickly found the servant's entrance to the southern side of the castle as though she'd known exactly where it was. She borrowed a fur-lined cloak from one of the hooks and plunged into the storm.

She stepped and slid down the pathway, and the thrill increased. It was as if the further she went into the cold, the greater the thrill.

The cold wind stung her eyes and ruffled the fur-lined collar of her cloak. She stopped, again feeling a slight hesitation, and squinted back up the trail toward the castle. Aside from her barely visible footprints, the path was covered with drifts and was slowly disappearing in the storm. Except for the barest shadow of the looming castle, she might have been in the middle of some distant woods rather than a stone's throw from the seat of power in the Kingdom of S'kai.

Her Father and Mother would follow her, of course, and soon. They'd send out the King's Scouts, men and women who could track a fish through water. But princesses didn't use servants' corridors nor servants' entrances, so that would throw them. It would take them time.

She tromped to the barely visible bend of the path and into

the forest, pushing her boots through the thickening snow. At first, she didn't know where she was going. The thrill pushed her forward and she felt enormously glad to escape heat of the feast, the bodies filling the hall, the happy smiles all around. Every face had seemed a twisted mirror that reflected her desperation to escape, to be free.

She stopped before a lake. A thin sheet of ice covered its surface at the recent plunge in temperature. Yesterday had been mild enough to walk in short sleeves and skirts, but that was the way the weather came in S'kai. One day it was warm. The next, winter was upon them.

She stared at the ice. The boys from the city surrounding the castle came here sometimes to engage in a daring game, imitating the King's Warriors. She had watched a group of them last winter from her high window. The day had been bright and clear, and the boys had stamped the ground with their boots and shoved each other about by the water's edge. Plumes of winter breath had drifted up from their mouths as they laughed and dared each other to break the ice, to bathe in the frigid water like the King's Warriors did after a bloody battle.

The men who had felt Creili's Song, who had slain their enemies and returned alive, would bathe the blood from their bodies in frigid water. The lives of the slain—enemies and comrades alike—were washed into the water, given as sacrifice to Creili, the Goddess of Battle, to demonstrate that they the warriors had walked through blood and fire and were still free.

The people of S'kai believed—and Creili demanded—that they should bend the knee only to Her. The mantra of the King's warriors was "Live free and die clean." Bending the knee to anyone besides the goddess meant you were a coward.

Kaela's new thrill pushed her toward the edge of the lake. She felt reckless, alive, and maybe for the first time she understood why the warriors laughed when they plunged into the icy water.

Without even knowing what she was doing, Kaela pulled the drawstring of her stolen cloak, letting it fall heavily into the snow. The cutting wind gleefully stabbed at her through her thin gown, made especially for today's event. It was an expensive piece, with the thin fabric of the south expertly sewn together with soft mink fur.

She shivered, but Kaela's fingers worked at the buttons that started at her hip, followed the curve of her waist, in front of her right arm, all the way up to her neck. One by one, the buttons released, and she wriggled free. The gown fell by her cloak. The shock of the air stole her breath, but it also swept away that stifling, crushing feeling she'd had. She stripped out of her small clothes and her boots, and she felt free for the first time that night. Free like the warriors who celebrated their battles here.

Her first step in the icy snow sent pins into her feet, but she walked naked to the water.

She stepped tentatively onto the thin ice, expecting it to break. It didn't. The wind swirled into her, each flake of snow like a tiny knife, again and again. She took another step further out, and the ice was so cold her feet began to lose sensation. She hissed and stepped again. Still the ice didn't break.

Her teeth began to chatter, so she clenched them, and her whole body shivered. She stomped on the ice. Still nothing. She took three more steps toward the middle and stomped again. Nothing.

With a cry, she jumped up and came down with both heels—

The surface broke so quickly and completely she dropped without warning, plunging into the icy water. The shock of it ripped the breath from her chest.

The murky twilight of the snowstorm vanished as paralyzing cold grasped her. It was absolutely dark beneath the sheet of ice, and for a moment she thought she had killed herself. She'd heard—everyone in S'kai had heard—the stories of the incautious who had traversed the frozen lakes too early in the winter or too late in spring. Those who fell through rarely survived.

And she had walked too far out.

She groped for the hole above, but she couldn't find it. Only a solid ceiling of ice. Her body felt like it had been poked with a thousand frosted picks. Her chest convulsed, wanting to draw breath, but she managed to keep her mouth shut. Her arms flailed. Her legs thrashed—

And her toe scraped through frigid mud.

The bottom! She pushed the same aching leg down, down toward that mud, and her foot smooshed into it. She swept down with her other leg, barely touching the mud, and she churned her legs in a running motion, praying to Creili that she was faced toward the bank and not away.

Luck—or Creili herself—came to Kaela's aid. Each foot dug deeper, and her body moved through the water. She swiped with her flagging arms.

Her head knocked against something hard, and her hands flew up to meet it. The ice. She slammed the heels of her palms into it.

It didn't break.

Her lungs burned, a mocking heat in the midst of the killing cold, as she ran out of air. If she didn't get free soon…

She banged again with her hands. The ice held.

Bubbles of panic escaped her mouth.

She set her numb legs to working again. They barely responded at first, but soon she had them churning, scraping mud with her toes. Slowly—terrifyingly slowly—she pushed her body further up the slope. Once she could push her feet solidly into the mud, she surged forward, wedging herself against the ice.

She shouted underwater, and rush of bubbles exploded around her as she pushed upward with her numb legs.

The ice shattered, and she surged upright. She flung her head back, gasping. She shuddered, then sucked in another desperate breath.

She stood there shaking, waist deep in the freezing water, surrounded by shards of floating ice. The snow fell harder now. Her eyelashes and hair began to freeze immediately and she frantically looked for her clothes on the bank.

She spotted them and tried to move toward them, but her numb legs were knotting up.

With a pitiful cry, she pulled her right leg up and out of the mud with her hands, and plunged it down again. Then the left. Then the right.

She punched the crust of ice around her with her fists, breaking it so it wouldn't cut her thighs as she surged forward. With every step it was easier to take the next. If she stayed still too long, she'd freeze solid, but if she could just keep moving, she could reach her clothes.

Finally, she emerged from the shallows and reached longingly for her pile of clothes—

A man stood behind them. He was tall, even taller than her father, with wide shoulders, a broad chest and the long, muscled arms of King's Warrior. But that was where his resemblance to a native of S'kai ended. The northern islanders of her homeland were fair haired and blue-eyed. This southerner had long, thick black hair tied back in a ponytail and black eyes that seemed to cut through the storm to drill into her. He wore no cloak, and the sleeves of his tunic were short, yet he seemed unaffected by the cold.

She gasped and recoiled.

"Avert your eyes, st-stranger!" She commanded through chattering teeth, twisting and covering herself with her hands.

He didn't turn away. Instead, he appraised her.

"D-Do you kn-know who I am?" She demanded. She realized she would hardly cut a royal figure mud covering her legs to the knees and her arms to the elbow, with her hair tangled and frozen. She undoubtedly looked anything but a princess at the moment, but her imperious voice was the only weapon she had.

His black gaze locked on hers, and she felt a chill. There was no lust in his stare. It was like he was judging a lamb shank.

Her shaking legs began to knot up again, and she knew she had to get to her clothes, get warm again, or she'd never take another step.

"If you d-don't want my f-father to c-cut your head from your b-body, you will t-turn and leave immediately," she chattered. She looked longingly at her clothes, half-buried in a snowdrift. Who was this man? What was he doing here? He didn't seem like a brigand, but neither had he been at the party, or at least she'd not seen him. Surely she would have noticed someone so tall and strange. Even the mainlanders did not look like this man.

"Princess Kaela," the tall man finally said.

So he did know who she was. His accent was something she had never heard before, dark and lilting. There was no trace of the harsh gutturals her people used.

"M-My clothes," she said. "If you p-possess even a s-sliver of honor, you will t-turn your back that I m-might dress. Or w-would you rather I f-freeze to death?"

"Ah," he replied, as though only now realizing she was cold. "Of course."

But instead of turning away so that she might dress, he raised his gloved hand.

Heat engulfed her. It was as though she suddenly stood in the corner of the royal kitchens between the two big ovens. The frost in her hair melted. The numbness in her frozen limbs turned to needles of fire as they warmed up in an instant.

She gasped, eyes flying wide. Even though she was knee-deep in freezing water, snow whipping into her, she could not feel the cold! The snowflakes that had previously frozen her hair and collected on her skin melted when they touched her.

The man was a mage, a powerful one! Aside from the discomfort of being thawed so quickly, the spell hadn't hurt her. Even Father's strongest Land Mages—men and women who could alter the elements—could not have done something so precise. Yes, they could conjure fire, but not this precisely. They'd have burned her to a crisp.

"Who are you?" she whispered, her modesty forgotten. This man wasn't just a stranger to S'kai. He was…something other.

He beckoned, gesturing at her clothes. The gesture was patient. But his eyes were not. They were black and depthless, and she sensed that a well of frightening power lay behind them.

She swallowed.

"Everything shall be revealed, Kaela Fjorlund. Information I have in plenty. Time, I do not. Please…" He gestured again at her clothes. "We must hurry."

He spoke so oddly, like he was born of another age. She had thought his strange accent came from one of the southern realms she had not yet visited, but now she wondered if it was not a different realm from which this man hailed, but a different time. A shiver went up her spine.

"Where are we going?" Her soul whispered to her that this moment was the most important that she'd ever experience.

"The world needs you, Kaela Fjorlund. You and you alone."

A fierce sense of rightness swept through her, as though her soul had been but an incomplete puzzle until now, and his words were the missing piece.

"Why me?" she asked.

He held out his hand. "Come, Kaela Fjorland."

She swallowed, and with legs that now felt more invigorated than they ever had, she picked up her undergarments. They, too, became instantly warm and dry, and she put them on. She dressed in silence as the man watched. Once she had buttoned the last button and thrown her snowy fur cloak over her shoulders, he turned and strode into the woods, away from the castle.

She looked back the way she had come, toward home, toward the castle.

"I should tell my parents," she said.

He kept walking. He was almost out of sight. Kaela felt her chest compress when she looked back at the castle, that same stifling feeling she'd had at the party. But when she looked after the stranger, the thrill raced through her. She ran after him.

"When will we return?" she asked as she caught up with him.

"A war is coming, Kaela Fjorlund, a war unlike anything the

world has seen for millennia. Your kin. Your nobles. The nobles of Pyranon. All will die, slaughtered in droves. Unless you do something."

Her eyes went wide.

"What...war? What can I do?"

"You can give your people a chance to fight it... perhaps even win it."

"How?"

He didn't answer, his long strides cutting through the snow effortlessly. She stumbled to keep up as he guided her through the trees.

They strode through the forest for what must have been an hour. By now Mother and Father would surely have sent a search party for her. Maybe they would have seen the broken ice of the lake. They might even now be dredging it, looking for her drowned body.

But still she followed him, followed that thrill that lit her up. The war he mentioned seemed alive in her mind. Flames and the screams of the dying. Father and Mother dying.

The man finally broke through the edge of the forest, and she suddenly knew where they were. A broken tower and the ruined walls of the ancient structure called The Scal Scorlix loomed in the storm. The Scal Scorlix was a nuraghi, a structure the soothsayers claimed had been built by Giants during a time before time, when the enormous man-like creatures had walked the lands.

"Why are we here?" she asked. A quick flash of fear raced through her. She was far into the wilderness with this man, far away from anyone who could protect her. But the fear came and went, leaving only the thrill of adventure again.

He strode up to the broken door, stepped through, and she followed. He wound his way through the hallways—with debris-strewn floors and cracked walls—like this was his home, like he knew every turn intimately.

They descended a set of stairs, then another, down into the pitch black.

"I can't see anything!" she said in a high-pitched voice. His hand closed around hers, and he gently pulled her forward.

"I can," he said.

She clung to his hand. It was neither rough nor smooth, almost as though it wasn't real, as though it had been made to be the perfect mold of a hand. She could see nothing, but she heard scuttling, breathing, even growling in that darkness. The quiet thumps of paws and clicks of nails crossed the stones nearby, and she cringed. Those were not small animals. Not just rats, but something large. Many of them, lurking in the dark. She could sense the hunger of the beasts as they whined, like they were being kept from a morsel they would happily devour if only...

But nothing attacked them, and she was certain it was because of the tall stranger. They feared the man with the dark eyes filled with dangerous power.

She didn't know how many staircases they descended. She became so disoriented by the darkness that she didn't even know how long they had been walking. It seemed a never-ending spiral into the bowels of an abyss, down and down and down.

Finally, they stopped and the floor flattened out. They seemed to be walking straight, perhaps down a hallway.

She began to think she could see faint lights, colored lights, and she wondered if her mind was playing tricks, conjuring colors because she desperately wanted to see something.

But the colors grew brighter. Green, red, blue and brown swelled in the ever-present darkness, coming from around a corner ahead.

Every person in the kingdom—whether they were a king's daughter or not—had wondered about this place. Where the nuraghi had come from, and what was inside. She had heard boys bragging about having entered the forbidding structure, but they had to have been lying. And if they'd dared enter, they'd certainly never come this deep. She doubted even Father's scouts had come this deep, or if he even knew about these catacombs.

The stranger rounded the corner and pulled her into a wide, circular room. On the far side stood an archway as tall as the ceiling, the source of the swirling colors. They filled the arch from side to side and top to bottom, like a vertical pool of colored water bordered by the arched stones.

The colors flared to life when they entered the room, as though greeting the stranger.

"What is it?" she whispered.

The stranger stopped before the archway, let go of her hand, and looked down at her with those depthless black eyes.

"Let us talk for a moment," the man said, turning to face her.

She looked up at him.

"You have heard of Giants?" he asked.

"Of course. Legends," she murmured. "Fictions made by soothsayers of old to scare children into obedience."

"Before humans ruled the peninsula you now call S'kai, before humans ruled the mainland of Pyranon, Giants did. Yes, Kaela Fjorlund, unfortunately for you and all the races on Eldros, we are very real."

She swallowed. "We?"

"My name is Nhevalos. I am one of the Noksonoi."

"The Noksonoi…" She drew a long breath and had difficulty exhaling. It was as though she wanted to keep drawing and drawing more breath. Commoners wouldn't know what the Noksonoi were, but as a member of the Royal Housse of S'kai, she had been required to read the old texts, the stories of the times before.

The Noksonoi were Giants from a continent called Noksonon. Just as the Pyranoi were the Giants who had supposedly lived on Pyranon.

Noksonon was supposedly a continent that S'kai—that all of Pyranon—had once had contact with. As were the continents of Shijuren, Drakkanon, and Daemanon. But…she'd thought those were only legends.

"You're saying you are a Giant?" she blurted.

He stared at her, his cold black eyes steady, and she saw that same frightening power. She saw a thousand deaths reflected there; she saw the passage of time, the ages of humankind this creature had seen flipping past one after the other like pages in a book. She saw fire and blood and screaming people. Her heart thundered in her chest.

"There are no such thing as Giants," she whispered, but without conviction.

"They want the world back, Kaela, and unless you truly wish for humans to prevail, they are going to get what they want."

"What can I do?" she whispered.

"Follow your heart," Nhevalos said. "As you followed it to the lake. As you followed it here with me."

She felt that thrill, that drive to continue forward, so unlike her. She'd never felt anything like it before, but he was right. It had pushed her here, and she wanted to go further.

He held out his hand.

The thrill leapt through her as she took it. He stood up and pulled a huge coin from a pouch at his side. It had the symbol of Pyranon engraved on one side—the five-towered castle engulfed in flames—and another symbol on the other side—a demon skull with seven horns around its face. He flipped the coin at the swirling surface of the archway. It rang as though the pool of colored water was solid as stone. The coin rebounded directly to his hand, and he pulled her forward. She gasped as they both went through the archway. It felt like she was submerging herself in oil.

They came out the other side and she gasped, grasping her arms, expecting them to be covered in colored oil, but they were dry. She looked back at the archway. Its swirling colors looked the same on this side, but this wasn't the same room at all.

First of all, it was filled with people, but they weren't like any people Kaela had ever seen. They were all shorter than she was, but almost as wide as they were tall, with powerful shoulders, stout legs and wide necks. There were close to a dozen of them, and each wore thick plate mail that would have crushed her to the ground if she'd put it on. Her people never wore plate mail, but she'd seen knights from the south in such garb. They always had visored helmets. These compact men did not. Their stout helms only covered the tops and backs of their heads, with flanges of thick steel protruding down to protect their ears and their noses. And every single one of them wore braided beards, much like the men of S'kai.

"My lord," one of the short, stocky men said, removing his helm and going to a knee before Nhevalos.

"Thorfyll, this is Princess Kaela Fjorlund of S'kai on Pyranon," Nhevalos said.

"Your Highness," Thorfyll said respectfully, bowing his head a second time. He stood up and replaced his helm. His full plate armor looked even heavier than that of his fellows, and the man seemed made of pure muscle. A symbol was engraved on the neck plate of his armor, a demon head just like on the huge coin Nhevalos had used on the portal, except this symbol had a dagger thrust up through the head.

"Kaela, this is Thorfyll, a Delver of the Klymrukaar and Warmaster to the Duke of Draksymsur."

A Delver! Kaela had a flicker of a memory. She'd read about men who lived their lives beneath the earth, cutting resources from the rock. More legends and myths…

"The Wergoi have broken through the perimeter in the K'uleth tunnels," Thorfyll said, his dark eyes intense.

"Are they near?"

"No, my lord. A skirmish, nothing more. We hold Nuraghi Jul'Torai and the keep of Kraken'Suun above. They cannot hope to breach these walls and reach the Thuros. But we will escort you to the surface nevertheless."

"Good. We'll use the north entrance. I have no wish to be seen today."

"Of course, my lord. It has been prepared."

Nhevalos nodded and strode to the doorway, holding Kaela's hand. Thorfyll and half the Delvers in the room fell in line behind, weapons drawn. Fear flickered through her. Had she emerged in this new place in the midst of a war? At first, the hallways seemed to be hewn from pure rock. That gradually gave way to blocks of stone and mortar meticulously placed and polished.

"Where are we?" Kaela asked.

"Daemanon," Nhevalos said. "Beneath the Sylverwylde Mountains in the kingdom of Pelinon."

Her fear transformed again into that thrill as Nhevalos led her forward. It seemed to take as long to emerge from the tunnels of this new place as it had to descend into the bowels of the Scal Scorlix.

Nhevalos and Kaela emerged from the dark stone corridors at last into the bright sun. The air was warm and humid, a stark contrast to the blowing winter of S'kai. Down the slope away from the cave's entrance lay a lush jungle and a single, well-worn road snaking between the trees and the slopes upon which they stood.

"Your mounts are refreshed and ready, my lord," Thorfyll said.

"Very good," Nhevalos said.

"The king approaches," Thorfyll continued. "You will find him just over the bridge spanning the Drakvoria River."

Nhevalos nodded, then turned to Kaela. "We will have to tear your dress so you can ride."

Thorfyll glanced at Nhevalos, then back at Kaela. He unsheathed a dagger and flipped it in his hand, catching it deftly by the blade. He extended the hilt to her. Kaela hesitated, then took the knife. She expanded the slit on the right side of the gown, popping buttons, until it freed up her legs enough to ride. She gave the knife back to Thorfyll, and he sheathed it.

"Your Highness." Thorfyll held one thick, powerful hand like a ledge next to a bay mare. She glanced at Nhevalos, who nodded, and she stepped into the Delver's hand. It was like stepping on a rock. He didn't even move as she put all of her weight on his hand and launched into the saddle. The thrill of the adventure washed through her again.

Nhevalos mounted smoothly. "Thank you, Thorfyll."

"Always, my lord. Godspeed." He thumped his fist against

his plated chest in salute, and it rang loudly.

She and Nhevalos rode. She had a dozen questions, but he seemed intent on setting a swift pace, so there was no time for talking. The sun had already set when they crossed a sturdy stone bridge wide enough for two wagons abreast. The stonework was the finest she'd ever seen, and the crystal clear river below flowed swiftly.

On the far side, they soon neared a huge encampment. At first she'd thought they were Delvers again, as so many of them wore gleaming platemail, but as they came closer, she saw they were clearly men. Others—obviously the lesser fighting men or camp workers—were dressed somewhat like the mainlanders of Pyranon. They wore more greens and browns, not as many yellows and reds, and their clothing was obviously of lighter, thinner fabric due to the pervasive humidity.

Nhevalos turned into the dense forest almost immediately after crossing the bridge and skirted the edge, staying just within the protection of the foliage. Soon, stopped at a spot overlooking the encampment, dismounted and helped Kaela down.

"It is time," Nhevalos said.

"For what?" she asked.

"To help the world," Nhevalos said. "To follow your heart."

"I don't know what that means."

He gave a reassuring smile. "I think you do. I did not choose you by accident, Kaela Fjorlund."

She held her hands out. "What must I do?"

"Have you felt anything unusual this night? A compulsion within you? A push in a particular direction?"

She thought of the thrill that had passed through her for the first time at the stifling betrothal party. Every time she thought of either going back to the castle or turning away from this adventure, the thrill had vanished. But every time she had followed Nhevalos, every time she had chosen to go forward, she'd felt that thrill.

"Yes," she breathed. "I feel it."

"That is what you must follow. It will guide you."

She looked down at the camp, men and women moving about their duties, tents everywhere. Her gaze fell upon the large tent in the center. A banner flew above it. It was twenty feet tall and six feet wide with a white, winged sword suspended amidst a field of blue, trimmed in gold. It was obviously the leader's tent.

"It tells me to go there." She pointed.

He nodded. "Then go."

"I just…walk through the camp? It looks like they are a war band of some kind."

"I will ensure that you arrive safely."

The thrill tugged expectantly, pulling her toward that tent.

"Go," Nhevalos murmured.

She descended the slope, every second waiting for the alarm to go up, for the armored men to notice and swarm to her, this strange woman in a gown emerging from the jungle.

No one did.

She walked right past them all, and a swift chill went up her back. Several times one of mailed soldiers or camp workers would look at her, then they would turn away as though they'd recognized her, as as though she belonged.

She went up to the large tent, and the two guards outside watched her pass, but then they stared into the night as though she was nothing more than a fluttering moth.

As she closed the flap behind her, the lone man wearing a king's raiment and a crown looked up at her in surprise. He stood behind a table with a map upon it. His eyes narrowed at first, a warrior's eyes, ready to slay, to defend. But as he saw her, his fierce gaze softened.

The thrill that had pulled Kaela to this place now vibrated through her whole body, as though nothing had ever been more right than this moment. The king's smoldering, coal-like gaze made her knees feel weak and buttery. With his dark, wavy hair and his short beard, he was the most handsome man she'd ever seen. But…there was a sadness to his eyes as well, something deep, something that she realized in an instant would never go away.

"I'm Princess Kaela," she said with a dry mouth.

"I am…King Saren II."

"King Saren II," she said, as though wanting to taste the words.

"No," he said. "Please. Call me Kylar. That's…what my friends call me."

"Kylar," she murmured, liking the taste of that much better.

"What are you…doing here?" He blinked as though struggling to hang onto his thoughts as they fluttered from his head.

"I'm here to save the world," she said. They were odd words to say, but it was as though her mouth knew they were the perfect words for this moment, even if her mind did not.

"Save the…the world?" he said with a trace of confusion, but the that quickly vanished from his face, slowly transforming to ardor. Color rose in his cheeks.

"I'm here for you," she whispered, her heart beating so fast she could barely catch her breath.

"And I you," he rumbled, all sadness and confusion gone. He moved to clear himself of the table and crossed the room like he couldn't get to her fast enough. She rushed to him.

He took her into his arms, and she melted into him.

⬟　⬟　⬟

Kaela didn't remember the ride back to the Delver's cave or her next trip through the Thuros. The thrill seemed the only important thing. It spun and whirled through her. She was certain of her purpose. It was to be in this new land Nhevalos had brought her, to pose as a servant within the manor of Duke Avendon. It didn't chafe her pride to suddenly be a servant instead of a princess because of the thrill. That seemed odd at first, but the feeling never lingered long. Every time she wondered at her new state of affairs, she thought of the look in the king's eyes—Kylar's eyes—his hands on her, and that the feeling of utter rightness.

She gave birth to a son nine months later, and she named him Khyven. Raising him became her new purpose.

After the first year at Duke Avendon's mansion in this kingdom of Usara—which was much like S'kai in some respects—she only had glowing memories of King Kylar. He was everything she'd ever dreamed about, and she longed for him every day.

The second year, her imaginings and longings for Kylar flowed through her like an epic tragedy. She imagined she and Kylar were like the sun and moon, forever bound to their endless promise to serve the world, but constantly circling each other, never to touch.

She focused on raising their son. That was what was important.

The third, fourth, and fifth year, when Khyven was a little boy, she wrapped herself in quiet pride. Her righteousness armored her against the lonely nights and the menial tasks she was forced to perform. She was an attentive mother, and she saw herself as the hand of the goddess Creili, moving events in the world that her employer, Duke Avendon, could scarcely imagine.

But in her sixth year since her meeting with King Kylar, the thrill within her faltered. For the first time since that fateful night when she'd plunged into the icy lake, doubt flickered to life in her mind. It began small at first, but it grew with each passing year. It was like she was waking from a long sleep, a little bit at a time.

Soon, as the thrill vanished completely, she began to review that fateful night when she'd left her betrothal celebration and had embarked on a completely new life. She couldn't remember why she had chosen to go with Nhevalos. For the life of her, she couldn't remember making that decision, only that suddenly the importance of following him was all-consuming.

She couldn't remember deciding to go into King Kylar's tent, either, only that she was pulled by that thrilling compulsion. She remembered only that when she looked at him, reason vanished and her desire went wild like a fire sweeping through a dry forest.

She couldn't remember wanting to come to this place, either, to be servant to a lesser lord.

Nhevalos returned during her eleventh year as a chambermaid. One moment, she was in her room, brushing her golden hair with Khyven playing with a wooden knight figurine on the floor, and the next Nhevalos stood there.

Her heart hammered, and she stood up to face him. She forced herself not to reach to her neck where the charm she had purchased rested on its chain.

"Nhevalos," she said. All the questions she'd wanted to ask him, all the way back to the beginning, surfaced in her mind. She would never have time to ask them all; she must choose the one, the right one.

Khyven looked up, surprised to suddenly see a man in their room. He started to get to his feet, but then, as if by magic, he blinked and went back to playing.

"Don't touch him," she said through her teeth. "Don't you do that to him."

Nhevalos's dark eyes narrowed. "Ah," he said as if he suddenly realized that something was amiss, that his spell upon her had somehow faded. "That should not have happened. I apologize."

The amulet around her neck felt warm. She'd spent a year's savings on it in the crown city of Usara. It warded spells, and it grew hot as she felt Nhevalos try to reestablished his control over her.

"What shouldn't have happened? That you ensorcelled me? That you stole my life from me!" she shouted.

Nhevalos sighed, and his gaze softened. "That was not my purpose. I did not mean for you to suffer. I have made a mistake and—"

"Stop trying to cast your spells on me and tell me the truth," she seethed. "I never loved this Kylar, did I? And I never wanted to go with you. That 'thrill' you told me to listen to, that was your spell, wasn't it?"

He watched her. "Yes."

It was the answer she expected. It was the answer she'd have demanded from him had he lied, but to hear it so blatantly spoken swept through her like a cold wind. She'd spent eleven years of her life in this place, serving, removed from her family and her friends.

"Why?" she asked, so softly she could barely hear it herself.

"Because you are important. Your blood is important. It is... necessary," he said.

"Not to me!" she exploded. Khyven played with his toys like he didn't hear her. It sliced her to the heart to see how he was already being manipulated by this horrible, magical creature, just as she had been.

"You can save the world," Nhevalos said. "I did not lie to you about that."

"You are twisted. You... can't play with people's lives like this."

"I can and will do whatever I must. The Giants are coming," he said. "And they will kill you all. All of you. Unless we kill them first."

"We? You mean my son?"

"Kaela, your blood is pure," Nhevalos said. "The purest I've seen in generations. And King Saren's blood...it contains the potential for what we need."

"Potential? Who is 'we?' Stop speaking in riddles!"

"The potential that, when the Giants come, the mortals of this world—every continent in this world—will have a chance to overcome them as they did seventeen hundred years ago."

"Seventeen hundred years?" she asked breathlessly.

"The Giants nearly destroyed you all during the Great Revolt. It was by the barest luck we defeated them. That will not happen again. We must prepare this time."

Kaela's swirl of questions roiled inside her, but she knew she'd never get the answers. Or if she did, she would hate them. The vendor of the magical charm had said it would only work once. She'd spent that. She had only a few seconds, maybe, before Nhevalos tried again. When he did, she'd go back to being the happy little thoughtless slave.

She couldn't ask all her questions, but she could ask one. In the end, it was the only question that mattered.

"My son," she said in a flat tone. "He's the one you need, isn't he? He's the one who can…help against the Giants."

"That remains to be seen. But he is the most promising."

The most promising… There were others. How many lives had Nhevalos ruined? How many children had he ripped away from their mothers? How many maidens had he plucked from their families and made them… Made them…

Kaela squeezed her eyes shut, and a single tear escaped, streaking down her cheek. "I see." She felt the hard reassurance of the ring on her finger. Another charm. More powerful than the first. It had taken the rest of her life's savings to buy it.

"Kaela," Nhevalos said, as though he could read her mind. "Don't."

She couldn't wait any longer. She'd waited too long already. If he suspected something, he would try to stop her. She couldn't allow that.

Turning her head so she could gaze upon her beautiful little boy, so that her last living vision would be of him, she said, "You will never manipulate my son. I'd rather he be dead than be your slave." She pushed the stone on the ring with her thumb.

"Incendius," she carefully spoke the incantation.

Fire exploded from the ring, and she screamed as it engulfed her and the entire room, blowing out the window and the door. She might die, but at least she would take this monster with her, and ensure he never had a chance to enslave Khyven as he'd enslaved her.

"Live free!" she screamed. "Die clean!" She had no water to bathe in, but she hoped Creili accepted the blood she was about to send Her.

With her last second of life, she looked at her son—

—and found him completely unaffected by the inferno, completely unaware of her screams. He continued to play with his toy while the blistering heat cracked the walls and turned the stones at her feet red.

Aghast, she spun to Nhevalos. He, too, was completely unaffected. As her eyes boiled in her sockets, the last thing she saw was Nhevalos's sad expression, as though he'd known this would happen all along.

And then Kaela knew no more.

● ● ●

Nhevalos watched as Kaela Fjorland burned to a cinder, becoming nothing more than ashes as the powerful charm spent its energy and the manor ferociously caught fire.

"It is necessary," he murmured to himself amidst the roaring flames.

He'd liked Kaela. But then, he liked most of them. The way they thought. The way they loved. Giants did not do that. Love was human creation.

Kaela was now dead, and he wondered if he should feel sad about that. A Human would have, he was sure. But Nhevalos couldn't afford to care about one human. He had to care about them all. He had only one slim chance to turn it around.

If he didn't clear the path to victory for the mortal races, they were doomed—Humans, Luminents, Delvers, Shadowvar, Brightlings, Taur-Els—all the mortals of Noksonon and every other continent. And so…no number of sacrifices was too small. For if he failed, they all died.

And beautiful mortal foibles like love would die with them. Raudokurdjom had taught him that. He could save them if he stayed strong, if he persevered, if he kept his eyes on the board.

Nhevalos turned back to the place Kaela had been. Could he have played this better? Did she need to die? Might he have taken her into his confidence and tried to convince her of what needed doing, rather than using his magic?

He shook his head and put the thought from his mind. Only a fool tried to change a decision already made.

The board was being set, and he was placing the right pieces. In the end, he'd made good use of Kaela, the best he could.

That was what mattered. That was all that mattered.

With a wave of his hand, he lifted the boy and sent him out the broken window. As the Khyven hit the ground, Nhevalos let the fog spell go, wiped the boy's memories, and filled him with a fear of the fire. With a cry, the boy bolted toward the woods like a dragon was snapping at his heels.

Nhevalos gave one last look into the fire. Where Kaela had stood. The bed behind her and the walls behind that were almost completely obscured by roaring fire and brutal heat. He turned away, floating through the window and landing on the ground outside. The entire manor burned now, flames licking a hundred feet into the air.

If there is an afterlife, brave Kaela, he thought. Perhaps I will see you there. Perhaps I will apologize, and you will forgive me.

He walked slowly up the slope toward his next task. Khyven must be made ready. They only had so much time, and Nhevalos had found a new ally to help.

Time to make the best use of him.

ABOUT THE AUTHOR

Todd Fahnestock is an award-winning, #1 bestselling author of fantasy for all ages and winner of the New York Public Library's Books for the Teen Age Award. *Threadweavers* and *The Whisper Prince Trilogy* are two of his bestselling epic fantasy series. He is a two-time winner of the Colorado Authors  League Award for Writing Excellence and two-time finalist for the Colorado Book Award for *Tower of the Four: The Champions Academy* (2021) and *Khyven the Unkillable* (2022). His passions are fantasy and his quirky, fun-loving family. When he's not writing, he teaches Taekwondo, swaps middle grade humor with his son, plays Ticket to Ride with his wife, plots creative stories with his daughter, and plays vigorously with Galahad the Weimaraner. Visit Todd at toddfahnestock.com.

AUTHOR'S NOTE

Writing *Rhenn the Traveler* broke my heart.

Oh, and if for some reason you're reading this Author's Note out of order, and you have not read *Rhenn the Traveler* yet, I urge you to go read the book. BIG spoiler coming up…

…

Okay, you've been warned.

Back to my broken heart.

So like *Lorelle of the Dark*, who stole the narrative away from Khyven (as one might expect a rogue to do), Rhenn actually took the narrative away from *me* (as one might expect a queen to do).

I wrote the first quarter of the story quickly. I knew what I wanted. I loved Rhenn's devil-may-care personality, acute intelligence, and natural charm. She flowed onto the page. And of course, being able to write on Quincy's continent was an added thrill. New lands. New cultures. A hot and humid continent instead of the cool, alpine Usara. And, of course, a land rife with water goblins.

So yes, writing Rhenn in her new environment was like a vacation.

As I approached the quarter pole of the story, though, I started having ideas for the ending. Before starting on "Act II" of the story, I jotted down a few of these ideas. Then I had a few more, so I jotted those down. To make a long story short, I finally gave up writing the book in chronological order and wrote to my inspiration instead. I plunged headlong into the end without having written the middle at all.

So yes, shortly after I wrote the first quarter of the book, I wrote the last quarter. And it tumbled onto the screen. It was rough, true, and I knew I'd have to adjust it once I filled in the middle, but this was the ending I wanted: heroic moments for Rhenn and Khyven in combat, Lorelle bouncing around with her cool noktum cloak, and Slayter using his big ADHD brain to solve the impossible puzzle.

Then I was left with the gaping, half-the-book hole in the center of the story. Now I'm a big fan of The Hero's Journey by Joseph Campbell, and in The Hero's Journey, the midpoint includes a death, usually symbolic, sometimes real.

As you know, Rhenn's death at the midpoint is all too real, but it didn't start out that way. I didn't want to kill her. I loved the Rhenn from *Khyven the Unkillable*, the Rhenn that shines through like a light in the beginning of this book. She is optimistic. She's fun, playful, and a bit saucy. No matter how dire the situation, she always seems on top of it. In short, she's full of life and love, and my inspiration was slowly settling on the idea of taking that away from her.

I resisted the notion.

I hemmed and hawed. I circled the mid point. I wrote a few lackluster chapters (later delcted) that took her in a different direction. Then I slowed to a stop.

Funny how the Muse stops talking if you stop listening.

So I turned to others for affirmation. We have an Eldros Legacy creative meeting every other Thursday, and I brought up the problem to the group.

"So… my book is full of undead bloodsuckers. People who have died and have been brought back. I'm toying around with an idea. I figure it can go one of two ways. I could have Rhenn have a near-death scrape, have her almost get turned into a vampire and escape through her own ingenuity and skills…."

Everyone listened. No one cheered.

"K," I continued. "I could also turn her into a vampire for real."

Lots of head nods. Clearly the preferred choice.

"The only problem is…" I said. "I have to figure out a way to turn her back. I mean, I can't have Rhenn end up a vampire. She's the quintessence of life and vitality. She's got to rule Usara. She can't do that if sunlight kills her. I can't have her *remain* a vampire."

As I said this aloud, though, I had the ephemeral feeling that I was wrong. My statement, while it spoke to the need of my heart, did not speak to the need of the story. This was *exactly* the kind of situation you want your character to go through. The crucible, the horrible fire they have to face, and then find a way to triumph over.

But I didn't want it. I didn't want to hurt Rhenn so badly. I knew she could never recover from something like this. She could never go back to what she was before. And I *liked* what she was before.

But when I said the words to the group, told them that I needed to find a way to return Rhenn to how she simply *had* to be, brake lights flared all over.

"No!"

"No way, Todd. You can't do that."

"You'll undo the magnitude of the sacrifice. That's bullshit."

I knew I could fight them off if I chose to. I've thrown off others' opinions before, stood firm in my conviction. The problem was… I had no conviction. Making her a vampire with no way out served the story. Keeping her the way she was served my personal need. I just didn't want to hurt her.

Who's the writer that says, "Kill your darlings…" Faulkner? Wilde? Chekov? King?

Oh, yeah. Like, all of them.

Clearly, Rhenn was my darling. And my creative group knew it.

I hung my head and sighed. "Okay. I'll write it that way. But if I hate it—and I'm going to hate it—I'm going to scrap it and rewrite the whole thing."

So I wrote it, and the floodgates opened. The Muse returned (as she does when you listen), and everything flowed. Suddenly the most uncertain part of the book became the richest, most daring part.

But my heart was in my throat when N'ssag gained the upper hand. I cried when Rhenn finally broke down and begged him to stop, begged him to spare her life. I felt like a monster when I took that life.

I had to walk away from the computer.

But I will tell you this… Later on, this made a different moment in the novel into my favorite part. Because of this cruelty. Because of all she lost in that moment.

That favorite part? When she escapes, of course. When she goes back through the Thuros to Usara. She's made it! She's free… but then her inherent nobility forces her to come back for E'maz.

And of course it's a trap. They grab her, hold her down, and even her supernatural strength can't save her. It seems she's not only lost her life but now she's going to lose her autonomy as well. N'ssag is going to turn her into a slave…

And then her friends show up.

Slayter's cleverness alerts them. Lorelle's cloak transports them in time. And Khyven brings the promise of mayhem to anyone who threatens his friends. I felt a deep satisfaction as N'ssag faced that frightening crossroads that all bullies must eventually face: meeting someone who's a bigger badass than you are.

Which led to my favorite lines of the book.

Khyven smiled his charming smile, the one that seemed friendly. The one that meant he was ready to kill.

"That's our friend you've got there." He pointed at N'ssag with his sword. "I suggest you let her go."

Those lines meant Rhenn wasn't alone anymore. They meant no matter what I'd had to put her through, she still had her friends, and they weren't going to ever let her go.

So that's how *Rhenn the Traveler* broke my heart and (mostly) mended it in the end. Rhenn's death was the right decision. It not only redefined her life from that moment forward, but the meta-plot of Noksonon as well.

I can't wait to show it to you, so stick around for *Slayter and the Dragon*, because that one's going to blow the doors off…

Also By Todd Fahnestock

Eldros Legacy (Legacy of Shadows Series)
Khyven the Unkillable
Lorelle of the Dark
Rhenn the Traveler
Slayter and the Dragon (forthcoming)
Bane of Giants (forthcoming)

Tower of the Four
Episode 1 – The Quad
Episode 2 – The Tower
Episode 3 – The Test
The Champions Academy (Episodes 1-3 compilation)
Episode 4 – The Nightmare
Episode 5 – The Resurrection
Episode 6 – The Reunion
The Dragon's War (Episodes 4-6 compilation)

Threadweavers
Wildmane
The GodSpill
Threads of Amarion
God of Dragons

The Whisper Prince
Fairmist
The Undying Man
The Slate Wizards

Standalone Novels
Charlie Fiction
Summer of the Fetch

Non-fiction
Ordinary Magic

Tower of the Four Short Stories
"Urchin"
"Royal"
"Princess"

Other Short Stories
Parallel Worlds Anthology — "Threshold"
Dragonlance: The Cataclysm — "Seekers"
Dragonlance: Heroes & Fools — "Songsayer"
Dragonlance: The History of Krynn —
"The Letters of Trayn Minaas"

Want More Eldros Legacy?

If you enjoyed this story and the world it's set in, then the creators of the Eldros Legacy would like to encourage you to don thy traveling pack and journey deeper into the mysteries of the world Eldros and all the myriad adventures set therein.

The mortal world of Eldros is coming apart. The Giants, who once ruled its five continents with draconian malice have set their mighty designs on a return to power. Mortals across the globe must be victorious against insurmountable odds or die.

Come join us as the Eldros Legacy unfolds in a growing library of novels and short stories.

More Novels in Noksonon

Relics of Noksonon Series by Kendra Merritt
The Pain Bearer
The Truth Stealer (Forthcoming)

Worldbreaker by Becca Lee Gardner (Forthcoming)
The Beacon by Rebecca K. Busch (Forthcoming)

Founder Series in Eldros Legacy

Legacy of Deceit by Quincy J. Allen
Seeds of Dominion
Demons of Veynkal (Forthcoming)

Legacy of Dragons by Mark Stallings
The Forgotten King

Legacy of Queens by Marie Whittaker
Embers & Ash
Cinder & Stone (Forthcoming)

Other Eldros Legacy Novels

A Murder of Wolves by Jamie Ibson
Deadly Fortune by Aaron Rosenberg
Stealing the Storm by Aaron Rosenberg
Dark and Secret Paths: Warrior Mages of Pyranon by C.A. Farrell
Stonewhisper: Crimson Fang by H.Y. Gregor

Other Eldros Legacy Short Stories

Here There Be Giants by The Founders
The Darkest Door by Todd Fahnestock
Fistful of Silver by Quincy J. Allen
Electrum by Marie Whittaker
Dawn of the Lightbringer by Mark Stallings
What the Eye Sees by Quincy J. Allen
Trust Not the Trickster by Jamie Ibson
A Rhakha for the Tokonn by Quincy J. Allen